DESTINED BY DRAGONBLOOD

BLOOD BORN 2

LYNN BURKE

DESTINED BY DRAGONBLOOD

I had given up hope of finding my fated mates until a gifted dragonblood showed me a vision of my future: an alpha, a beta, and a female bonded by dragon flames and fulfilling our role in preventing the extinction of the Blood Born.

The violet-eyed beauty I seek and follow from the shadows is everything I and my beastly nature long for. Although past trauma has destroyed Ashley's desire for physical connection, an inner force drives her toward healing.

The man offering her the pain she needs to find pleasure is a human dominant who calls to my primitive instincts. Master Vanni makes my weak inner dragon yearn to submit.

But I kneel for no man.

I am of royal blood, born to rule, and my future was determined long before Ashley or Vanni drew their first breath.

When insecurities about my royal heritage arise, I begin to question everything Father promised me as a child.

Will I find peace with my beastly side and accept who we are? Or will indoctrination keep me from the arms of the two destined for me?

CHAPTER 1

DOLYN

I shifted into my dragon form, which ripped through flesh and bone without pain. For the first time in over a decade, pleasure welled inside me as I shot like a golden comet southward through the afternoon sky. Emotional torment slid from my mind as the brisk wind swept over my heated scales and spines like a lover's soothing touch.

I'd found out moments earlier that Elijah had replaced me with two other lovers, and I could still feel his female's hand on my chest like a fiery brand. The visions that had flitted through my mind at her touch remained crisp.

Blindingly brilliant in color.

Vivid images of the two creatures she stated were intended for me remained ingrained in the deepest parts of me.

Elijah's female, Dakota, had a gift of old due to the ancient dragonblood flowing through her veins. A minuscule amount, however, not even enough that I had been able to scent it on her. I'd declared her unworthy of my ex-lover, but

1

he'd been adamant in his claiming of both her and the woman's husband, Jon.

Fated mates, he'd called them, the ones meant for him—drawn to him by his alpha dragonblood.

With Elijah's sexual prowess and his beast's desire to dominate, I didn't doubt he had bonded with the couple seconds after I'd thrown my human body off the veranda of his home deep in the White Mountains. I'd done so in order to shift and escape the pain of seeing them complete Elijah in ways I had never been able to but also to seek out my own destiny.

Cloaked from human eyes, I flew toward where I would find the female dragon in the vision Elijah's mate had shown me. While I'd seen a pale gray beast, purple-blue eyes were a rarity and ought to make my female easier to identify in human form. Further description and a name known to Elijah had offered me all the information I needed to locate one of the two who belonged to me.

Ashley O'Connor, according to my ex-lover who employed her as one of his secretaries, was a petite brunette, demure and fragile in her emotions, a woman who would require gentle handling from a traumatic past he wasn't fully aware of.

Like Father before me, as alpha, it was my responsibility to protect the female fate held in wait for my future. But *unlike* Father, I would treat the third party in our triad, my beta, differently than he had. I'd endured watching Father belittle his subservient male mate with unkind words that rang through my mind centuries later.

Unworthy.

Inferior.

Both of which, in my opinion, applied to the two Elijah had chosen.

They were nothing more than mere humans who didn't

have the ability to shift, two beings who would never be a good match other than to make him feel he owned the alpha status he'd always claimed during the years he and I had spent together.

My human flesh and mind refused to bow to another, but my dragon used to purr with delight over every lash of Elijah's whip, every crack of his cane across my backside, every thrust of his hips that had buried his long length deep inside me.

It had been twenty years into our relationship before I initially submitted my body—never my mind or status—out of desperation to bond with Elijah. I'd only done so in the hopes that we would find our female and breed her since no other shifters walked the earth. It took three dragonblood to create life, and I'd instinctively done what was necessary to see our species survive. But all the sacrifices I had made, the past I'd left behind to be with Elijah, and he'd still chosen Dakota and her husband over me, one of royal blood, their superior in every way.

My alpha father had told me from the time I could remember that I had been born to dominate, and he had raised me to be a protector. An assertive leader. A man who wouldn't bend the knee to another.

While soiled by Papa, my beta father's lesser bloodline, the fact Father used to rule the Western world made me his sole heir, the last alpha of our line no matter what others believed.

Elijah had shown no desire or intention to submit to me, and while he could have coerced me into being his mate as Father had claimed dragonblood of old used to do, Elijah hadn't. My lover of seventy years had gifted me the right to choose, and our coming together had been a battle from day one, a delicious tug-of-war that had always ended up with our bodies sated and covered in cum, sweat, and once, tears.

The final war between us had left my soul broken and bleeding, and I'd flown from our home in a last attempt to find our fated mate who would recognize me as the alpha and help Elijah see the truth of his station beneath me.

And in my absence, while I'd given up the comfort of our home hidden in the mountains to scour the entire earth for the one who would make us whole, he'd taken up with mere *humans*.

A wind gust slammed me in the face, causing me to blink and spin toward earth. Rather than lament being replaced, I allowed myself a moment of freedom from despair while tumbling through the sky, imagining myself grappling midair with the beta I would soon claim if Dakota's vision held true. Once I owned my violet-eyed Ashley, fate would no longer hide its gift of a beta from me. I would locate the bridge between me and my female, and we would finally be brought together in perfect timing to ensure our mating lasted for centuries.

The images Dakota had shown me flashed through my mind, revealing the slender gray beast with light purple eyes, the beat of my heart, one of my reasons for existence. And the other who would bring us together to breed...a lithe, black-scaled creature with brilliant green orbs.

Dakota had claimed him to be my alpha.

A snort erupted from my nostrils, steam rippling through the air behind me as I sped above thickening populated land with a flap of leathery wings. *Beta*, I had corrected her immediately because no partially human dragonblood would ever rule over a royal Blood Born. I'd been raised to be an alpha in our triad, and nothing would convince me otherwise.

I snapped my tail and careened into a gleeful roll, but fate called. Another strong push of my wings rushed me through the cold toward the cityscape on the horizon—New York.

Lower Manhattan and Tolzman Industry's building specifically.

Five o'clock neared, the time of day when Elijah's employees spilled onto the streets, bustling to return to their peace. The perfect hour for me to hide myself and watch for the woman I would soon claim as my own.

Towering sky rises above me blocked out the final rays from the sinking sun. Brisk wind continued to buffet through the streets as I stood in front of Elijah's building, the main entrance glass doors allowing me a peek into the brightly lit lobby. Warmth flooded my bloodstream, in contrast to the sinking temperature on my human skin.

Naked and camouflaged, I leaned against a light post, hidden from sight to those scurrying past in their rush to return home after a long workday. I'd come directly from Elijah's, not having time to stop by the penthouse suite I owned but rarely utilized. It was one of many escapes I'd kept from Elijah's knowledge along with the rest of my physical assets and wealth from having invested in America's stock market since its inception. As alpha, I'd never felt the need to include Elijah in the various outlets of my life outside the physical, same as Father had done with Papa.

But there were other secrets I'd hidden from him.

I chose to put the past behind me when I'd finally submitted my body to Elijah that wintery day in 1962, after agreeing to pursue companionship with each other since there were no other of our species that we'd found in our years together prior to that day.

But my heart and head refused to submit fully, thus the constant battle for dominance between us.

Now, a fresh start lay before me where not even the sky was the limit.

Something far greater than a tumultuous relationship with another self-proclaimed alpha awaited me, a gift from fate for having lived too many centuries seeking to bond and breed as a Blood Born's instincts demanded.

A low whine drew my attention off Elijah's building. Some sort of raggedy, downtrodden dog peered up at me. Hunger shone in his eyes, bones protruding along his gray-speckled chest, further evidence he hadn't eaten in a while.

I bent, running my hands over his filthy head. "Who's a good boy?" I murmured, keeping my voice low so no one became aware of my invisible presence.

A lick over my face made me smile, and I scratched behind his matted ears. "You need someone to take care of you, don't you, boy? Hmm?"

He rolled onto his back, giving me his belly, and I scratched, glancing over at Elijah's building.

Employees began their exodus from Tolzman Industries, and I inspected every dark-haired woman for a glimpse of the one Dakota's vision had revealed as my new friend continued to gladly accept my weighted strokes and murmurs of praise.

Minutes passed without my female's arrival beneath the evening sky, and the rush of people turned into a trickle, unease prickling the back of my mind. Had I somehow missed Ashley in the throng? Was her dragonblood of so little potency that she had escaped without me catching the scent of her? My forehead etched into a deep furrow.

No. I refused to believe she would be unnoticeable, that she could have slipped by me countless times in the final month I'd spent in this very city searching for Elijah's and my female. I had admitted defeat and returned to him empty-handed, determined to offer him every part of me in the hopes we might find some sense of contentment together.

I hated to believe my human side's alpha nature hadn't been able to locate Ashley after ten years of searching, but I'd grown desperate. Eyes closing, I sought out my inner beast, the one Father had taught me to rule with an iron fist—the lesser beta-like creature within me that I refused to bow down to. Rarely did I allow him equal rein, but I felt I had no choice.

"I need you." I muttered defeat I rarely admitted to, unleashing his instincts instead of only his beastly form I required to take flight.

Embers hot as lava flared in my gut as I lowered the walls between us, a rumbling of life cracking through the manacles I used to shackle his natural inclinations.

Yips sounded and quickly faded, saddening me for scaring my new friend away when I could have provided a better existence for him.

A cackle of glee over sudden freedom flared like flames in my chest, nearly bursting through my skin, but I managed to retain my human form.

Relief oozed through my pores as my inner beast settled, shivers pebbling my skin. A sense of rightness I despised began to weave our minds into each other, allowing both of us equal control. He tended toward greediness, so I lay in wait, ready to smother him at a moment's notice if necessary.

I quickly glanced around, heart aching over the missing dog.

Breathe...

Embracing our true self, we opened our airway fully, drawing oxygen deep into our lungs, scenting through the beast's senses rather than our lesser human's. Clogging exhaust burned our nostrils. A wafting stench of sewage curdled our guts. Putrid traces of body odor and cigarettes clung to those passing us by. Cloying perfume and spiced aftershave hit our nose, both of which caused a grimace to stretch our lips.

Vanilla, sweet as syrup—

Our eyelids snapped upward. Movement slowed as though we'd suddenly been submerged in water. Silence descended, stifling regardless of the beauty before us.

Like a siren, our female called to us while stepping from Tolzman's doors into the breeze, dark strands floating past her face, covering the eyes we lusted to see. Flushed, high cheekbones, a dainty, pointed chin...full lips our tongue lusted to stroke and taste, urged us to drink our fill and flooded our senses with everything that she was and imprinted them for all of eternity into our memory.

Arousal swelled through our groin like a tidal wave, causing an instant ache as she paused mere feet from us. We leaned toward the source of our need, energy rippling outward like a massive swell, attempting to drown us in desire. While my human half disliked anyone touching us other than those worthy of our attention, this female made our skin itch for caresses and kisses.

Need.

She lifted a trembling hand to tuck nearly-black hair behind a perfectly formed ear, baring what we longed to see.

Dark lashes framed the violet-colored eyes our human side had caught a glimpse of in Dakota's vision. Though less in brightness and intensity, there was no mistaking the irises of the woman before us. The faintest scent of her dragonblood filled our merged noses and lungs, assuring us she was our female. She was much more human than beast, but her beauty, the allure of her scent, caused my superior half to not care about her lesser blood as much as I'd expected.

Ours.

Indeed, she was.

The instinct to hold and protect her set like stone in our mind and heart. We would move heaven and earth to see her safe from harm, content with life, and smiling with joy.

Ashley stared at us—no, *through* us—as though the essence of our presence escaped her. She didn't feel or recognize the energy fate wished to utilize to weave us together, same as I wouldn't have done without my beast's instincts. The draw of dragonblood fated mates went completely unnoticed to the one meant to be by our side.

She blinked and turned away, giving us her back as though we meant nothing to her.

Pain ripped through our chest, and reality snapped back into real time, bringing with it the vivid bleak city surrounding us that reiterated our loneliness we'd fought to fill for too many years.

Nothing would offer release to our aching cock but her wet warmth, her submission to our tender touch.

Follow.

While in flight to New York, we had already made a plan for claiming her. Like Elijah's, my beast wasn't above coercion, but the human half of us preferred to have our female come to us willingly. Softened for our gentle initiation, accepting of her place—recognizing who owned her body and soul. That part of us didn't want her obedience and submission given unknowingly or grudgingly.

Accomplishing such a task required a firm grip. Control.

And patience, which our beast side struggled with.

I shackled my inner dragon's instincts before he realized what I did, taking charge. He grumbled at me in my head, but I muzzled him, my sole focus on the one hurrying down the sidewalk in front of me.

She kept her head lowered and could easily disappear into a crowd undetected. But not to me. Having seen and scented Ashley through my beast's senses, she stood out like a beautiful rose among thorns, the brightest star in the night sky. She was a beacon of hope, the promise of a new beginning.

Ashley and I might be meant for one another, but I wanted contentment and perhaps a true love like I longed for yet had failed to see or feel in. And that needed to be earned above the supernatural draw between us that I hoped she would experience when I was ready to reveal myself to her.

After a childhood of having to watch a disjointed triad of Blood Born fated mates, I yearned for the type of harmony spoken of in poetry and songs. Equal give and take on all three sides, a sharing of hearts atop minds that would be linked once we properly bonded.

While severely less in intensity without my beast's abilities to smell, hints of vanilla continued to tease my nose and keep me aroused as I followed my sweet female through the mass of people hurrying to escape the bustle of the city.

Ashley descended into the depths of the subway, and I shut out the rest of the world from my mind. A dark blue peacoat covered her narrow shoulders and the top half of her backside. Black slacks with a wider leg around her ankles brushed against what appeared to be leather boots. Even with the inch or so heel, the shoes wouldn't bring the top of her head to my chin.

She was a delicate little thing in need of an alpha of my stature and strength, but not enough dragonblood swam in her veins to inform her the one she must long for stood an arm's length behind her.

Even shut into a stifling subway train, Ashley took no note of me on her right side or how my naked body craved hers with pulsing throbs throughout my cells. Through clicks and clacks of the rails, we moved, the bumps shifting us side to side but not bringing us into contact with each other where we huddled amidst the crowd.

I couldn't tear my gaze off the paleness of Ashley's cheeks, the ripe pink of her mouth, and the hint of freckles over her nose. She didn't attempt to cover what some would see as blemishes with makeup. No fake contour shaded her skin, nor did mascara clump her lashes together. Ashley O'Connor bled beauty from every pore, the kind of perfection others paid thousands to achieve.

Even with her curves hidden by the coat keeping the fall chill at bay, I found her more alluring than any human I'd set eyes upon, and traveling the entire planet had allowed me to behold every race known, every species *unknown*, to man.

She made my mouth water, my groin ache, and my heart race.

A muffled voice announced we'd entered New Jersey, and I stuck close to Ashley as she exited the train a short while later. I followed her down Walnut Street on silent, bare feet, continuing to drink in her luscious scent, my thick shaft pointing toward her like a homing beacon. We slowed at a row of condos, and I moved farther into the shadows even though she wouldn't be able to see me with her human eyes until I uncloaked myself, which was out of the question in my current state of undress.

With a quick glance around as though finally sensing a stalker, Ashely quickly unlocked her front door and slipped inside her home, which was bracketed on either side by others of similar build and color. The sound of various bolts slid into place behind her, prohibiting me from entering without force, which I refused to do.

As the minutes passed, daydreams flooded my mind, and I allowed myself to fantasize over our future. Far beyond merely sinking into her tight heat and flooding her with my seed but building a life together. Cooking alongside each other. Cuddling on the couch, sharing about our day. She was employed by Elijah, which meant she held a good work ethic. She also hadn't cut out early but must have stayed to finish up whatever task she'd been assigned for the day.

I allowed myself to envision our beta between us, creating the bridge that would physically and emotionally tie us together for life. I could only imagine how the bond would snap into place, dropping all walls among us, allowing thoughts and feelings to flow through us like an unhindered stream, healthy and vibrant, full of life.

Euphoria would be found in her arms, heaven on earth alongside our beta.

A real smile curved my lips for the first time in too many years to count. Hope swelled inside me to the point where I inadvertently lowered my guard, and my inner beast whimpered his need to know such happiness.

I want.

Refusing interaction with my dragon came easy. Not hearing him when he reminded our human half of his existence proved harder since I'd removed the walls between us while in Lower Manhattan, thus granting him power that would linger for a short while.

I yearn.

Closing my eyes briefly, I allowed him to further experience the misery I'd managed to shed from my mind while flying away from Elijah's mountain home. We'd been found wanting and set aside, but I wasn't jaded enough that I didn't desire the same as my beast did. I longed to share in the physical as well. The touch of skin I rarely allowed, the heat of arousal, the release of climax that had been brewing in my sac since first scenting Ashley.

Take what belongs to us.

I'd given the bastard an inch, allowing him speech, and he took a mile. Using full sentences to make demands hadn't been tolerated in close to a decade.

However, the temptation to do as he pushed tensed my

body toward action rather than stifling his voice as I ought to. The truth that I could easily break into Ashley's condo without raising alarm and claim her before she thought to scream caused my muscles to tremble and shaft to throb. I had yet to sniff over her skin and fully indulge in her scent. I didn't yet have the pleasure of tasting her sweet breath on my tongue. But the idea of doing both hardened me to the point of pain, and a bead of pre-cum welled on my swollen cockhead. I ignored the lone droplet sliding down my length. A pulsing stream should have oozed from my body like Elijah's had done whenever he'd experienced arousal.

Proof we are beta.

"Be *silent*," I growled. I disregarded him and the lack of moisture as I'd been doing since learning about an alpha dragonblood's sexual mechanics, focusing on the dark panel of glass keeping me from fulfillment.

The beast began to hiss and claw at his inescapable bonds instead of insisting on what I refused to accept.

"We will study Ashley's ways," I stated, hoping to shift his focus to what truly mattered, same as I had done. "Learn about her life, those she surrounds herself with and loves. Her habits, what she does for enjoyment. Only then we will decide on a course of interaction."

Curses over my flesh's dominance echoed in my head as my dragon shrieked his displeasure.

"You forget yourself." Centuries of practice made keeping hold on my inner beast easy once I muzzled him.

He sulked in silence as I tore myself away from our female's presence for the nearest intersection. I shifted skin and muscle, elongated bone into the shape that allowed me flight, all while retaining control over my beast. One leap upward and a flap of wings shot me into the dark sky. Night caressed my scales as a lover might, something I hadn't had the pleasure of enjoying in far too long of a time.

No one since Elijah had touched my flesh—dragon or otherwise—because of their unworthiness, and both my beast and I trembled in our shared need for release.

We had found our female, but every part of me craved more than softness and gentleness. My skin tightened with the need to feel biting pain. Stinging lashes. Impact play that would send endorphins rushing throughout my body and empty my brain of unceasing thoughts.

With Ashley located, I expected to soon cross paths with my beta, the submissive male who would complete us. He would have no interest in inflicting what the secret part of me sometimes craved, therefore, I would allow myself a single night of weakness before fate settled into place.

Since Elijah was no longer an option to give me what I ached for, I would have to locate a club in New York that catered to those who preferred pain with their pleasure. Surely, finding a human dominant wouldn't be difficult. I would allow him to hurt me but without skin-to-skin contact. He would offer the kind of release I needed one last time before I walked away from that part of me.

Then I would prove myself worthy in Father's eyes by claiming my place as alpha over my destined mates.

CHAPTER 2
VANNI

I sipped my tonic water, the hint of lime a pleasant zing over my tongue while gazing through my office's one-way glass, keeping me hidden from sight.

The lounge below me was busy for a Wednesday night. Couples and singles looking for a hookup or simply enjoying the dimmed, sensual atmosphere of my sex club mingled around the large room. Leather couches and chairs created more intimate areas, breaking up the space. A bondage frame, St. Andrew's cross, and whipping post along with various types of spanking benches sat atop daises throughout the open area, available for those with exhibition and voyeur kinks.

Two pieces of the furniture meant to bring pleasure were currently in use, but no part of my body aroused at the sight of the wielded flogger or whip. Even had the sound-proofing of my office been absent, the cries of both pain and heightened desire wouldn't have affected me.

My mind remained focused on the cell phone I'd left atop my desk and the news app I'd checked as I always did when the evening hours drew closer. Hand steady regardless of how my insides shook, I sipped my tonic again, fighting to remain calm and in control.

After ten years, Caroline finally married my best friend, the man who'd stolen the one I'd thought had been the love of my life.

The tumbler shattered in my clenched hand.

"Fuck." I pursed my lips, my focus dropping to the hard-wood flooring littered with bits of glass and clear liquid. The lime wedge sat atop my soaked black dress shoe. Lifting my left wrist, I stated an order into my watch that would bring someone to clean up the mess.

I eyed the two small lacerations on my right palm and turned toward the full bathroom attached to my office. Neither cut was deep or stung, but I washed thoroughly, making sure no glass shards remained imbedded in my skin. I'd always been freakishly strong, but never had I ever squeezed a glass until it broke into pieces.

A knock sounded from out in my office.

"Come in!" I hollered while checking to make sure the bleeding had stopped.

"Master Vanni?" one of the submissive employees who kept my club pristine called.

"I dropped my drink by the window, and the glass shat-tered." I explained the reason for my summons, leaving out the part where I'd broken the tumbler in anger.

They took care of the mess I'd made while I finished with my injury before glancing up at the mirror. The ten years since Caroline left hadn't exactly been kind. At forty-two, I grayed at the temples, but I kept my dark hair on the longer side and over my ears, which hid evidence of my aging from sight. Slight lines marred the skin at the corners of my eyes, but there was no sagging on my face or the rest of my body, for that matter.

Having lost my wife to another man, I'd focused on bettering myself in every way. My darker desires had led to my marriage's ruination, but I no longer had to restrain myself or give up my need to dominate. I sought out knowledge and mastership of the kinks that had turned her off. I'd also honed myself into a machine built of muscle and sinew by cleaning up my eating, hitting the gym every day, and treating my body like the gift it was.

Depression had threatened initially after the betrayal, but I'd strived to keep my mind off Caroline's infidelity, going so far as to seek out therapy for the grief. She'd wanted a side dish, and because I adored my wife, I had invited Jackson, a gentle soul, to join us to fulfill her fantasy of a threesome. He had been the one man I'd trusted, the best friend I had made my first million with. I'd bought him out of the software company after catching him and Caroline fucking, without my knowledge or consent, two weeks after he and I had shared my wife. He'd agreed to less than half of the company's worth. Out of guilt, I expected, and we hadn't spoken since.

Over ten fucking years, and no matter the hours I'd spent chatting with a shrink, the sting of betrayal still struck whenever I came across either of their names anywhere online.

Left alone in my office once more, I wiped off my shoe and settled into my chair, eyeing my cell phone where it lay, its screen dark.

Swiping would only keep me rooted in the past, a painful void I hated to revisit. And while I feared vulnerability, living in emotional isolation would never give me what I truly wished for.

I desired a love I could trust to remain faithful. A partner who accepted every part of me, kinks included. While I'd become confident in the aspects of my life I could control, the absence of someone to share it with continued to nag at me like my mom did to my dad.

A shudder rippled through my spine, and I grimaced. Pulling open the bottom drawer of my desk, I blamed my parents for being the final trigger to make me go for what I'd wanted earlier rather than that damned tonic.

The welcomed burn of whiskey coated my throat, and I put the flask back where it belonged, closing the drawer. Liquor had no place in my club or inside what I considered my temple, which housed my liver. But once in a while, shit happened, and the thoughts of my parent's marriage of convenience atop Caroline made for a good reason to enjoy one shot.

I pushed aside my cell and opened my schedule for the night ahead, ready to turn my focus elsewhere.

Eight months earlier, I'd sold off my company for twice what it was worth, leaving me with nothing to occupy my mind but my money, the sex club, and fanciful dreams of finding contentment with a submissive who would match perfectly with my strengths and weaknesses. I'd since seemed to flounder, a sense of…*something* hovering on the horizon, but what it might be, I had no clue. Itchiness lay beneath my skin, making me restless, and more often than not, I yearned to take out my aggression on a willing body.

While I rarely allowed people in the lifestyle to drop in without a membership, a man with deep pockets had inquired about a caning from the most sadistic dominant on staff.

That person would be me.

According to the paperwork he'd filled out and returned in a matter of hours, he was desperate for pain—my kryptonite and exactly what I needed tonight. Even better, he had very few limits, penetration being one I myself held when it came to men. While I enjoyed anal sex, no man's asshole, or body for that matter, had ever tempted me to question my sexuality.

According to this man's file, his second hard limit was skin-on-skin contact, same as my favorite little submissive I would be sceneing with again next Friday night.

Ashley had witnessed countless club members on spanking benches getting their asses handed to them while moving through the lounge the previous five evenings she'd come to my club, but I never allowed myself the hope of seeing her give herself to me in that way. So far, she'd asked to be tied down spread-eagle on a bed, behind closed doors where I could use toys to give her what she wanted, but never touched in the way I desired.

Timid and shy, kind and sweet, she submitted beautifully to the pain she required in order to feel arousal and eventually find release. I hadn't been informed, nor was it my place to ask about her past or what had led to her need to be dominated, but I knew it stemmed from far more than mere kink.

Ashley had been referred to me by Doc Hasslet, a sex therapist and good friend of mine who hadn't told me more than the fact she had major PTSD triggers she wished to overcome, including no skin contact. While I knew she dealt with trauma from years earlier, I honored her privacy and never asked—merely gave her what she required to get off.

I rarely scened with a person more than once unless they signed forms clearly outlining my own hard limits of getting emotionally involved and dating. But something about the woman roused my protective instincts, and I had agreed to Doctor Hasslet's suggestion of meeting with Ashley on a monthly basis. She had stolen my breath at first sight and part of my heart the Friday before. She had finally allowed aftercare, so I burrito-wrapped her body to keep her skin safe from touching mine and cuddled her tight against my chest.

Holding her had been heaven, far more fulfilling than I even remembered my ex-wife feeling in my arms.

I wanted more with Ashley, even though I feared lowering my walls would lead to heartache and humiliation. Had I been able to trust a person with my heart and thoughts, she would be the woman I would choose.

Heaving a heavy exhale, I focused on the computer screen in front of me rather than continuing to linger on wishes and dreams I longed to see fulfilled yet feared to the point my stomach tightened. Triggered by my own past trauma I had sought out help for years earlier, I was more than in the mood to have someone submit to my hand. Beg for release while crying for mercy.

A sense of power rose up inside me, a desperate craving to dominate and relieve that itch I'd been craving to satisfy.

I eyed the man's name.

Dolyn.

Warmth I hadn't felt since sceneing with Ashley infiltrated my body, heightening my pulse.

Never had a man physically turned me on, but I reasoned my arousal away due to my intense desire to dominate after the shit day I'd had.

Hopefully, this Dolyn guy and I would be able to fulfill each other's needs tonight without issue, and we would both leave my club satisfied.

The sight awaiting me in my private play room pulled me up short inside the door.

Rather than kneeling in wait as a submissive club member would have done, Dolyn remained standing, every inch of his hairless, golden skin on full display. He appeared like a statue chiseled from stone—cock included—and my mouth filled with moisture.

Heat rushed through my body, settling into my groin and making my leather pants suddenly way too tight. Perhaps going commando hadn't been the best choice, but I hadn't been expecting this type of physical reaction toward a man.

Dolyn was a magnet, drawing me closer and tempting me to partake of something new, and I had no qualms about exploring this awakened part of me. Since I wasn't sure how to do so without physical touch, I would rely on intuition more than logic.

I shut the door, leaving us in silence, completely cut off from the outside world. A hush, full of tension and expectation, flooded the room and made the hairs on my nape stir.

Our gazes held, sending a zing of pure lust straight to my cock and causing a full hard-on, which I didn't mind in the slightest. His audacity to keep his golden brown eyes latched onto mine, however…

I raised an eyebrow, but he didn't drop his focus to the floor as one ought to do when their master for the next hour entered the room.

Dolyn's chin tipped upward in a slight hint of defiance, almost like he…looked down at me. As if those two inches he had on me made him superior. He didn't realize exposing his neck in such a way suggested the opposite.

Giddiness lit in my stomach, spreading throughout my limbs, but I bit my grin back while blatantly adjusting my bulge. I approached, already knowing from his file I'd gone over a few times before dressing in my leather pants and harness that Dolyn disliked submitting.

And yet he'd paid to feel the bite of a cane.

A puzzle for sure, unexpected and thoroughly exciting. Also none of my business. I was in this room for one purpose alone: Give him his money's worth of pain while enjoying the hell out of my mental release or more, depending on how our scene progressed.

Dolyn stared straight ahead as I slowly circled him, taking in his muscled mass. His shoulders, set back in confidence, were wider than my own. The V shape of his back would cause any bodybuilder envy, the dimples and swell of his ass a dominant's dream. Thick thighs, bulging calves...hell, even his feet were perfectly formed.

Sex on a stick took on a whole new meaning, as did Greek god. Dolyn was the perfect specimen of a man, but nothing about him intimidated me or suggested he had a dominant bone in his body, regardless of his stance and the claims he'd made on the forms.

Something inside me insisted I let out that damned chuckle, but I stifled the sound for the second time, sure he would be offended by my amusement over the front he attempted to put on.

I rounded Dolyn to face him, and as though drawn to me, he leaned closer regardless of him attempting to peer down his nose at me.

Less than a foot separated our flesh, and heat zaps like lightning ignited between us.

And I thought I'd experienced lust and desperation to dominate before.

Nothing compared to the intense want vibrating inside me. Dolyn's unconscious desire to submit begged me to attend to him, explore the desire he attempted to deny, and reward him for yielding to me. Every cell of my being craved to command him, mark his skin, and watch him sink into subspace, which I sensed he yearned for regardless of his facade.

I despised being lied to, and this man reeked of dishonesty.

Or perhaps he simply didn't yet understand the depths of

his true self, thus denying he was a submissive creature by nature.

"Why are you here, Dolyn?" I had no right to his personal business, but if there were triggers he'd left unlisted and I inadvertently ignited, shit might get ugly. I refused to have that kind of drama in my club.

A muscle ticked in his jaw, and he either showed his first outward sign of submission by shifting his focus to the wall behind me or he did so out of guilt for lying.

I wasn't convinced he would know the real reason if I asked.

"I crave pain and am allowing myself one last night to indulge." His low voice, husky as though he'd smoked for years, slid over my skin, awakening every hair follicle on my body.

I breathed deeply, filling my lungs with the scent of fire and smoke—but not tobacco. More along the lines of...cedar embers.

Delicious.

The unexpected descriptor whispered through my mind, but I studied Dolyn's full lips, somehow knowing he would be the embodiment of that word and so much more.

"*Master Vanni,*" I murmured the title he'd forgotten when addressing me.

"No man is my master."

I looked forward to proving him wrong. "Sir, then," I stated firmly, giving my attention to the rest of his face to see what other tells he gave away.

Jaw clenched, Dolyn nodded, the golden glints in his whiskey-colored eyes giving way to swelling pupils. Pink flushed his cheeks, the throbbing pulse in his neck suggesting he was as equally affected by our proximity as I was.

I crowded his personal space, loving how my body

responded. I felt *alive* for the first time in years, completely enthralled and focused on my purpose. Horny as fuck and ready to give this man whatever he requested.

"You listed two limits," I stated, needing them repeated out loud considering the undeniable attraction between us.

"Skin contact and penetration, Sir." He echoed what he'd written on his forms, much to my disappointment. "I have an aversion to the first when it comes to humans, which makes the second an impossibility."

"Humans," I repeated, perplexed, but not inflecting my voice with a question for clarity. "Have you ever been fucked, Dolyn?" I found myself asking, my shaft bucking at the thought of sinking my length between his ass cheeks, past his tight ring, and into the silken heat of his core.

"Yes, Sir."

A low hum rose past my lips as I pressed in even closer, mere inches separating us. My heartbeat throbbed in harmony with my groin, much as it did when I pushed Ashley's limits. "Did you like having a hard cock thrust deep into your guts?" I murmured, hands fisting to keep myself from caressing over his stiff length.

He swallowed audibly, a slight tremor rippling over him as his hands clenched briefly before releasing. "Yes," he whispered, once more forgetting to address me properly.

I eased back slightly since biting his lower lip in punishment was off-limits, and I needed some space to breathe, as did he.

If Dolyn had enjoyed having his ass owned, why did he use the word "aversion"? Past trauma, I supposed, same as Ashley, but suspicion had me believing Dolyn's issue stemmed from more. Did he crave the pain as some form of penance? The hard length straining toward his belly button and the droplet of pre-cum oozing down his shaft suggested he was here for more than a punishment.

Like me, he ached for relief.

I had no right to question why he'd come to my club. Opposite in their desires to submit, Dolyn and Ashley were two peas in a pod with their distaste for physical contact, and while both of them intrigued the hell out of me, only one stood ready to be taken care of tonight.

Dolyn deserved my full focus, and I would gift it to him.

I straightened my spine in readiness to give this man exactly what he needed from me—a cold-hearted beating that would ease his conscience and maybe empty his firmed ball sac if he could come untouched.

The conflict over his written answers and tells, however, required a verbal response to a question he hadn't provided on his forms.

"What is your safeword?"

Dolyn returned his gaze to me, and I swore fire flashed in his eyes and blinked out. "I don't need one, *Sir*."

"The fuck you don't," I whispered, leaning closer. "What you crave, the lust for agony I feel radiating off your skin like electricity, will be a pleasure to inflict on your gorgeous body, but I promise I wield more than you could ever handle, boy."

He snorted, the scent of burning cedar flooding my nose.

My cock pulsed inside my leathers, releasing an unnatural and unusual flood of pre-cum. God*damn*, this man worked me up inside like no one had before.

"I can't be broken," he claimed, his chin lifting, exposing even more of his neck.

I withheld my own snort at his gesture of submission and hissed as another burst of pre-cum slid down my thigh. "I use the stoplight system for checking in, but red won't cut it tonight. I won't give you what you need without a safeword, Dolyn." It pained me—literally—to state the truth, but I was a respected Dom and I would have an answer, or he could walk out the door unfulfilled.

The muscle in Dolyn's strong jawline ticked again. "My safeword is *beta*, Sir."

Interesting choice. Fitting, as the puzzle pieces of him moved around in my mind.

My instincts demanded I order him to his knees. My fingertips tingled to grasp hold of his hair and shove his face into my groin and command him to use his tongue to clean up the mess he'd caused inside my leathers. But, without the right to touch him, I had to ignore the hungry inferno he kindled inside me.

"You requested a caning." I double-checked, my focus back on the task at hand.

"Yes, Sir."

"And do you have a preferred position?"

"Over a bench, wrists and ankles shackled." He didn't hesitate to speak.

A shot of adrenaline rushed through me at the exact position I'd always craved to see Ashley displayed in.

I strode toward the bench where she had yet to kneel for me, the fantasy of her pale, off-limits skin intensifying the ache in my groin. I'd never lost myself in a scene and orgasmed unintentionally, but if anyone could take me to that point, it would be her.

I could now add this conundrum of a man to that small list.

But he alone deserved my attention tonight regardless of how the thoughts of the two of them wove together in my mind.

"Come," I commanded quietly, curious to watch how he responded.

Dolyn hurried to do as told, further revealing his true nature.

Satisfaction welled up inside my chest, and I swallowed what would have been a purr of delight had I allowed the noise to pass my lips.

With fluid grace, he lowered himself to rest against the angled bench, hands grasping the holds, knees spread but not quite far enough to expose the dark recess between his muscular ass cheeks.

My cock throbbed at imagining what his pucker might look and feel like stretched around my girth.

I practiced deep breathing for a full thirty seconds to settle my mind back on the task at hand. "Dolyn."

He turned toward me, attempting to keep his face a blank slate, but I'd been dominating willing participants for almost a decade. Rarely could a person hide their vulnerabilities or internal struggles from me.

A weight lay on Dolyn's mind or heart. Something seemed not exactly *off*, which would require that I end our scene before it began, but…unsettled? Or perhaps my attraction clouded my usual discernment. A yellow moment for sure, and I needed further assurance he knew what exactly it was he'd requested from me this evening.

"You're sure you want the cane?"

"I *need* the pain, Sir," he insisted, his tone rough.

I nodded, still not completely convinced we ought to continue, but I couldn't smother the lust heating my blood to inflict on his body what he'd asked for. "Tell me your safeword, Dolyn."

"Beta." He bit the word out, fire once more flashing in his eyes, assuring me of his hatred for the meaning behind it.

More pieces of his puzzle shifted around inside my brain as I studied his face. The twitch of the muscle in his jaw. The flare of desire in his swollen pupils. The slow bob of his Adam's apple as he turned his gaze to the floor, brow furrowing deeply.

Dolyn craved more than the torment of his skin and muscle, and he despised that part of himself.

For whatever reason, this man had called *my* club. Fate had placed him in front of *me*, and I would do everything within my power to set this man free. He'd captured my fascination and woke up an obsessive side I'd only experienced once before with Ashley.

My balls tightened at the mental reminder of her, and I clenched my teeth while taking care to buckle Dolyn's wrists tight without touching his skin. I longed to lean in and brush against his hip or shoulder, a mere whisper of contact, to experience that physical link for the first time.

The same damned desire I felt for Ashley but couldn't enjoy.

Would I pant for breath?

Leak enough pre-cum it would slip all the way down inside my leathers to my boots?

Grow feverish, a sudden flush of warmth spreading out from my aching groin?

Focus.

I knelt to buckle around Dolyn's ankles, and once finished, I glanced over to find his body rigid, knuckles white from clutching the holds.

That red flag sense rose again, but I looked at it from a different angle while pushing up to my feet.

A war raged inside Dolyn, one I recognized. I'd dealt with the same since Caroline had left me for a man who had no interest in exploring my kinks, which she considered disgusting.

The absolute need to be in this place clashed with both my and Dolyn's desire to escape what haunted us. Whether from shame or dislike of the lifestyle we both couldn't help but want, these yearnings stemmed from who we were in the deepest parts of ourselves.

While I didn't know how to bring peace to either of our minds, I could offer some respite from the noise in our heads we hadn't yet conquered.

I chose a synthetic cane since it packed more of a punch than wooden. High-strength, the stiffer rod would take us where we needed to go. A gentle Dom would aim to lay strokes out neat and parallel, but I was in the mood for a messy, angry caning, and Dolyn expected pain.

I would deliver—gladly, but still carefully land the lashes intentional and precise at first. And I would warm him up slowly to see how much he could actually take.

I hoped he could handle everything I had in me, because he'd woken a beastly aspect to my sadist side I'd never experienced before.

"Are you ready, Dolyn?" I asked quietly, my body vibrating, needing to let loose.

"Yes, Sir."

Go easy, I reminded myself while pulling my arm back and setting my sights on the thickest part of those round globes I wanted to bury my face between.

The first crack of my cane against his flesh made both of us flinch, but we remained silent.

"Color?" I asked, shifting my feet slightly while eyeing where I would land the next stripe given the go-ahead.

"Green, Sir."

Grinning, I hit his ass twice in a row, one lash right beneath the other, earning delicious grunts from the pain I'd gifted him. "Color?"

"Green," he stated through gritted teeth. "Now quit asking, stop holding back, and give me what I want, *Sir.*"

The petulant brat didn't know who he messed with. I let a chuckle loose along with a fourth swing across his upper thighs.

"Fuck," he muttered beneath his breath, his head finally tipping forward to hang.

Two more gorgeous red lines decorated his golden skin before sweat beaded his shoulders.

"Please," he whispered, and I knew without question he asked for more strength behind my hits rather than mercy.

Dolyn was a perfect fit for my sadistic side.

Time to give this boy what he begged for.

CHAPTER 3
DOLYN

My backside stung with a luscious burn, but I wanted to snort at the man's insistence he ought to be called my master.

Crack!

Another hit landed on my lower thighs, and I groaned, the power of his swings weakening my human form and loosening my tensed muscles.

While sceneing with Elijah, I'd never had issues keeping my beast's voice and natural inclinations to submit shackled up tight. I had always been in charge of our responses so I could control the outcome, something Father had taught me to do.

But this dominant called to my dragon, and the beast prowled beneath my skin with ravenous hunger, desperate to consume my human half. He fought for freedom the second my Sir for the evening had stepped into the private room one of his employees had shown me to.

Please.

An echo rather than a shriek broke through the muzzle,

and I clenched my eyes shut, my mouth repeating the word aloud.

I didn't beg.

Ever.

But the deep impact, the thumps that reached beneath the surface of my skin were more intense than anything I had experienced beneath Elijah's hand.

Vanni DiLoreto, self-proclaimed Master and owner of this club, gave me exactly what I craved.

Hyperaware of his movements, I sensed and tracked his arm drawing back.

Crack!

"Fuck," I groaned, shuddering as my cock bucked, hitting my belly. A lone droplet of pre-cum dripped to the floor.

Beta.

I clenched my jaw to keep the beast's whispered word off my lips. The pain, while exquisite, hadn't yet reached the pinnacle I'd sought this Dom out for, the consuming, mind-numbing agony that would shut down my senses. But I couldn't allow myself to go that far, which I feared would release the beast inside me.

My inner dragon continued to yank against his restraints, his pleadings for dominance over my human side whispering through my brain, but I wouldn't give over completely.

Couldn't.

Elijah might have stupidly shared a conscience with his beast and made decisions as one, but I chose to remain in charge so I could influence all outcomes, exactly as Father had taught me.

Every time Vanni checked in with me, I moaned an easy "green." I lusted to have his hands on me, his fingers in my ass, palm coaxing my balls to release while rubbing that magic spot inside me. My backside burned, every hit atop already bruised and stinging skin clouding my mind further as my body chased release without touch.

Need.

I ignored the inner whisper, concerned yet unable to be bothered he'd somehow removed his muzzle. While I'd never managed to come without a hand on my shaft, the tingling in my spine indicated I wouldn't be able to stop my reaction to the loveliest pain I'd ever endured.

More.

"More," I repeated my beast's pleading, and Vanni finally hit me like he meant it. "Fuck!" I hollered, limbs jerking in their restraints even though I had no wish to escape.

"Color, Dolyn?" Vanni demanded in his smooth-as-whiskey voice that caused another droplet to well at my slit.

"Green—please...*Sir*," I whined, too far gone in desire to care I sounded weak.

"You're doing so well for me, boy," Vanni murmured, his words like a soothing balm to my stinging skin, sweet as ambrosia on my tongue.

I whimpered at the words of praise I had been desperate for in my strive for perfection throughout my life. Nothing gave me more pleasure than knowing I pleased—

Another hit to my thighs cut off the thought, and I silently thanked my Sir for keeping me from spiraling deep into my shame.

Vanni didn't hold back but crisscrossed slashes over my ass and thighs in what would be the most brutal beating I'd ever taken. I lamented the fact my dragonblood wouldn't allow bruising to remain into the next day to remind me of the pleasure I'd been gifted.

I trembled in my bonds, my inner dragon slashing at my will, shrieking and begging me to fully give in.

There would be no true submission on our part.

Ever.

"No," I whispered at my beast, barely audible, but Vanni heard.

He immediately ceased striking me.

"Don't—please don't stop." I swallowed against the dryness in my throat, shaking my head as tremors rippled through me. "I need more," I begged.

A low growl, reminiscent of a true Blood Born, sounded from behind me, causing my cock to jolt again.

I moaned, goose bumps shivering over my skin.

Another hit landed lower than the rest, and I pressed back, widening my thighs as far as I could. Cool air slid over my desperate hole, and I shook my head against the desire to be penetrated with a single thrust that would send me over the edge.

I had no words left in my mind, no ability to speak what I lusted for, but I bit my tongue until the tang of metal coated my mouth to keep from asking for what only Elijah had ever been allowed.

Vanni smacked the tip of his cane against my exposed pucker with the perfect amount of sting, ripping all thoughts of anyone or anything but him and his delightful torture from my mind.

"Again," I gasped, and he gave me what I needed—but harder, with a sharp snap of his wrist.

Cum erupted up through my shaft, and I roared as white light flashed behind my eyes. Spunk continued to spurt from my body, a consuming release like I'd never experienced before.

I'd come completely untouched.

Yessss.

I groaned in agreement with my dragon, holding tight to my control over him as I shuddered with every pulse of seed through my shaft. Couldn't slip into subspace and be vulnerable to a beast who lusted to kneel for a master.

A grunt sounded behind me as I sagged against the bench, and I turned my weary head, blinking and panting as Vanni jerked himself off. His cock was perfect in length and girth, and even though the man had made me drain my balls without a single caress, my hole fluttered with want to feel him buried deep inside my guts.

"Fuck," Vanni muttered as though he considered the same, his focus on my ass.

"Come for me," I gasped, still out of breath but needing this to end before I caved to my beast's baser desire to be owned.

A deep groan rose past Vanni's lips, his eyes closing, veins popping along his forearm as he stroked over his length. His first wave of spunk shot five feet from his slit, a milky rope that had to be a few weeks' worth of cum.

I ignored his massive load, choosing to watch my Sir's face as he painted the floor with stripes of white.

His dark eyebrows furrowed as though he was in pain, full lips parted as he struggled to fill his lungs. A flush coated his cheekbones above his neatly clipped beard, a slight sheen of sweat worked into the long strands of hair hanging around his face. Muscled as though he spent hours every day in the gym, Vanni made leathers look good. His prominent pecs and abs that humans fought hard for were also covered in sweat.

I allowed myself a few seconds to imagine licking over every indent of his torso, tasting his salt. Licking his cum—

No, I mouthed the word rather than give it tone, refusing to interrupt Vanni's prolonged release.

The man was gorgeous, no question, and upon first laying eyes on him, I'd been tempted to do away with the two limits I'd listed for the evening.

But I was saving myself for my fated female and beta.

No one would touch me but those destined for me, nor

would any other male's cum slicken my lips or coat my tongue.

Vanni finished, and I slumped in relief of having escaped temptation, my eyes closing as I enjoyed the tingles settling through my limbs. As a dominant, I expected Vanni would feel cheated by not attending to aftercare as he did with others who submitted to his hand, but my no-touch limit still stood firm.

I heard him zipper up, curse, then chuckle.

"Never came so hard or so much in my life," he muttered before walking around the room, every shift of his leathers keeping me aware of his presence. "Drink."

I pried my eyes open to find a bottle of water in front of me and didn't hesitate to obey Vanni's command as he tipped it to my lips. A few pulls emptied the bottle.

"Good boy," he murmured, and for one heartbeat, I yearned to feel his hand stroking over my sweaty hair.

Another bite to my tongue stopped me from asking for the type of affection Father would consider needy. A weakness that led to ruination.

Both of which he'd claimed of his beta mate.

Vanni crouched down beside my head, and I met his mossy-green gaze. Yellowish star bursts radiated from his pupils, creating the most gorgeous eyes I'd ever seen the like of.

Except for my female, of course. Her beauty was unrivaled.

But I anxiously awaited finally standing before my beta and seeing in person the brilliant green orbs I'd caught sight of in Dakota's vision. I couldn't imagine my beta being any more beautiful or enticing than this human male kneeling before me, but he *must* be.

"Okay?" Vanni asked, his voice rasped as though he'd been the one crying out during our scene.

My inner beast stretched too close to the surface of my skin, and having regained some of my strength, I took the opportunity to shove him back into the prison where his weak ass belonged.

"I'm fine," I rumbled my reply, growing antsy over being tied down. "Unbuckle me."

Vanni didn't speak while releasing me from my bonds, and I pushed upright, swaying on unsteady legs. He reached for me, but I held up my hand to keep him at bay.

"I'm *fine*," I insisted as my dragonblood warmed, the ability to heal faster than mere humans pumping through my arteries.

He glanced down over me, gaze lingering on my flaccid cock. "I won't argue that fact."

His flirting caught me off guard, and I fucking smiled. Flashed my teeth at a mere human for making me feel good.

My inner beast purred and settled in his prison at the deepest reaches of me, tail curling around his body, a huffed exhale emptying his lungs.

Alpha.

Ignoring his whisper, I erased the smile from my mouth.

"Are you sure you're all right?" Vanni checked in with me again, handing me a second bottle of water, careful not to touch my hand in the exchange. "No one has ever taken my full strength, and the fact you're standing and lucid..." Lips pressing together, he shook his head as I guzzled his offering. "You're one hell of a man, Dolyn Kemmerly."

I had endured and stood strong so quickly after the beating because I was Blood Born, but this human didn't need to know that.

"It would take a lot to drop me to my knees," I informed him while re-capping the empty container.

Lust flared in his steady gaze, and I cursed that nothing

about this human's body suggested dragonblood flowed in his veins. He would be a prime candidate—

I cut the thought off. This man, while smelling of delicious musk, was a dominant and, like me, would never submit himself to another even if he had been a fated beta mate.

He gestured toward the bottle, and I handed it over, escaping temptation to simply brush my fingertips over his.

"Will I see you again, Dolyn?" A hint of insecurity inflected in his tone, and I allowed myself a single fantasy of grabbing hold of his black leather harness and riding his ass from behind.

My cock didn't so much as twitch but not surprising considering the release Vanni had gifted me through pain.

"I have no intentions of returning," I stated firmly, retrieving the robe I'd been given for walking through the lounge. My clothes were in a locker room off the entryway to Vanni's club. Showers were also available, but I preferred complete privacy for bathing.

"Thank you for gifting me what I requested." I shoved my arms through the sleeves and settled the satin material over my shoulders. The hem hung beneath my ass but only barely. The cane marks on my lower thighs would be visible to anyone who cared to look, and while I hated to have other patrons know I had submitted my body to *anyone*, I would avoid their gazes and stride with purpose toward my destination.

Turning away, I lifted my chin and let myself out of the private room, shutting the door firmly behind me.

My dragon whimpered, but I ignored him as I did the club members and employees.

One last night, I had told myself, and it'd been so good, better even than any pain Elijah had inflicted. Although days had passed, it seemed mere hours earlier I'd been heart-broken over the loss of my lover.

Thanks to Vanni, I now felt confident in taking the next step toward my destiny.

Wanting to stretch my wings, I camouflaged once out of sight from other night owls in Manhattan, shifted on a quiet corner, not bothering to save any clothing. The shredded material and boots lay below as I escaped like a rocket into the night sky.

I allowed my inner beast a little more freedom than usual, his heightened sense of smell drinking in the cold air, tasting every subtle hint of the city far beneath us on our tongue.

Wanted to scent him.

I ignored the voice radiating through my head. My serpentine body moved through pockets of air, every flex of muscle in my lower half a sweet, achy reminder of Vanni's heavy hand.

Submit.

Master Vanni.

I told the beast to shut up, but he persisted in complaining that I hadn't allowed him a taste of the domi-nant who'd given my human half pleasure. After a solid ten minutes of manipulative whispers trying to convince me that submission would have been sweet and rewarding, I had enough.

We are *alpha*, I reminded the beast while muzzling him.

I flew eastward in peaceful silence, banking and dipping in the cooling Atlantic before bursting back up through its surface, salt water snorting from my nostrils. Talons skim-ming the surface, I took the time to reflect on all of the emotions that had been roused in the previous couple of days.

Anger and hurt over Elijah claiming someone other than me.

Elation at his female's vision of the two mates destined for me and locating one.

Relief for never having submitted fully to my ex-lover whom I had considered settling for.

Excitement and absolute joy when stalking my own female to and from work the past couple of days, longing while watching her move beyond her curtains while hidden in the shadows outside her condo at night.

Absolute pleasure in the release of a lifetime.

Confidence that my fate lay within my grasp.

By the time I hovered near the balcony off my penthouse's bedroom, my dragonblood had healed the delicious pain in my backside and thighs.

I grabbed hold of the railing with one clawed foot and started to shift. Once bone and muscle shrank enough I would fit, I leapt onto the sturdy platform off my suite's bedroom to finish the transformation.

Stretching my neck side to side, I assessed my human form as it solidified into completeness.

All traces of the torture I'd allowed to my body had dissipated. A glance over my shoulder revealed the markings were gone from what I could see of my thighs. At least I'd gotten a good look at them before changing in the locker room. I held a deep appreciation for the club's owner, respect as well, for his precise hits.

My inner beast moaned his misery, a mere whisper of tone in the back of my head, but I wouldn't be swayed into letting him have further say.

Two steps took me to the glass slider. Having my suite on the top floor of the building across from Tolzman Industries,

I never bothered with the lock, which made for easy reentry into my Manhattan domain.

Silence clung to my bedroom, and for the first time, I missed the comforting noises of having a companion.

"Soon," I murmured to myself.

My inner dragon hummed his agreement, which was rare and always tended to loosen my rigid hold over him.

"Argue with me, and I'll silence you," I warned him, deciding on leniency while removing my restraint on his voice.

He didn't offer further sound, so I allowed him his quiet freedom to reflect verbally if he so desired. The beating and flight had eased him thoroughly, and he curled up inside, content. But not for long. Eventually, he would attempt to coerce me into doing his wishes.

A long, hot shower eased the tension in my shoulders, but sleep eluded me once I rested upon my king-sized mattress. Exhaustion clung to my bones regardless of my active mind considering how I would reveal myself to Ashley now that I was ready.

Steal.

The beast took advantage as he always did once my human side experienced tiredness, however, he stated what *was* my right as an alpha.

Force.

I rolled to my stomach, planning to ignore him since he didn't argue our status for once.

Ours. Take.

Ashley did belong to us—was destined to stand by my side, exactly as he insisted.

"I thought I'd wanted that with Elijah too, though," I grumbled into my pillow and punched the fluff that wilted quickly beneath the weight of my head.

She is a fragile thing, isn't she?

I growled at the beast's sudden eloquence but didn't silence him since he spoke the truth I didn't mind hearing. Knowing him, he would push things too far in attempts to get what he wanted, same as he always did when I offered his voice freedom. But until then, I would allow his waxing poetic. Perhaps his soothing tone would ready me for sleep.

Like a spring flower rising out of the frozen depths of the earth in desperate need of sustenance and care.

"I won't be swayed by pretty words," I warned, my words muttered into the pillow.

As beautiful and glorious as the rising sun.

"I will not be manipulated into doing as the Blood Born of old did," I told him what I'd said countless times already.

Soft, supple...she will be as refreshing as the finest wine, the sweetest honeysuckle on our tongue.

My cock swelled again as I imagined my face between Ashley's thighs, lapping at the arousal her body wouldn't be able to help but produce from her alpha's touch and scent once the beginnings of our bond bloomed.

Addictive nectar. A wet, clutching pussy to ease our ache.

My balls drew up, my shaft throbbing over my beast's whispered suggestions, and I rolled once more, unable to help myself. Giving in to my body's need, I wrapped my hand around my swollen length, knowing any release I found wouldn't be nearly as satisfying as my last beneath Vanni's cane.

Brow furrowing, I focused on what my inner dragon whispered about our female rather than how my backside's desire to be filled wakened.

Imagine the clutch of her inner walls around us, drawing us deeper against her womb, the contractions of her body begging for our seed.

Erotic imaginations of sinking into her, again and again, flooded my mind, enticing pre-cum to well at my slit.

Flood her. Breed her.

A tight grip while working myself ensured a climax within a few strokes. Growls rumbled in my chest, and I bit my tongue to keep from roaring as disappointing shots of white laced over my lower abs. Grunts accompanied every pitiful spurt, and my body contorted, muscles flexing with my unsatisfying release.

Soon, my human half?

I gasped a ragged breath as the last of my hot seed dribbled over my knuckles instead of against the opening of Ashley's womb where it belonged.

"Yes," I managed while struggling to fill my lungs. "Soon."

CHAPTER 4

ASHLEY

For over a week, every time I left my condo, I swore someone watched me. The feeling remained throughout the walk then subway ride into Manhattan. But no matter how often I scanned my surroundings or checked from my periphery, I never saw a hint of suspicious intent from anyone around me.

Considering the trauma I'd endured as a child, fear over having captured someone's undivided attention should have kept me on edge each and every moment out among the masses of the city. Instead, I found myself intrigued, worriedly wishing for…more.

I stood beside my office window hoping for a hint of warmth to kindle between my thighs. Coolness remained in my blood as it always did once I entered Tolzman Industries.

Sighing, I pressed my forehead to the glass, watching tiny people far below hurrying to get home after a long day of work. Only a few minutes remained before I was off the clock and join the masses where my watcher's eyes would send delicious shivers down my spine.

It had been years since I'd experienced arousal on its own and for good reason.

Was my body responding to mere fantasy because I'd been seeking healing for my distaste for physical touch? Or had the sexual nature within me finally begun to bloom how it ought to had I not been ruined as a teenager?

I'd made a wrong decision when physical desire had first roused in my body, and no amount of meetings with my sex therapist, Doctor Hasslet, had healed the resulted brokenness from messing with fire back then. No attempts at self-pleasure had coaxed arousal to life let alone allowed me to climax. No vibrator, dildo, or solo finger-fuckings encouraged wetness to dampen my thighs or send me tumbling headlong into relief I barely remembered enjoying prior to the assault.

But this sense of being stalked while outdoors stirred something up inside me that I couldn't wait to share with my therapist next week.

While readying my things to head home a short time later, I shivered in anticipation of feeling my follower's full focus, his desire for me. That sense of power I'd experienced as a teenager upon drawing the attention of an older, well-respected man had returned but grew more potent with every passing day.

At first, tingles of awareness had raised the hairs on my arms and sent a pleasant shiver down my spine.

The second through fifth mornings I had left my condo for work, my nipples had grown tight, and warmth settled low in my belly.

The last two days, my body had become fully stimulated, the feeling intense and consuming. Slickness coated my panties, and my nipples tightened to aching buds from my stalker's want that I swore I could taste on my tongue.

But once in the privacy of my home, fear of failure to get

myself off kept me from reaching between my legs to seek out relief from the new stirrings inside. I'd been celibate for close to a dozen years, and I swore a lifetime of the same lay in my future unless some magical dick healed my trauma.

As if.

I enjoyed reading stories and watching movies that suggested happiness and healing could be found beneath or riding a man's cock, but those escapes I allowed myself inside the pages of a book or on screen weren't reality.

Healing wouldn't come overnight, Doctor Hasslet had said when I'd first started meeting with him a few years ago, but he assured me it *would* eventually. I needed to keep pushing myself and taking strides toward the future I desired, one that included a sensitive, patient man who had the ability to love me regardless of my brokenness. In the meantime, Doctor Hasslet recommended meeting monthly with a Dominant to help me on my walk toward wholeness.

He had suggested his friend, Master Vanni. A hotter-than-hell Dominant with a sexy, short beard and unbearably beautiful green eyes, he owned the sex club I'd been gifted a membership to through my doctor. I'd learned in the hours I'd spent with Master Vanni that he was trustworthy and respectful.

Our first sit-down to go over the intake forms and my experience, of which I had none in the BDSM lifestyle, had been disagreeable to say the least. During the scene that followed, I'd been too self-conscious to let go and enjoy any aspect of the training for submission. The second Friday night we'd met, I was comfortable enough to accept a bit of pain. I'd also experienced hints of real arousal stir between my thighs over the crop he'd taken to my backside.

The third, fourth, and fifth scenes, Master Vanni and my growing trust in him had allowed me to find greater pleasure in the pain he gifted me. The last time we had scened together, he'd brought me to climax with a flogger and given me joy I'd never hoped to experience. Tears had coursed down my cheeks during aftercare, but he'd held me wrapped up in a blanket to keep our skin from touching, his deep, soothing voice like honey coating a sore throat. He'd also given me his private number and ordered me to reach out if I ever needed him.

Although we had learned ways of shutting off my mind in order to climax, I had yet to allow skin-on-skin contact, nor was I ready for penetration of any sort. Regardless of my forward progress, I feared such intimacy would send me spiraling back to that weekend I'd been tied up and used to fulfill a sick man's fantasies.

Master Vanni and I were scheduled to meet tomorrow at his club, and the combined thoughts of my stalker and the expectation Master would set me free in just over twenty-four hours caused my core to throb.

I entered and stood impatiently in the elevator, waiting to arrive at the ground floor, my heart palpitating. Never had I looked forward to a Friday more.

People took too long exiting the elevator, and I grumbled my impatience in my mind while buttoning my coat closed against the impending winter evening awaiting me outside.

My stomach tightened as I stepped into the cold air, my gaze darting up and down the street. Barely able to breathe, I sought out the sense of being watched, waiting for pleasure to wash over me, turning my core to lava and easing the tension in my entire body.

Frigid shards of awareness lanced at me instead, freezing me in my tracks. Alarm skittered along my spine, threatening to loosen my bladder.

This feeling was *distinctively opposite* from what I'd become familiar with.

My instincts screamed at me to flee the stare that had

turned chilling, but what if he was a chaser? What if he had a predator kink and saw me as his prey?

A shudder rippled through my body, leaving my core dry as a desert. Alarming red flags raised and snapped inside my mind, causing me to shrink into myself in desperation to hide.

My throat tightened as I pretended to fix my coat's collar while discretely glancing around. People brushed past me where I stood in the middle of the sidewalk, the right side of my face burning like ice pellets slashed at my cheeks. Stomach tight, I swallowed hard and fully turned my focus northward, needing to face my stalker rather than run.

A dark shadow a block away drew my attention like a beacon but slipped into the alleyway.

Immediately, the sixth sense of uncomfortable awareness dissolved, allowing me to draw breath. My lingering discomfort insisted I move. Turning in the opposite direction, I hurried for the subway entrance, chin tucked to my chest, ready to escape the bustling crowd of people and hide away in my condo.

What happened since that morning when I'd sadly entered work and left my sweet stalker's stare behind? Had his seemingly harmless thoughts toward me turned violent? Were intentions developing in his mind that went beyond attraction and longing from afar?

Warmth caressed my face, and a recognizable shiver of awareness slid over my skin. My skin pebbled as heat kindled between my thighs. My lungs opened fully, allowing oxygen to flow freely.

There he was.

The familiar sense I'd been looking forward to, the same one that had accompanied me to and from work for a week.

Were *two* men watching me?

I lifted my focus directly ahead from where I could sense

the good eyes, but no one seemed to pay me any mind. No orbs stared at me from the backs of heads. No person craned their neck to meet my gaze while making their way deeper into the bowels of the city.

I considered the idea of a second man's gaze pinned on me while slipping beneath Manhattan's streets for the subway. Whoever had been waiting outside my work was definitely not the man who made me feel protected and instilled a craving for physical fulfillment rather than release brought on by pain.

Rather than making me feel like a bug beneath a telescope, my stalker's study caused arousal to dampen my panties, and I bit the inside of my lip to keep from moaning in my desire for his touch. My insides purred as I waited for my train and continued my search for what felt like warm sunshine on my face.

No one within sight seemed to give two shits about the petite woman hunkered in her coat along with the others anxious to leave the workday behind, but I swore someone did.

Somewhere.

I couldn't wait to meet with Doctor Hasslet to share with him what I'd been experiencing. Perhaps he would think the broken parts of my mind caused my body to respond to an imaginary presence, but until that time, I would gladly partake in what could very well be fantasy.

Telling myself I had imagined the *bad* set of eyes, I focused on the daydream of the good eyes drinking in the vision of me. He appreciated my lack of makeup, something I'd given up in *the after*. The less I did to draw attention to myself, the safer I felt.

Rumbling grew, the clack of metal wheels on tracks announcing my ride drew close.

The warmth of his presence followed me through the

opened doors of the train once it stopped, and I continued to experience arousal yet comfort from his nearness. I swore he stood inches away, perhaps breathing my scent deeply into his nose, but neither the teenaged kid with a backpack or the thirty-something businessman flanking me indicated interest in the woman sharing space with them. People sat directly behind me with barely any room between their knees and my legs, and another glance over the three in close proximity showed two wrapped up in their phones, the third with her nose in a book.

I turned back around to face the doors, sighing that I couldn't see who affected me like this. Perhaps my brain *had* invented this stalker as a coping mechanism or distraction—

An exhale ghosted over my nape, and I spun, jostling against the legs of the elderly woman behind me. She glanced up from her cell.

"Sorry," I murmured, my face heating, before facing forward.

Perhaps a ghost followed me.

An angel?

Demon?

I shook my head at the possible scenarios, my lips pursing. My traumatic past had directed me toward atheism, and I no longer believed in spirits along with the god and book my parents had used to brainwash me. Indoctrination was the worst evil, not allowing for critical thinking and personal growth.

Both my mother and father had been part of my abuser's faithful flock and worked in his church. When I'd returned from my weekend sleepover at a friend's house I'd lied about going to, neither believed me when I told them about the assault. I'd begged to go to the hospital and have a rape kit done to prove I didn't lie about having my virginity stolen from me, but they'd refused.

Sitting in my physical and emotional pain, I had accepted that I was to blame for what had happened. Our beloved pastor had been tempted and fallen into sin because I'd flirted with him, enticed him with my budding curves. Both of my parents had been employed by the church and still were last I'd heard. Speaking up to anyone else would have brought about dire consequences that probably would have left my family destitute.

I'd chosen to keep my mouth shut since I'd been taught children were meant to be seen and not heard, and I feared hell as a consequence of my supposed disobedience to that leather-bound book.

From that day forward, I'd stayed home as much as possible, sticking to my mother's side whenever we were at church, even though something inside me insisted she wouldn't protect me in the way she ought to if needed.

I graduated and escaped to the Christian college my parents had insisted I attend, happy to be eight hours away from home. Four years of rarely returning to visit, and I received a degree in missions, something I'd never wanted but had agreed to in order to please my parents. With indoctrination's claws still in me, it wasn't until a friend I'd secretly found online had asked me to come visit her in New York—fuck my religious upbringing and college education— that I realized the lies I'd been fed since birth.

I left the Bible Belt behind and began my religious deconstruction while sleeping on my friend's couch. Two years and three base-pay jobs later, fate slammed me *literally* into a rich man, the coffee to-go tray in my hands smashing against his chest and emptying hot liquid down the front of his suit that probably cost more than both of my parents made in a year combined.

Elijah Tolzman had smiled rather than cussed when our gazes locked, and I immediately felt a strange connection to him, as though he was a kindred spirit. Perhaps I'd known him in another life, but he was like the older brother I always wished had been around to protect me from those in spiritual authority I'd been manipulated into submitting to.

Mr. Tolzman obviously sensed the same, because he had hired me as one of his secretaries, and my new life began. With twice the salary I'd made anywhere else, I eventually saved a small nest egg and had decent enough credit that allowed me to purchase the condo in Jersey. I finally had silence and space to just *be* and explore who I wanted to become.

But the trauma had continued to hold me back until the previous five months when I'd started visiting a BDSM club where I'd met another man I felt a connection with. While enjoying the warmth of the good eyes still caressing over my nape as the train clacked along toward Jersey, I considered Master Vanni.

His soothing presence never failed to make me wish I was stronger than my fear of touch. If anyone could help me break down those walls, it would be him. He had my full trust, and now more than ever, I wanted to move another step forward. Perhaps I would ask him to push me tomorrow. Or maybe I would take the initiative and put my hand on his sexy forearm and the veins I'd been dying to trace with a fingertip.

My core pulsed, and I swallowed a sudden rush of saliva. I'd found Master Vanni alluring since day one, but this was the first time desire welled over thoughts of him. Elation rose, fluttering my heartbeat.

Things were going to change.

I would hang onto this physical excitement and the positive feels from my stalker and carry them with me to Master Vanni's club tomorrow night.

The train slowed for my stop, and I slipped out onto the platform, heading toward home, unaware of the cold.

Good eyes trailed along behind me into the quieter neighborhood, the gaze keeping my skin alive, pulse heightened, and my core just as wet as Master did once he started to hurt me with the most exquisite, stinging pain.

A few glances over my shoulder assured my vision that I walked alone, but I refused to believe the empty sidewalk that my eyes suggested.

I let myself into my condo, hating how the sixth sense shut off once the door locked behind me.

"Until tomorrow," I murmured, already looking forward to leaving for work in the morning. While peeling off my coat and sweater, I snuck a peek past my curtained front windows. Neither glass panes afforded me an eyeful of the man I wanted to see more than the dinner of beef stew I'd put in my slow cooker earlier that morning.

Sighing, I went about my evening routine, settling in for the night.

An hour later, my belly full and dressed in fleece PJs instead of work clothes, I lounged on the couch with my e-reader. At reading about the lead character forgetting to take out the trash, I realized I'd done the same.

"Damnitalltohell," I muttered, forcing myself to be responsible and get up.

Still grumbling at myself, I gathered every bit of refuse from the condo, emptying my fridge of leftovers too.

I stepped outside, intent on hurrying to the sidewalk where I usually left my weekly bag of trash.

The bad vibe I'd felt earlier hit me full force in the face like a slap, pulling me up short on my stoop. Heart racing, I glanced up and down the street. Too many shadows lurked, offering hiding places for whomever meant me harm.

My skin crawled, my breaths heavy and puffing in white clouds in front of my mouth.

Movement captured my attention, and I whipped my head to the left, the trash bag slipping from my grasp and tumbling down the stairs.

Someone stood near the corner of Walnut and Deerfield Avenue but back enough out of the way that the streetlight didn't offer me a good look at their face.

They stared my way, keeping me frozen like a deer in headlights.

Hairs rose all over my body, and I squeezed my core's muscles to keep from peeing myself.

He took a step toward me, and I stumbled backward over the threshold, slamming the door as I went.

A sob ripped from me as I attempted to lock up with shaking hands. A frigid chill settled into my bones, and for the first time in years, I wished I didn't live alone, that I had a companion to help calm my rising panic.

The lock finally slid into place, and I ran on weak legs from window to window, making sure they were locked, curtains closed, flicking off lights as I went deeper into my condo.

This *was* real, definitely not a figment of my imagination.

I pushed into my closet, knees drawn up to my chest, my eyes clenched shut while rocking back and forth.

Visions of the past crystalized like jagged ice pelting the inside of my head.

Burning rope wrapped around my wrists and ankles. Aching throat from having been gagged over and over again with a rigid piece of flesh that had violated my other private areas as well. I was sore between my thighs and in a hole I hadn't known until that night could be utilized for anything other than an exit.

My stomach heaved, and I tore from the tiny space, barely making it to the bathroom in time.

Vomit erupted up my esophagus, burning and choking, and I sobbed once finished, flushing the dinner I'd eaten while attempting to distract my mind with what tomorrow held in wait.

Master.

The echo in my head gave me strength and courage to crawl into the living room, my wary gaze flitting from covered window to still-locked door.

Silence rang in my ears, and tears dripped down my face as I fumbled on the coffee table for my cell phone.

He answered after the first ring.

"Help me," I managed to whisper before breaking down into sobs again.

CHAPTER 5
VANNI

I'd been daydreaming about Dolyn and Ashley both on their knees for me while caressing over the hard-on inside my sweats when she called.

Two whispered words set off my protective instincts and deflated my dick in a heartbeat. "Where are you? What's wrong?" I hopped off my couch and strode toward my front door, stomping into my workout sneakers on the way as she quietly cried and attempted to answer my questions between hitched breaths. I grabbed my keys and wallet from the table in my entryway before hurrying into the private elevator that would rush me to the ground floor.

Ashley continued to whimper but finally managed to whisper something about a stalker outside her home.

Rage erupted in my guts, causing my jaw to clench and my eyesight to go red. I smashed the first-floor button, swallowing down a curse, thankful as *fuck* I'd insisted she take my cell number in the event she ever needed me outside the club.

"Are you alone in the house, Ashley?" I asked, my calm tone far from matching the fire stirring inside me.

"Yes." She fumbled with her cell.

"Did you call the police?"

"I—I'm p-probably overreacting. What would I t-tell them?" She let out an unsteady exhale in an attempt to control her emotions. "That I've been feeling t-two sets of eyes on me? That one arouses me and one t-turns my b-bowels to liquid?"

I rubbed a hand over my face, cursing beneath my breath. Was there more to her trauma than the physical? Did mental instability cause this? She'd shown no signs of such an illness, and surely, she would have informed me of something that serious when we'd sat down and negotiated moving forward with sceneing together.

"Trust your instincts and stay put," I ordered. Ashley was always a good girl for me and would do what I said. "It's going to be a little before I get to you, but I'm on my way."

"Okay." She sounded broken, and my heart ached to hold her tight, wrap her up in my arms to make that feeling of a boogeyman disappear from her conscience.

But she'd been off-limits from day one, and I refused to cross boundaries until invited to step over those lines.

As though connected by a living cord, I'd felt Ashley's presence the instant she'd entered the lounge on the Friday night Doc Hasslet had first booked for her. She had called to me like a siren to a man floundering about at sea as I swore I'd been until that moment. The scent of sweet vanilla had filled my lungs once we stood in close proximity, and I hadn't been able to tear my focus off her beautiful, tortured violet eyes as my mouth watered to lick into hers.

Focus.

"Where are you right now?" I asked while hitting the fob on my keyring, my Mercedes beeping loud in the quiet parking garage I hurried across.

"Living room—behind the couch." Ashley's lack of stuttering eased some of the tension in my face.

"Can you see out your windows?"

"No." She continued to keep her voice low, going on to explain about the shades being drawn.

"I'm going to stay on the phone with you until I get there, okay?"

"Thank you, Master Vanni, I—I know I'm being ridiculous, but something is just *wrong,* and I don't have anyone else—"

"You're not ridiculous," I stated firmly, "and call me Vanni right now. Please."

She exhaled quietly, a soft sigh I dreamed of hearing in my bed beside me at night, but all thoughts of fantasy and somehow magically healing her needed to stay in the backseat until we got to the bottom of this shit.

"Now be a good girl and tell me about your day, Ashley. From the time you woke up until now."

"I can do that," she whispered.

I listened as she explained this "feeling" she had concerning a sure stalker from over the previous week and a newer, different one from today that had raised every red flag imaginable. A strange occurrence, to be sure, especially the sense of someone hovering close on the subway train. Her tumbling emotions caused by both supposed stalkers made my chest tighten—but the thought of another man watching...*waiting* for a vulnerable moment to possibly rip her out of my life?

Fuck that shit.

Possessiveness burned in my veins, molten lava oozing beneath my skin and wanting to erupt in searing flames to devour anyone thinking they could get close to her. I'd never felt so protective over someone I'd scened with, an instinctive *knowing* that she'd been meant to walk into my club and submit to my dominance.

Same as Dolyn.

Fuck.

I rubbed a hand over my face as Ashley's quiet voice continued to fill my ear.

Perhaps it really was time to invest more of myself with her and allow some vulnerability. Maybe a good, long talk was needed to settle my mind—pursue a possible relationship or insist she find another Dom to submit to.

My lip curled.

That second option? *Definitely* a new hard limit of mine. No way in hell could I bear the thought of Ashley gifting her pleasure and release to someone other than me.

I turned onto Walnut Street and focused on my immediate surroundings. I let Ashley know I approached, driving slowly, head swiveling so I could scan every inch of the condos lining the road.

A young couple walked a dog, bundled in puffer coats with beanies on their heads. One middle-aged man dragged his trash can to the end of his drive as others had done earlier in the night for the morning pickup.

Other than those three, I didn't see another soul in the areas lit by streetlights.

"I'm here—sit tight while I check things out," I told her while pulling up to the curb in front of her walkway. "I'm going to hang up now, and don't open your door unless you hear my voice on the other side."

"Okay," she stated quietly, sounding a little less sure than she'd been moments ago.

"See you soon." I ended the call and turned off my car.

Silence lay heavy over the interior, and I attempted to even my breaths while peering in all three of my mirrors and through the windshield. I'd only gotten off the phone with

Ashley because I wanted to have both fists available for anyone sneaking around thinking they could take what didn't belong to them.

But I didn't see a living soul or evidence of one nearby.

The dog walkers had gone around a corner, and the neighbor shut himself back behind his front door. No puffed white exhale rose from someone in shadow. Not even a breeze traveled down the empty road stirring leafless branches from the few trees alongside the street.

I opened my car door and stood tall, actively scanning with a lifted chin and shoulders back.

Stillness and a sense of solitude surrounded me.

Turning, I examined the front of Ashley's condo, the dim light atop the stoop, the curtained-off windows, and the darkness beyond. Other units were pressed up on either side of hers: two on one, three on the other. I strode up her sidewalk, retrieved the dropped bag of trash, and took it to the sidewalk like her neighbors.

No unease made my hair stand on end, but I remained vigilant, looking into every dark shadow lining the street. Still not seeing anything unusual, I returned to Ashley's door and knocked.

"Who is it?" Muffled through the door, Ashley's voice shook.

"It's me, Ash—Vanni."

Two locks disengaged before the door creaked open a few inches.

Pale, eyes wide, Ashley peered at me through the crack. A rushed exhale left her, and she yanked open the door, huddling behind it.

I quickly stepped over the threshold and carefully pulled the door away from her and locked us in.

She hugged herself, her shoulders hunched beneath a purple pajama top made of flannel.

Hands fisted at my sides, I fought off the need to grab her in my arms and hug her unease away. "You okay?"

A harsh swallow sounded before a keening noise rose from her caved-in chest.

"Ash." My voice broke, and I held out my hand. "Can I…"

Ashley threw herself at me, fingers grasping at my coat. She buried her face in my chest, and I gently wrapped my arms around her, eyes closing and heart racing as a sense of rightness flooded through me. Ashley fit perfectly against me, fulfilled the part of me that longed to have someone to hold. "I've got you, baby girl. You're safe now." My voice rumbled low and soothing, full of promise and firm in confidence.

Sobs ripped from her as I clutched her close without touching her skin, her petite body shuddering along my front.

I'd heard her cry every time she'd been tied up and beneath my flogger, and same as then, the soft scent of vanilla swarmed my senses and dizzied my brain, tempting me to run my fingertips over her throat and into her hair. Bury my face against the satiny strands and breathe her deep into my lungs where that piece of her wouldn't be able to escape me.

No doubt, I was gone on the woman, and that truth turned my stomach to a rock no matter how much I secretly longed for true love and a sense of belonging.

Ashley had major issues, and not being able to fuck her, watch my dick disappear down her throat, or mark her skin with my cum, stung like a thousand hornets attacking at once. She was untouchable in every sexual manner except for receiving pain—and even then, I couldn't use my palms or fingers.

But maybe moving forward we could be more vulnerable with each other. Perhaps grow together and learn how to lower our walls. Doctor Hasslet had assured me healing could be found, but I had to want it.

Ashley created that yearning inside me, and I would be a fool to ignore the draw.

But first, we needed to take care of the matters at hand.

"What do you need from me, Ashley?" I asked once her cries faded to sniffles and I expected she could speak clearly.

"I—I don't know, Master."

"It's Vanni right now," I reminded her, rubbing my palms over the softness of her long-sleeve shirt, wishing I caressed her skin beneath.

She inhaled deeply before stepping away from me and wiping her eyes.

The front of me went cold, and I forced my arms to my sides, hands fisting to ward off the temptation to pull her back where she belonged. "I would invite you to spend the evening at my penthouse, but I think you'll be more comfortable here with me on your couch rather than in an unfamiliar place. It's your decision, but either way, I'm not leaving your side tonight."

Nibbling her lower lip, she nodded. "Thank you. I'd rather stay here if you're sure you don't mind?"

"Not at all." I glanced through the entryway into the living room and the wide couch she'd been hiding behind. "We could sit and talk for a while?" I suggested.

Ashley emptied her lungs with a strong exhale. "I should probably call my therapist."

"It's okay if you'd rather do that. You don't have to share personal information with me."

She huffed a shaky laugh, her violet eyes glancing at me and away again. "Pretty sure we've shared more personal things than most acquaintances."

"You have me there," I said with a smile, wishing she could have me other ways.

"Want a drink?"

"Water would be great," I replied, slipping off my coat and hanging it on a hook beside hers.

Ashley shuffled into the kitchen in the cutest pink bunny slippers, and I trailed after her, scanning the interior of her home while she flicked on lights. She had blinds and curtains drawn over every window, their drab tan color matching the rest of the interior. Few personal items littered the area, and not even the kitchen appeared lived-in with how clean it was.

Was she a naturally tidy person, or did her trauma inflict the need for control over her environment?

She handed me a glass of water, and I followed along behind her into the living room.

"Can I sit with you?" I asked as she settled on the couch, slippers shucked and socked feet tucked beneath her.

A lone hardback chair, appearing unused, sat across from her, a plump pillow atop the seat.

Ashley glanced at it before nodding consent for me to share space with her.

Either she wanted me close by or was pushing her boundaries as she'd said Doc Hasslet had recommended she do. Perhaps both, but I wasn't going to look a gift horse in the mouth.

Settling into the opposite corner as her, I sipped my water. "I'm no therapist, but I've seen and heard a lot in my years as a Dom."

Ashley glanced at the barricaded window, wrapping her arms around herself again. "I can imagine."

More than anything, I yearned to place demands on her so I could turn her mind off, but she wasn't the type of submissive looking to be bossed around twenty-four-seven. Unlike with Dolyn, I'd never gotten the sense she looked for direction in our scenes, but they both submitted beautifully to the pain I gave, which allowed them release.

"I'm broken," she whispered, bringing my full focus back on who needed me right now.

Not sure of her background or issues, I didn't argue. But I'd seen worse trauma-haunted individuals come through my club's doors over the past decade and find partial healing. "You're a beautiful soul, one of the sweetest women I've ever met."

A soft smile curved her generous lips I'd dreamed of countless times seeing wrapped around my cock.

She caught me staring, her cheeks flushing as she glanced away again. "You might not think that if I told you how and why I ended up at your club."

"Nothing about your past will change how I feel about you." I tore my focus off her mouth.

Ashley turned her gaze on me, searching my eyes as though desperate for connection yet suspicious as hell.

Fuck, could I empathize with both.

She started picking at her pinkie finger, something I'd noted before when she grew uneasy. "You know what grooming is?" Her question released as a ragged whisper, causing my insides to tighten.

I nodded and sipped to keep from cursing as my mind went in ten different directions, each and every one dark and disturbing.

"The pastor from my parents church was a revered man."

Her truth hit me like a fist to the gut, and I listened as Ashley explained in detail about the lies he preached from his pulpit and how his flock was blinded to the truth of the evil man feeding them bullshit.

Feeling powerful for having caught his attention, she'd initiated their flirting, but resulting manipulation on his part landed her tied up on a basement bed for two days, lured in by promises of enlightenment and worship. Not one inch of her body had been ignored, her three holes used without permission, and all the while he'd blamed her "Eve nature" and budding body for his sinful downfall. But once finished, he'd praised her for being so perfect an angel that she ought to sit by the right hand of God.

Had I believed in his god, I would have agreed with the sick fuck.

Ashley *was* a divine creature.

The rapist had released her, threatening her with eternal damnation if she spoke a word of what had happened in those torturous forty-eight hours.

Regardless of his attempts at coercion, she'd told her parents of the assault, and blinded by their faith, they didn't believe her. Not realizing others outside the church would have listened and advocated for her, Ashley had chosen to keep quiet and count down the days until she was old enough to leave what she realized a few years later was a cult.

The man hadn't physically come after her again before graduation, and she'd escaped without further trauma. However, twice in the following year, he'd managed to get in contact with her through different social media platforms. She'd finally deleted her online presence and changed her cell number.

Still, the effects of the assault lingered, the reasons for her hard limits. Physical arousal hadn't been possible until I'd gifted her the pain she required to lower her mental defenses, and anytime someone of the opposite sex intentionally touched her without permission, she had flashbacks of what she had survived. Thus, the reason for the no skin-on-skin limit.

The traumatizing tale had me cringing, raging to rip that fucker's head from his body. I longed to hold her again, erase the memories of how he'd hurt her, but I sat, empty glass on the coffee table, hands on my thighs.

"I'm sorry for spewing all this shit on you," she whispered, rubbing over her arms, gaze on her lap.

"Don't be," I said, my tone low. "I'm here for you, Ashley—no matter what for or when, okay?"

A tentative smile curved her lips, and she nodded. "Thank you. You're one of the few people I trust."

I didn't need to imagine why.

She retrieved a pillow and blanket from the linen closet, bringing them to me where I remained seated. "Can I get you anything before I try to get some sleep?"

"I'm good, but thank you."

She nodded and straightened her fleece top. "See you in the morning." Ashley slipped back down the hallway, arms wrapped around her center, shoulders hunched in on herself.

I lounged on the couch as promised, reliving her story and searching through my feelings. What she'd told me intensified the growing attraction and desire for connection even more.

There was no way I could let Ashley go. If that meant another broken heart, so be it.

She needed me as much as I did her, and I was willing to sacrifice whatever was necessary to help us both feel whole again.

CHAPTER 6

DOLYN

The Mercedes out front of Ashley's condo hadn't been there when I'd left the night before once she'd locked herself away after getting home from work.

I eyed the dark, sleek car, evidence of its owner's wealth, wondering who visited at so early of an hour. The sun had barely crested the horizon, and I waited in cloaked form for her to leave for Manhattan.

Sleep had eluded me the night before thanks to my inner beast, who'd grown restless again. He had begged for the chance to submit our physical form to pain once more, lamenting the loss of bruises and aches from ass to thighs from Vanni's cane.

My human skin grew itchy as well, and I moved from where I leaned against a light post across from Ashley's condo. A short walk landed me beside the Mercedes, and I perched my bare ass on the cold metal of its hood facing her front door, arms and ankles crossed.

Part of me hoped whoever owned the car visited someone on the street other than my female, but I doubted it. Why park directly in front of her door otherwise?

My insides twisted into a knot that caused my forehead to furrow.

Inner dragon thoroughly muzzled thanks to his grumbling since I'd crawled into bed last night, I waited for Ashley. A trash truck approached and grew louder with every stop closer, deepening my frown. The stench of garbage wafted like putrid fumes as the truck idled beside the Mercedes. Two guys hopped off the back to grab bags left on either side of the road, completely ignorant of the naked, cloaked shifter feet away.

I snorted at their weakness, the lesser blood flowing through their veins making them impervious to the dangerous predator who could incinerate their bodies with a mere wisp of dragon flame.

Eventually, the truck turned off Walnut Street, the air clearing and sounds fading.

Dogs barked.

A baby shrieked while being buckled into its car seat off to my right.

The vehicle beneath me beeped twice, and the engine turned on thanks to a remote start.

My focus glued to Ashley's closed blinds and the front door, uncaring of the car warming up under my ass or how the neighborhood woke around me.

She was running later than usual.

Perhaps something had happened—

My pulse picked up, rousing my dragon, and I strode up the sidewalk on instinct, intending to...I didn't know. I couldn't exactly reveal my nakedness, knock on the door, and check in with her. An attempted peek through one of the front windows' blinds didn't offer any indication of what went on inside her condo, so I went to the other side of the stoop, my muscles tensing.

Feet crunching on wilted, frozen flowers, I craned my

neck but couldn't see anything. I growled, a combination of human and beast, releasing steam into the air.

The front door locks clicked, and I turned to face the door as it pulled inward.

A man in gray sweatpants and a coat stepped out first, and another low growl, much more menacing, rumbled in my chest.

His dark head swung my way.

Vanni DiLoreto.

Like a punch to my gut, he stole the oxygen from my lungs and loosened my hold on my inner beast, who purred at the sight of his heavy-lidded eyes and the square jaw beneath his short facial hair. Just as bad, my cock swelled to rock hard in less than two fluttered heartbeats, bucking up to tap against my clenched stomach.

Alpha.

The fuck he was.

I gritted my teeth, swallowing the curses I wanted to rain down on my beast for taking advantage of me being off-kilter.

Vanni's starburst green eyes scanned where I stood, his brow furrowed. Not seeing who had made the instinctive noise that had escaped my mouth, he turned his focus around the rest of the front yard and walkway, to the street and condos beyond.

Who the hell was Vanni to Ashley, and why was he at her place so early in the morning?

Regardless of my lust for the man, a burning sensation roused to life in my chest. Like a swarm of hornets, his presence stung, causing a scowl to pull my eyebrows inward.

Want.

My beast hungered for Vanni and Ashley with the same intensity, but I kept my human half in check even as my groin throbbed for release.

Ashley was already destined to be mine. This human male was nothing to either of us, or at least, he wouldn't be once I claimed Ashley and we found our beta.

Muscle ticking in my jaw, I watched as Vanni coaxed Ashley out into the cold, hurrying her to the Mercedes. I refused to consider how well they fit together. Their shared beauty, even while wrapped up in winter gear, was a perfect concoction that would inebriate any unsuspecting victim.

Imagine sipping from the chalice of their combined sweetness.

I would do no such thing, but temptation welled inside me at the beast's unexpected, poetic words.

Neither human spoke, but with how Vanni kept watch like a sentinel, I wondered over his actions, attempting to shut down the beast and the deep yearning to taste and touch them both. My inner dragon went quiet, but my cock continued to strain upward.

Had Ashley realized someone—some*thing*—had been following her, and she reached out to a man she trusted to protect her?

Sudden fear I might have caused her distress lanced pain through my heart, and as they pulled away from the curb in Vanni's car, I stared, unmoving in the cold, dead flower bed beneath Ashley's dark window.

I had waited too long in my pursuit, enough that she must have sensed her alpha's presence. But if so, she would have been drawn to me, not scared enough to call on…a friend?

Her lover? Her…*Master*?

I groaned at the thought of their bodies entangled but cut the tone from leaking past my lips a second later.

Something wasn't right with my reaction. I should have been raging with jealousy. Anger. A protective instinct to rip Vanni to shreds for touching what belonged to *me*.

Every part of me yearned to be closer to him.

Unsettled in mind and body alike, I strode into the center

of the street, made sure the beast half-inside me was properly bound, and shifted into dragon form. One leap took me into the sky. I scanned Jersey beneath us until spotting the Mercedes. Vanni drove Ashley across the river toward where I'd expected. A short while later, he opened her car door in front of Elijah's building and escorted her to the entrance.

Once she passed inside to safety, he left, and I followed since I wouldn't lay eyes on Ashley again until after work and the man intrigued the hell out of me.

Vanni pulled into a parking garage of a building I'd visited the week before. Blood still pooled in my groin, keeping me hard as nails as I landed, shifted into human form, and trailed after him. Stalking on Vanni's heels as he walked through the parking garage, I stared at the back of his head. My beast rolled belly up and purred while I considered every way of making Vanni bleed out. The man had no right to touch what belonged to me.

Ours.

I cursed my beast and his ability to weasel into my mind when I grew preoccupied.

My fingers should have itched with the need to elongate, claw Vanni across his face. Disembowel him. Slice through his carotid artery. Tear his lower half off and feast on his flesh.

No.

Biting my tongue to stop myself from growling at my dragon half and revealing my flesh to Vanni, I snuck into the elevator behind him, expecting he planned to visit his sex club.

The ignorant, weak human had no clue about the danger hovering over his back. How easily I could end him. Erase his existence from the face of the earth.

But something stilled my hand—and caused pre-cum to pearl atop my cockhead.

The elevator took us two floors higher than the club, sliding open to reveal the penthouse suite, yet another array of evidence Vanni had money to spare.

Who the fuck was this man who made me ache with lust?

He passed by the sprawling living space with its two couches and massive TV screen, walking through double doors that led to the master suite. A navy bedspread covered the king-sized mattress, the frame beneath wooden and thick, sturdy enough to easily survive a harsh fucking.

Vanni stripped, leaving his clothes where they fell, and my cock slapped my belly again at the sight of his naked backside and the dark crevice between his cheeks. I chewed on my tongue to quiet my inner beast's whimper for a taste.

I moved closer, hot on Vanni's heels, staring as he climbed into the master bathroom shower and tipped his head back into the spray. Eyes closed, his lithe, muscular build as close to perfection as a human could get, he captured my undivided attention. He shampooed his hair and reached for bodywash. When he began to lather smooth pecs, as hairless as mine, I finally managed to turn away, intent on ignoring the draw of his body and learning what I could about him while he finished showering.

Files sat atop Vanni's office desk, and since his laptop required a fingerprint to open, I inspected every scrap of paper in sight.

Vanni owned the building I currently stood in.

His wealth afforded him more than ninety-nine percent of the population—but not me.

Pride boosted, I rifled through his refrigerator to find he ordered pre-made meals, all healthy and macro-balanced. I entered the master bedroom again, looking through his closet, breathing in the delicious scent of expensive cologne with a hint of earth and spice. Further evidence of his wealth hung on hangers, sat on shoe racks, and lined velvet cushions in the form of expensive watches and cufflinks.

I scoffed at his taste, refusing to acknowledge how he smelled almost as delicious as my Ashley. I assured myself our beta would be ten times as alluring as Vanni once I finally allowed my inner beast to scent him properly as we had our female.

Sounds from the bathroom assured me Vanni finished, and I made myself comfortable in a corner of his bedroom, arms crossed, looking down my nose at him as he exited the bathroom, towel wrapped around his waist.

My mouth did *not* water.

My cock did *not* leak or flex with want.

And my beast sure as hell did *not* weep with need.

Vanni dropped his towel, and I allowed myself to soak in and appreciate his olive skin and the sleek mass of muscles beneath. Bulging calves and thick thighs suggested he daily spent hours in the gym. An ass meaty enough to withstand a pounding flexed as he pulled on a pair of boxer briefs.

Tingles came to life in my lower spine, and I grabbed hold of my cock, squeezing the base.

Vanni disappeared into his closet, and I waited, body on fire, mind stalled out on everything but the lust consuming me. Visions flashed in my head of him writhing between me and Ashley as we bonded.

My inner beast growled a resounding, *No.*

Another image of Ashely being filled by us both while we bred her made my dragon purr with pleasure.

Vanni appeared in his closet entryway, attaching cufflinks to the starched button-down covering his sexy, veined forearms. He wore the suit well, the lines and precise cut further evidence of the man's wealth.

But I still had better in my own closet.

A smirk on my face and chin lifted slightly, I trailed after

Vanni as he readied to leave his suite. He skipped breakfast but took the time to utilize his French press, which I could appreciate. He filled a travel mug with black coffee, his lips against the rim, and the resulting hum of satisfaction over the taste made me reach for my hard cock again.

Back in the elevator we went, but and I continued to imagine sinking my shaft into his tight ass. Biting his neck until he bled and lapping at the coppery tang of his blood as the wound healed from my saliva. The atoms in my body ached to mesh with his, become one—

"No."

Vanni's head jerked my way, and I cursed myself for unintentionally muttering my refusal of want over this man. His gaze hard, not startled or wary in the least, scanned over every inch of the elevator's interior as it descended.

I stared back even though he didn't meet my eyes, a cocky smirk growing as his lesser human abilities didn't allow for him to see me.

The bell dinged, and he shook his head, lips pursed, while exiting on the floor housing his sex club.

I considered following him inside, learning every last detail I could about the man who more than piqued my interest. Whimpers inside pushed for me to do the same, but we had a female to win over and plans to consider on how we might locate our beta.

Vanni, while a tasty morsel, was no longer of importance.

I needed to focus on the destiny Father had assured me of and the two fate had in store for me.

CHAPTER 7

ASHLEY

Vanni had slept on my couch, allowing me to get some rest. Still, we ran a little late getting to work in the morning, and I'd given him my promise to call if I felt threatened at all during the day.

The hours dragged, my thoughts on how comfortable I'd been alone with him in my condo, how he'd been tender and careful about no skin contact while holding me. More than anything, I knew I could trust my master in every way, and the warmth that instilled deep inside me overshadowed fear from the cold, bad eyes.

Five o'clock finally rolled around, and I shut down my computer, so ready for Vanni's flogger on my back that my hands shook and twinges of arousal woke between my thighs. I had two hours before our scheduled appointment to scene, and I planned to do as I always did to waste time. Even though I needed release from the week-long buildup of sexual tension riding me due to the good stalker, my body required sustenance first.

When I stepped out beneath the darkening sky, both sets of eyes burned from opposite sides, one warm and honey-like, the other cold and biting. A shiver slid over me, pebbling my skin from desire and unease alike.

Master Vanni had insisted I reach out to him if I experienced the same sense as last night, but I only had to walk two blocks to the cafe I visited every Friday before meeting with him. His club sat closer to Midtown, an easy walk on crowded sidewalks where no one would attempt to kidnap me.

If that was their intention at all.

And for some reason, the good eyes made me feel safe, protected from the other. As long as I continued to sense him along with the bad, I didn't need to bother Vanni.

I turned north, shoulders hitched and chin tucked into my coat against the cold, keeping a sharp eye out. Like me, dozens if not hundreds hurried through the biting air, done with the work day and ready to head home. Traffic jammed in the streets, horns, and the occasional curse were nothing new under Manhattan's buildings reaching into the dark sky.

I made it to the cafe unmolested, and a blast of heat warmed my face as I pulled the door open. I shuffled inside, erasing the opposing feelings of my stalkers.

After ordering my usual chicken Caesar wrap and green tea, I took the only table available to me—in the front window.

Immediately, goodness rather than the chill I'd feared radiated through the glass, and I hid my smile by ducking my head and sipping my piping hot drink. Sweetness slid over my tongue, and I licked my lower lip before turning to look out the window fully.

People hurried past, most of them on their cell phones, a few abnormal meandering souls checking out the sights rising high overhead regardless of winter's wind. I scanned everyone who passed by, hoping for a glimpse of eye contact, a hint of whose stare I'd felt walking the mere two blocks from work.

A couple stood across the street on the far corner to my left reading a brochure. Another woman lingered far to my right, just outside the window casing, a frown on her face as she mouthed into the cell held between her cheek and shoulder.

The soft music overhead was lost in the buzz of voices as people came and went the same as every Friday I visited the establishment. Usually, I read on my e-reader until the hours passed, but I found myself unable to focus, my gaze flitting from its screen to the glass beside me more often than not, my skin tingling with awareness.

I gave up on my fairytale book of happily-ever-afters and turned my attention to the crowded sidewalks. The stationary couple and woman had disappeared, but others had taken their places, lingering here and there while more people pushed past in their hurry to get to wherever they needed to go.

Picking mindlessly at the small wart on my pinkie, I scanned toward the left. A solitary figure leaning against the building across the street snagged my attention. He gazed in my direction, and even though I couldn't make out his face or be sure he even looked at me, my breath caught as a rush of arousal swept over me. I straightened in my chair, my hand falling to my lap.

Wide shoulders encased in a gray coat drew my gaze first, the thicker material doing nothing to hide the fact he spent his working hours in a gym rather than behind a desk.

I craned my neck as people slipped past, cutting him from sight for brief moments.

Casual jeans couldn't hide the powerful-looking thighs beneath.

A bus rumbled by, and I bit my lip while shifting on my

chair, cursing the slow-moving vehicle from hindering my view.

The gorgeous man still stared my way once the vehicle moved on, and my mouth dried as the moisture in my body pooled between my thighs. I pressed my legs together, hoping to relieve the sudden, pulsing ache. Heart thrumming, I took in his dark blond hair and strong jawline, wishing like hell I could make out the color of his eyes.

A filthy dog sat at his feet, head tipped while peering up at the man, tongue wagging—almost smiling it seemed from that distance.

The man absently rubbed the animal's head with gentle strokes.

Surely if a dog wasn't fearful of his looming presence, he couldn't be that bad of a person.

My hand itched to wave, to motion the stranger across the street to join me, but I knew better. Initiating was a thing from my past, something I would never do again.

Tearing my focus off the man and his dog didn't come easily. My chest ached and breaths came choppy from trauma's reminder. For fifteen minutes, I wished him away. For fifteen minutes more, I longed for him to approach. Flitting my gaze out the window on occasion allowed me to find him squatted beside the dog he held against his chest, but his focus was still on me.

Or, the cafe, at least.

A quiet ding from my cell reminded me it was time to face the cold for another walk that would lead to warmth and the chance to find relief from the lust burning throughout my body.

Shaking, I cleaned up my dinner things and stepped out onto the sidewalk, expecting to sense both stalkers. No trace of the one that instilled fear remained, thank goodness.

The man who had flooded me with desire no longer

stood across the street, but the warmth of his presence continued to caress my face. His dog sat unmoved, peering up at the building behind him.

I swiveled my head side to side, looking for the man, feeling as though his disappearance had caused a piece of me to be stripped away and tossed far into the ocean. Where had he gone? Had I been wrong in thinking he'd been the one following me?

Swallowing back disappointment yet still thrilled I felt my comforting stalker's presence, I turned and hurried northward through the cold.

Nose half-frozen, I pushed into the lobby of the building housing Master's club.

The good eyes followed me, and I hid my smile by ducking my head while climbing onto the first elevator empty of those ready to leave the sky rise.

Other people pressed in to stand in front of me, and the stare of my stalker continued to warm me even though no one had given me a second look before turning to face the doors. We sped upward, people exiting one by one until I stood alone.

Every inch of my body tingled with awareness.

I sensed another presence, but my eyes assured me no one rode the elevator with me. Deceit at its finest. Or perhaps I was losing my mind.

"Who are you?" I whispered, refusing to believe the latter.

Of course, no one answered, nor had I expected a voice to reply.

Blowing out a heavy exhale, I straightened and faced the doors as the elevator slowed.

An exhale over my nape caused a shudder to ripple through me, and I squeezed my thighs tight as a whimper slid past my parted lips.

Want.

The word whispered through my mind, a perfect description for the ache in my body. Never had I ever desired physical touch so much in my entire life. My skin burned for contact, my core pulsing around emptiness that needed to be filled.

The door slid open, and I forced myself forward into the club's entryway.

Lust followed, hot on my heels, and I shivered, thankful my stalker hadn't left me.

I took my time in the women's locker room, stripping out of my work clothes until I stood completely naked. My breaths came in pants as my insides jittered and fluttered like butterflies on crack. Swallowing hard, I glanced around the open room, taking note of a few other women in states of undress. No tall blond in a gray coat watched from the shadows, no hulking figure leaned against a wall, arms crossed, intense stare soaking me in even though I could feel him.

Every inch of me wished for him to be real.

I wanted him to follow me into Master Vanni's domain, to watch how I found release. Clenching my eyes shut, I fought off an instinctive desire to be owned by him—a complete stranger, a creepy yet hot-as-hell stalker my body had no business being turned on by. My pussy dripped over the image of the man etched into my brain.

But part of me longed for Master Vanni as well. Something deep-seated from having bonded with him through our scenes. When I fantasized over him laying his bare hand on me, even more wetness roused, and I bit my lower lip to keep from whimpering.

I needed my master.

Now.

I slipped into the blue silk robes provided by the club and took out the clip holding my hair tight to my head. A few trembling finger combs fluffed the dark waves to the middle of my back, and I hurried toward the door leading into the lounge, my pussy aching to be filled.

Delightful goose bumps licked over my skin at the thought of allowing Master Vanni to fuck me with the huge cock imprisoned inside his black leather pants. Long and thick, his bulge had caught my eye a few times, and I wondered at his desire for me even though he'd never once voiced it, nor did he push my limits.

It wasn't yet seven, and patrons already littered the lounge. My stalker's eyes cut off as the locker room door shut behind me, and while I would have preferred for him to stay close, Master Vanni waited for me. He would take care of me as only he could. His pain would have to be enough for tonight.

A redheaded submissive was shackled to the cross on the dais straight ahead, her bear-like Dom using a flogger to stripe her back. The sex swing was also in use, where a male sub strapped in and wearing a cock cage was getting pegged by his mistress.

Both sights caused more arousal to slip from my body, and I stifled a needy moan.

"Ashley." Master Vanni had caught me unaware while I stared, his low voice on my right sending a shudder through me.

I lowered my head rather than lift my gaze higher to look into his arresting, mossy green eyes. "Good evening, Master," I whispered, unable to hide the craving for him from my voice.

He touched my lower back, the satin robe between our skin, but a jolt of electrical current raced through my blood. I needed more. "How are you?" he murmured near my ear, sending ripples of goose bumps over my skin.

"I'm ready." Never had those words been truer.

"Do you wish to sit and talk first?"

I shook my head. "I'm good. Work was fine. I—I need you, Master. I'm so green I can't think straight."

Master Vanni cursed under his breath, his fingertips pressing tighter against me as though to order me toward his private play-room.

I moved beneath his steering, but halfway across the lounge, a shiver licked along my spine like what a warm, wet tongue might feel like. I lifted my head.

Master Vanni moved like a predator beside me, dark hair curling at his nape, olive skin covering wide shoulders I suddenly wanted to clutch while he sank into my body. Swallowing hard and not nearly as freaked out as I would have been over that thought a week ago, I looked beyond him.

A few people gazed after us, but they were patrons I recognized from my prior visits to the club, and not a single one of them caused the arousal inside me to intensify. *That* sense came from a presence heading toward the corner grouping of empty seats.

He watched.

Whoever—*whatever*—this creature was, it stared as it took up residence on a leather chair, causing another wave of desire to make my skin itch for physical touch.

An idea flitted through my brain, and feeling reckless with instinctive need, I reconsidered the limits Master and I always discussed before sceneing together.

Yessss...

The whisper slid through my mind, more potent than my subconscious voice. Rather than freak out over the voice in my head, I sank into the word still hissing like curling smoke through my blood, heart, and lungs. The suggestion gave me strength, and I made up my mind.

CHAPTER 8
VANNI

Tension had seemed to ride Ashley's shoulders from the second she'd walked into the lounge, same as always, but she held herself differently tonight as I approached from her blind side. No longer did she cower or stare at the floor, ignoring the sensual delights of my lounge.

Her gaze had slid over the two apparatuses being utilized in the common area, the pulse in her neck suggesting arousal had begun to warm her blood before my flogger even licked over her back. Her nipples pebbled and tightened beneath the robe, causing my mouth to water.

The sight of her in nothing more than satin always thickened my cock inside my leathers, but my groin ached over the interest she showed and that she was turned on without pain. What had happened over the workday to cause the change?

The evening prior, she'd told me the full extent of her trauma, her inability to experience desire without what I'd given her. I struggled to believe a transformation could take place from the idea of someone simply watching her as she'd claimed. But seeing her now, I realized the idea of her stalker had definitely awakened her body. Her response went beyond having an exhibition kink. She definitely felt *something*. I just wished I knew what it was so I could somehow cultivate it. Her acknowledgement of my greeting then stating how ready she was for me caused hope to rise in my chest.

I hadn't been able to hold back a curse when I touched her back, her skin burning my fingertips through the thin material separating us. The warmth of her continued to radiate into my palm as we moved through the lounge. Her proximity lured me closer, insistent and tempting, making my hair follicles come alive. Staying focused on my professional role became more difficult with every scene between us, doubly so tonight because of her blatant arousal and unhindered willingness to submit.

I wanted to strip her down, tie her up tight, and dominate in every way I craved. Breathe in the scent of vanilla while running my nose along her neck. Lap at her sweetness, my face buried between her thighs.

My cock jerked in my leathers, releasing a thick stream of pre-cum, same as it had for Dolyn. That man had definitely woken up something inside me. While I grimaced over the unnatural slickness, I wouldn't trade my time spent with him for anything.

I directed Ashley toward the private rooms where we always hid behind closed doors.

She pulled up abruptly, and I stumbled to a stop, glancing down at her. "Ash?"

Ashley lifted her head, offering me an onslaught of violet eyes overflowing with desire, fear, and excitement.

Lust kicked my groin like a hoof to my balls, but the pain radiated sweet need rather than agony.

She licked her lip, glancing to the left and the unoccupied spanking bench. "Can we use that?"

My brow shot upward. One of her hard limits had been sceneing in public. Not that I was complaining over her question, but what the hell was going on with her tonight?

She stared at the bench, the pulse in her neck thrumming in time with mine, pupils dilating to eat up the lightness of her eyes.

How far was she willing to go, and could I trust her to make the right choice when aroused so potently?

"Are you sure you're ready for that?" I forced myself to check in when all I wanted to do was tie her down, push my granite-like cock into her pussy, and stroke her silken walls, my fingers thrumming on her clit, until she found release.

She licked her lower lip again and nodded. "Yes, Master Vanni."

Fuck. Yes.

I wanted every patron in the lounge to see how sweetly Ashely obeyed her master, how generous she was with her submission. A discreet palm to my bulge shifted my strangling cock.

"And what do you want me to use tonight to give you the pain you need?"

"Your hand."

My balls tightened in a flash, and I hissed through clenched teeth. "You're *sure*, Ashley?"

She nodded.

"Words." I insisted when she didn't give me the necessary verbal response to cross this line.

"Yes, Master." She stared up at me with vulnerability and assurance in her gaze. "I want you to mark me with your palms tonight."

Fuck, as her friend and master I should talk to her about it further, find out her reasoning, and assure her she made a good choice for her journey toward healing. I'd yearned from day one to get my hands on her, wanted her ass showcasing my prints.

And tonight, that fantasy could come true.

"Ash…"

"Please, Vanni—I trust you explicitly, and I feel ready for your touch."

A deep, gratifying warmth spread through me. "Then I will give you what you desire." Pressing firmly against her lower back, I angled us toward the empty bench.

She moved without hesitation, grace in her body, swaying even though sexual tension crackled between where we touched. Our deviation from the usual drew attention, but I thrived on people watching me take apart my submissives and put them back together again.

While I felt a connection with Ashley, I had no wish to hide her beauty from interested eyes.

They just weren't allowed to touch.

"Give me your robe," I commanded, my voice low with authority. Rarely did I consider using my Dom voice with Ashley, but tonight, among the other members of my club, I needed to show the part of me they expected to see, the dominant who hadn't been out to play in public for far too long.

Her hands shook as she slipped the knot free and let the satin slide down over her milky shoulders. Breasts high and full, rose nipples furled tight caught my gaze, and my tongue flicked over my lower lip. They would fit perfectly in my palms, and the cherry-like nubs would be sweet to suckle.

Maybe someday.

I let my groan escape into the mix of slapping flesh, moans, and quiet overhead music filling the lounge around us.

"Knees here," I said, patting the leather cushion of the angled spanking bench.

Skin pebbled, she rested where I'd indicated, moving without a hint of trepidation or lack of surety. Ashley must have seen countless patrons getting spanked while moving through the lounge the other nights she'd come to me for therapy because she arranged herself perfectly where she needed to be without me having to intervene.

Restraints rested near her ankles and wrists. Watching her emotionally fall apart the first time I had tied her down—and unable to wrap her in my arms to provide comfort—had been like a knife to my chest. If that happened again out here where everyone could see, my inability to hold her as her Dom ought to would kill me.

"Do you wish to be tied down tonight, Ashley?" I asked quietly, hopeful she would refuse.

She opened her mouth to reply, glancing across the lounge toward one of the far, empty corners.

"Ashley?" I checked in when she didn't respond.

"No, Master," she finally whispered what I wished to hear, making my next inhale easier.

The roundness of her backside faced one side of the lounge, a beautiful heart-shaped ass with its hole hidden by plump cheeks I couldn't wait to see marked up by my hands.

I swallowed both a moan and growl, prowling around the bench to fully take in the gorgeous sight of her complete submission that Dolyn had denied me in holding a part of himself back.

At the thought of him, another pulse of pre-cum slid down the inside of my leathers.

Ashley had lowered her head, dark hair framing her face, slender hands gripping the bench. Shivers twitched the skin across her shoulders and along her spine. The swell of her ass once more drew my attention.

"I'm going to put my hands on you, Ashley."

"Please, Master."

I rubbed over my bulge, grimacing at the sticky mess inside my pants. Dolyn and this woman could very well be the death of me given the chance. I didn't give a shit that Ashley held my already fragile heart in her hands. If she told me to stop breathing, demand the blood cease pumping through my arteries, I would grant her wish.

Whatever she wanted, I would willingly give.

Cream smeared along the insides of her thighs suggesting she would eventually try for more than pain.

"Fuck," I whispered and swallowed hard as fire shot through me, overheating my skin from scalp to toes. Insides quivering, I leaned down near her ear, leather strangling my cock. "You know your safeword."

She turned to rest her cheek on the headrest and met my steady gaze. "It's *red*, Master."

I wanted to lick the words off her lips, plunge my tongue inside and taste her sweetness.

Ashley enjoyed pain, but I wasn't about to fuck up and ruin my chances with cultivating our friendship into something more unless she showed interest. Neither would I let loose with six months worth of sexual tension with one blow just because she and thoughts of Dolyn had me worked the fuck up.

I eyed her pale flesh and lifted my arm. My palm landed with a decent crack, enough to cause her to gasp. I immediately stepped away without lingering over how warm or soft she felt.

"Color?"

"Green, Master—so *very* green." She sighed and sank onto the bench as though one swat had leaked all of the tension from her muscles.

Two more hits in quick succession earned me a spine-tingling moan and a full-body shiver.

"Ash?" I whispered, my chest fluttering, palm itching, ears desperate to hear her cries of release.

"Green, Master."

I landed a few more blows, satisfied at seeing my print bloom across her pale skin but itching to go further than she'd asked for. She'd taken one hell of a step tonight, and I couldn't help myself from pushing for more. "Can I soothe the sting away, Ash?"

"Mmm." She wiggled her hips as though already searching for release.

"Words, Ash," I demanded, my voice low and ragged.

"Yes, Master—touch me. *Please*." Her whimpered reply caused my stomach muscles to clench and cock to throb in its prison.

Another curse hissed through my brain, and I reached out, coming into direct, lingering contact with her skin. She was silk beneath my fingertips, softer than anything I'd felt, the redness of my prints warm and delicious as sunshine. I took my time caressing over her backside, staring at the wetness seeping down the insides of her thighs.

The cells in my body vibrated, my subconscious insisting I touch her there. Slide my fingers through her wet folds, stroke deep into her slick channel until she climaxed.

Holding tight to my restraint, I removed my hand, hauled off, and whacked her again, teeth clenched.

Ashley whimpered, a sheen of sweat dampening her skin. She trembled against the bench, and I selfishly leaned in close, allowing my straining dick to brush against her thigh since leather separated our skin. "Tell me what you need, Ashley."

"I—I..." She swallowed and moaned, pressing against my dick, dark strands of hair sticking to her sweaty face.

"Ashley," I growled, forcing myself to move away.

"More pain, Master," she whispered and licked over her lower lip. "Please make me come."

Every muscle in my body tense and straining, I gave her what she asked for, turning her cheeks a deeper shade of red.

She bucked against the bench, weeping, but didn't safe-word or attempt to escape the blows I rained down on her sweet ass.

The musky scent of her arousal permeated the air, mixing with her natural vanilla in my nose. I lusted to taste, to plunder, barely managing to keep myself restrained from devouring her like a ravenous animal. The furthest reaches of my soul pushed to claim, mark, and own. Like a beast waking from a deep slumber, craving attempted to take over my brain, insisting I do all three.

Ashley cried out, shuddering with her climax before my body caved to its need.

Another rush of pre-cum slid along my left thigh, and I hissed, rubbing over the welts on her backside as she came down from her release, trembling—and not crying.

Our scene had ended.

But a newly awakened, unnamable part of me roared for satisfaction.

CHAPTER 9

DOLYN

I watched as Vanni brought my mate release and caressed over skin he had no right to touch.

And strangely, I did. Not. Care.

Jealousy should have roused my beast from his purring delight into raging fire and brimstone. I should have burned the sky rise to the ground until nothing but glowing embers and ash remained as I took to the sky, my female clutched to my chest.

Instead, I sat camouflaged, my cock hard and aching inside my jeans, eyes riveted on the gorgeous sight of Vanni gifting my female pleasure without a single touch between her thighs.

He'd done the same to me.

Growling beneath my breath, I pressed down on my shaft, thrusting into my grip.

I'd decided to continue my pursuit slowly and only reveal myself from a distance to Ashley to see how the sight of me would affect her—if at all.

She'd felt my stare and had taken note of where I'd stood outside the cafe for nearly two hours watching her eat, attempt to read, and keep an eye on me. I hadn't yet felt ready to approach and enter the cafe and realized she might be uncomfortable with a man starting at her for so long. But she hadn't appeared unsettled by my presence or my focus being solely on her.

The same dog that had come across me on my first night in New York had found me again, keeping me company as I watched.

Once she'd exited the establishment, I'd made myself disappear from sight so I could loom closer. Sniff her. Follow feet away as she walked Manhattan's sidewalks. The filthy dog had trailed after me, loyal even though we'd only just met. His presence had made my heart ache, and I promised myself I would look after him as soon as I could.

Rather than go to the subway as she always did at the end of the workday, Ashley entered the building I'd followed Vanni into earlier in the day.

Once more, I'd been forced to leave my new K-9 friend behind in pursuit of my female. Even knowing her destination and who she intended to see, I hadn't been jealous. Simply curious and a whole lot turned on.

Ashley had been aware of my presence the entire elevator ride upward, going so far as to ask who I was once she thought she was alone. I could have appeared out of thin air and answered, but she would have freaked for sure. I couldn't have any fear consume her from my presence. Instead, I stayed close, following her like a lost puppy straight into the women's locker room where she continued to act unbothered by my presence, which she most certainly took note of.

As though feeling my stare like a caress, she'd watched the corner of the changing area where I leaned against the wall, my body vibrating with need to lower my walls and allow my inner beast the joy of scenting her again.

With every piece of clothing she removed, Ashley

flushed a deeper red, her lips parting as she glanced at me. She didn't attempt to hide herself while baring her skin or even appear uneasy about someone staring as she stripped down.

She'd left, and I snuck into the lounge a few seconds later, thankfully no one seemed to notice the door open and close without anyone visibly coming or going.

Vanni had his hand on her lower back, leading her toward the private room where I'd allowed him to bring me to release.

My inner dragon had whimpered, horny as fuck from the reminder of that night with Vanni, but thankfully he remained silent in his desire for the bite of pain. I'd been too far gone in my own head and lust to fight with that half of my being. Giving in to what he wanted would be bending over alongside Ashley and begging for Vanni's cock and cum to fill me.

I hissed, tearing my hand off my groin for the arms of the chair where I sat enthralled over the sight of them together.

What made Ashley trust Vanni?

How had he weaseled his way into her life and suspicious mind?

Nothing about my female suggested she was a masochist until I'd seen with my own eyes how easily Vanni's sadistic side matched her darker desires.

Other than rubbing over her reddened skin, Vanni didn't touch her intimately. He didn't offer the usual aftercare a submissive deserved after sceneing with their Dom.

Perhaps she *didn't* trust the man she'd called master, as I had refused to do.

I frowned over the puzzle in my brain, watching as he carefully replaced her robe, now taking care to keep from touching her skin as he'd done with me. He retrieved a bottle of cold water, barely any words passing between them as they sat in chairs across from each other a few feet closer to me than the dais they'd scened upon.

He should have been cradling her in his arms. Soothing his palms over her skin, murmuring against her ear. Slowly bringing her back…

I took in her relaxed body, her face still flushed and blissed out from release. She hadn't fallen into subspace, which meant she withheld a part of herself from him, same as I'd always done with Elijah.

I relaxed into my chair, my chest puffing out, wishing I could unhide myself, tell her who she belonged to, the only alpha she would ever fully submit to.

My beast hissed disagreement at my thoughts, but I ignored him, watching as Vanni led Ashley to the door of the women's locker room a short while later.

I should have followed on her heels, but I wasn't yet ready to leave.

She disappeared from sight, and I turned my watchful gaze onto Vanni, who spun to take in his lounge, hands on his hips, his bulge thick and inviting.

My backside ached, my empty hole desiring to be stuffed full while glides over my prostate caused pre-cum to pulse through my shaft.

"No," I muttered even though my beast hadn't spoken a word. But I *did* want release. Desperately. And a hot, willing Dom stood across the room from me.

Did he have another submissive to care for tonight now that Ashley was gone?

Would he agree to scene with me if I asked?

With how his body had responded to beating me with that cane, I didn't doubt he would, given the chance to hurt me.

I would see Ashley home and return for one more taste of his heavy hand.

And tomorrow?

I would stride forward toward my destiny with no further hinderances, approach my female, and finally speak with her face-to-face.

Decision made, I strode across the lounge and waited silent and invisible in the entryway.

Both Vanni and Ashley appeared a few minutes later, bundled for the cold weather. I stood in the corner of the elevator they shared, watching as his hands fisted and released a few times. I understood his fight to keep from touching her.

"Are you sure you're alright, Ash?" he asked once the doors closed, leaving them supposedly alone.

"Yes." She smiled up at him but shivered as though aware I shared space with the two of them. "A little sore, but I love the reminder of what you gifted me."

"Good." The starburst in Vanni's eyes seemed to glow as he looked down at her, warmth and more than affection lining his face.

Their gazes stayed locked, the taste of sexual tension sweet on my tongue.

Vanni lifted a hand as though thinking to tuck wayward strands of dark hair behind her ear but hesitated.

"Go ahead," she whispered, and he gently did as I'd expected.

Both exhaled heavily as his hand dropped to his side, fingers curling inward. "Thank you."

Her smile radiant, Ashley peered up at him.

Nothing in me demanded I step between them, tear Vanni's focus off my female's face. Continued lust, still raging from the spanking he'd gifted her, kept me hard and throbbing. I was curious over how far he would go in his desire for her and how hot they would be writhing together while I watched. The scent of lust intensified in the air, stirring my skin toward pebbling, and my body flushed with heat. Charged moments passed in silence, and I swore I could hear all three of our rapid heartbeats.

"Are you sure you're comfortable staying at the condo alone tonight?" Vanni asked, his voice low and ragged as though experiencing the same need as I did.

Ashley's smile faded slightly. "I felt that second presence tonight after work but only until I got to the cafe, then it disappeared."

Lips pursed, Vanni nodded.

Second presence? My brow furrowed. Someone *else* stalked her?

Hackles raising, I bit back a low, animalistic growl as tension rippled over my body.

"I'm only a call away," Vanni assured her, lightly touching her elbow.

She leaned in a little closer. "As long as the cold one isn't around, I'll be fine."

"And the good eyes? Have you felt them at all today?"

A flush crept up Ashley's neck and face as she glanced toward the corner where I lurked. "I don't mind his presence in the slightest. He's…well, it's why I asked for you to touch me tonight. Something has woken up inside me I haven't experienced since—you know." She returned her focus to Vanni's face, searching his eyes. "You truly don't believe I'm losing my mind, do you?"

"Not at all," he assured her.

The elevator slowed, and a couple climbed aboard with us, ending the conversation I was desperate to hear more of.

My muscles quivered as anger simmered inside me, embers ready to flare into flames if needed over this second person following my mate.

Who was it, and what were his intentions toward her?

For a brief moment, I imagined the creature to be our

beta, but he wouldn't instill fear or unease in our female if they were fated to be together. If this second presence caused her minuscule amount of dragonblood instinct to raise a red flag, I ought to trust her judgment.

I stalked close to both of them as they made their way to his Mercedes, finding myself thankful she had a human man she could call on to keep her safe until she grew comfortable with my presence at her side. Without a second thought, I shredded my clothing and took to the dark sky, following overhead as Vanni's car eventually crossed the bridge into Jersey.

Having become aware someone else had their eye on Ashley, I felt even more driven to reveal myself to her.

But tonight, I needed to be tied down onto Vanni's bench to experience the same release as my female had. Besides, she said she would be fine once home.

I watched Ashley shut herself up for the night in her condo, listening from beside the stoop where I hid in plain sight as the locks engaged. Vanni hesitated in leaving, same as I did, but eventually, he returned to his car and pulled away, red tail lights fading from view.

I stayed put in Ashley's flower bed, lest the cold presence she'd spoken of lingered nearby and dared approach.

A half hour of peaceful silence and a lack of movement on Walnut Street passed. Feeling confident in her safety, I shifted and shot into the sky. A slow, low fly over the surrounding area didn't allow my enhanced dragon sight to pick up anyone hovering in the shadows. I flapped my leathery wings harder, intent on Manhattan and Vanni's club.

Minutes later, in human form and still camouflaged, I snuck into the men's locker room, pleased to find it empty. Willing myself into sight, I slipped into a blue robe identical to the one Ashley had worn. More people gathered in the lounge when I entered, my presence drawing a few sets of eyes as I had last week. Ignoring their hungry stares, I scanned the room, intent on one man.

Vanni sat broodingly in a chair in the far corner, a tumbler with clear liquid and lime wedge in his hand. He lifted his glass to drink but caught sight of me and paused.

Our gazes held, and he finally sipped, holding my eyes in place—and my body—the entire time. He swallowed, Adam's apple bobbing, hand lowering. Lifting his chin and widening his thighs, he narrowed his gaze. A come-hither look and demand to submit if I'd ever seen one.

Too desperate from the buildup over the last two hours, I strode toward him with sure steps, uncaring of other patrons' eyes following me as I passed them by.

"Dolyn." He all but hummed my name, pleasure in his low tone as I stood before him.

Kneeling wouldn't happen no matter how much my beast whimpered for me to obey the alluring human.

I dipped my head in greeting but held his stare rather than sinking down and presenting myself. "Sir."

He drank from his tumbler again, eyes flicking down over me and back up. "Do you need something from me, boy?"

My molars ground together.

A slow smile curved his lips, his mossy green eyes lighting with excitement. "I don't suppose you would get on your knees for me while I finished my drink."

He didn't ask a question, so I didn't bother responding.

"Fine." Vanni set his tumbler aside and stood. Two steps forward brought him into my personal space.

I lifted my chin to look down my nose at him, loving the fact I had a couple of inches over his human height.

His smile widened as his gaze drifted over my neck. "You reek of lust and need."

There was no questioning the truth.

"Come."

My balls tightened at his command, but I ignored my beast's instinctive desire to climax since Vanni meant for me to accompany him to the private room he started toward. Same as with Ashley, I followed like a needy puppy, close to his heels, desperate for the pain and release he would help me find. His ass flexed beneath his leather pants, that damned harness making my human side's fingers itch to grab hold and command *him*.

But I remained quiet and kept my fists at my sides.

The private room hadn't changed since I'd last been inside, and I shrugged the robe from my shoulders, ignoring its silent flutter to the floor while striding toward the bench.

"So hungry," Vanni mused behind me, but I didn't argue his assessment.

Famished better described my current state.

"What's your safeword, boy?" he asked while buckling me to the bench, taking care to keep from touching my skin.

"Beta," I stated clearly without any intent of saying it while he gave me what I desired.

"Cane?"

"The whip tonight, Sir," I requested since I was more in the mood for stinging pain rather than the rod.

"Mmm." He hummed his appreciation. "Have your hard limits changed, Dolyn?"

My beast hissed for me to give more tonight, and I reminded him that we would wait for our beta for penetration. This human didn't deserve to touch royalty. "My limits remain the same," I informed Vanni, while my inner beast grumbled at me.

"Shame." Vanni sighed and moved to the wall where various toys hung. He returned, shaking the whip's coils loose. The tip dragged on the ground behind him, and I shivered in anticipation, well aware of his every move. "How badly do you need the pain tonight?"

"I want release more than agony."

"Sir," he reminded me.

"*Sir*." I echoed his title with a bite to my tone.

Vanni chuckled. "Hold on, boy. Let your master bring you to your knees."

"You aren't—"

A whooshing sound led to a stinging stripe over my ass cheeks, cutting off my denial.

I hissed at the delicious sensation, my beast purring his delight over being strapped down and at a dominant's mercy. Staring straight ahead, I flexed my cheeks, my hole clenching.

"Color?" Vanni asked, voice low, his face near my ear.

"Green, Sir." I made myself snip rather than moan and settled in for what wouldn't take too long.

Pre-cum dripped from my slit before the fifth slash over my skin, and by the tenth, I sagged, panting and sweating, beast roused and begging for more.

"The sight of you like this undoes me." Vanni's ragged voice flooded through my entire being, and I shuddered, biting back a deep groan. "What I wouldn't give to soothe and lick the marks I've put on your skin."

His words caused a shudder to ripple through me, those slashes tingling in desire for the same.

"No," I forced through gritted teeth.

"Do you want more, boy?" Hot breath ghosted over my neck, awareness of his proximity causing my overheated skin to tingle as my beast pushed to make himself known and scent the man.

I shoved him down, his hiss loud in my ears regardless of him being locked up tight. "You know I do—just do. Not. Touch. Me."

"Pity." Vanni's presence beside me disappeared, allowing me to breathe.

Three more quick stripes over my back pulled grunts from my lungs.

"Again. Please," I hated how my voice sounded like a whiny, needy bitch, the type of man Father would despise.

My inner beast hissed at the thought, and I shoved Father from my mind, focusing on the heat growing low in my groin. Another hit sent shivers down my spine, settling at its base.

One more, maybe two would tip me over.

"Fuck yes." I gulped and shuddered.

Another—

Cum erupted through my shaft at the next hit, and I roared, spurts of white pulsing in a stream from pent-up lust and longing. I jerked against my bonds but only with human strength so as not to escape. My muscles twitched until I finished, gasping for breath. Satiated bliss buzzed through my blood, allowing me to sag against the bench. Tingles raced through me, settling into my fingertips and toes.

A heavy sigh left me completely depleted and at rest.

Soon.

Yes, it wouldn't be long before I would fill our female with my seed, I assured my inner beast, my cock attempting to thicken again.

Master Vanni—watch.

I cut my beast's fantasy short, his manipulation rousing my lax muscles to wakefulness. He continued to purr with satiated bliss from his curled-up position deep inside me, unaffected by me setting him straight.

Vanni could give my female the pain she yearned for until the time she accepted me as her alpha. The thought of hurting her churned my guts, and I questioned my ability to gift her what she desired.

Beta.

I wondered if my inner dragon suggested our beta might

be a sadist even though I'd never read throughout history of such a Blood Born existing. Or perhaps, he meant what he usually did—that *we* were the lesser of worth.

Awareness of Vanni behind me sent a rush of energy through me, pebbling my skin.

Beta.

My beast's echo assured me of his intention in speaking.

"Release me," I demanded, and Vanni submitted to my command without argument.

Shedding my shackles, I told myself that tomorrow I would reveal myself to the female destined for me and take my place as alpha, no matter my inner dragon's desires.

I was in charge, and *I* would control the outcome of our future.

CHAPTER 10

ASHLEY

I slept better than I had for over a week.

The sun shone bright through the winter sky, and I opened my blinds to allow the light and bit of warmth into my east-facing condo. Within sight of those outside, I stood still. Waiting. Scanning the length of the street out front.

Neither set of eyes made me feel any particular way.

Soothed yet a little saddened, I returned to my bedroom and changed into something comfortable since I needed to get groceries.

I started my small Coop I rarely used by remote, looking through my front window as the engine came to life.

No one but neighbors busied themselves beneath the winter's sun from what I could see, but a rush of warmth far beyond golden rays slid over me.

Good eyes hovered nearby and watched me, same as last night.

Smiling and core warming, I hit the unlock button on my car with expectation he would accompany me and turned away, excited to step outdoors and gladly yield to his stare.

While sceneing with Master Vanni, I'd felt my stalker's comforting presence. Got off on knowing he watched, a sense of his appreciation over my submitting to pain a turn-on so great that I'd asked for Vanni's touch.

His fingertips on my backside hadn't brought about revulsion or curdled my stomach as it would have done a week prior. I'd wanted to press into his hand, beg for more. Ask him to put his hand between my thighs. It wasn't fear that had kept me silent but recognition that one step at a time would ensure I healed properly without falling backward into my trauma.

Next Friday, I'd told myself once I had locked myself in for the night.

But I didn't want to wait a week to meet with Master Vanni and strive forward in the progress I'd been making.

Ten minutes later and considering a request to visit the club sooner than scheduled, I opened my front door. Sweet heat flooded through me, and I wanted to bask in the double dose of sunlight caressing my upturned face. I checked the back seat, finding it empty as I'd expected but hopeful my invisible…friend? awaited me. I climbed into my car, my smile widening over his close presence. Either he could pass through metal and plastic, or he'd snuck in while I'd still been out of sight putting on my coat and hat.

My body tingled with the desire to see him in the flesh.

Maybe even touch.

But more than anything, assurance of his presence filled me with peace and a sense of rightness, allowing me to move without fear of harm.

"Hi," I whispered, straining to hear the slightest shift or breath behind me.

Silence met my ears, and I laughed at myself rather than be disappointed. Incandescent happiness flooded through me with sweet warmth. A torturous yet delicious tension filled the interior of my vehicle, causing dampness between my thighs. I rubbed them together, believing I could get myself off if I tried.

But I wanted more than self-care. Needed physical touch like a seed buried underground required sunlight to grow. The yearning inside me strengthened with every passing minute, settling my mind on what I wanted even though logically, such a step toward healing seemed more like a leap off a cliff.

I drove toward the closest grocery store like I did every Saturday morning, wishing for conversation throughout the entire five-mile trip.

His presence disappeared when I entered the store but returned minutes later, solidifying in my mind that he had to open doors instead of passing through them. Otherwise, awareness of his being close wouldn't have waned.

He followed me through the store, my grocery cart a lame one, the front left wheel squeaking and tugging me to the right. But I was too amped up with a heightened heartbeat and impatience for the unknown to be annoyed with the faulty cart. I meandered up and down every aisle even though I didn't need to, enjoying the eyes on my back and the arousal in my core. Comfortable with the fact I would never see my stalker if I looked for him, I finished up with my chore, not bothering to glance behind me.

I loaded the groceries into my trunk but hesitated in returning home immediately. If he couldn't pass through metal in his invisible form, I would be driving to the condo on my own. Perhaps I could open the backdoor and invite him in.

I nibbled on the inside of my lip, wondering if Doctor Hasslet would think I was insane. Without evidence of my stalker's presence, how would anyone but myself believe I didn't imagine him?

A Dunkin' Donuts sat beside the grocery store, and as my gaze landed on the coffee shop, another option presented itself. Hoping my thought might pay off how I hoped for, I made my way across the parking lot. A hot chocolate and donut would be a nice weekend treat and also a good excuse for me to keep him around a little longer.

I entered the shop, the door closing behind me, hiding me from the view of good eyes. Breath held, I moved forward, joining the line waiting to place their order.

The door opened behind me, letting in a blast of cold air.

Warmth flooded my veins with more intensity than usual.

He was here—but the strength of his presence suggested he would be visible if I looked over my shoulder.

My heart rate spiked, a rush of adrenaline weakening my limbs in the best way possible.

The person in front of me moved forward to order, and I attempted to do the same but stumbled.

A firm hand grasped my elbow.

Even through the coat prohibiting skin contact, I felt a sense of connection with him as I had with Elijah two years earlier. A strange recognition of a similar soul, or perhaps we had known one another in a previous life. That awareness of my stalker's invisible presence heightened and solidified into knowledge he stood behind me in the flesh.

I lifted my head, turning slightly.

The blond god I'd seen outside the cafe in Manhattan peered down at me, his grip on my arm holding me upright.

A rush of saliva flooded my mouth, and I swallowed hard as a shudder quaked me in my boots.

Amber eyes seeming to flicker with golden fire roamed over my face as though drinking me in as thoroughly as I did him. High cheekbones flushed from either the cold or nervousness. Nostrils flared at the base of his Grecian nose.

His deep inhale, as though scenting me like a shifter in the romance novels I read, sent shivers down my spine.

My good eyes, my desire-inducing stalker, was beauty personified. Perfection unknown on Paris runways and across magazine covers. Tall and heavily muscled, he loomed over me but didn't feel threatening in any way. If he asked me to sink to my knees, I wouldn't hesitate to gift him my submission.

The truth of how he physically and mentally affected me caused my mouth to water rather than raise the hairs on my nape with alarm. I bit the inside of my lip to keep from whimpering from the overwhelming need.

"Are you all right?" His low voice was husky yet smooth as silk and as tantalizing as a lover's caress I hoped to enjoy one day soon.

"F-Fine," I sputtered, my face hot and insides fluttering.

His hand slid down my coat-covered arm, and instinct didn't allow me to flinch away from the stranger's touch.

Warm fingertips ghosted over mine—

An onslaught of energy whipped through my body, ripping a gasp from my lungs as his hand fell to his side. His flesh coming into contact with mine triggered some sort of reaction throughout my nervous system.

Was that how true attraction affected a person?

A sense of comfort flooded me, and I relaxed into the tingling vines wrapping around my body like a cradling hug. The scent of campfires on cool nights and cedar filled my lungs on my deep inhale, and I whimpered as a rush of wetness soaked the cotton of my panties.

I stared, smitten by the sight of him, aroused beyond what I'd ever experienced before. Surely, a gentle caress over my clit would send me careening into a flood of sensations only Master Vanni had led me toward.

A slow smile curved my stalker's generous mouth as though he knew exactly how his touch affected me.

"Can I help you?" A muffled voice barely reached through my concentration.

Good eyes stood close to a foot taller than me, and every cell inside my body yearned to move into his embrace. Grab hold with all my might and never let go. Lift my face for his kisses. Allow him to push against all of my limits and take what belonged—

"Excuse me?" An annoyed tone yanked me from my fantasy.

Blinking, I became aware of the scent of coffee and donuts. I glanced behind me to find the cashier's one eyebrow raised as she glanced between me and…

Mine.

Awfully presumptuous of my mind to whisper such a word, but I couldn't help the sureness of who this man was to me.

But I'd thought that once upon a long time ago when I'd first experienced arousal, and initiating contact with that man had ruined me for life.

Swallowing hard, I turned my focus on the blond god, more than anything wanting to trust more the sense of safety I felt from his proximity.

I'd never believed my pastor would hurt me either though.

"Two hot chocolates and…" He glanced down at me, waiting for me to complete our order.

"Boston cream donut," I whispered, my insides no longer completely at rest.

His golden gaze twinkled down at me, his grin causing my belly to flip upside down.

"Two Boston cream donuts," he told the woman behind the counter while pulling a wad of cash from his pocket.

His profile etched into my memory as he paid and dropped the change in a tip jar.

Our gazes clashed, and I lost my breath over the vulnerability he showed rather than arrogance I expected from a man with his beauty.

He grasped my coat-covered elbow, but I wished for skin contact to experience that electrical connection again.

"Who are you?" I whispered as we stepped to the side to wait for our drinks.

Still holding my arm, he turned and faced me fully, moving into my personal space so I had to tip my head back to hold his gaze. "My name is Dolyn Kemmerly."

"You've been following me." I didn't ask a question, but he nodded without hesitation. I appreciated his truthfulness. "Why?"

A slow exhale from his parted lips tickled sweetness over my tongue, and he opened his mouth further to reply.

"Your drinks, sir."

I glared at the cashier who'd dared to interrupt us but swallowed my annoyance rather than sounding like a deranged animal by hissing like a cat.

Dolyn released his hold on my arm and accepted the two cups, a bag already tucked between two of his fingers.

I hadn't even seen the exchange of donuts at the counter.

Dolyn's arresting eyes searched my face, inducing a deep ache in my core that my instinct suggested only he could ease. "Would you sit with me?"

I nodded, earning another slow smile. I bit my tongue to stop myself from begging Dolyn to flood me with so much of his cum that my DNA was forever changed because of it being inside my body. A shudder ripped through me, mostly pleasant, but traumatic memories attempted to leak through the consuming, unexpected want, demanding I remain on alert.

Dolyn led the way toward a table tucked in the corner, far from any other patrons, and I followed on his heels as though his nearness could protect me, that he could assist me in what I attempted to heal from.

He set our drinks and the bag down before pulling out one of the corner table's two chairs for me. Heat rushed to my cheeks, and I slipped out of my coat before sitting, laying it across my lap.

Dolyn settled on the other side, gently pushing one of the hot chocolates toward me, the scratch of the cardboard cup over the laminate surface loud between us.

His soft smile and unguarded gaze suggested he meant no harm.

Trust.

Why did instinct demand such a thing when I ought to be wary considering my past experience? Suspicion weaseled its way through the comfort Dolyn's presence attempted to offer. The sure sense of good eyes following my every move lately couldn't stop hesitancy from invading my thoughts.

Dolyn's smile faded. "I won't ever hurt you," he murmured as though reading my mind.

"I've heard that one before," I said, my voice only slightly shaky from the adrenaline's slow decrease through my blood.

His full lips pressed into a thin line, another flash of that fire flaring to life in his eyes before blinking out. "Who was it, Ashley?"

He knew my name without my having to speak it, proof he'd been the one stalking me. Why didn't *that* truth make me skittish and send me rushing out the door?

My butt remained planted in place as that awakened instinct and my usual better sense warred inside me. This intense energy, the potent desire between Dolyn and I wasn't...normal. Something pinged in my brain as though *off*, but I couldn't make sense of what it was I felt.

"My past is none of your business," I answered, deciding to stay put for now. Curiosity demanded it alongside desire to learn more about this man who befuddled my senses. Walking away without answers was not an option.

Dolyn nodded and turned his attention to the bag, taking care to remove both donuts, place them onto napkins, and slid one my way. A slow exhale loosened the tension from his shoulders. "I am sorry for causing you discomfort," he murmured, his tone soothing as honey.

I nodded my acceptance of his apology. "Tell me about yourself, Dolyn. Who you are and why you've been following me for over a week." My voice didn't shake, nor did I leave space for him to brush me off. I would know this man who'd been stalking me, who'd gifted me the ability to experience arousal without the bite of pain.

Regardless of the safe sense of having his attention, awareness of something strange going on shivered in my belly.

Was he both the heat *and* cold I'd been feeling? Did some sort of bipolar or psychological issue cause him to have two distinctive sides that affected me in this way?

It was time for answers.

CHAPTER 11

DOLYN

Ashley didn't trust me, and although that was to be expected, I couldn't help the disappointment pinging through my chest.

Force.

Clearing my throat and slamming the muzzle closed over my beast's sneaky mouth, I attempted another smile at the tiny woman sitting ramrod straight in her chair across the table from me. Purple-blue eyes hinted at unease, as did the tension in her shoulders, and I wished more than anything to erase both.

She'd been hurt by someone in her past, and I would eventually root out that truth and make them pay. For now, I would answer her questions about who I was as truthfully as possible and hopefully set her at ease as to my intentions for watching her.

"I'm simply a man from Lower Manhattan who enjoys traveling, investing, and supporting dog shelters." None of that was a lie, but there was much more to me.

Blood Born.

Dragon shifter.

Her fated alpha.

My inner beast hissed at the third truth ringing in my head, but I ignored him.

Ashley would need time to grow comfortable with my human half before I revealed all of who I was and how we were forever tied to each other.

"Dog shelters?" she asked, blinking some of the wariness from her beautiful eyes.

I sucked in a lungful of vanilla and her underlying musk that hinted of desire. My cock had been hard since I'd first seen her exit her house, and the length trapped inside my jeans continued to throb over her nearness. I eyed her hand wrapped around the steaming cup of chocolate wishing to touch her again, my beast side whimpering his agreement.

A mere brush of fingertips had cemented the fact of who she was to me the second we'd come into contact. I'd been sure she also felt the connection destined by fate ignite between our bodies, the beginnings of the bond we would one day complete.

After we found our beta.

Alpha.

My jaw clenched as I attempted to muffle the voice whose opinion I did not need. Touching Ashley's skin had somehow strengthened his part of our dichotomous nature.

Focusing on our female, I offered what knowledge I could. While not actually forcing her hand, perhaps I could sway her toward assurance of my intentions.

"I'm a very rich man," I stated since women tended to swoon over that fact.

Ashley's face didn't so much as twitch at my revelation of being her possible sugar daddy. Perhaps she didn't care about wealth, or the status riches awarded one in society.

Truth.

Yes, I had ways of appealing to her softer nature, the

compassionate side I witnessed through a brush of finger-tips, but I hadn't ever shared that part of me with anyone—Elijah included.

She is ours and will one day know our every thought.

My inner dragon didn't lie about the bond that would eventually link us together with Ashley, but fear of rejection tied my tongue.

Our fated female will never turn her back on us.

Throat tight, I nodded over what Father had assured us of. Still, my stomach roiled. "I'm a philanthropist and donate to those in need," I continued, my voice barely above a whisper. "Especially to dogs that deserve to be cared for when their owners abandon them."

"Dogs?"

"Yes. I've had two shelters built and continue to cover all expenses for the aging and sick, the unselfish creatures no one can be bothered to love."

I didn't share that I'd adored one such creature decades earlier and had left them behind out of selfishness and a broken heart.

My beast didn't mourn that part of our past as much as my human side, the cold bastard. He didn't give two shits about domesticated animals, cats especially. As for the homeless creature who'd found me twice while trailing after Ashley, I planned to locate him and take him north of the city to one of the shelters where he would be properly looked after.

Waste.

Liar, I wanted to speak to my beast but kept my lips sealed. Nothing about caring for needy dogs was a waste of my time or money.

Ashley stirred her hot chocolate with a shaky hand, still studying me intently enough I shifted my weight in the plastic chair beneath me.

"You're suspicious," I stated, easily reading the wariness on her face.

"As any woman in her right mind *would* be."

I nodded, leaning forward onto the table. "How can I prove myself to you, Ashley? What do I have to do to earn your trust?"

She glanced around the nearly empty seating area but didn't make a move to leave as I got the impression she suddenly wished to do. "That's the second time you've called me by name when I didn't supply you with one," she accused, meeting my stare.

Curses rang through my head from both my beast and human side alike.

Partial truth.

"An old friend of mine shared your personal information with me," I answered, believing the proposal that Elijah would be willing to vouch for me since his female had revealed Ashley to be my fated mate.

"Who told you about me and why?"

"Elijah Tolzman because I lost my heart the second I first saw you."

Ashley blinked, settling back into her chair. "Mr. Tolzman? I'm one of his secretaries."

"I'm well aware."

"I've never seen you in his office before, nor have I heard him mention your name."

"Even though we don't have in-person interactions at his building, I have known him for many years. We were even roommates for quite a few of them." Elijah and I were a lot more than that, but my female never needed details about how her alpha had submitted his body to another.

"Huh." A hint of a smile flitted over her face, relieving some of the tension in my stomach. "That man saved my life. Well, not really, but I smashed into him with a tray full of coffee a couple of years ago. He hired me hours later. Elijah, while my boss, is like a big brother to me, the one I never had but always wanted."

Elijah must have unknowingly sensed the hint of dragonblood in her veins and instinctively looked out for her.

Such knowledge had taken first scenting her then skin contact in order for me to sense she was more than human.

Because Elijah is in tune with his inner beast, and you selfishly keep me shackled up inside, only allowing me out to play when your human half is too weak to obtain what you want.

I fought to keep from clenching my jaw over my beast's spewing of bullshit. Ashley's presence lowered my defenses and gave him more strength than usual, but as long as I held control in my hands, he would remain unable to affect my physical body.

Ashley might be mostly human, but the fact I was now convinced her line had spawned from dragonblood generations ago, I told myself I could accept her lesser bloodline as my mate. Some might think me arrogant to believe destiny had allowed her to be born specifically for me, but Father had insisted I remember who I was.

Worthy.

Wanted.

Deserving of greatness as a pure Blood Born.

But the gentleness of her spirit...

Yes, I sensed that of her when we touched, spurring a deep desire to connect far beyond the physical in both parts of us. I wished to know my mate's emotions and desires. Take her under my wing.

Protect her at all costs.

Shower her with the love she deserved for belonging to us as Elijah's female had shown in the vision that had drastically changed my existence.

"Elijah is a good man," I stated the truth even as my beast acted petulant over Elijah having known her first.

"He is." Ashley sat quiet for a few seconds, watching as I sipped my too-sweet drink. She did the same. "You've been following me."

I wasn't ashamed for trailing after her or camouflaging myself from her human eyes that weren't yet ready for the truth. "I have."

"Why couldn't I see you?"

"I'm good at hiding in shadows."

She pursed her lips for a moment. "And the sense of eyes on me while I was in my car?"

My inner dragon chuckled his approval over her wily attempt to corner me with questions.

"Did you notice the vehicle following you?" I asked, skirting the truth.

Ashley's eyes narrowed as she glanced over me. "You aren't a ghost."

I tapped my chest to prove her right even though most humans would believe my other half dwelled inside me as a separate presence, invisible unless I allowed him partial freedom.

"I don't believe in spirits anyway," she muttered and bit into her donut, tongue flicking out over her top lip at a smear of chocolate.

My groin tightened, and I tore my focus off her mouth to find her still studying my face.

Intuition, while appreciated in a mate, promised a chat to become familiar with one other would not be easy.

"Why didn't you walk right up to me and introduce yourself like any other normal guy would?"

Lie.

A grimace marred my mouth over my beast's fear she

grew too disbelieving and would soon leave us. "You're… intimidating."

"Yeah, okay." She huffed a sarcastic laugh. "Try again."

I stared at her face, drinking in the sight of her flawless beauty. "There are no words to describe your perfection." My dragon side hummed his agreement although he'd waxed poetic about her looks before.

Ashley's smile dissolved, and the hand lifting her donut up for another bite settled back onto the table.

I ran my gaze over her face and neck, soaking in the sight of her. "Beautiful pale skin. A glorious shade of eyes I've never seen the likes of. An imperfect nose that only adds to the draw of your heart-shaped face. Your full lips. Dainty chin. The spackling of freckles over your nose. I love how petite you are, the height difference between us. Makes me feel…strong. Protective. My instinct is to wrap you up in my arms and carry you through life."

She straightened in her chair. "I don't need a man in order to survive in this world."

"I didn't say that you did." I'd seen Ashley take more pain than a lot of women could possibly tolerate. "You're tougher than most would assume. You have an inner fire—a beast, if I had to guess—inside you, gifting you not just strength but grace. You, Ashley, are a queen, and I would love nothing more than to be your king."

My inner half held his breath, cursing me for going too far.

Wetness welled in Ashley's eyes, but she forced a laugh, tearing what remained of her donut in two. "I don't like to be touched, so making a pass like that won't get you into my panties."

Fingers aching to dip into her arousal I could scent in the air, I swallowed hard. "I have an aversion to physical contact as well."

She jerked her focus up, her dark brows furrowing. "You do? Why?"

Partial truth.

"Like you, it's personal, but let's just say that I tend toward feeling more than mere warmth or smoothness when I touch another person's skin."

"So, you're like an empath?"

Inner beast silent, I considered Ashley's comparison. Since there really was no other way to describe a supernatural bonding of mates, I nodded. "I guess you could call me that. What about you?"

"I'm not done with my interrogation."

I chuckled along with my beast and bit into my own donut, the burst of sweetness not nearly as delicious as Ashley would be on my tongue. "Then ask away, beautiful."

She did—and I answered the questions that I could and brushed off those I couldn't.

Like how she swore she felt me watching her throughout the week even when I wasn't within sight.

I had been close enough to touch, but she wasn't yet ready for that revelation.

"Perhaps you enjoyed my longing stare from those moments I was physically present that you imagined them when I wasn't," I suggested.

Ashley narrowed her eyes again and popped the last bite of her snack between her lips. "Something is…not right with you Dolyn Kemmerly."

Stomach turning to rock, my smile faded. The beast within me curled in on himself deep inside me. "What do you mean?"

She worked her lips side to side as though nibbling on the tender flesh inside. "You aren't being completely honest with me."

"Would you be open and vulnerable if I asked *you*

personal questions?" I shot back, not unkindly but hoping to make her see my reasoning for silence on certain topics.

"You have a point." She crumpled up her napkin and pushed it inside her empty cup.

I filled my lungs as my inner beast's tension eased slightly. "Perhaps we could meet again and get to know each other better," I offered. "In time, you will come to realize that my intentions toward you are pure. I will never manipulate, coerce, or force you against your will."

Her eyes grew misty, and my instincts growled deep inside. Who had hurt her? When, why, and how? They would know the sharpness of our claws, the power of our jaw, and our ability to rip a human limb from limb without effort.

Yessss.

"I would like to see you again," Ashley finally said, "but don't get your hopes up."

Regardless of her warning, my heartbeat stuttered. "Everyone could use another friend."

"That is true." A soft smile, one without a trace of unease, curved her mouth, causing renewed warmth in my groin.

"Can I have your number?"

She hesitated. "Give me yours, and I'll contact you. Maybe we can meet for lunch next Saturday?"

A huff of dissatisfaction sounded inside me, but I refused to push Ashley until she was ready for the full truth between us.

"I would love nothing more." I recited my digits once she had her cell in hand.

"Thank you for the opportunity to get to know you better," I said as she put her phone back into her purse. "And for not running away while I worked up the nerve to finally talk to you."

"Thank *you* for the drink and donut," she replied. "But honesty from here on out, okay?"

I nodded and stood to help her with her coat, careful to keep from crossing the line she'd set between us about physical touch.

Someday, I would be gifted the opportunity to feast on every inch of her. But until then, I would practice patience no matter how desperate my instincts were to claim and breed the precious one who belonged to me.

CHAPTER 12
VANNI

I studied my hand, remembering the feel of Ashley's reddened ass cheeks. Satiny smooth. Hot and deliciously fleshy. My index finger had later grazed the top of her ear while I'd tucked back strands of her hair.

Tingles still raced up my arm whenever I relived those moments from Friday night.

Before dropping her off, which I hadn't been comfortable doing, I requested she keep in touch with me over the weekend. She'd insisted on going home alone and had texted me as she'd climbed into bed later, safe and sound.

I hated her being by herself, believing someone—*two* someones according to her strange sixth sense—stalked her every move.

Ashley had only felt the good eyes after climbing from my car and as I'd walked her to her front door. She seemed pleased by the supposed presence. I had no say in her life, but if I'd had my way, Ashley would have been safe and sound in *my* bed where I could keep her close and protect her.

But her independence won out, and I felt as though a

piece of my soul lay too far away with every night that passed.

Heaving a heavy exhale, I got up from my couch and went into the kitchen, needing another glass of water. I'd worked my body hard in my home gym earlier in the day and had run five miles atop the weights I'd lifted. Exhaustion should have put me down for the night, but my body vibrated with excess energy as it had since I'd first come into contact with Ashley's skin.

I guzzled the water and looked down at my hand again.

How could one scene impact me so deeply that I couldn't think about another female? Even memories of my ex didn't rouse bitterness with how caught up I'd become in my desire for Ashley.

That other pea in the pod though—Dolyn...

Blood pushed toward my groin, and I cursed, pressing down on my swelling cock. That man. Infuriatingly sexy as fuck, enticing enough I practically had begged to touch him as I had Ashley.

His refusal had stung, and his inability to slip into subspace, even though I'd given him everything I had packed behind my whip, confused the hell out of me. What had caused such strength to build up that his natural submission gave way to stubbornness?

I lusted to peel back his layers, dive deep into his psyche. Break him down and rebuild him into the person he yearned to be.

Same as I wished for Ashley.

Shaking my head, I meandered back into my living room and slouched on my couch, head tipped back, legs spread, ignoring the ache growing inside me.

Dolyn was a stranger, a two-time scene and done guy.

Ashley held the possibility of a future, and even though I allowed myself vulnerability with her, I would attempt to make myself content with crumbs if that was all she offered.

My cell rang, and I leaned forward to grab it off the coffee table.

Ponder on my beautiful angel, and her name appeared on my screen.

"Hey," I answered, hoping for the best. "Everything okay?"

"I met him."

The stalker. I sat upright even though she sounded pleased, happy, even, rather than scared.

"What happened?" I asked, my tone barely regulated.

"He approached me in Dunkin' Donuts," she continued, her voice almost purr-like, twisting my guts up tight.

I frowned as she went on to describe how gorgeous he was, how the sight of him, his proximity, caused her heart to beat too fast. How his smile and steady gaze made her feel the same as when she'd felt his watchful gaze—aroused.

My muscles tightened, and spots flashed in my vision. I would rip him apart. Tear off his head—

"He was a perfect gentleman, and yet something felt...off about him."

I clung to her cautious tone, desperate to keep this man away from her. "You have to trust your instincts."

"See, that's what's strange," Ashley said, thoughtfully. "My instincts say yes, and my past trauma causes my head to say no."

Her explanation made sense because of how I was torn between her and Dolyn but also sounded alarms in my head. The connection growing between her and I felt threatened by the introduction of a second man.

Fear over experiencing similar heartache to what my ex had caused demanded I protect myself and stay in the friend zone until Ashley decided what and who she wanted.

That encouragement I'd offered her to move forward had

backfired, and the sense of floundering even worse than before learning more about Ashley returned tenfold.

"At therapy the other day, Doctor Hasslet suggested I meet him again in a safe place," Ashley went on, and I could tell from her voice she had every intention of doing so.

A burn lit inside my chest, and I bit my tongue to keep from demanding otherwise. She might submit herself to me once a month, but Ashley was not mine.

Yet.

I appreciated the quiet thought in the back of my mind.

"He also asked how I felt about you now that this new man has come into my life," she continued.

Of course Doc Haslett had. He knew everything about me and probably assumed correctly how I would respond to another man entering the picture. I'd only just become comfortable with the thought of opening up my heart again and had told him as such during our virtual chat a few nights earlier.

"What did you say?" I asked, my voice rasping with desperation even though I tried to hide my emotions.

"I'm drawn to the guy, but I…I feel the same way about you too, Vanni. Is it wrong to be interested in two men equally?"

My eyelids slid closed as I rubbed a hand through my hair, thrilled to finally have the truth of her feelings for me yet torn over her heart being divided in who she ought to pursue. "I have to tell you something, Ashley."

"What?" Wariness bled over the line.

"I told you I'm divorced, but I never shared the reason behind our split."

"Shit," she whispered as though knowing where my tale went before I said a word.

"One of my ex-wife's fantasies was a threesome, and I

invited another man into our bed to give her a night to remember."

"Oh no."

I'd considered my gift the mistake of a lifetime but lately had been rethinking the entire event that had led to me meeting Ashley.

And Dolyn.

"She left me a short time later to pursue a future with him."

"I wouldn't ever play you like that, Vanni," Ashley said.

"We aren't in a relationship that you should feel the need to persuade my thoughts."

"Ouch." Her tone suggested she grimaced over my blunt words.

Swallowing hard, I forced myself to go on. "You are free to travel your path toward healing without interference on my end."

"It sounds as if you'd *like* to interfere?" Her voice hinted at a question.

I held my breath for a moment before emptying my lungs and deciding on honesty, since she obviously needed reassurance. "More than anything, I desire a deeper connection with you, but I want what's best for *you*, Ash, and if that's him…" I couldn't bring myself to finish.

"I'd like to get to know him better, but something inside me suggests you're both equally important in my life." She exhaled loudly as though as troubled over the entire affair as I was. "Are you available to meet with me this Friday night instead of waiting another three weeks?"

A low chuckle escaped me, and I rested against my couch, eyes wide and staring at the ceiling. "I closed my schedule down after you allowed me to touch your skin."

"Oh." I could imagine the flush on her cheeks. "That's… wow. Okay."

"Don't ever question how I feel about you, Ashley, but I'm not telling you that because I'm one of those pick-me guys."

"You definitely aren't," she laughed lightly. "So, um, Friday?"

"I'll see you at seven," I stated rather than asking if our usual time worked for her. She would obey like the good girl she always was for me.

Ashley requested to be showcased on the lounge dais again, her graceful body draped over the same bench we'd used the week before.

My heart thundered in my chest, my mouth drier than a damned desert while taking in the flush over her pale skin. "What is your safeword, Ash?"

A shiver rippled goose bumps over her arms and legs that were unrestrained. "*Red*, Master."

"Are you sure about this?" I checked in one last time while circling her bent form, appreciating every swell of her flesh I wished to mark.

"Yes, Master. Please use your hand like you did last week."

Hissing quietly, I stood beside her backside and pulled back my right arm. My palm landed against her flesh with a loud crack.

Ashley jolted forward and moaned. "Again, Master."

I allowed her to top me from the bottom, giving her everything she asked for.

My handprints littered her ass cheeks and thighs within minutes, and tears dripped off her chin to the floor. Tremors rippled through her, the scent of her arousal and the smearing between her thighs testament to her pleasure.

"Master!" She cried out when I paused for too long enjoying the sight of what I had done to her.

"Yes, sweet girl?" I crouched beside her lowered head, careful in brushing back her hair to better see her face.

Wet violet eyes met mine, and the level of her need slammed into me, stealing my breath.

"T-Touch me, Master," she begged, another tear sliding down her cheek.

"Ash…"

"Please, Vanni—I need." She swallowed hard and shuddered. "P-Please."

"You're asking me to push your limits while you're high on endorphins and out here where everyone can see."

"I'm green, Master Vanni. Promise."

Cock hard and leaking inside my leathers, I reached around her body, gently trailing my fingertips over her heated backside. Every part of me longed to touch, to caress, same as I'd been desperate for with Dolyn the last time I'd scened with him. I'd lusted to nut on his back, paint his whip-lashed skin with my cum. The drive to mark him, make him smell like me had been almost too much to withstand.

I wanted him then with as much longing as I did Ashley.

She shuddered and moaned beneath my gentle touch.

"Color, baby," I whispered.

"The most glorious shade of green imaginable," she said on a sigh.

I barked out a laugh, unable to help myself over the fact she wasn't sold on this other guy and was gifting me the opportunity to touch her before he even got a chance. Still, the knowledge she felt drawn to him unsettled my soul. "Ash."

"Put your hand on my pussy, Master."

Fucking *hell*. How could I deny this woman what she desired and found the guts to voice?

My head swam, my breath coming in pants as I slid my fingertips over her plump ass cheeks.

She leaned into my touch rather than jerking away like she would have done a month prior. "Yes—there."

I ghosted my touch between her thighs to her core, finding slippery arousal. She was waxed and smooth.

A pulse of pre-cum erupted through my shaft, and I bit my tongue to keep from taking more than she'd begged for.

"Inside me." Ashley backed against my hand, and I dipped a single digit into her tight heat.

We both cursed, hers more of a moan to my bitten-off word.

I swallowed hard and pushed in a little farther, her body so damned responsive and silky soft.

"M-More, please, Master." She writhed against the bench, trying to fuck herself on my finger.

I gave her another, gentle while sliding in deep until my knuckles rested against her wet flesh.

"Tell me what you want, Ashley," I growled near her ear, hardly recognizing my own voice, my entire body tensed and trembling. "Use your words, sweet girl."

She panted, trying to lick the dryness from her lips.

"This?" I asked, pulling from her tight grasp and easing back in, searching out the roughened patch of flesh inside her.

There—

A whine slipped from her mouth, causing my cock to throb against its leather prison.

I stroked over her G-spot then withdrew, sliding my finger up over her puckered hole.

"Oh, God." Her breath caught as I circled my finger around her rim, smearing enough juices I could have fucked her ass without a single drop of extra lube.

"Fuck, Ash." I tenderly cupped her entire sex, her heat singeing my hand.

Eyes still clenched shut, she arched her back like a sensual cat needing to be fucked until she screamed. "P-Please, Master."

"Please what?"

"I need to come."

I flicked my middle finger over her swollen clit, back and forth, my balls on the verge of explosion.

"M-More…"

I rubbed my thumb along her pussy while toying with her hardened nub. "This what you want?"

"Mmm," she hummed, head jerking in a nod.

"Words, Ashley."

"Put your fingers in me again."

My dick bucked again, and I slowly pushed into her with my thumb.

She gasped, lifting her hips toward me.

"Like this?" I stroked her sensitive nerve bundles inside and out, and she groaned, her core fluttering.

"Yes. There. Oh, fuck, *yes*."

The scent of her arousal and the sweetness of vanilla flooded my senses, and I stared at her panting mouth while fucking her with my fingers.

"You have my permission to come." I said the words she always needed to let go, and Ashley bowed, shrieking her release, a rush of cum soaking my hand and dripping to the floor between her thighs.

I cursed and grabbed hold of my bulge to ward off my own climax. "Such a good girl for me, baby. So sweet and obedient. Look at you," I crooned, so goddamned proud of her my chest swelled and eyes stung. "You're absolutely stunning when you let go for me."

I continued to coax every last pulse from her pussy until she lay spent, hair plastered to her damp forehead. She hadn't fallen into subspace, but she rested, a smile on her lips as she attempted to catch her breath.

"My beautiful girl." I reluctantly removed my hand from her body and eyed the cream smeared over my fingers. The musky scent of her cum flooded my nostrils, and a growl rumbled low in my chest. I shoved my thumb into my mouth, sucking her essence down my throat, eyes rolling back into my head.

Every part of me ached to thrust into her tight wetness, stroke myself against her cum-slickened walls. Shoot copious amounts of thick spunk against her womb—claim her.

Mine.

My skin on fire, I licked my other fingers clean while staring at her peaceful face. How far would she be willing to go? Could I rouse her need enough again that she would allow me to at least blow my load all over her reddened skin?

I reached out my hand to caress the prints on her ass—and, I hoped, bring her back to the state of need where she might beg for my cock.

CHAPTER 13
DOLYN

I'd followed Ashley after work but stayed invisible as she ate in the same cafe as the week before. She'd sat in the front window again, searching the bustling side-walks for me as I was sure she sensed my presence.

My old, what turned out to be sickly, dog friend now rested in one of my shelters in upstate New York. Two nights ago and unable to sleep, I'd gone in search of him, allowing my beast to simmer close to the surface so we could scent the animal together.

I'd found him in a dark alley, damp and shivering, huddling in a pile of rubbish.

He'd allowed me to pick him up and cradle him to my chest. My beast had been bothered by the animal's stench, but I'd kissed the dog's snout and promised him food and warmth.

A few hours later, he curled in a kennel in the back of a hired van, licking me one last time on my fingers as I stroked his forehead. I'd told him to be a good boy.

He'd woofed his promise.

While I'd have preferred to keep the animal in my own

care, my suite and current situation didn't allow for such a pet. I'd called the shelter I financed and informed the overseer of the dog's impending arrival and insisted they spare no expense in seeing to his health.

Even knowing he'd arrived and was being looked after, I'd missed his cold nose against my hand as I watched Ashley finish her meal. Same as before, she'd headed northward, entering the doors of Vanni's skyrise as I'd expected.

I'd waited to enter, not wishing to be all up in her space again where she might be tempted to speak to what she considered thin air. If she'd simply reach out an arm or wave one quickly around her, she would come into contact with my body, and I couldn't have that until she first accepted the truth of what I was.

Once the elevator doors had slid shut and hid her from sight, I'd hurried to another, waiting for the people around me to crowd in. Riding upward to the floor housing the sex club took a bit of time with various ups and downs since I couldn't very well push past people and excuse myself to exit. Once finally alone, I hit the button for Vanni's club, cursing over every minute wasted.

Still invisible, I'd made myself at home in the men's locker room, the only place I felt sure I could reveal myself without the possibility of a camera catching me in the act. Seconds later, I'd stepped over a threshold leading to a sinner's delight. I moved deeper into the lounge as though I had every right to be there even though I hadn't paid for a membership. Surprisingly, or luckily, Vanni hadn't questioned my presence the last time I'd bent over and presented my ass for his whip. I expected his need to test my submission had been too great.

Musk, sweetness, and the scent of anxious perspiration slithered up my nose, hardening my already thickened cock as I moved deeper into the lounge.

Humans, dozens of them in all sorts of dress and lack thereof, mingled in the open area as with the other nights I'd been there. Dim lights teased with the suggestion of what went down in the shadows. Low music lay like a silken sheet beneath the rising moans and crack of instruments of pain upon supple flesh. The St. Andrew's cross held a woman moaning beneath a Dom's ministrations.

Chains clanked from a man strung to the ceiling directly on my right. Groans rose from two men getting their cocks sucked by kneeling submissives as they lounged by the bar.

My gaze returned to the cross and the woman strapped to it.

Please.

My dragon's whimper to play hit me hard, the fact he requested to submit rather than dominate pressing even harder. "*Alpha,*" I muttered aloud, my hands fisting at my sides.

A fierce frown dented my brow as I licked my lips, hoping for a taste of Ashley's sweetness in the air while scanning the room.

Cries of ecstasy jerked my head to the left to the lounge's far corner where Ashley had submitted to Vanni last week. Once more, she'd given her pleasure to him, and from my view, it appeared his hand still stroked between her thighs.

Slickness oozed from my slit, and I groaned, pressing down against my cock.

What a sight they were together. Both dark heads, hair dampened by sweat, skin shimmering from exertion. My feet moved me forward, and I drank them in, listening as Ashley whimpered and came down from her high.

Vanni pulled his hand away from her pussy and studied his glistening fingers.

The scent of her cum slammed into me with a wave, and

my dragon growled a rumble deep in my chest I couldn't hold back.

Ours.

Yes—she was, and I questioned the lack of jealousy over Vanni touching what didn't belong to him.

He sucked each and every digit clean, and my mouth drooled for a taste of her. My dragon should have shrieked and clawed at my brain to explode in a mass of muscle, sinew, and scales. We should have torn the building down around the man who dared to taste my mate.

Need.

Teeth gritted over my beast's whimper, I moved in close, doing as Father would have done.

I grasped Vanni's bare shoulder, intending to pull him away from Ashley—

Electrical currents shot up my arm and split toward my brain and chest, allowing my beast full control for a mere heartbeat.

We scented the man we touched, and knowledge slammed into us that couldn't be written off as desire or mistake.

"No," my human half gasped as fire swept through us. We dug our fingertips into Vanni's skin, yanking him around as tension crackled through the air like static electricity.

Hissing, I shoved my inner beast back in his prison, barely able to gain control.

Vanni scrambled to get his feet beneath him, breaking the connection between us, but the damage had been done. Same as with Ashley, the imprint had taken hold in our mind. "What the fuck—Dolyn?"

Our gazes caught, and he stilled.

Green orbs, brilliant like spring grass glared at me.

Yessss.

I growled and shook my head, blinking the sight of what Elijah's female had shown me clear from my memory.

Vanni DiLoreto stared at me with his usual mossy colored eyes, but because my inner dragon had come into contact with him at the same time as our human half, I could no longer deny who—*what*—the man before us was.

Even if only a minuscule portion, Giovanni DiLoreto was part dragonblood.

My beast purred, and I broke into a cold sweat as every muscle in my body tensed.

"No," I growled yet again, my vision going red.

Our alpha.

"No!" I let out roar to assert my dominance and snapped. My fist shot out, connecting with Vanni's cheek and slamming his head to the side. Rippling currents of awareness pulsed through where our skin had collided for less than a second.

The fucker kept his feet and simply worked his jaw while straightening and meeting my gaze head on.

Fire flared through his eyes, and there was no mistaking the inner beast's presence prowling beneath sinew and bone.

I faltered, frozen for the space of a heartbeat, as the realization his other half had possibly roused from its deep sleep due to my touch settled in.

Vanni barreled forward, taking me down before I could blink.

I slammed onto the floor, his weight forcing a grunt from my lungs.

My aching cock pressed against his, and a wave of desire stole my breath. "Fuck. Me," I gasped, the second I could speak.

A cocky grin lifted his lips, and he shifted his hips in a grinding motion that tempted me to unfurl my hands and grasp at the harness strapped to his bare chest. "You know

I'm the one in charge here, Dolyn," he murmured, leaning close to my ear, "but that's one command I would *love* to obey."

His low voice slithered over my skin like an erotic caress.

I shivered, and the bastard chuckled.

Two sets of hands grasped my arms from behind, yanking me from beneath Vanni. Both men, bodyguards mostly likely, were fully human, their touch lacking the awareness that had crashed into me when my skin had met Vanni's. I couldn't tear my focus off him as he slowly stood, adjusting his bulge. I didn't fight. I froze at the flash of green fire in his steady gaze.

Those eyes had haunted my dreams, same as Ashley's had.

I jerked my focus off Vanni.

My female stood beyond the spanking bench, a blue robe wrapped tight around her trembling body. Lips parted, she gaped at me, her eyes wide and fearful, luminous in the light above her. A hint of her emotions slid over my mind like a warm blanket thanks to the small touch we'd shared last Saturday, rousing my dragon's instinct to protect her.

Need.

I tested the firm grips holding me, aware I could easily toss both men aside, but the desire to pull Ashley into my chest, hide her from the stares licking at every inch of her kept me in place.

"Ashley," I whispered, the fear of violence and confusion overwhelming her widened eyes.

She shook her head and hurried toward the women's locker room.

"Ash!" Vanni, her Dom, my beta, called after her but didn't give chase.

Not beta.

Vanni turned his harsh glare on me, and my inner dragon

purred with desire to feel his strength as he punished me for causing our female unrest and a ruckus in his club.

I held Vanni's gaze, every cell in my human form questioning the authority in his stare.

Even with his minuscule amount of dragonblood, Vanni would never be able to dominate a creature such as myself. I looked forward to owning him, having him on his knees before me, begging for me to claim him.

"Who the *fuck* are you?" he asked, drawing near and getting in my face.

Sexual and violent tension radiated between us, and I locked my knees to remain upright. "Your alpha," I stated my claim through clenched teeth.

His head tipped back, and he roared with laughter, pure enjoyment and disbelief ringing throughout the silent lounge.

I strained forward against the bodyguards' hold, my body temperature rising as my inner beast echoed his response.

"Oh, that's good." Still chuckling, Vanni wiped at the blood dripping from a small cut on his cheekbone where I'd hit him. He eyed the smear of red on the back of his hand before glancing up at me through his black lashes, a sexy smirk taking over his mouth. A glint of promise lay in his vibrant eyes.

"Master Vanni?" Someone stepped into my periphery, handing him a towel.

"Thank you." He cleaned himself, a smile still on his lips.

He will be sweet on our tongue.

Perhaps, but most likely, he would be all fire and brimstone, biting and gnashing as I dominated him.

My dragon slithered sensually inside me, tempting me to fuck and find out.

Fear kept me planted.

I was royalty. A dominant alpha dragon shifter in need of his beta to bridge the gap between me and Ashley.

My dragon sneered at the thought but moaned with arousal as Master Vanni drew close enough that his heat wavered like the sun's rays over every inch of my skin not covered by clothing.

"You're my alpha, huh?" His gaze caressed my face with a knowing look. "Like you, I bow to no man," he murmured, his eyes glinting green fire as he peered into mine. "She never told me your name, but I have this strange feeling you're Ashley's stalker, the one she finally met last Saturday in a quaint little coffee shop where you enjoyed hot chocolate and Boston cream donuts."

I kept my lips sealed even though I found pleasure in hearing she'd spoken of me.

"Hmm, what a conundrum this has become," Vanni mused. "Tell me, Dolyn, how did you get into my club?"

His club.

Master Vanni.

He might be an admired Dominant, but not nearly enough dragonblood flowed through his veins for my liking.

Our destiny.

I clenched my eyes shut as my dragon cackled in glee.

CHAPTER 14

ASHLEY

The locker room door shut silently behind me, erasing Dolyn's presence from my skin.

My hands shook as I tore off the robe, my mind at war with my body.

I'd been aware the second he'd spotted me bent over the bench, and reborn arousal had caused my core to clench in need.

Master Vanni had been the first man to touch me in over twelve years. The first to give me a climax through pure pleasure alone. I'd wished to linger in the bliss of another step toward healing, but Dolyn had attacked him.

My stomach knotted, bile bubbling up my throat at the memory of his fist connecting with Vanni's face. Swallowing a few times kept me from vomiting, but the nausea remained as I struggled to dress in my work clothes.

Seeing the two men alongside each other, touching even in anger, the stare that had latched them together immediately after they'd tumbled to the floor, had my instincts insisting I slither between them.

I'd burned with desire to have one of them—both of them —buried deep inside my body.

But Dolyn's brutality toward Vanni meant to instill pain without pleasure had also put me on edge.

Vanni had called him by name, but I wasn't about to question their connection when every patron stared at us.

I'd chosen to re-robe and had put distance between us, saving my questions for later. Fleeing the lounge hadn't been enough space to stop the conflict battling in both parts of me.

I grabbed my bag and hurried to the door leading into the club's reception area but paused before touching the handle.

Had the bouncers dragged Dolyn out there? Did Vanni wait along with them to check on me?

Had both men been…playing me?

I shut that thought down as both of their touches gave me assurance they'd done no such thing. Vanni and Dolyn cared for me. Wished to protect me with animal-like inclination. And yet they would battle in anger over who had the right to touch me.

Off-kilter and torn between residual fear from my past and desire I'd never experienced before, I sagged against the wall, unsure of what to do.

A knock sounded from the door leading into the lounge opposite me.

Vanni stuck his head in. "Ashley?" His low tone soothed my heightened nerves and relit the heat in my core.

A hint of dried blood smeared over Vanni's cheekbone, the beginnings of a bruise already discoloring his usual olive complexion. Other than that, he appeared to be fine as he stepped fully into the locker room.

I glanced beyond him but couldn't make out much of the lounge behind him before the door shut quietly, leaving us alone.

"He's being held in my office," Vanni informed me, as though he'd read the question in my mind. He crossed the locker room, and energy snapped between us, familiar and yet different—more intense, as though our intimate contact had somehow brought us closer together.

I'd clearly read too many fairytales.

He peered down at me, his dark brow furrowed.

I gently touched his bruise, my hand still shaking. He held his breath as warmth crept up my arm from the physical contact between us. "Are you all right?"

"Are *you*?" he asked with a rushed exhale.

"I think so?" I tried for a smile, one he didn't offer in return.

His hands clenched and released at his sides. "Can I…"

I dropped my bag and stepped into him, laying my cheek against his bare chest between the straps of his harness. His heart beat heavy in perfect time with mine, the musky scent of him flooding my nose and causing unrest between my thighs regardless of the comfort I received from being pressed against him. My inner turmoil calmed enough that I drew a breath without hindrance for the first time since Dolyn had hurt him.

Vanni settled his arms around me, nose in my hair, a shudder ripping through him. "He's your stalker, isn't he? The man you met on Saturday."

"Yes. Please don't call the cops on him."

"Security already did."

I heaved a heavy exhale, exhaustion creeping in thick enough I couldn't think straight. Tears clogged my throat—hazed my sight. A sob rose past my lips, and I clung to the only unmovable rock I had in my life.

Vanni didn't shush me or attempt to stop my rolling emotions, simply allowed me a different type of release than the usual he gifted me.

Nothing made sense anymore. My heart and body were torn in two directions, and I had no clue what to do about my feelings for both men. I didn't even know Dolyn, yet sensed a strange connection with him, as though our souls had been entwined before time. And nothing had ever felt more right than Vanni's hands on me, his arms holding me close, and the thump of his heart beneath my ear. Any fear I'd had of skin-on-skin touching had long since disappeared with this man.

I should have been glorying in the next step toward healing, but the mess with Dolyn didn't allow for any happiness or satisfaction.

My tears eventually quieted, and Vanni gently cupped my cheeks in his palms to lift my head.

I blinked up at him, the desire swirling in his eyes—my need to close the distance between us and taste his lips—mirroring his.

"Ashley." He swept his thumb across my lower lip.

I shuddered. "Green, Master—Vanni. Please kiss me."

A small shift on his hold angled me perfectly for his descending mouth.

"Mr. DiLoreto?" a man called through the closed door beside us, and I huffed, pouting.

Vanni heaved a sigh and stepped back, cupping my elbow. "Yes?" He lifted his voice in return but didn't take his focus off my lips.

"Cops are here."

I peered at my master, my insides beginning to twist into a knot, all trace of arousal from our near-kiss evaporated.

"Let's go get this straightened out, and then we'll have a nice glass or two of wine to unwind, okay?" Vanni pushed my hair over my shoulder and smiled softly.

My insides swooned over the desire in his eyes, but the tension remained.

Was I healed?

Still broken?

Jenna gave an encouraging smile from behind the desk when we entered the receptionist area.

The security guard led us through a door behind her and up a set of stairs.

My thoughts replayed the last twenty minutes, and my insides continued to shake with the need for rest and lust alike. Forget the glass of wine Vanni had suggested. I would be drinking an entire *bottle* to escape the conflicting feelings ravaging my insides.

A cock buried deep inside my body would be just as good. Slow, lavish glides against my inner walls heightening my arousal until I climaxed around the thrusting length, lost in pleasure. I would gladly accept every drop of cum gifted to me.

But from which man?

I caught the moan rising up my throat and swallowed as the guard ushered us into what I assumed to be Vanni's office.

The scent of fire, smoke, and sex flooded my nose, and my gaze landed on Dolyn across the room. He sat in a leather chair, hands gripping the armrests. Cops flanked him, both with firm grips on his shoulders. As with when we'd first made eye contact in the coffee shop, golden fire swirled in the depths of his orbs, terrifying yet beautiful.

Mine.

The same word whispered in my brain, and even though I didn't understand where the voice originated from, I knew without a doubt my instincts spoke truth.

"Who are you really, Dolyn Kemmerly?" I whispered, starting toward him, but Vanni tightened his hold on my arm, keeping me at a distance.

Longing beyond sexual gratification filled Dolyn's eyes. "I'm your mate."

"Oh, for fuck's sake, Dolyn, enough of this nonsense," Vanni muttered.

"Miss O'Connor?"

I jerked my head toward the voice to find a third cop stood on my right. "Yes?"

"Can you tell us what is going on here? Mr. DiLoreto's bodyguard informed us that Mr. Kemmerly has been stalking you?"

"I…" I glanced back at Dolyn to find his stare unchanged.

The trauma of my past screamed I request they take him away. A deeper part of me needed everyone gone—but him and Vanni, the three of us writhing on the floor in a tangle of limbs and grasping hands.

A vivid vision of us entwined so fully I couldn't tell where one began and the other ended flashed in my mind, catching my breath.

Thighs clenching together and core pulsing, I blinked away the fantasy and glanced up at Vanni. He would be horrified, perhaps heartbroken over my desire to be with them both at the same time.

Vanni stared at Dolyn, but I couldn't read his thoughts. Eyes shuttered behind the mask of Dom, Master Vanni didn't reveal a single thing about what was going through his mind.

I refused to hurt him, but I also couldn't allow Dolyn to be taken away before I had answers to all the growing questions in my mind.

"There has been a misunderstanding," I said to the cop, hoping my wobbly smile appeared genuine. "Dolyn is…he's an acquaintance of mine. I—I'm sorry. I shouldn't have invited him here tonight without Master Vanni's permission."

Rarely did an outright lie pass my lips, but I had no other option.

I glanced up at Vanni to find his focus on me, eyes softer, almost as though he understood my dilemma.

"Mr. DiLoreto, do you wish to press charges?" the cop alongside us asked.

He studied me quietly as my pulse thumped in my ears. I held my breath.

"No," he finally said, and my body sagged, tension leaking from me on my exhale. Vanni released his hold on my arm, another show of trust.

Voices muttered as the two cops left Dolyn's side, but I shut them out while slowly approaching my stalker.

Who was he *really*? Why did I feel as though I knew him, as though we belonged to each other as the voice inside me and his own rumbling one had declared?

The office door snicked shut, but I didn't turn to see who all had left.

Master Vanni had given me space, but I could sense him behind me, could still smell his delicious musk.

I peered into golden eyes, sensing a giant crack in the earth had opened up before me. I stood on the edge of something that called to the deepest part of my heart and soul.

"Tell me the truth, Dolyn," I whispered, itching to reach out and caress his face. "What is this between us? This... longing to be close to you? The deep unrest you've roused to life inside me that seems unquenchable, something I can't even put a name to?"

Dolyn studied me in silence before his gaze softened from pure need to gentle assurance. "I am your fated mate, your alpha. I am a shape-shifter, one of two remaining full Blood Born left on this earth."

I blinked and burst into laughter. "You're *what*?"

"Dragonblood—same as you."

Yes.

Truth.

My lips flattened. I swallowed hard against my throat closing off at the voice echoing in my head. "I—I don't…"

Darkness crept in around the edges of my periphery as I suddenly struggled to breathe.

I wavered on my feet, reaching for him, my heart racing and lungs aching for oxygen.

Dolyn leaped from his chair, his strong yet gentle hold on my arms keeping me from harm. For the briefest of seconds, I gloried in complete peace.

I collapsed to the floor and knew no more.

CHAPTER 15
VANNI

Dolyn caught Ashley before I reached her fainting form.

"Goddamn you," I growled, kneeling in front of them and ripping one of his hands off her before jerking my touch from his skin.

Same as when he'd grabbed my shoulder down in the lounge, currents of some weird-as-fuck shit rippled throughout my body. Almost electrical but without the hair-raising charge. A deep longing and unrest exactly as Ashley had whispered to him seconds earlier continued to radiate throughout me as though time had somehow bound our fates together.

I'd never been into destiny and that sort of shit, but this affinity...there were no words to describe what I felt.

Skin contact with Dolyn had opened me up in ways I'd only heard about in the supposed supernatural world. Colors had become more crisp, my sense of smell heightened. I could literally taste Dolyn's radiating anger and lust on my tongue, and my slit had leaked in response.

The mess smeared inside my leathers as our gazes clashed. "What the hell is going on here, Dolyn?"

"I won't hurt her," he said, gathering her tight against his chest. At least they were both fully clothed so she might not freak out when she woke up to find him holding her like that. "She is my female." His eyes glowed golden with swirling darkness in his pupils for a split second, and I blinked to clear my focus.

Blood Born, he'd said. Dragonblood.

"The fuck is wrong with you?" I glared, unintimidated, intrigued, and horny as hell wrapped up in one gigantic ball of tensed nerves. "You're a sick fuck, and she should have told the goddamn cops the truth of how you've been stalking her." My focus jerked from each of his hands atop Ashley's coat, to his eyes, and back down again, unsure of his intent. I wanted to be ready to flatten him if he made a wrong move.

"I'll explain soon enough." He kissed her forehead, his eyelids closing briefly as he lingered, inhaling her scent.

My hands should have been fisted over how he held her without her consent. My blood should have boiled with rage over his mouth touching her skin. But the way he cradled her with tenderness, how the two of them fit seamlessly together, held me in check. I'd been thinking about both of them, getting myself off to fantasies that had included their images flipping back and forth. A few times, I imagined them both in my bed, the three of us gasping for air as we came down from powerful orgasms, our bodies covered in sweat, sticky with cum.

Where nausea from my past should have had me hugging a toilet and heaving, yearning to crowd close and join in their sharing of comfort had me reaching out.

Ashley stirred and whimpered.

"Ash?" My fingertips came into contact with hers, and as though she was a conduit of the otherworldliness emanating off Dolyn, I could sense his concern for her. His adoration for the woman he called his female was a damned love bomb of emotion crowding my chest.

But something darker, completely foreign, yet not alarming, lay deeper beneath whatever it was connecting the three of us. Almost as if…Dolyn was split in two. Bipolar didn't fit the sense I got. There were definitely opposing sides to him that I'd experienced while sceneing with him.

Was he both the hot and cold eyes Ashley had told me about?

Did something inside him wish her harm?

My hackles should have raised at the thought, but assurance he would give his life before he allowed someone to hurt *his female* settled over my mind, putting my questions of her safety to rest. I believed his protective nature extended to every part of her, same as mine did.

I lifted my gaze off Ashley's peaceful face to find Dolyn staring at me, those golden flames in his eyes again. As though his focus on me changed my vision, I saw clearer. Brightness lit in my periphery. I expected I could peer through the wall beyond Dolyn if I focused hard enough.

His gaze dipped to my mouth, and a trickle of heat slid through my fingertips from Ashley's skin, a reaching out of sorts that wound its way through me, settling in my groin.

Lust, a desperate need, flooded my dick with blood, mutual desire waxing and waning in the air between us.

My abs tensed, balls tightening.

Ashley shifted, breaking the moment.

Dolyn and I both gave her our undivided attention, and I threaded my fingers thoroughly with hers to hopefully help ground her emotions when she came fully to. He shifted her in his arms, sighing as she blinked her eyes open.

"Dolyn," she murmured, her pupils dilating and pulse beginning to thrum in her neck. She went lax against him when not so long ago, she would have been scrambling away from the near-stranger holding her.

She wanted him, and that truth made my chest ache in memory of the hard lesson I'd learned a decade earlier.

Before I could untangle my fingers from hers, Dolyn cupped her cheek, palm resting fully against her skin, linking all three of us through direct contact.

A zap shot through me, burning like fire, jagged as shards of glass.

The breath ripped from my lungs. That sense of connection I'd felt seconds earlier intensified. I could fucking *feel* Dolyn in my head as though Ashley acted as a conduit between us.

His heart beat in time with mine…a whispering echo deeper in his core humming its approval.

A sense of Ashley's peace trickled in, soothing and sweet, when she should have been freaking the fuck out like I should have been doing. Her desire for both Dolyn and me followed on its heels, assuring me I would never have to fear her abandoning my heart for his.

While my eyes welled with tears, a prickling of my skin caused my stomach to tighten.

Who was this man that he affected her and me in this way?

"Otherworldly" flitted through my brain again as his words about dragonblood echoed through my mind.

Yessss.

I ripped my hand off Ashley's, but the hissing assurance Dolyn spoke truth had come from within me not through our connection.

We were no longer touching, but whatever funky voodoo Dolyn had done while the three of us had been in physical contact with each other lingered. While less in potency, I could sense them both as if some sort of residual energy of theirs had attached itself to my cells.

"What. The. Actual. Fuck?" I spat through clenched teeth.

Dolyn peered at me, brow furrowing as though he hadn't felt the same goddamned thing.

I had to get us from this creep who fit my sadistic side like a glove and turned my cock to granite. "Ash." I grabbed hold of her hand again.

The strength of our connection snapped back into place, and Dolyn's thoughts hazily flooded my brain, taking mine along for the ride.

A vision of him settled between her thighs made my cock buck in its tight prison. I saw my cane marks on his ass as he flexed, burying himself deep inside her pussy I'd been the only one to touch in over a dozen years.

A similar darkness to Dolyn's center roused inside me when I remembered the satiny folds of her tender skin sucking in my thumb while I'd played with her clit. But I wanted to sink into her slick sheath alongside his cock, filling her at the same time, flooding her with our seed.

Another vision flooded my brain of thrusting into Dolyn's ass while he fucked her, green fire flaring around us like a vortex of passion that would bind us forever.

"No," he hissed over our shared fantasy, but I was too far gone in understanding how the three of us would fit together.

Dolyn would be the bridge between Ashley and I, the channel of our emotions, our pleasure. He would flood her womb while I emptied my balls deep in his guts, marking him as mine.

Yessss.

The echo caused my balls to draw up tight, pulling me out of the fantasy.

I squeezed my junk to keep from blowing my load, groaning through my clenched teeth at the ache in my groin.

Dolyn stared at me, pupils blown, showing his teeth and growling.

He hated how we fit perfectly together and longed to exert his dominance, but I didn't doubt what I'd seen. The darker part of him lusted for what had played in my mind. Dolyn fought an inner battle, and I wanted to devour his lips. Hold him down and fuck his ass until he submitted and begged for relief.

I eyed where he clutched her lower back, the fingers of my free hand itching to complete the circle among the three of us. This strangeness would become more empowered, I didn't doubt.

A sharing of mind, body, and spirit.

More.

Blinking hard at the strange inner voice, I tore my fingers from Ashley's, backed away, and scrambled to my feet. Where had the raspy voice as though newly awakened come from? Was I losing my goddamned mind?

"What are you feeling, Vanni?" Dolyn asked, his voice wary.

"*You,*" I spat. "Up here." I tapped at my temple.

He blinked, muttering under his breath about that not being possible.

"Trust me, it is," I hissed. "I saw that same fantasy you did, Dolyn."

A muscle ticked in his jaw. "We're destined to be together. I will claim what has been gifted to me, and *you* will learn your place regardless of what our inner beasts believe."

I opened my mouth to curse him out, but snapped it shut when Ashley sighed, burrowing in closer to his chest. She trusted this madman wholeheartedly. That truth had burrowed deep in my soul when we'd been connected.

Strangely, I knew I didn't have to fear her safety as long as he was around.

Dolyn might be crazy in the head, but I'd never met a more loyal soul. He reminded me of those dogs Ashley had told me he cared for.

Beta.

Dolyn's safeword echoed in my brain.

"I—I have to go," I sputtered, my chest constricting and blood rushing through my ears.

Ours.

"Vanni." Ashley held out her hand to me, violet eyes shining and vulnerable as though she could empathize with the tumbling emotions crowding my chest.

"I... My goddamned brain won't shut the fuck up." I shook my head, backing away even though the draw to be one with them felt like chains wrapping tight around my free will. "I'm sorry, Ash—I don't understand. Can't..."

I grabbed my cell off my desk.

Ripped my office door open.

My boots thundered down the stairs as I attempted to escape them—my desires, the racing thoughts.

"Sir?" Jenna called to me as I strode past her desk, intent on the private elevator that would take me to my suite. "Is everything all right?" she asked as I closed my eyes, cursing at the slow ding of numbers while shoving my phone into my back pocket. "The cops left, and I wasn't sure..."

"Everything will be fine." I lied through my teeth and swallowed hard. The doors slid open, and I stepped in, jamming the up button. "Come on," I muttered under my breath, body trembling, hands squeezed into tight fists.

Want.

Need.

Similar words continued to ring in my ears, ones that couldn't *possibly* be true, but I felt them resonate deep inside my soul where that shared darkness with Dolyn lingered.

There was no fucking way that man was fully human—if at all—and he owned Ashley's heart, her body, as did I.

He also threatened my self-control in a way no one ever had before. I wanted to dominate the *fuck* out of him. Crush his stubborn spirit and put him back together again as he was meant to be.

Mine.

Ashley's.

Ours.

Goddamned *fucking* voice in my head sounded as far from human as possible. But was it residual shit from Dolyn…or had he somehow implanted a beast inside me?

I needed a drink.

CHAPTER 16

DOLYN

As alpha, I should have sensed both of my mate's emotions once we came into contact all at once. Father had assured me of that truth.

The lack of Vanni and Ashley's thoughts and feelings, the missing beginnings of our bond upon touching, raised alarms in the back of my mind, causing my dragon to chuckle. Perhaps it would take more time, or maybe acceptance was needed on both of their parts before the sharing began.

But Vanni had seen the vision I had, the one put into my human brain from my other half. It'd only been a few heartbeats that I'd been aware of him. While I hadn't appreciated the false imaginings of a weak inner beast, I comforted myself in having felt my beta.

Vanni would submit and be mine.

Eventually.

I moved back onto his office chair, Ashley still curled up tight against me. We hadn't spoken a word since our mate had stormed off—fleeing from the questions that probably plagued his mind he wouldn't have answers to until I set him straight.

Regardless of his minuscule amount of Blood Born DNA, after having touched him, I now at least felt the draw, the lure of it, pulsing through his body—same as Ashley's.

Eventually, he would believe we were destined by dragonblood. He would offer himself to me. But I was no sadist and wouldn't be able to gift him the pain and pleasure he would long for as my beta. Ashley had already submitted herself to him, so how could I change their dynamic to set things right as Father had always assured me awaited?

Maybe our triad could be different.

My beast lay curled in delight, for once keeping silent over my musings of our destiny. He gloried in having our female in our arms where no one could harm her.

She trusts.

I couldn't yet feel her emotions, but I believed my instincts. Her relaxing against me rather than pulling away assured me my inner beast spoke truth.

How our relationship would play out as the days passed, I wasn't sure. But hope rested in my chest that Vanni would prove satisfying in our giving each other mutual pleasure. He might not have enough dragonblood in his veins to fulfill the requirements Father had always insisted I stand firm on, but the sex would be earth-shattering.

And with our tender female's vulnerability and the empathetic nature she seemed to possess, I wouldn't have to emotionally connect with Vanni, same as Father had refused to do with Papa due to his lesser lineage.

Elijah had looked at Jon with more emotion than he'd ever shown me, but Elijah still considered himself an alpha. Not that the human male mate of his would ever dominate a royal Blood Born. Theirs was a match I would never understand. I would focus on what Father had assured me of.

While my role model throughout my earlier years hadn't always been kind or understanding, I'd had no better examples of an alpha in my life to follow.

My inner dragon huffed a snort strong enough that my human body jostled our female.

Ashley sighed heavily, shuddering against me.

I continued to caress my fingertips over her cheek, wishing to experience more of her inner workings but glorying in the warmth that moved between us like a lazy river on a summer day. "How are you feeling, my female?" I asked, closing my eyes and nuzzling my nose into her soft hair again.

"Half-okay, half-freaked-out." She rested against me, her fingers lying lightly on my chest. Her sweet breath rose to make my mouth water with the need to taste. "I'm sitting on the lap of a man I hardly know and I'm not even the slightest bit scared. But some of the shit you've said, Dolyn...I'm concerned."

More than anything, I wished to be bonded so I might hear her thoughts. "You believe I'm insane, but I've spoken nothing but truth to you this day." I made an assumption for which she needed assurance.

"I'm sure you believe you have." She pulled back to focus on my face, causing my hand to fall from her satiny skin.

My beast mourned the loss, and I bit my tongue to keep from whimpering like someone with a weaker nature.

"Until tonight, I hadn't allowed a man to touch me in twelve years."

My brow furrowed, head cocking to the side. Not that I would complain, but how had such a beautiful woman escaped notice for a decade? Her statement suggested she'd been intimate before that time, but surely she'd experienced attraction since? "Would you explain why?"

A shuddering breath, and she climbed off my lap, leaving

me bereft. She stood before me, and my heart seized as I peered at her, trying to read through the purple-blue of her eyes and deep into her soul. I wished for the full bond between us, one I'd been promised would allow feelings to emanate with clarity and allow me to know her—communicate in the way she needed to understand without having to speak a word.

"I was raped when I was sixteen," she whispered.

Instant red hazed my eyesight, and I fought to keep my inner beast tamed as he roused in a flare of heat.

"He tied me up and beat the hell out of me, promising me I would like it. He played at being a Dom, bruising me, taking every last bit of my innocence."

I clenched my teeth to keep my roar contained but couldn't help the fire in my eyes and how my skin and bones itched to expand and shift.

She studied my flaming eyes closely but didn't back away at what must be a strange phenomenon to her. Vanni hadn't been put off by my dragon attempting to make himself known either, which gave me hope they would come to accept the truth sooner than later.

"Who was it?" I growled, ready to rip through the building and go in search of the one who'd traumatized my female.

"The pastor of the church I attended as a child." She shuddered.

"Where?" I bit the word out, fully intending to file the information in the back of my mind for further musing.

"A small town in Jonestown. We were the only independent bible church there, and it was more of a cult than an actual following of Christ."

I would peel the skin from the man's bones.

Incinerate him to ash with a blast of dragon fire.

"But I've been going to therapy for years because the thought of a man's hands on me made me sick," Ashley continued. "I've only recently found pleasure—through pain."

"Vanni," I said through clenched teeth, angry for a whole other reason. I could appreciate he was able to help her in a way I never could, but I hated she required enduring torture in order to find release.

"Yes. Master Vanni."

"He isn't your master," I spat, my insides still fire and smoke over her trauma, my claws and aching jaw desperate to tear into flesh.

"He is when I submit here in this club," Ashley said. "Outside, he is my friend. Confidant. And I care for him deeply."

I didn't need the bonding to recognize she spoke truth.

"How do you know him?" Ashley questioned.

I couldn't tell her how he and I had met. She would see me as unworthy to be her alpha, a weaker vessel than I'd been destined to attain.

Lying now would only cause mistrust later once we'd bonded as she might find out the truth.

But Ashley wasn't aware of Blood Born history, she knew nothing of our people, or the dynamic in a triad of dragonblood. And, while communication would be easy once bonded, neither Vanni or Ashley need ever hear or read an alpha never submitted to another.

My beast snickered, and I slapped his muzzle in place, firm and unyielding, my ire still burning.

"I followed you here a few weeks ago," I answered, my voice surprisingly calm. "Vanni and I...met and spoke briefly."

Ashley continued to study my face without a hint of fear. "Why didn't I see you?"

My female had already been through a lot tonight, but

one more upheaval of her reality might be exactly what she needed. Honesty—evidence of my non-human blood—would sway her toward accepting the truth.

I shimmered out of sight, and she gasped, stumbling backward. Leaping forward, I revealed myself, grasping her forearm to keep her from falling over.

She blinked at me, pulse throbbing in her neck, swallowing hard. "I'm dreaming." She pinched her hand and laughed, near hysterical. "I'm losing my damned mind is what I'm doing."

"Ashley." I cupped her cheek, hoping to calm her.

"Do it again."

I obeyed without thought, and her gaze went hazy once I shimmered back before her eyes. "Listen to the inner creature whispering my honesty," I begged what I hoped to be true—that her beast had woken from my touch, same as Vanni's had.

"Dragonblood—you're a shifter, and I'm your mate." She woodenly echoed what I'd declared.

I nodded.

"So you're saying that…I'm a shifter too?"

A grimace twitched my mouth. "You're more human than dragon, and I doubt you will ever have the ability to morph into your beast form."

She gently took hold of my wrist and pulled my hand from her face. "I—I'm going to need some time to process all of this, Dolyn."

"I understand." I stepped back, allowing her space even though every part of me wished to pull her back into my arms and hold her close.

"You…you wouldn't ever harm me, would you?"

"Never," I swore.

"Then those other eyes weren't you, were they?"

The second gaze she'd felt—I'd forgotten she'd spoken of it to Vanni.

My inner beast growled, and I silently assured him nothing and no one would ever hurt our female again. "I will watch over you day and night, Ashley. You needn't fear anything or anyone as long as I'm near."

"And what about Vanni?"

A shot of lust punched through my gut. "What about him?"

"He's a part of this." She didn't ask a question, but I nodded. "The three of us are meant to be together. I can sense the connection deep in my bones."

"We are."

"But what if he never accepts us?" Her voice wobbled, and she clutched her hands in front of her.

"Why wouldn't he?"

"He...well, something in his past wounded him deeply, and while it's not my story to tell, I'm afraid it would keep him from wanting this."

I expected a lot more than our pasts would cause speed bumps along our road toward bonding, but the reward would be worth the effort we put in.

"Give me space for my emotions to settle while I process all of this, okay?"

I nodded rather than argue like my dragon side begged and whimpered for me to do.

"I'll talk to Vanni."

A bite on my tongue kept me silent. I'd rather have tied him up and beat the truth into him—if only I truly had the desire to do such a thing.

My goddamned masochist beast snickered, but his amusement faded to quiet longing when the door to Vanni's office closed behind our female.

I gave her ample time to descend the stairs before cloaking myself and following at a far enough distance she wouldn't feel me as intensely as before. But the hint of my presence would assure her of safety until she was ready to accept what we'd been destined to become.

CHAPTER 17
ASHLEY

Dolyn seemed farther away than usual, and I appreciated his agreeing to my needing space yet still watching over me.

While my dreamer side sighed in bliss over the rubbish I'd been told tonight, the part of me who needed to stay grounded in reality frowned.

I longed to believe Dolyn. Hell, his magic trick of blinking out of existence for a few seconds pushed me to give in. I wanted to accept the fact I'd met the one destined for me, who would heal all my wounds and make me whole again. Why I'd spewed the shit of my past to him, I didn't know. Like a mental tether connected us, I hadn't been able to stop from spilling my guts.

Crawling into bed didn't allow me to escape the thoughts in my mind, so I focused on an event that flooded me with warmth.

Vanni had touched me.

A much more enjoyable moment to think on rather than confusing explanations.

I relived my time on the bench, the pain of his hand, and the soothing caress of his palm. The fingers he'd teased through my soaked folds. The one he had pushed into my body, bringing me to my first climax without pain since I'd been a teenager and had realized what happened when the clit was given attention while aroused.

I had found release through Master Vanni's gentle touch alone. No pain. I'd already been turned on prior to arriving at the lounge, and the scent and closeness of my master had intensified what Dolyn's presence had roused to life once I'd left work.

The feelings were the same type of tension, sexually charged, that had landed me in my abuser's hold all those years ago. The urge, the driving need to get off, had cuffed me to a lumpy mattress I could still feel beneath my backside when the dark memories built in my head. The lashes of his belt, the buckle still attached…

I shivered, all trace of desire ripped from me. The scars he'd left on my body had faded, but those inside me remained regardless of the gains I had made toward healing.

Tears pricked my eyelids, and I rolled, stuffing my face in my pillow, but memories and fears continued to haunt me, refusing me rest.

Morning found me bleary-eyed and exhausted. I couldn't rouse myself from bed but stared at my ceiling, cursing the sun filtering through my blinds.

Who could I go to for answers?

Vanni had seemed horrified by what would sound like bullshit to any other rational thinking human. Doctor Hasslet might finally start to question my sanity when he hadn't earlier in the week. Dolyn would only spew more of his nonsense—

Truth.

I swallowed hard, eyes clenching shut at the whispered

suggestion coming from deep inside me. It was almost like I'd finally located my soul, and that part of me was a separate being.

Dragon shifter, Dolyn had claimed.

He'd also told me other things I hadn't thought to check into.

I grabbed my cell off my bed stand.

It wasn't yet nine in the morning, but I doubted my boss would mind me calling. It'd been weeks since he'd been in the office, and although I had communicated with him via email while he worked remotely from his home in the White Mountains, I'd never before brought my personal life up to my employer.

"Ashley?" Elijah answered, his deep voice easing some of the tightness in my chest.

I sank back into my pillow. "I'm sorry for using your private number."

"You don't have to apologize when I offered you the ability to contact me whenever you had need."

Closing my eyes, I breathed out slowly. "Who is Dolyn Kemmerly, and how do you know him?"

The sound of a door closing reached over the line. "Are you all right, Ashley?" he asked rather than answering me.

"I'm…yes. Physically, at least." I huffed a small laugh that had nothing to do with amusement. "Mentally, not so much?"

"Talk to me—tell me what is bothering you."

Exactly as a caring older brother would do, Elijah listened without interruption as I explained what I had felt, seen, and heard since he'd last been in the office. I tried to verbalize the sense of being watched. Followed. I shared about seeing Dolyn for the first time outside the cafe. How talking to him and being in close proximity assured me of a connection between us, yet the feeling of something being off that made me question his intentions.

I even opened up about my past so Elijah might understand why I spent time with a dominant. I withheld speaking of the sexual intimacy I experienced, but I did admit to feeling desire for Dolyn and my master both. At my telling Elijah about how Dolyn had punched Master Vanni the night before, he chuckled.

"I hope your alpha makes him pay," Elijah murmured, still laughing lightly.

"Alpha—he threw out that word along with beta." Seated against my headboard, I wrapped my free arm around my drawn-up knees.

"Of course he would." Elijah sighed heavily. "Are you questioning Dolyn's intentions toward you or his explanation of his existence?"

"Both," I whispered, for some reason, my throat growing tight and eyes stinging.

"Dolyn has never listened to his instinctive side, which a royal Blood Born is supposed to be in complete harmony with. For him, there is a constant push and pull that exhausts his human half. He has no trust in who he is."

"Which is?" I pushed even though I already suspected Elijah would assure me Dolyn hadn't lied.

"We are not fully human."

"We—you're a dragon shifter too?" I asked even though I'd already come to the conclusion myself.

"I am." Elijah spoke with finality, the same strong tone and assurance of authority that I had heard in countless boardrooms. Grown men tended to quake in my boss's presence when he took on that air, but I'd never once felt threatened by him.

I rubbed a hand over my neck while trying to swallow. "This isn't all a dream?" I rasped. "Some fantasy I cooked up in my head to give me healing and a happily ever after of my own?"

"What you're experiencing is *reality*," Elijah stated. "You saw the power within his eyes, but I promise that Dolyn will *never* hurt you, no matter what form he takes. He could reveal his golden beast—which is quite lovely, I must say—and be full of rage but not lift a razor-sharp claw your way."

I blew out a slow exhale, wiping the back of my hand over my eyes and stretching out my legs beneath my warm blankets. "This is real."

"Indeed it is."

"Shit!" I straightened. "I just…the *armor* you manufacture! It's made out of dragon scales, isn't it?"

Elijah chuckled.

"Oh my God!" I huffed a real laugh. "Who else knows? Does the government? You have countless contracts around the globe—holy *shit*, Elijah!"

"No one is aware of the truth, and I would ask that you do not speak of it. As a human with dragonblood running in your veins, you must protect yourself."

Racism among humans was bad enough. I couldn't imagine bringing sentient creatures into the toxic mix.

"Damnitalltohell." A shudder rippled through me, raising the hairs on my arms as possible futures flitted through my mind. Shackles and bars. Solitary cells. Hundreds of tests, probing and unpleasant. "I won't tell a soul," I whispered, wiping a damp palm over my top sheet.

"It would be for the best. Now, let's discuss moving forward in your relationship with Dolyn."

"We're not exactly *in* one."

"But you're his fated mate."

I tipped my head back and closed my eyes. "That's what he said."

"He speaks truth, Ashley." Elijah's warm voice wrapped around me like a brother's arms probably felt like. "But there is no rush, regardless of how he pursues you or pushes your boundaries. Hold firm in your own desires but listen. Learn. Share your truth and ask for his. I assure you, once the bonding occurs, honesty will be easy."

"Bonding," I repeated, my brain taking off down the route of paranormal romance. "Does that, um…including biting? Sexual rituals?" My voice was more a squeak than tone.

Elijah chuckled. "That topic, I believe, should be discussed between the three of you."

"Three?"

A slight hesitation on Elijah's end caused my heart rate to pick up.

"It takes three dragonblood to create life. Alpha, beta, and female," he explained.

My eyelids popped open as a rush of adrenaline heightened my pulse. "Vanni."

"I've never met the man, but considering the interactions between him and you, along with Dolyn's…*not* so pleasant reaction to the man, yes, I believe you may have guessed right."

Pulsing twinges between my thighs made me swallow hard. "Okay. Good. Yes, I mean, that sounds perfect. I think?"

More deep, rumbling laughter filled my ear. "Be patient with Dolyn as he comes to terms with his destiny, Ashley. He is stubborn. Blinded from the truth because of his past, I expect. Perhaps he'll share with you those parts of himself he mostly kept hidden from me. Doing so prior to bonding would doubtless create a far superior future than a mating based on instinct and lust alone."

Elijah went on to explain how he'd met Dolyn decades ago, how they believed themselves to be the last two Blood Born alive and shared a relationship while attempting to find a female to bond with. He told me about his fated mates he'd met in the mountains near his home, the married couple who completed him in every way. His mate, Dakota, had an ancient gift that had allowed Dolyn the opportunity to see the female fate intended for him. Elijah had found his happily ever after and again encouraged me to trust my instincts in moving forward with Vanni and Dolyn.

His advice lay heavy on my heart and mind throughout the morning. I crunched on some toast while sitting at my kitchen table writing out my shopping list since life went on regardless of my heavy eyelids and bleary sight. My cell dinged, and I set aside my pen, taking another bite of my breakfast when I just wanted to go back to bed and forget the world for a few hours.

Vanni: **Please tell me you're okay, that I didn't make a mistake in leaving you alone with that otherworldly madman last night.**

I snickered over his description. Until speaking with Elijah, I'd thought the same. This morning, however, I found myself believing the unbelievable.

Me: **I'm fine. We discussed some things, he saw me safely home, and I went to bed.**

While waiting for Vanni's reply, I considered calling him and telling him everything Elijah had shared with me, but if my boss and I were both wrong in our thinking—if Vanni wasn't dragonblood or my and Dolyn's fated third...

I shook my head and swallowed down my breakfast with lukewarm coffee.

If our assumptions were correct, the truth needed to come to light in ways that wouldn't put my or Dolyn's life at risk. Fate had brought Dolyn and I together, I truly believed, and I had to trust the cosmos to finish what she'd started.

Vanni: **When can I see you?**

Now, yesterday, forever, I wished to reply, but didn't. I wanted to speak with Dolyn first, learn everything I could before asking him about our...beta? Alpha?

Master Vanni was a dominant through and through, and

even though Dolyn radiated similar confidence, I wondered over his understanding of the dynamic in a D/s relationship. Perhaps he knew nothing about the BDSM community and wasn't aware the submissive held all of the power.

Me: **I'm going to meet with Dolyn next week and talk this through first.**

Vanni: **You believe his horseshit?**

Without having the knowledge I'd gained from Elijah, Vanni probably wouldn't believe the best of me if I said I was convinced Dolyn hadn't lied. Hopefully, the truth would reveal itself, and Vanni would be my other...*mate*, and the three of us could be together.

Yessss.

Warmth flooded between my thighs, and I sighed while shifting in my chair.

Me: **I'm willing to listen to him with an open mind.**

There. That wasn't even a partial lie.

Vanni: **Call me if you need me. I care about you, Ashley. If anything happened to you, I would be devastated. Please be careful.**

That heat in my core turned into butterflies rushing toward my chest.

Me: **I care about you too, Vanni. More than you know.**

Vanni didn't respond, and I hoped I hadn't said too much.

I went grocery shopping a few hours later, thankful to feel Dolyn's presence even though he stayed at a distance rather than sitting in the back of my car as I was sure he'd done the week before. No trace of cold eyes chilled my blood, and I breathed freely with a slight pep in my step.

Possibilities made my heart race.

Hope flooded my mind.

Sunday, I stayed indoors regardless of the warmer weather and sunshine, losing myself in a dragon shifter book, an intentional choosing on my part from a new-to-me author.

The polyamorous tale between three men and one woman leaned more toward straight-up erotica rather than romance, but by the time I finished late into the early morning hours, I was hot, horny, and feeling emboldened by the events of Friday night beneath Master Vanni's hands.

I lay in bed, flushed and needy between my thighs, my pussy empty and weeping with desire to be filled. Stuffed full. Maybe *double* stuffed like the female main character. Trailing fingertips through my folds didn't lessen my arousal like it used to. Thinking of both Vanni and Dolyn pleasuring me with their mouths and hands made me skirt the edge of climaxing. Remembering the release Vanni had gifted me while bent over his bench, I gently eased a finger into my soaked pussy.

"Oh." I gulped and bucked, pushing deeper into my core. "Oh *God.*" A gasp flew past my lips, and I writhed against my hand, desperate for more. Two fingers eased the ache but didn't offer me what I chased.

I slid my other hand down my belly to my pubis I kept bare. My clit lay hot and swollen, protruding from my labia.

"Yes," I hissed while gently rubbing over the nub, slowly fucking myself with my fingers. "God, yes. So good." I licked dryness from my lips, whimpering over the exquisite tingles racing over my skin and leaving goose bumps in their wake.

I was going to come—

A shriek fled my lungs as my core pulsed, needing a solid shaft to flood me full of seed.

Yessss.

I cried out again, bucking and chasing every last clench of my core, the rush of adrenaline and satiated bliss.

Master.

Dolyn.

Both of their images hovered in my conscience, the scent of their musk heavy in my nose regardless of their absence.

My body sagged onto my bed, both hands easing from between my thighs.

I'd masturbated successfully for the first time since my teenage years, and while I expected having two hot men to focus on while toying with my body helped, I was starting to believe that complete healing would soon be found.

But one step at a time.

During my lunch break on Monday, I texted Dolyn, asking him if we could meet.

He suggested a restaurant on the first floor of the building across from Vanni's. Temptation to include my master had me toying with my cell, but I'd been truthful with Vanni. I needed to settle things with Dolyn before moving forward toward a possible triad.

My insides jittered throughout the rest of the day, but upon feeling Dolyn's warm gaze on me once I exited Tolzman Industries, I settled inside. Exactly as I'd done upon leaving my house that morning intent on making it into work on time. His proximity, while arousing, was the thickest blanket on a cold day. Comfort I'd come to trust in the deepest parts of my soul—separate being or not, we were in agreement Dolyn belonged to us.

I wasn't sure when my thought patterns about there being two parts to me had changed, but it felt right to converse in my head, the occasional whispers of agreement or single-worded answers bringing peace rather than fear.

Clinging to my newfound inner friend I wasn't ready to tell my therapist about, I headed north on foot, my coat unbuttoned, the warmer air a pleasant gift after the chill of a long winter.

Spring still lay weeks ahead, but the teaser from Mother Nature was deeply appreciated.

I filled my lungs with exhaust and the scent of rubbish, unable to stop smiling as Dolyn's presence drew close enough behind me to cause my pulse to race.

A hand slid into mine, the skin contact racing delicious shivers over my skin.

I squeezed, glancing up to find golden eyes full of warmth drinking in the sight of me. "Hi," I whispered.

"Hello, my beautiful female." Dolyn's husky yet rumbling voice raised goose bumps over my arms, and I bit my lip to keep the flutters in my belly from bubbling up as giggles.

Our bodies bumped as we walked the remaining few yards to the restaurant.

Dolyn released his hold on me to pull open the door, and although I missed his touch, I appreciated the fact chivalry was indeed not dead.

"Table for Kemmerly?" Dolyn told the hostess who stared at him like he was a piece of chocolate cake and she'd been dieting for six months.

Mine.

I hissed beneath my breath, and she glanced over my peacoat, plain black slacks, and worn boots, her nose wrinkling.

"This way." Chin high, she moved like a model on a catwalk, every step accentuating her lush curves I wished filled out my slender form.

Dolyn gathered me against him, tucking me against his side.

Appreciation over his possessiveness filled me, far more than any physical desire. I felt seen, heard, and accepted as-is. Wart on my pinkie finger and all.

Once seated, we stared at each other from across the table in the back corner of the restaurant. Quiet instrumental music played, and the dim lights set a scene for romance and intimacy.

"Thank you for watching over me this weekend."

"Thank you for allowing me the pleasure."

I smiled, my face hot.

Dolyn's gaze dipped to my mouth but lifted as a waiter approached.

I drank in Dolyn's profile as he spoke in perfect…French. My insides swooned. Sweat dampened my palms, and I leaned the slightest bit closer to him, breathing in the scent of campfire and cedar.

Our gazes met and held as the waiter moved off. Dolyn reached over the table, palm facing up.

I slid my fingertips over his, my heart thundering in my chest as tingles raced clear up my arm, spreading through every limb in my body before settling between my thighs.

His gaze darkened as though aware of what his touch did to me.

Breathing deeply, I filled my lungs, held it there for a brief moment, and slowly leaked it past my lips. "I spoke with Elijah."

Dolyn didn't flinch.

I threaded our hands together, and he gently squeezed. "I believe you," I murmured.

Tension I hadn't realized had kept him rigid eased from his body, slumping his shoulders. Wetness coated his golden eyes, but his smile was glorious, brighter than any sunshine shooting rays through the clouds.

This gorgeous man—*not* man—belonged to me, and what a glorious future we would enjoy at each other's sides.

Tears stung my eyes, and I gave him a watery smile of my own.

"He convinced you." Dolyn's ragged voice hadn't sounded a question, but I shook my head.

"His explanations helped settle my mind, but my heart already knew the truth of who you are to me."

Dolyn lifted my hand and brushed his soft lips over my knuckles. "And who might that be?"

"Mine." My insides purred like a happy kitten. "But there is so much to learn, Dolyn—"

The waiter appeared with a bottle of wine, and Dolyn and I sat back, hands in our laps as the middle-aged man made a show of opening and allowing Dolyn to taste the offering before trickling a small amount in each of our glasses.

Once he was gone, Dolyn lifted his wine, and I did the same. "To new beginnings."

We clinked at his toast, and I sipped, the red wine dry and heady. No way in hell I would be drinking more than a single glass of whatever this stuff was. "Tell me your greatest fault," I demanded.

Dolyn blinked, then stared.

"What?" I smiled, leaning forward and wishing there wasn't a table between us. "Haven't you ever played fifty questions to get to know someone better?"

A haze slid over his eyes briefly, and he shook his head, focusing clearly on me. "Never with someone as lovely as you."

Flushing, I coated my tongue with the rich wine.

"I am stubborn beyond what is healthy. Selfish and needy to a fault." His blunt honesty surprised me, but the descriptors did not.

"I appreciate your determination and how much you crave my attention," I said as he swirled the small bit of liquid in his glass.

"You have no idea." His stare turned molten enough my panties almost burst into flame.

I shifted on my chair, and he chuckled, setting his wine aside.

"Tell me yours," he murmured, once more reaching for my hand.

I gladly gave him ownership of all five fingers, shivering over how he caressed my skin with his thumb. "My greatest fault has been believing that trusting people ends in hurt."

"A fear that your past dictated to be truth."

"Yes," I whispered, my focus falling to where he continued to caress over the skin he'd kissed. "But I'm learning suspicion shouldn't be held against everyone."

"Thank you for gifting me the opportunity to earn your trust, Ashley."

I nodded and lifted my attention to his face.

"You don't owe me any explanations about your past as we move forward," Dolyn said, his voice gentle as his touch, "but I would ask, should I push your boundaries or do something that is triggering, you'll be honest with me. I have no wish to hurt you. Ever."

"I know you don't." I squeezed his fingers.

"I—I am not enough for you." Dolyn swallowed hard, his forehead furrowing, amber eyes troubled. "As a dragonblood's fated mate, you will yearn for another, a beta who I hope can gift you what I am unable to."

"And what is that?" I asked, my own heart aching over the clear insecurity in his gaze.

"The pain you crave."

An image of my master flitted through my mind, longer hair damp with sweat as he watched me come undone on his fingers.

Yessss.

A shiver pebbled my skin. "So what happens now?" I asked, my tone unsteady.

"That all depends on him." Dolyn glanced away, and I followed his gaze toward the bar.

Master Vanni sat with his back toward us, shoulders slumped, an empty tumbler in his hand.

Mine.

A deep seated knowing radiated through every cell in my body.

"Yes," I agreed, my tone near silent.

CHAPTER 18
VANNI

'd done pretty much nothing but drink since leaving Ashley with Dolyn in my office Friday night. Turned out, whiskey slurred the voice deep inside me enough I could ignore it. Him. Whatever the damned creature was inside me. My sloshed brain couldn't find a fuck to give over pronouns or trying to identify if I'd picked up some sort of parasite or spirit.

But the sole fault belonged to Dolyn.

I dreamed of beating him senseless then fucking him until both of us dropped from exhaustion. I'd woken so damn hard Saturday morning I shot off at a mere brush of my fingertips over the soaked crown of my dick. Throughout the day, unrelenting need haunted me. No matter how drunk I got or how many times I jerked off, the semen came like a wave, a well that refused to dry.

Satisfaction, however, eluded me with every jetted spurt up over my hand and abs.

I wanted Ashley. Longed to be with her, beside her, breathing her in. Her quiet gentleness would soothe the demon in me, but she'd rested in Dolyn's arms. Hadn't made an effort to crawl from his lap for mine.

She'd chosen him over me, exactly as my ex had done.

Was tender loving care her thing now? Had the pain I'd gifted no longer hit the mark?

But I'd brought her to climax with my fingers. Hadn't hurt her then, right?

"Last one. You've been sitting here since noon. I'm cutting you off."

I blinked rapidly to focus on the bartender as he poured another shot into the glass I clutched. "Thanks," I slurred.

Once he ambled off, I attempted to stare at my waving reflection in the mirror beyond the bottles lining the bar in front of me. My suit was a rumpled mess, tie loosened and askew… Had I worked today?

Was it Monday?

Where had Sunday gone?

I looked like an absolute mess, but at least I couldn't feel shit.

Tipping back my last shot of whiskey didn't burn my throat as it ought to, and I grinned at myself. My head swam in empty vastness. Zero tension clenched my guts and hitched my shoulders. Even my dick lay soft inside my slacks.

Perfectly numb, I chuckled to myself. My liver was going to hate me, but I didn't care. At least silence finally settled in my head. All that vivid color shit making me see through walls had dissolved.

Blessed whiskey had deadened my senses—

A hint of vanilla and cedar wafted past my nose.

"Fuck." Eyes clenched shut, I cursed a few more times as my dick swelled. "The fuck is wrong with you?" I muttered at my lap and its obscene bulge. How long until I started leaking?

I needed to get laid, thrust my dick deep into the first willing, wet pussy I could find. An angry sea rolled inside me at the thought of anyone but Ashley—and Dolyn.

My memory teased me again with their combined scents, and I attempted to rub a hand over my nose to rid me of the hunger rousing inside me I wanted *gone*.

A shiver slid down my spine as awareness awakened in my liquor-muddled head.

Goddamnit—

A hard, heavy hand grasped my shoulder and squeezed, and I groaned at the scent of pre-cum flooding my nose.

His.

Hers.

Mine.

Growling, I turned to find Dolyn crowding my stool. Golden eyes full of lust caught and held my attention—or whatever brain cells weren't drowning in alcohol. "The fuck you want?" I made a fumbling grab at the bulge between his thighs. "This?" I grinned as his jaw clenched.

His pissiness rolled over me, but I could barely feel it.

"Not here, not now." Low and rumbling, his voice licked over my skin, causing a pulse of premature ejaculate to soak my boxer briefs.

"The fuck?" I muttered, glancing down to see if the wetness seeped through my pants.

"Come on." Dolyn slid an arm beneath my shoulder, pulling me off the stool. Like a mountain, a steel beam, he handled my weight as I struggled to find my feet.

Ashley's gasp had my head attempting to twist, my eyelids blinking to make out where she was.

My other side. My other half. Third?

Whatever.

Gorgeous violet eyes studied my face like I was a book loaded with text. Did she like my story? Could she sense my emotions like I had theirs on Friday night? Dark hair spilled over her shoulders and caressed the swell of her pert tits and tight nipples.

Drool flooded my mouth, and I snickered, struggling to find my feet so I didn't lean so hard against Dolyn even though he felt delicious as fuck all up in my space.

Pink flushed Ashley's face, and my nostrils flared as I sucked the scent of her arousal deep into my lungs. "You're so goddamned luscious, beautiful," I declared, probably too fucking loud, but I didn't give a shit. "Can smell how much you want me. Him. Both of us." I imagined, or tried to, rather, the three of us locked together, dick in ass and dick in pussy. "Hmm. Yeah, a fuck train would work, wouldn't it?" A chuckle burst from me at the memory of how badly Dolyn had fought against the desire while sharing his fantasy with me on Friday night.

Otherworldly bull-fucking-shit.

Dolyn steered me away from Ashley, and I stumbled, grasping his arm holding me upright. Hard and unbreakable...

I snickered, knowing I could break him—I could break anyone.

"Where we going?" I glanced over my shoulder to make sure Ashley followed us out of the restaurant, my head lolling rather than moving as it ought to.

"My place."

Fuck me, he smelled divine. I ran my nose along the warmth of his neck, groaning from another ooze of spunk in my pants. "Mmm. Gonna let me fuck your ass, boy?" I murmured against his ear. "I'm leaking so goddamned much I won't need lube to push into your tight hole."

"Shut the fuck up, Vanni," Dolyn growled, hailing a cab. Or was he waving at the people across the busy street?

I lifted a hand at them too, grinning.

Blinking, I found myself squished between Dolyn and Ashley on the backseat of... I looked around, my vision swimming. Not a limo, that was for goddamned sure. Rancid onions overpowered the sweetness and brimstone of my mates.

Mates.

I barked a laugh even though the word made me think of Dolyn on all fours like a dog while I made him mine.

"Gonna fuck you, Dolyn," I said, tipping my head back against the car seat as my eyelids slammed shut. "And you're gonna like it—and beg for more."

Ashley panted beside me, her arousal making my mouth water.

Or was the whiskey I'd downed all afternoon ready to erupt from my esophagus?

Dolyn simmered like a rage-filled tension rod on my other side. Fuck, did I want to break him.

Our female would watch and get off. Then we would love on her. Penetrate her together. Fill her. Flood her womb with our seed.

I groaned, grabbing hold of my leaking cock. "I'm soaked, and it's all your fault. Fuck."

Someone cleared their throat.

Swirling thoughts and feelings wove together in my head, and I couldn't tell which were mine, if any of them. The memory of satiny, slick flesh, slick slid through my brain.

"Ashley?" I groaned, squeezing my junk.

"What?"

"You let me touch you when we scened."

"Yes," she whispered, and heat swelled inside my chest.

"I made you come so hard." My words slurred, and I blinked into focus the hand I lifted. "Sucked your cream off my thumb." I wiggled the digit. "You're so sweet, Ash."

"We can talk once you're sober, Vanni." Her attempt to sound bossy made my cock buck.

"Mmm." I stroked myself lazily as we rolled, rolled, rolled along the road.

Dolyn grabbed my wrist. "Calm the fuck down," he growled close to my ear. "We are not alone."

"Don't give a shit. Got an exhibition kink." I grabbed my balls with my other hand and squeezed. "Touch me, Ash. Touch your master."

"Vanni!"

I grinned at her hissed admonishment. "She has a backbone, Dolyn." I tried to peel my eyelids open to look at her but only managed to flop my head to the side. "What a perfect angel you are. So soft. I've been craving to drink your sweet cum straight from between your thighs."

Someone coughed, and the motion beneath me stopped.

I blinked but couldn't make out shit through the watery colors in front of my face.

My feet swayed.

We took another ride.

Up, up, up.

"Weeeee!" I called out like a kid and laughed even though my stomach churned.

A grumble sounded on my right, a sigh on my left.

My stomach fucking flipped.

"Gonna be sick." I tried to warn them—I think?

Fire raced up my throat, and I coughed and spat, cursing the day I was born, groaning over how my knees ached where I knelt on tile.

The scent of lemons and bleach burned my nose.

I wiggled my feet in my socks beneath my backside.

Had I lost my shoes?

Rubbing my forearm across my lips made me aware I no longer wore a shirt.

"Are you okay?" Ashley's soft voice sounded behind me.

I blinked my eyes somewhat clear.

A bathroom surrounded me. White porcelain in front of me. Sink to the right.

The toilet flushed.

"Here." A warm, wet cloth rubbed over my mouth. Fingers combed through my hair, causing my eyes to slide shut.

Comfort flooded through me at her gentle touch, and I sighed, leaning into her. I sensed her disappointment, but couldn't tell if it was because of what I'd done or that I couldn't fuck in my current state. At least, I didn't think I could?

"I drank too much," I muttered.

"Understatement," Dolyn snipped from somewhere, his annoyance itching my fingers to grasp his neck and push him to his knees before me.

I chuckled, but Ashley's fingertips slid down my whiskered cheek. Warmth flooded my chest. "I can feel you in here." I tapped my sternum then temple, my skin still numb. "Fucking love it. Soft and gentle. Arousing as fuck."

Dolyn yanked me upright, but my legs noodled beneath me. The heat of his hand on my bare arm burned like fire and caused my dick to flex in my pants. "Let's get you in my bed."

"Mmm," I hummed my agreement, leaning against his hard body, wanting to stretch like a languid cat in the need rolling off him. "I turn you on."

"Shut the fuck up."

"Don't tell me what to do, boy." I grabbed his bulge and squeezed.

A strangled groan sounded against my ear. "Get your fucking hands off me."

"Nope." My grin widened, and he tossed me like I didn't

weight over two hundred pounds. Softness met my backside, and I fought to bring the beast towering over me into focus while sinking down, down, down. "You're a fucking animal," I mumbled.

"You have *no* idea." His growl barely registered.

Darkness closed in on me before I could order Ashley or Dolyn to suck me off.

CHAPTER 19

DOLYN

Drunk Vanni was almost amusing.

My dragon chuckled along with him, gleefully enjoying his mutterings and complete lack of control over the words spilling from his lips.

Mind a jumbled mess of desire and stubbornness, I stared at my beta as he faded into oblivion.

Vanni's jaw lay lax, and my ass cheeks clenched at the thought of beard burn on my skin. His thick, black hair grayed at the temples and spread over the pillow in a rumpled, sexy mess. Long black lashes rested, hiding the most arresting green eyes I'd see in my four hundred plus years.

My gaze slipped over his neck to the smooth, olive skin of his arms, chest, and abs. The man was ripped. All cut muscle and a trim waist with its dark trail of hair disappearing beneath his slacks.

Kneel.

Worship.

There was no denying the draw. But could an alpha do those things and still hold his status?

I considered a true submissive's lifestyle subservient, complete obedience. Such expectations could not be placed upon a royal Blood Born. Father had told me we bowed to no man.

Lifting my chin, I considered the frailty of the body before me. Vanni's instincts were shut down, and had I desired, I could break his bones with a snap of my fingers. I could burn him to ash with a mere wisp of dragon fire from my lips.

The man wasn't *worthy* of my worship, nor did he deserve for me to bend a knee.

"Do you think he'll be okay?" Ashley threaded her fingers through mine, and immediate calm snaked through my cells, easing my frown and heavy thoughts.

"He vomited until his stomach emptied. I'm sure he'll be fine except for a ripping headache when he wakes." I sank onto the bed's edge, unable to leave Vanni. Pushing aside my thoughts on how I wanted him, I tugged my female toward me.

She settled onto my lap, snuggled against my chest, and released a sigh, her sweet breath and slight scent of arousal making my mouth water.

My cock thickened beneath her backside, blood heating.

I expected my inner beast to demand we claim what was ours, but he lay quiet, his purr a soft rumble in my head.

Eyes closed, I rested my lips against Ashley's forehead, breathing in the scent of vanilla and the underlying musk of her body's desire for me.

Pre-cum smeared inside my slacks, and I groaned, shifting my female away from my aching length.

"I'm not afraid of intimacy." She tilted her head back to meet my gaze. "I want this—you. Vanni. Yes, I'm nervous that ugliness from my past might try to erase my ability to enjoy sex or reach climax with you."

I cursed quietly along with my dragon half at the thought of her wet heat clenching around my shaft.

"But I'm going to try if you'll have me."

"You already own every part of me, Ashley." I cupped her cheek, drinking in the sight of her swelled pupils, the flushed skin beneath my touch. "I will give you the world. Make myself available to you in every way you need to find contentment and happiness."

"Will you kiss me?"

I stared at her parted lips. She had told me that no one had touched them since her abuser. Embers of need flared in my gut, a driving force demanding I consume. Devour. Fill and flood with my seed. Wetness slid from my slit, and I hissed.

The pulse jumped in Ashley's neck as though she felt what I did, the same energy, the magnetic pull to come together and cement our souls for all time.

I thumbed over her mouth, tugging down slightly, revealing the pink inner skin beneath her front teeth. "Hold still for me."

Ashley whimpered as I lowered my head.

A gentle lick over the softness inside her lower lip burst sweetness along my tongue, and I groaned, tightening my hold on her back.

With a soft sigh, Ashley clutched at my hair, and our mouths sealed. She was ambrosia, divine sustenance. Cool water on a hot day, and I thirsted, the fire inside me needing to be doused.

More.

Vanni shifted in his sleep, his knee pressing against my hip. Even through the fabrics separating us, heat and a ripple of awareness slid to my groin.

I groaned into Ashley's mouth, licking, suckling, and nipping.

My cock throbbed on the verge of release from a mere sip of my female's sweetness.

Need to bury deep.

Release against her womb.

We did.

Desperately.

I allowed my beast to rise closer to the surface so he might enjoy our female too.

The scent of Ashley's arousal intensified, flooding my senses, and I tore my mouth off hers, trailing my tongue and lips along her jaw and down her throat.

She tilted her head, granting me access, and I grazed my teeth over her soft skin.

No.

Swallowing hard, I refrained from biting as my human side lusted for. "I need to taste you as he did."

Ashley shuddered. "Yes."

I stood and turned, laying her beside our passed-out beta. The loss of his heat against my leg made my inner beast whimper, but the one awaiting pleasure peered up at me with bright violet eyes, needy and ready for my attention.

I ran my hands down her clothed body, atop her pert breasts, along her tucked waist, and over the swell of her hips. While tiny, I didn't doubt she would be able to carry our young.

My cock bucked inside my pants, and I pressed hard against my bulge.

Ashley watched, her tongue flitting over her lower lip.

Yessss.

"You wish to put your mouth on me too?"

She nodded, panting and rubbing her legs together as though seeking relief.

I released my shaft from its prison, hissing as I gripped the base tight.

"Dolyn," Ashley whispered, fisting the comforter.

"I will take care of you, my female. Promise." I thumbed over my slit, gathering the wetness, ignoring the fact I didn't leak nearly as much as I ought to. "Taste," I murmured, smearing the slickness over her lower lip, choosing to focus on Ashley rather than my shortcomings.

Her tongue flicked out, and she moaned, suckling on my thumb.

A rush of desire rolled over me, and I groaned, leaning over to taste myself on her tongue. Salt and sweet mingled together.

"Dolyn, please," she mumbled around my kiss.

I nipped her lower lip, held her gaze, and slid my hand down her front. Her buttonless slacks from work had an elastic waist, easy to slip my fingers beneath.

She gasped as I feathered over the satiny material covering her core. Heat and wetness met my touch, and I swallowed hard, her panted breaths rushing over my lips inches from hers.

"Can I take them off?" I asked, my tone low and ragged.

Rather than answer, she lifted her hips and shoved her pants and panties to her ankles.

The scent of her musk swelled in the air, and a shudder rippled through me. I stood, running my hands over her legs, my eyes feasting on her pale skin and the delicate flesh awaiting my tongue. My inner beast growled and moaned, panting and salivating.

Taste.

Breed.

I shimmied Ashley's pants and panties completely off her legs, and she lifted her feet to the bed's edge.

Vanni grumbled in his sleep, but I couldn't tear my focus off our female and how she bared herself to me.

"So beautiful," I murmured, sliding a single finger over her damp, pink petals.

Ashley shifted, her hips seeking more contact. "Dolyn, *please!*"

I dipped into her slickness with a single fingertip and, cursing quietly, sank to my knees. I grasped her hips and pulled her closer to the edge of the mattress. Her legs wrapped around my shoulders.

Yessss.

My mouth watered, and I nipped the inside of her thigh. "Can I put my mouth on you?"

"Yes. Please."

Skin pebbling, I placed a chaste kiss on her wet labia. So soft. I breathed her in, my eyes closing in absolute euphoria while sucking her essence off my lips. A long lick from her pucker to her clit coated my tongue with her sweet cream. I swallowed her arousal down, a growl rumbling in my chest.

She is perfection. Succulent and sweeter than any honey.

Ashley ran her fingers through my hair, yanking me back to where she needed me, and I gave her my tongue.

I was the first to taste her nectar straight from the source.

My chest swelled while licking her clean and probing for more.

Ours.

"Mmm," I agreed and settled in to drink her down, toy with her flesh, until I wrung every last bit of pleasure from her body.

She writhed in my hold, trying to chase my mouth as I teased over her hardened nub, gentle flicks keeping her on edge but not allowing her to climax.

"Dolyn—more." The tortured plea poured from her lips. "*Please.*" Her broken sob sounded like the sweetest symphony to my ears.

Take her. Own her body.

I ignored my other half and focused on bringing her pleasure.

Ashley ripped at my hair, whimpering senseless words, but our connection dictated my moves.

Latching my lips on her clit, I slid two fingers deep into her tight core.

She gasped, hips lifting.

My eyes rolled back into my head, my cock aching. Throbbing. Ball sac drawn up and tight.

"Oh…yes. Yes!" Ashley's back bowed, her thighs clamping tight against my head. Her core sucked around my fingers in milking pulses, her cum dribbling over my knuckles. I lapped around her entrance, gently fucking her through her climax, devouring every drop she gifted me. Swallowing ensured a part of her would always be with me.

"Need—you." She gasped and shuddered, coming down from her high but evidently not finished.

"What, my female? Name it, and it's yours." My voice was ragged with desire.

She scooted around, still on her back, feet against our snoring beta, her head hanging over the bed's edge. A beckoning of her fingers explained and enticed me to obey her command.

"Fuck." I stood, grabbing hold of my cock in a death grip. If she drank her alpha's cum, she would grow desperate for more, addicted to our life-giving seed.

I longed to give her what she desired, but…

I glanced at Vanni.

Lips parted, he emitted evidence he wouldn't rouse anytime soon.

As their alpha, I had hoped to bestow the gift upon them at the same time, but my need along with our female's had grown too great. We could wait to fuck, but this, I would allow.

I slid my pants to mid-thigh and moved closer to cup the back of her head in one of my hands. "Is this what you want, my female?" I murmured while rubbing my leaking cockhead over her lips.

She flicked out her tongue, shivering hard enough goose bumps rose along her bare legs. "Please." Ashley opened her mouth and stuck out her tongue.

Teeth gritted, I slid partway into her mouth, stretching her lips with my girth.

She moaned, laving at my shaft.

I growled, backed out, and pushed in. Head tipping skyward, I stilled, memorizing the soft, wet heat of her. So perfect. I pulled out fully and tugged down on my sac, hissing at my lack of restraint.

"I can take all of you, Dolyn." Ashley's voice suggested assurance, but a hint of fear rested in her eyes.

I knelt immediately and cradled her head in both of my hands. "He did this to you."

She nodded, a tear sliding down her cheek and into the river of black hair dangling toward the floor.

Red heat flared in my guts, and I couldn't keep the fire from my eyes.

"You won't hurt me," she murmured, her voice small like a timid mouse.

I should have gathered her into my arms. Sheltered her from the torment of her past.

"Help me make new memories, Dolyn. Please. I'm ready for this step. Want you in my mouth and your cum in my belly."

My dragon groaned, and I shuddered. "I'm so close."

"Then hurry up and feed me your cock, my mate."

Wetness stung my eyes at her declaration, and I stood, swallowing hard to keep my emotions contained. All I had longed for, the words I'd never allowed myself to believe would caress my ears, had emitted from this gorgeous creature's perfect lips.

Our gazes locked, the energy between us potent and life-giving as tears coursed down my cheeks. "I'll be careful," I choked out and slid my length over her waiting tongue.

She grasped my hips and pulled me inward, and I cursed as my cockhead slid straight into her throat without resistance.

Wetness coated her cheeks as well, but her eyes shone with inner peace. Happiness. I swore I could almost feel her already, her emotions seeking me out, attempting to assure me of her being okay.

I fucked her mouth gently, my muscles tensed. "Won't be long…"

Ashley reached between my thighs and rubbed over my sac and taint.

"Fuck." I tipped my head back, eyes closed, losing myself to her touch. "Yes—fuck, yes."

My brazen female searched higher, fingertips fluttering over my pucker.

Vanni grunted in his sleep—and I came, roaring my release.

Shudders owned me, my hips stuttering in attempt to bury my cock inside Ashley's body. Spurt after spurt of seed shot deep inside her, and she swallowed, coaxing my balls to gift her all of me.

"Mine—so sweet." I dropped to my knees and devoured her mouth, my chest heaving, tingles still racing through the cells of my body. "Mine," I murmured against her lips before licking deep, needing to check for myself she'd devoured very drop.

Ashley cried out in ecstasy again and shivered, her hand between her thighs.

Groaning, I yanked her off the bed and into my arms,

burying my face in her neck as I sank onto the mattress's edge. We both breathed heavy, our hearts thudding in time with each other.

I wasn't sure exactly what the word love meant, but Ashley owned half of me. Lifting my head, I took in our sleeping beta who had rights to the rest.

Submit.

Turning away from Vanni and my inner beast, I closed my eyes and basked in what fate had destined me and how easily Ashley and I had come together.

CHAPTER 20

ASHLEY

"You're happy." Dolyn kissed my hair and squeezed me tighter.

"Very." I leaned back and looked him full in the face, needing to see the same joy radiating through what seemed like a tether between us. "So are you."

"I am."

The unspoken *but* lingered between us, something I swore we felt at the same time as we continued to stare at each other. I was bare from the waist down. He still had on all his clothing, but his pants were down around his knees.

And my bare ass sat on his warm, solid thighs, his soft cock nestled against my leg.

My inner friend's purr filled my chest, but I heard another. From Dolyn? His lightheartedness matched mine in a sense of contentment I wanted to bask in like the summer sun.

"Are we... It's like my mind is connected to yours," I said, not as bothered as I should have been by the supernatural I'd found myself a part of.

"Our inner beasts can sense one another." Dolyn brushed hair off my forehead before pressing his warm lips against my skin. "Coming together must have caused the beginnings of a bond."

Awareness of his emotions lay in the back of my mind, as though swallowing his seed had somehow attached us together. I imagined the biting and claiming from the book I'd read over the weekend, and my body ached to be filled.

"How intense will it grow once we complete whatever the ritual is?" I asked, my voice unsteady with renewed arousal.

"Enough we won't need to speak."

"Damn." I exhaled heavily. "There won't be room for misunderstanding. No lying."

"That is correct."

I smiled. "I think I like that."

Vanni shifted, emitting a heavy breath, and although I longed to look at him, to touch the bent leg near my hip, I couldn't tear my gaze off Dolyn.

I opened my mouth to ask how we would bond, but desire radiated off him with an intensity that…hurt my heart. Like Elijah had said, I had a feeling Dolyn fought what he wanted, what part of him longed for.

His yearning to submit to Vanni made my backside tingle in memory of my master's hand, however, a sense of distrust slithered into my mind. Was that the part of Dolyn Elijah had told me about? It almost felt like…he warred with his deeper desires.

Alpha.

Beta.

My friend whispered in my head, and I found myself wondering over Dolyn's claim about his station among us that night in Vanni's office. I doubted Vanni would submit. That hazy connection to Dolyn assured me one half of him had zero intentions of giving up complete control.

But Dolyn and Vanni's relationship would have to be worked out between the two of them.

I decided not to question or probe too deeply into his unrest like I wanted to. All would be made known the day we properly bonded. "Kiss me," I demanded instead.

He obliged, and I found myself falling all over again, his gentleness—and my body's response to it—making me realize Dolyn had definitely helped bring more healing to my life. Tears slid down my cheeks, and expecting he might feel a little of what I did, I waited for him to pull away.

Instead, he worshiped me with his mouth, tasting my dampened skin with open-mouthed kisses down my throat, sitting me up straight so he could finish undressing me. He stared at my small breasts once they were bared to him, his thumbs feathering over my nipples.

My breath caught.

"Can I taste you here?" His tone suggested he was entranced, like I was perfection in his eyes.

"Please." I grasped his head as he dipped to take one of my aching nubs into his mouth. He nibbled, and pulses shot between my thighs. "Dolyn." I whispered his name, my head tipping back.

He cupped my sex, and I shifted, needy as hell. He slid two fingers into me and suckled on my nipple at the same time with deep, coaxing pulls.

Whimpering, I grabbed at his hair. "I'm gonna come again," I half-choked on the words, laughter and a sob of astonishment and complete joy mixing inside my throat.

"Mmm." He hummed, crooked his fingertips inside me, and I cried out, my core clenching, desperate to keep a part of him inside me. Shudders rippled through me, but Dolyn held me firm, cradling me until I settled.

I blinked, my eyes and mind sleepy from pleasure as I peered up at him. "This is brand new, and I'm scared as hell about what I'm feeling, but I'm falling in love with you, Dolyn Kemmerly."

A soft smile made his eyes glow—and my pussy squeezed around his fingers again. He stroked me twice through the wetness. "I've already fallen, Ashley O'Connor."

"Will you get naked with me?" I asked, tugging at the collar of his shirt. "I want your skin against mine."

He pressed a chaste kiss to my lips and lay me down beside Vanni.

I rolled to my side, my back against my master's warm body, hands beneath my cheek as I watched.

Dolyn took his time unbuttoning his shirt, his focus on my face as he stripped. I'd expected arrogance, a knowing look in his eye, as he unveiled his god-like body to me. He simply peered at me with adoration, the warm fuzzies in my belly tingling from our happiness like a rainbow swirling around us.

Smooth, hairless skin covered muscle and bone. His upper body appeared to be sculpted out of pure gold and hard as granite. A waterfall of muscle led down his core to his groin. His naked cock hung heavy between thick thighs.

Arousal attempted to wake me up, but a yawn cracked my jaw as my body settled deeper into the mattress.

Dolyn smiled while climbing onto the bed and fitting me against his chest. Regardless of his firm muscles, the warmth of his skin made me want to snuggle in closer. Deeper.

How had I gone without physical contact for so many years?

My throat tightened as I rubbed my face over his pec, the thrum of his heartbeat soothing to my ear.

We touched from shoulders to knees, and he slid one of his legs between mine as though feeling the same need as I did. "Is this all right?" he murmured against my hair, his breath hot enough shivers slid down my spine.

"More than," I murmured, snuggling into his warmth. The scent of campfire and cedar filled my lungs, and I sighed as a sense of coming home swept over me.

"Sleep, my female." Dolyn kissed my hair again, and I obeyed like the good girl Vanni always claimed me to be.

CHAPTER 21

VANNI

I dreamed of a golden dragon capturing my gaze—ensnaring me entirely—and he held me enthralled with his sheer size looming over me. The energy emanating off him caught my breath. His scales rippled like a bend of light beneath my hand, and he purred as though enjoying my petting as much as I did the heat beneath my touch.

Fear of such a beast should have made me sweat, quake in my dream—I definitely wasn't awake. No such beast existed in real life.

I grabbed his lower jaw in both my hands and peered into his glowing gold eyes, the black slits of his pupils swirling with a darkness I recognized in myself.

Mine, a voice deep and full of conviction spoke inside my head.

"Mine," I echoed out loud, peering into those arresting eyes of singeing sunlight and heat.

The dragon's hot breath woofed over my face, scented with brimstone—and sex.

My cock hardened to stone in a mere heartbeat, and the beast growled as I stroked along the tiny scales beneath his jaw. His great length trembled, and a sense of mistrust washed over me but not from my own mind or heart. He and I were...connected. I *felt* his desire to be dominated, to be owned by a heavy hand. Thoughts of a whip, a cane, spiked the arousal coating the cord between us.

I pressed my forehead to his snout, needing to climb inside his head and root out all his insecurities so I could lay them to rest.

Female moans caressed my ears, drawing me away from darkness around the beast, and I went willingly. Desire, potent as what I felt for the beast, led me toward light.

I blinked in the glow of a lamp atop the bed stand beside where I sprawled. The mattress, while soft, wasn't mine.

My head fucking *pounded*, and my mouth tasted like the bottom of a trash can.

The bed shifted.

Soft warmth pressed against my side, and the scent of vanilla and burning embers wafted past my nose, making my aching cock throb.

"Fuck," I rasped and grabbed hold of my junk. I still wore slacks.

Another feminine moan, more like a sigh slid over my ears, pulling my head toward my left.

Ashley slept curled up beside me.

A bulk of golden skin and muscle lay behind her.

Dolyn.

Pre-cum oozed from my slit, and cursing, I carefully shoved off my pants until I lay as naked as the two in the bed with me.

Talk about a dream come true.

And my head, while hurting like hell, was quiet. Fucking silence between my ears.

Had the whiskey cured me of that damned voice that had

come to life on Friday night? I'd done nothing but drink since then to be rid of it.

I grimaced at the rancid taste in my mouth. No doubt, the rest of me smelled as bad as my breath. I remembered sitting at the bar around lunchtime, and here it was a solid twelve, if not more, hours later.

Darkness lay behind the pulled blinds, and a shift onto an elbow and a glance across Dolyn's massive body revealed a clock on the far bed stand.

Two in the morning.

I lay back down and rubbed a hand over my gritty eyes. Goddamnit, I was going to be absolute shit for the next forty-eight hours from how much I had poisoned my liver. Heaving an exhale, I slid from the bed to find I wasn't yet completely sober. We weren't in a hotel either.

Dolyn's place, most likely.

I staggered into a bathroom that looked vaguely familiar from earlier in the night. Emptying my bladder, I peered around, taking note of the marble flooring and walls, high-quality towels similar to mine, and the fancy-as-fuck sink. Took me awhile to figure the thing turned on by touch.

I washed my hands and used my finger to scrub my teeth with toothpaste I found in the vanity's top drawer.

Feeling somewhat more human—I snorted a laugh at that one—I returned to the bedroom.

Ashley still curled up like a cute kitten. Dolyn cradled her backside, his arm now over her waist in a possessive hold. Dark and light, they were a perfect combination of everything I thought I would never want again.

A threesome.

My stomach should have churned, my flight instinct kicked in, sending me running in the opposite direction. But a longing deep in my bones that I didn't recognize or understand kept me rooted in place. I didn't question the sense of rightness easing through my chest that I rubbed without realizing. Brow furrowed, I simply accepted the desire and *life* welling up inside me.

Dolyn's mouth parted in sleep, his face relaxed for the first time since I'd set eyes on him in my club. The sight of him alone made my cock perk up, and I lazily stroked my hard-on that hadn't relented. My gaze flicked between the two I wanted to be my lovers for who the fuck knew how long.

Forever?

I hadn't thought a future outside my ex could exist.

Could I be vulnerable and open myself up fully to these two seemingly perfect submissives fate tempted me with?

Yessss.

The voice didn't send me down a path of panic like it had before. Instead, I listened. Chose to accept this new part of me. While it didn't speak again, an instinctive urge to join the sleeping beauties who lay on top of the bedding sent me into motion.

Cock hard, I lay in front of Ashley without touching her satiny skin. Even though she wasn't conscious, I could still somewhat feel her inside my head. She seemed content and peaceful, her mind quiet with sleep.

Dolyn emanated a similar restfulness I'd never sensed in him before. Sleeping Dolyn was definitely my favorite—nah. Nope. I *liked* him sassy and stubborn, challenging my authority while secretly lusting to drop to his knees for me.

My shaft bucked against my belly, and I released a slow and steady hissed exhale.

I didn't want to rouse either of them, but the urge to touch controlled my body. I traced over Ashley's arched eyebrow, along her cheekbone, and over parted lips. A trickle of energy radiated between us but not nearly as potent as Friday night.

Fuck, did I want to lick over her mouth, taste her on my tongue.

She stirred, blinking violet eyes open until she focused on my face. Her pupils swelled.

"Hi," I whispered as that hazy connection between us woke as well.

A quiet hum from her accompanied a rush of feelings through my fingertips lingering on her lower lip.

Sleeping definitely lessened the emotional connection because desire suddenly slid between us like a living, breathing entity, needy as fuck.

I shifted closer, pushing her hair over her shoulder.

Dolyn's arm lay between us, and a brush of my stomach against his skin caused a current to rush through my body same as it had Friday night.

The three of us were physically connected.

The vision of burning green fire like a vortex around three writhing bodies flashed in my head again, and I groaned, my lust so great I had to close my eyes to keep from spilling my release all over the bed.

Ashley moaned as though my desire roused hers further, pressing against me.

Dolyn shifted, his arm caressing along my skin before disappearing, taking the awareness of him with the movement.

I jerked my eyelids up.

He'd rolled onto his back, still sleeping.

Ashley nestled right into me, shifting one slender leg atop mine and higher until smooth skin cradled my hip. "Touch me, Master."

A gush of pre-cum erupted from my cock onto her leg, and I cursed, sliding my hand between us to her core. Slickness coated my fingers.

"You're so wet for me," I murmured, inches from her face.

Pupils blown, she stared at me. "Make me yours, Vanni." She swallowed hard. "Please."

Groaning, I took her mouth in a bruising kiss, all thoughts of still being buzzed and headaches long gone. The scent of vanilla and sex swarmed me, the softness of her skin, the tight clench around my fingers as they sunk into her heat.

She. Was. Delicious.

A five-course meal I lusted to gorge myself on.

Never had I wanted a woman more. Even my ex hadn't instilled this kind of yearning for physical connection, intimacy of not just body but mind and soul. I licked into Ashley's mouth, suckled on her tongue, and memorized the feel of her satiny flesh moving along mine as I finger fucked into her wet heat.

"More," she whispered against my lips, grinding herself against my hand. "Need your cock in me. *Please.*"

Mine.

Fucking right, she was.

I pulled my fingers from her body and slid her closer until her slick pussy kissed the tip of my leaking cock.

Both of us moaned, and I exhaled heavily, pulling my head back enough that our gazes locked. "You're sure you want this?"

Ashley hummed her agreement, her smile radiant. "More than anything."

Still, I hesitated to slide into what I knew would be heaven on earth. Becoming one with her would break down barriers, demand vulnerability, and although I wished for nothing more than to worship this gorgeous woman, memories of devastating consequences stalled forward motion.

"Fuck her, Vanni."

My gaze jerked beyond Ashley to find Dolyn watching, his eyes fire. I'd been so caught up in Ashley that I hadn't realized the cord between him and I had awakened fully. Need vibrated off him in unrelenting waves, demanding yet filled with assurance of this being right.

I said I would never be bossed around by the man, but this was one command I couldn't say no to even if I thought I should. Submitting myself to Dolyn's desire, I held his gaze and flexed my ass, sinking into exquisite warmth.

Ashley clutched at me, moaning, and I tore my focus off Dolyn to watch her eyes as I pushed in fully, until our groins came together in a sticky mess.

A rush of adrenaline raced through me, spiking my pulse and drying my mouth. "I'm inside you, baby," I whispered, the flow of what felt a lot like love swelling between us like a gentle, warm tide.

She shuddered but held my stare as I backed out and slid once more into exquisite torture.

"That's it—be a good girl and stay with me," I murmured, repeating the action, the sense of her spiraling backward toward the trauma in her mind snaking in like a disease.

I slapped her ass.

She jolted and cried out, her mind fully in the present.

Dolyn cursed.

I grinned, heart racing, but kept my eyes on Ashley, whose gaze remained clear, the yearning she had for me returning tenfold through the cord binding us together. "Just giving her what she needs from me, boy."

"Do it again," Ashley whispered.

I slapped her other jiggly ass cheek.

She hissed, but her pussy pulsed around my girth.

"Such a good girl for me," I crooned, slowly fucking in and out of her tight clasp, my hand in a bruising grip on her heated backside.

An ache rose in my chest—Dolyn, I realized. "Come closer," I demanded. "Need to feel you too."

Swallowing hard, the unease in his mind reaching through to mine, he did as told, his lower abs pressing against the back of my hand.

A rush of lust swept through me, and I groaned, spunk gushing from me even though I didn't climax.

"Oh, my God." Ashley groaned and shivered as though she felt the unnatural release from my cock. Or maybe, she, like me, experienced Dolyn's intense craving for us both. One thing became clear as fuck—Ash's focus was with us one hundred percent, her need as vibrant as the sun.

"Want to roll in here between me and our female?" I teased the vision we'd shared Friday night while burrowing deep against her womb.

She gasped and arched.

Dolyn's hackles rose, and he growled, flames flickering in his eyes. But a rush of desire from deep inside him zapped through me, assuring me I guessed right.

"Yeah." I smirked and thrust again. "You know you do."

He palmed my ass and yanked me closer with supernatural strength, making me fuck into Ashley.

And his hand? A fucking *brand* on my skin of searing heat.

My heart raced, thoughts fled as lust and deep longing to be one wrapped the three of us up in a tight hold.

I let go of Ashley's plump backside and grabbed Dolyn's dick, earning a nice hiss. He shuddered as I jacked him in time with his fucking me into the whimpering woman between us. I allowed Dolyn to use me to pleasure her for no other reason than the fact I wanted to come. Hard. Deep inside—

"Fuck. Condom." I tried to pull out, but Dolyn's hold on me firmed with unnatural strength.

"We are dragonblood," he murmured, his tone sure, feelings about his factual words settling deep inside me regardless of my suspicion.

Yessss.

"We cannot catch vile human diseases."

Vile humans or vile diseases? What the fuck ever. I needed to fill Ashley up and feel Dolyn's release coat my fingers.

He made me fuck into Ashley again, and I gave her my attention.

"He's not lying," she whispered, her voice wrecked.

"I was tested three months ago," I told her. "Haven't been with anyone since."

"You know the truth of my last time."

I gritted my teeth at the unease slithering between us. With my free hand trapped beneath her hip and the mattress, I considered a way to give her pain. Our height difference didn't allow me to bend my neck in order to reach her nipples while my dick was swallowed up in her pussy.

Fingers it would be.

I shifted my left shoulder, easing my lower arm up her body while Dolyn fucked into my other.

"Yes," she hissed as I closed my fingertips around one of her ripe buds. "God, yes."

I pinched, and a rush of wetness coated my shaft.

Dolyn dug his fingertips into my ass, yanking me toward him, effectively stuffing her full with my cock again.

Felt so fucking good. Wished he could be in her tight heat with me.

"Put your dick in here with me, Dolyn," I ordered, tugging on his granite shaft hard.

Ashley moaned like the good little girl she was, her desire spiking.

"No."

I cut my eyes to Dolyn's, hating how dead set he was against double penetration. Lust radiated in his eyes, and the yearning to obey rolled off him in waves. "Why not?"

"It isn't time," he stated through gritted teeth, fucking into my fist with a snap of his hips.

Meaning he hoped to own her along with me in the *future*.

I could wait.

I toyed with Ashley's nipples, breathing her harsh exhales from being fucked on my dick into my lungs. "You gonna come around my cock, baby?" I murmured, licking over her parted lips.

"Mmm."

I grabbed hold of Dolyn's tight sac, and he cursed.

"Want my cum inside you? Dolyn's all the fuck over your cute little ass?"

"Yes—please, yes!" Ashley attempted to writhe, but she lay trapped between two hard bodies chasing release.

"You first." I pinched her furled bud as hard as I could.

Ashley shrieked.

Dolyn grunted.

Wetness coated my shaft, and my hips moved on their own as his seed erupted over my hand and her skin.

"Oh God!" Ashley cried again, her pussy pulsing around my shaft as I pumped in and out of her with steady stabs.

"That's it. So good for me." I clenched my teeth as my taint spasmed. "Here it comes, baby. Gonna fucking flood you." At the first shot of cum erupting deep inside her, I hissed. Curses spilled from my lips with every vicious spurt.

"So hot inside me." She moaned, head tipped back against Dolyn's chest, pulse throbbing in her neck. "Oh, my *God*."

Dolyn shuddered, his dick still hard in my hand.

I gripped him tighter, stroking him in time with my thrusts, my balls refusing to empty.

He hissed, but I didn't give a fuck he grew sensitive.

Another pinch to Ashley's nipple, and she came again,

milking me dry. The clench of her pussy forced my cum to leak around my cock.

Dolyn released his grasp on my backside and put space between us. He swatted at my wrist until I released his shaft.

Chuckling, I finally relaxed, dick still buried in Ashley's soaked sheath, her trembling body wrapped around me. "Okay, baby?" I whispered, panting against her hair, arms holding her tight.

"Mmm."

"Words."

"Yes—I'm perfect."

I hummed an agreement, my dick thick enough I could lazily fuck in and out of her body. More wetness leaked from her core.

Reaching between us, I felt around to where I penetrated her. As expected, I'd given her the nut of the century. Not surprising considering how much I'd been ejaculating over the weekend. Steady fucking stream, the never-ending well.

But I was sated for the moment.

Ashley pushed her hand between our bellies, and I backed out, releasing a rush of cum. "Holy shit." She huffed a laugh, soaked, sticky fingers brushing over mine, her sense of astonishment making me snicker. "It's...tingly."

A slam of anger and spine-tingling fear crashed into my brain, and I glanced over at Dolyn. The man, or not man, hovered on the edge of losing his shit, mouth gaping.

He stared as Ashley lifted her hand between us. Swallowed audibly as she eyed the evidence of how hard I'd come on her hand.

"Don't," Dolyn whispered, but the connection allowed me to sense how focused Ashley was on tasting my seed.

Yessss.

"Yes," I echoed.

Dolyn's eyes widened as Ashley shoved two fingers deep into her mouth.

She shuddered, moaning around her mouthful of flesh, body undulating as though I still fucked into her.

Feeling her need, I pushed three fingers deep into her core.

Dolyn went pale.

Ashley came from a single stroke, gasping and scratching at my chest.

"My cum tastes that good, huh?" I murmured against her hair as she finished, my gaze on Dolyn, whose emotions roiled so damned thoroughly I couldn't make heads or tails of them.

"Fuck you," he rasped, and I wasn't sure he spoke to me.

Still, I grinned while narrowing my gaze. "It'll be the other way around—I promise you that."

He shivered, the unrest inside him thick like billowing smoke between us.

"Next time, I'm going to spurt every drop of cum in my balls into her throat, and she's going to beg for more."

"No." His word, like a whimper, furrowed my brow, but Ashley rolled, reaching to thread her clean fingers with his, bringing awareness of him back full force as the three of us connected.

"Are you all right?" she asked him even though she had to feel what I did.

He hovered on the edge of a chasm in his mind.

Dolyn nodded, a blatant lie that dictated I beat his ass.

I could sense Ashley's concern over his fib and hated how it made the pleasure of her release fade. "You've smashed down your walls in so many ways," I said, pulling her face toward me, needing to keep her riding her high a little longer. "I'm so damned proud of you, sweetheart."

A heavy sigh rested her onto the mattress, and I gathered

her into my arms away from Dolyn, where his emotions couldn't touch us as potently.

Dolyn slid off the bed, heading for the bathroom. Every flex of his ass was like a goddamn shot of adrenaline to my system. I wanted to bury balls-deep in his tight hole, dig my fingers into his flesh, bite into his neck and ride him until we both roared.

The vivid image of the dragon I'd dreamed about flashed in my mind, stealing my breath and killing the semi I'd begun to sport.

Fucking dragonblood.

Blood Born.

Other-fucking-worldly.

What the hell had I gotten myself into? Some weird alien shit? Fucking Twilight Zone?

"Yes," Ashley whispered, drawing my focus off Dolyn.

"Yes, what?"

"Dragonblood. Otherworldly."

My brow furrowed. "Did I mutter that out loud?"

"No. I...felt some of your thoughts. In here." She laid a hand over her chest.

I breathed in and out, steadily and quietly as the bathroom door clicked shut behind Dolyn. "This is real? Everything he said?"

"Yes."

"He's not wholly human?"

Ashley shook her head, biting back a smile even though her eyelids grew heavy. "None of us are, but I'll tell you all about it later. Promise. Right now, I just need to sleep."

"The bed is wet. You're leaking."

"Don't care," she muttered, snuggling against my chest.

My focus fell to her twitching lips as I soothed my hand along her spine. "You tasted my spunk, Ash."

"So good." She hummed. "Tingly on my tongue." A soft

sigh ghosted over my chest, her breaths evening out. That strong, weird cord between us grew quiet, numbed by sleep.

Dolyn came out of the bathroom, towel in hand. He refused to look at me, jaw flexed, shoulders high around his ears.

Could he feel how badly I lusted for him? I wanted his cock up her ass, a mere thin wall of Ashley between our thrusting dicks. I needed him buried alongside me, shooting cum against her womb when I did.

He growled beneath his breath, and I grinned at his burst of desire even though the high of release had begun to fade from my own system. Awareness of my headache returned. My muscles relaxed into the mattress.

Dolyn gently shifted Ashley so she lay against my chest. He wiped between her thighs, taking care of her needs when I'd been too caught up in my own selfish thoughts.

"Thank you," I murmured, having no wish to wake her.

He set aside the towel, but I didn't chide him for ignoring the mess smeared on my groin. Dolyn lifted his focus to my face.

A fury of emotion slammed into me. The pain, the hollowness of his chest, the tumult of feelings inside him laid waste to me. His hurt reverberated through my mind like an ancient voice without tone, a hundred times worse than any I'd experienced. My heart ached with him.

For him.

"Lie with us." I begged with my eyes, clutching Ashley's sleeping form close and wishing I could do the same for Dolyn.

But he wasn't yet ready for my soothing or comfort. Aftercare, I expected, would be the last thing he would ever allow me.

He settled slowly onto the bed, a couple of feet away. On his back, he stared at the ceiling.

"Please stay," I murmured, closing my eyes and drifting off to sleep.

CHAPTER 22
ASHLEY

Warmth and the most alluring, musky scent of male surrounded me. Lingering traces of sweetness coated my mouth, making me hunger for more. Worse than the desire for coffee, my body craved…something I couldn't quite place.

I blinked my eyes open, gaze falling from the white ceiling to a small balcony outside the slider—and the Tolzman Industries building beyond.

Dolyn.

Vanni.

Mates.

Arousal flooded through me as the evening before caught up to my sleep-addled brain. I bit my lip to keep my whimper contained while rubbing my hand along the hard cock clutched in my grip. I turned my head to take in the body facing mine.

Vanni stared at me, his mossy eyes clear of sleep and full of lust. He grabbed my wrists and rolled atop me, pinning my arms overhead with a single hand. The head of his cock pressed against my soaked, aching pussy. "You've been touching me in your sleep, naughty girl," he claimed, reaching between us.

I arched on a gasp as he teased my opening by sliding his cockhead through my soaked folds.

"Moaning and whimpering your need for me." He groaned the statement a breath away from my mouth.

"Yes." I wrapped my legs around his waist, trying to pull him closer.

"And for Dolyn." The rumbled tone, the desire Vanni had for Dolyn, washed over me, releasing a rush of wetness around the head of his cock.

"Need…" I licked my desert-like lips. "Need you. *Him*."

"Inside you." Vanni read my mind, gifting me a mere teaser of his thick length, turning my blood to burning flames as he notched inside me. "Filling your tight pussy at the same time."

My eyelids fluttered shut at the delicious invasion, the stretching fullness as he eased in another inch.

"Ash."

I blinked up at him, his concern flooding my heart with what felt a lot like love. He wanted words like I'd given him last night, but surely he could sense how I longed to give him everything. "Yes."

He pushed forward, slowly filling me, allowing me all the time in the world to tell him to stop.

Never.

In full agreement with my friend, I lifted my hips until Vanni's swollen cockhead rested against my womb.

His length jerked inside my body, and we both groaned our shared yearning.

"Don't hold back," I whispered, and he gave me power over my hands so I could clutch at his shoulders, clutch him against me.

Planked on his elbows to keep his weight off me, he slid

his fingers into my hair, cradling my head. "Ash…" Swallowing hard, he backed out, and I clenched around him, desperate to keep him inside me.

"Fuck." Vanni slammed into me so hard I slid along the mattress. "Jesus, Ash—you're so hot and tight on my dick." He held my face against his hard chest and ground his hips against mine, hitting my clit just right.

I moaned, overwhelmed by a driving force I didn't recognize. A deep craving far beyond a mere climax swept through my body, a need to be one, wrapped up in the two meant for me.

The energy flickering back and forth between Vanni and I allowed me glimpses of his desire for his beta, his lust to shoot his cum along with Dolyn's deep inside me.

"Dolyn," I groaned a plea for him as Vanni stabbed into me again.

"He's gone."

A wave of heartache slammed into me at Vanni's declaration, his similar emotion amplifying my own. But the feelings didn't keep him from fucking me or my body's reaction to the torturous gyration of his hips.

Arousal, hot and thick, slid around his shaft, and I teetered on the edge, panting and moaning against his skin but unable to leave thoughts of Dolyn alone. He should be with us. In the bed, in our hearts—his emotions in our minds where they belonged.

"Where?" I gasped, fingernails digging into Vanni's back as he thrust.

"Don't—" he stabbed into me, dragging his cock slowly outward again "—know." A deep growl vibrated his chest against my cheek as he slammed into me again. "Fucker left." In one swift move, Vanni sat on his haunches, bringing me along with him so I sat impaled atop his hard shaft. "Not one single fucking word, no goodbye."

He lifted me up and slammed me down onto him, cock-head jabbing my cervix.

Exquisite pain caused shudders to ripple along my spine, and I gasped at the heat rushing through my limbs.

"Going to beat his ass."

Another deep-seated thrust jolted a cry past my panting lungs, and I grasped at his bulging shoulders.

"Cane him so he can't walk for a *week*."

Vanni's fingers dug into my hips, and my head tipped back, eyelids fluttering closed as my climax tingled, hovering beyond reach.

"He will submit," Vanni vowed, authority in his tone. "My beta, the link to our female." He pinched my nipple without warning, and my body convulsed, darkness creeping at the edges of my mind as I climaxed around him, milking, demanding he give me his seed.

"Ash…" Buried deep, he squeezed me tight, heat erupting from him to coat my womb.

I clung to him as wave after wave of shared emotion shot into me with his cock jerking and spurting between spasms of my pussy.

He captured my mouth, rough and fierce, and I melted against him, zero resistance or trace of the past haunting my mind.

"You're mine," he growled into my mouth, but I felt he meant the words beyond just me. Renewed heartache from both of us over Dolyn's absence made my eyes sting and throat thicken.

But Vanni's cum tingled inside me like it had the night before, sending shivers of delight up through my belly— and making my mouth water for another taste of its sweetness.

As though reading my mind, he lifted me off his still hard length and sprawled back like a dark, deviant god, eyes glinting like green fire, his smirk sexy as hell. "Clean me with your tongue."

Already drooling, I slid down his body, uncaring of the tang of my own cum mingled with the sweetness of his. I took him into my mouth, lapping and sucking every trace of his pleasure from his flesh, but like an addict, I needed more.

Vanni groaned and grabbed hold of my hair, tugging and thrusting. "Going to give you what you want, baby."

I hummed around his girth as his cock buried deep in my throat without resistance.

"Fuck, yes." He pulled my hair, lifting me off him.

I whimpered at the sting along my scalp, digging my fingernails into his thighs to fill my mouth with him, his scent, his taste.

He held me firm. "You're so greedy for me."

"Yes." I couldn't tear my gaze off his glistening cock, the long length bobbing, twitching as though lusting for me to consume what my taste buds craved.

"Be a good girl and take me deep. Suck me dry."

Wetness gushed from me as he shoved my gaping mouth down over him. My throat opened with ease, accepting every inch. Cum erupted down my esophagus, Vanni's hoarse shout causing my body to climax without a single touch between my thighs.

I drank every drop with greedy swallows but still hungered for more upon falling lax between his thighs.

Gentle fingers carded through my hair, soothing the sting away as we rested in our shared release.

Vanni and I snuggled on Dolyn's couch, the glass wall in front of us overlooking Tolzman Industries. I told him everything Dolyn had shared with me and filled Vanni in on my conversation with Elijah as I'd promised to do. My lover didn't argue who and what Elijah had claimed we were—alpha, beta, and female. Three fated mates with the ability to continue an almost extinct bloodline. Truth rooted in our bones, our strengthening connection assuring we both believed the unthinkable had become reality.

A deep ache lay in my breast, quiet whimpers of longing whispering through my head. I felt as though a piece of me was missing. So far gone beyond my reaches that my eyes stung.

Why had Dolyn left us, and where had he gone? The space between us seemed like a crater, its distance unfathomable, completely cutting his energy off from my mind and body.

"He's running scared," Vanni said as though hearing the question in my head.

I didn't argue with his assumption because it felt right.

"I sensed his conflicting desire to submit the first time we met, and even then, I could tell he'd rather have been anywhere but strapped to my spanking bench."

Arousal slid through my veins, and I swallowed hard. "When was that?"

"A few days before you finally let me touch you. He came into my club, desperate for pain, and I'm wondering now if fate led him to me. Like you did, I sensed something was off with him. Conflicting desires didn't allow him to submit fully."

"Did he allow you to touch him?"

"No. It wasn't until he attempted to rip me away from you that our skin came into contact. That connection is what had unsettled me and sent me running from my office."

I sighed, running my fingers over his hard pec.

"Even now, I can still sense him in the back of my head."

"I can't," I murmured, my throat tightening.

Vanni tightened his hold on me. "Text Elijah. Maybe he'll know where the bastard's gone."

I didn't question Vanni's order but grabbed my cell off the coffee table and did as told. We both hurt, and only Dolyn's presence would right what was wrong. Sighing, I snuggled back against Vanni's hard chest again, phone clutched to my abdomen.

He soothed his hand over my bare arm, awakening goose bumps and need between my thighs. Neither of us made mention of the continuous arousal between us, its presence more of a comfort than demand to fuck in the moment. He pressed a kiss to the top of my head, and I closed my eyes, pained yet thankful beyond belief for where we were. What we'd found together—and the possibility of an even better future.

"Did he come untouched from the pain?" I whispered, mind stuck on what Vanni dominating Dolyn would look like—sexy. Hot. Beyond arousing. I shifted on Vanni's lap, and he hissed, his cock thickening.

"Yes. I've never met a masochist such as him. He accepted every lash without begging for mercy. I put all of my strength behind the cane and whip, and still he begged for more. He is…"

My core pulsed, wishing to be filled.

Vanni sighed and nuzzled against my hair.

A notification dinged.

"Grand Tetons." I read the text and paraphrased the rest of Elijah's message as my need cooled. "It's where his family originated from—get this—thousands of years before humans made their way to this part of the world. When we'd spoken on the phone, Elijah had told me about Dolyn going missing for ten years, and he hadn't been able to find him anywhere near the mountain range. He's not sure where the home is for certain, but it would be either in the rock or beneath."

Yessss.

We both cursed quietly at the echoing voices and the reminder of how old the Blood Born were. There was so much we didn't know about the species we belonged to.

Vanni's narrowed gaze lingered on the sliding door's view. "Grand Tetons," he muttered, shifting me a little closer. His semi dug into my hip, his flesh warm and damp.

I stared at his length, remembering the sweetness of his cum and wondering why the need for more kept me in a constant state of desperation for another taste. My desire for Dolyn rose in equal measure, and pain pinged my chest while tingles of awareness raised the hair on my arms.

"I can smell your want."

I jerked my head up, so far lost in conflicting feelings that I'd lost touch of the energy sharing Vanni's thoughts. "You can?"

He breathed deep, his wide chest swelling, his brow smoothing, and a cocky smirk lifting his lips higher. "You can't get enough of me."

I shook my head as a shiver raced over me.

"You want me to hold you down and spank your pretty little ass red while you fantasize about Dolyn submitting to me, don't you?"

I wished Vanni would erase my mind for a while, and he was well aware of *that* fact too.

He shifted me from his lap to stand, took the coffee mug and cell from me, and set them aside. Leaning over me, he placed his hands on the back of the couch beside my head. Fire licked at my skin as darkness swirled in his pupils. "You want the sting of my flogger. The bite of my cane. But you *need* my seed on your tongue."

My backside squirmed on the couch beneath me, and my

thighs fell open in invitation. "Please, Master. I'm so hungry for you."

"Mmm." Vanni tipped his head to the side as his gaze traveled down my neck to my pebbled nipples. "You ought to get these pierced," he said and flicked one hardened nub with his tongue, "so I can tug the rings with my teeth. Give you the kind of ache in your clit that you crave."

I grabbed hold of his head to keep his lips and teeth against my sensitive buds.

Without preamble, Vanni shoved two fingers inside my sopping core, biting hard on my breast.

My climax ripped the air from my lungs, unexpected and with the force of one long denied, even though it had only been hours since he'd been inside me. "Master—Vanni!" I cried out, back arching, pulses wracking through my pussy.

He thrust deep into me, curling and stroking, prolonging my pleasure until I lay spent.

I whimpered when he removed his touch from me, staring at him as he licked his fingers clean.

"So delicious."

One last spasm rippled through me at his rumbled words, and my focus dropped to his other hand stroking down his slick cock. I sat forward, greedily taking him into my mouth before he could voice the order he planned.

"The fuck is wrong with us?" Vanni muttered on a groan while bottoming out against the back of my throat.

Dragonblood.

He hesitated briefly as the truth played, echoing between our minds. "Otherworldly bullshit." He thrust, stabbing into my throat with ease. "Goddamned—fucking perfect. Love it. Can't. Get. Enough."

His seed shot straight into my belly, warm and delicious.

I moaned around my mouthful of his cock, my throat

accepting all of him as though I'd been created to service him.

"Fucking hell," Vanni bit out the words, milking one last spurt onto my waiting tongue. "Swallow."

I did as told. Licked my lips and sent that last bit of his essence where it belonged with the rest. Humming my happiness, I slumped onto the couch, sated even though between my thighs felt too empty.

"Ash." He choked on my name and stretched out beside me, gathering me into his arms again.

The scent of sex, sweaty male, and remnants of Dolyn's cedar lay thick in my nose. My chest ached with the kind of pain that didn't bring pleasure. "Where do you think he went?"

"Don't know. I'm sober and can't get a sense of him, so he's definitely not nearby."

"We need to track him down."

Vanni heaved a sigh and squeezed me tight. "I'm not enough, am I?"

"It's not that." My brow furrowed as I considered Dolyn and the emptiness he'd left behind. Vanni and I together were nothing short of magic, the sweet magnetism, the ease with which our bodies and hearts fit together.

But a piece of our puzzle was missing.

"I understand," Vanni murmured, his lips against my hair. "I feel the same way. If he's not back by tomorrow morning, we'll go find him. And I'll make sure he never questions who he is ever again."

"And if he safewords?" I asked quietly, aware of the depths of Dolyn's denial and fear.

"I won't allow it."

But he would. My master would honor the one holding power over his heart.

Even if it wrecked us all.

CHAPTER 23

DOLYN

I set down on the cloaked veranda facing my cavern-like home and shifted to human form. A rush of wind lifted snow and freshly fallen sleet, blasting my naked body, but I didn't feel the cold—or even the frigid stone of the mountain beneath my feet.

Fire burned in my guts, ignited by a combination of rage and fear I couldn't stomach thinking about. Anger became my focus. Father had promised me so many things. Assured me of my station, how as the only spawn of one of the final royal bloodlines, I would take my place as alpha. A triad looked over by me, protected by my dragonblood, loved with every part of my being.

My inner dragon whimpered his sorrow, pulling my attention toward the other emotion swamping my brain regardless of my desire to ignore it.

I'd hoped to watch Ashley drink down my cum and find herself addicted to my life-giving seed. Instead, a single taste of Vanni's had made her hunger, desperate for more on her tongue and in her belly. According to her, his cum had been sweet, hot, and tingly inside her body.

Beta.

Swallowing hard, I shook my head, refusing to believe my inner beast's declaration about who we were. Forcing a bond even if I had wanted to rightfully claim myself as alpha over Vanni and Ashley wouldn't have worked. There would be no manipulating them.

So, I'd left. Fled like a coward to the only place no one would think to look for me, a mountain range I had avoided for decades.

A dozen strides landed me beneath crumbling archways worn by centuries of wicked weather, and I laid my hand upon the oaken door tucked beneath. The wood came alive beneath my touch and pushed open in silence.

I had expected warmth on my naked skin from the fires deep in the bowels of the mountain of my ancestral home but not the lack of dust and cobwebs that should have accumulated in my long absence. Or the lantern hanging above the kitchen island fighting off the oppressive dark.

My heart beat heavy in my chest, and I stepped over the threshold, the door swishing shut behind me on its own and entombing me in silence. Breathing deeply, I categorized every scent, searching for verification those I had provided for and visited on occasion while living with Elijah were still alive even though it wasn't humanly possible.

Lemon and rosemary.

Chicken and freshly baked bread.

A few steps into the living area of the massive cavern added more hints of life through my nose. Vinegar and hints of orange.

I filled my lungs until they burned.

Female.

But not the one I had abandoned.

My gaze narrowed while taking in the immaculate condition of my home that hadn't changed since I'd last stood in this spot.

The décor matched what had been popular in the fifties when I'd updated the space. Garish yellows and blues added color to the living area on my right. Wooden cabinets curved along the rock wall to my left. The Home Comfort wood cookstove in their midst still gleamed as though straight out of a catalogue rather than decades old from when I'd brought it up the mountain side and set it in place.

My home carried more unsavory memories than good. Heartache and bitterness lay upon every surface, thick enough to tighten my throat. The cavern had been the place of my birth, the prison where I'd been unable to escape Father and his teachings.

Unlike Elijah's place in the White Mountains, my ancestral home hadn't been updated with the latest technology. I didn't even have electricity or natural gas—I'd never needed it. A flicker of dragon fire lit candles, lanterns, and kindling as quickly as a thought.

After having experienced Elijah's comforts, however, I realized how badly I had ignored what was my birthright, even if the mountain surrounding me hadn't ever *felt* like home.

She approaches.

The scent of female strengthened in my nose at the same time my inner beast spoke. I flitted my focus toward the dark hallway directly ahead of me. A sense of familiarity lay beneath her flowery scent, causing my stomach to tighten.

She materialized like a wraith, a smaller lantern in her hand glinting highlights of gold in the pale hair shimmering down to her waist, a Burmese dog heeling at her side. Light brown eyes took me in from head to toe without a hint of fear or concern over my nakedness. She was tall and curved like the women I used to be drawn to prior to meeting

Ashley. I remained upright and unmoving, hands at my sides as the young woman turned off her smaller lamp, set it atop the table, and came to a stop a dozen or so feet away from me.

"Who are you?" I asked, keeping any trace of violence over her trespassing from my voice since her presence wasn't any threat to me. Neither was the cute dog, considering how it seemed to smile up at me, its tongue lolling out the side.

The young woman's gaze flicked over my face as though categorizing every pore and line. "Primrose Cadet."

Cadet...Dahlia.

The blood seeped from my upper body, leaving me lightheaded. "Dahlia," I heard myself whisper even though the woman couldn't still be alive—could she?

"My grandmother." Head cocked to the side, the young woman continued to study me. "She was ninety-four when she passed, and even on her deathbed, she hoped you would return. That was four long years ago."

"Joseph?" I managed to ask past the lump in my throat.

"My grandfather." Her gaze flitted down over my nakedness, but I couldn't read a single thought or feel any energy emanating from her.

My beast lay silent, even though I could sense the whimper he withheld since I wouldn't yet allow us to grieve over the loss of our old lovers.

The dog woofed and peered up at Primrose.

She absently touched its head, trailing fingers over its fur. "You *are* Dolyn, aren't you?"

I nodded, unsure what to think or how to stop the rush of emotion swarming my chest. Too much had been tossed into my face in mere minutes, and I floundered to find any sense of calm.

"Go on." She encouraged the dog. "His name is Tiggy," she

told me as he ambled close to sniff fingers I hadn't realized I'd stretched out.

Swallowing hard, I knelt, taking his face in my hands. "Who's a good boy?" I asked, my voice ragged.

"The summer before grandmother passed, I felt a driving urge to get this creature. She named him—for you."

"Tiggy," I rasped.

"Short for Antigone," Primrose said. "It's Greek and means worthy of one's parents."

A tear slid down my cheek, and Tiggy whined as though experiencing my pain. His wet tongue on my face offered comfort when I needed it most.

"I had a dog when I was a young boy," I whispered—to the animal or Primrose, I wasn't sure. "My alpha father had it killed because he said loving the lesser being as I did would make me weak."

"He was wrong." Primrose's voice wavered along with mine, proving she wasn't as stoic as she projected.

"Father made me focus on growing stronger, not soft toward cute, fluffy creatures that were beneath us." I murmured the words that had hurt more than any fist.

Tiggy rubbed his nose into my chest, and I scratched behind his ears before wrapping my arms around him. "Such a good boy," I whispered against his fur.

"He was meant to be yours."

I pulled away from the dog and stood, eyeing the woman before me. She wore billowy pants and an old sweater that looked homemade. No frills—lace, jewelry, or makeup— adorned her body, but she was as beautiful as her grandmother.

Memories flooded through me

Dahlia and Joseph chained in the playroom far below where Primrose and I stood, sweat and cum dripping off their bodies. The soft sighs as they had come down from climaxing beneath me always made me hunger for a deeper connection. The two humans had relieved my itch for fucking but hadn't been able to fulfill my need for the mates and offspring I'd longed for.

Elijah and I had never agreed to exclusivity, so I never told him about the two lovers I kept across the country for the first half of our relationship. I'd visited with Joseph and Dahlia in the early sixties in one last attempt to make them mine.

The ancient ritual to bind Dahlia, Joseph, and I together hadn't worked. Even after they'd drunk my cum and *wanted* the bond, our hearts and minds hadn't cemented together. No bursting golden flames had wrapped around us. No mental connection had been born in that moment and given us access to one another's thoughts. No shared emotions had radiated among the three of us.

Feeling unworthy, I had abandoned them, left my ancestral home for good, and submitted my body to Elijah—and my inner beast's desire for pain. But what I'd left behind…

Primrose's slightly crooked nose was all Joseph. The same pointy chin I'd always found so alluring on Dahlia lay beneath Primrose's full lips. The yellow hair and the glint of gold in her thickly lashed orbs were identical to mine.

"You're of my blood," I whispered, realizing I *hadn't* failed in producing offspring.

"I am."

My eyelids slammed shut, and I allowed my sorrow and rage to roar through my inner beast and back out again, rattling the cavern around us.

If only I had the gift of sensing Blood Born as Elijah's female did, I would have known I'd somehow managed to impregnate a human female. If I had stayed and accepted their comfort, within a matter of weeks, I would have recognized Dahlia miraculously carried Joseph's and my child.

A Blood Born of Father's royal line.

I had *succeeded* in producing longed-for offspring even though doing so with humans was unheard of.

It took three dragonblood to create life, I'd been told by Father.

What else had he been wrong about?

I opened my eyes to find Primrose still watching me, unconcerned and unmoved. "You know who and what I am?" My voice broke as I brought to question my entire damned existence.

"I do." Primrose moved into the kitchen with grace as though I hadn't nearly brought the mountain down on our heads with my roar. Her bare feet stepped silently on the stone, but Tiggy's nails clicked as he followed at her side. Primrose even walked with Dahlia's gentle sway, her head slightly canted to the side like Joseph's had always been.

Dahlia had been a girl of the streets, downtrodden and in need of shelter, food, and protection from the john, who thought to abuse her body. Having not seen or heard of another Blood Born in over a century after my parents' passing, I'd taken Dahlia in and shown her how a human male ought to treat a woman. Only once she had fallen deeply in love with me, did I reveal the truth of my inner beast.

She'd chosen to stay because she had no life to return to. We had discussed a third, my beta, and hoped he would be the missing link I craved. We dreamed of creating a bond between human and Blood Born for the first time in history. Desperate, I'd stolen Joseph, a simple and beautiful man with no family, one who wouldn't be missed.

"She and Joseph were mere humans. We tried to bond so we might procreate, but they failed me time and again," I murmured as memories continued to flood my brain.

"Perhaps *you* failed *them*."

"I did no such thing." I frowned at Primrose's back as she

put her hands into threadbare oven mitts. "I left them, yes, but without knowledge we'd conceived and not without having provided for them—generously."

"You are hungry."

I had expected anger on Primrose's part, annoyance at the very least, but not an abrupt topic change. "What?"

She merely glanced over her shoulder at me from her place by the stove, her face devoid of expression. "You. Are. Hungry." She enunciated each word as though I were a child.

My spine stiffened, but she opened the oven door.

My dragon salivated at the blast of scents filling the air.

"I baked a chicken and potatoes," she said, pulling a roasting pan from the oven. "With rosemary and thyme."

The same way Dahlia had made my favorite meal. "Dahlia taught you to cook?"

"Grandmother taught me everything I know."

Grandmother...not mother.

"Your mother is my daughter," I said as my inner beast's reminder clicked the truth into my brain. I glanced at the dark hallway Primrose had come from but couldn't sense another female in the cavern.

"She *was*."

I jerked my focus toward Primrose.

She set the roasting pan atop the stove and pulled the mitts free, placing them in a drawer. "My mother didn't live through delivering me."

A pang twinged my chest, and I rubbed absently at the ache, the knowledge of all I had missed out on due to selfishness. "Who was your father? And where is Joseph?"

"My bloodline, we'll discuss over dinner. As for Grandfather, his heart gave out on him a few years after I was born. I don't remember a single thing about the man Grandmother claimed to be a sweet, giving soul."

I swallowed against another roar building deep inside me.

Joseph and I had always been close. From day one, I'd felt affection for him even though he'd been far below my station.

"I'm so sorry," I murmured, not sure who I spoke to.

"Sorry I had to grow up without my mother or sorry you never got to meet her?" A hint of anger laced Primrose's words, and she set the platter in the center of the small table set for…two.

"Both," I murmured my answer looking at the table, eyebrows furrowing. "Were you expecting company?"

"Yes. You." Without glancing my way, she returned to the kitchen counter for a bread basket. "There is still clothing in your closet and dresser. It's all outdated, but it will cover your nakedness. Dress, and I will settle your overwhelmed and tumbling mind."

I moved to obey, striding back the pitch-black hallway—

My feet abruptly stopped.

Primrose had *sensed my thoughts*. She had also somehow known I approached.

"She has dragonblood gifts," I rasped in the oppressing rock tunnel.

Yessss.

"Not possible." I stared down the hallway that my other side's abilities allowed me to see without illumination. "If the history of our species is correct, she shouldn't even be *alive*."

My inner beast remained silent.

Primrose held the answers but had clearly wished for me to clothe my body first.

Shaking my head, I continued on, letting myself through an old oak door. My bedroom hadn't changed since I'd last been there, but as with the rest of the cavern I'd seen, it smelled of cleaning products, without a lick of dust on every surface—large bed frame, bed stands, and three bureaus.

As Primrose had said, clothing still hung in my closet,

severely outdated but free of dust. The thought of wearing polyester against my skin again after decades of going without caused a grimace to twist my face.

I pulled open the largest bureau's bottom drawer. Old jeans, worn and supple, lay piled unused and untouched since my days of playing at being a Greaser. While no fresh scent of laundry detergent clung to the threads, I found they fit as comfortably as they always had. Tight, white T-shirts along with a dozen other shirts lay in the drawer above. I pulled one on, the neck stretching from age.

Far from my usual attire, but I couldn't blame anyone but myself for not coming prepared.

Barefoot, I made my way back to the kitchen. Dahlia might have shown our granddaughter how to cook, but she hadn't taught her shit about manners. A chicken leg, half-devoured, lay on her plate along with a heaping pile of potatoes.

While chewing, she pointed at the empty chair across from her with her fork, and again, I found myself obeying, my gaze glued to her deadpan face as she swallowed.

I settled into the indicated chair but made no move to serve myself.

"What?" she asked without looking up from her plate.

"Primrose." I tried her name out loud, expecting she had been named for the flowers I used to bring back to Dahlia from excursions beyond our cavern.

My granddaughter lifted her head, golden brown eyes eerily similar to my own piercing me.

"Who were your fathers?"

"French Canadian twins," Primrose said while spearing a potato. "My mother met them while in town getting supplies with the truck one fall. She ended up staying with them for a week before returning home."

"Do you know their names?"

"No, and she never told my grandmother more than that."

"Were they properly bonded?"

She shrugged and tore a bite of chicken off the drumstick in her hand and chewed. "I've read most of the books down in the library, so I know it takes three dragonblood to procreate. I'm assuming my fathers were Blood Born, otherwise, I wouldn't be here, would I?"

"Joseph and Dahlia were not, and yet we created your mother."

"You're wrong." She speared another potato.

I sniffed. "And what gives you *that* confidence?"

"I…know things about people."

Crossing my arms, I raised an eyebrow.

"You don't believe me." She didn't ask a question.

"Are you reading my mind?"

A slow smirk curled one side of her lips. "Maybe."

"And what am I thinking now?"

"Beneath your wondering over my parentage, my Blood Born gifts, and longing for a certain someone—no, *two* someones—you're questioning how I lived and survived in these high reaches of the Grand Teton. Oh, and the truck? I upgraded years ago. It's in the garage far below, but you're well aware of how the winters are here." She busied herself with her food, ignoring my stare and continuing to spew out answers without me asking. "I know these things because we share blood. And you, Grandpapa, are very chatty between the ears."

Grandpapa.

My inner beast snickered.

"Grand*father*," I corrected.

She tilted her head to the side, finally looking me full on in the face. A soft huff left her mouth. "Whatever you say."

I pressed my lips tight.

She rolled her eyes. "Yes, I'll stop now. Feel free to ask

your own questions. Hearing another voice here in the cavern is better than focusing on the whispers in your head."

I wondered at the true strength of Primrose as my heart beat heavy in my chest. I had missed out on so much, so many years with my blood, the child I'd longed for—because I'd thought Elijah more worthy of me than the humans—or possibly *not* humans—I'd left behind.

A frown dented Primrose's brow as she peered at me.

Although she could read through the haze of my mind, I needed physical contact with my blood to gain all the knowledge I longed for. My mouth watered for the food she'd cooked, but I held out my hand and waited, anxious to have even the slightest connection with my granddaughter so I might have some sense of her thoughts and emotions.

She stared at my palm, knife and fork still clutched in her white knuckles.

"Please," I murmured, a slight flickering of energy between us in close proximity buzzing with anxiety. "You're my blood, which means our inner dragons will be able to communicate what I'm struggling to fully comprehend— answer all the questions I have."

"You don't deserve my memories."

"You're right." Shame flooded through me, causing my eyes to burn, but I kept my hand, palm up, on the table between us. "I have missed out on so much because of my own selfishness. If I had been aware—" My voice caught, and I swallowed the pain attempting to choke me. "I would never have left them. I'm begging you, please, allow me this gift."

A heavy breath lifted Primrose's chest and thinned her lips. She set the utensils down and slid her palm along mine.

Electrical currents shot up my arm, straight to my chest.

Our inner beasts sighed in unison, but rather than speaking, they shared memories with each other. Visions zapped through my head, and I grunted at the rush of emotions flooding my mind. All were of Dahlia and Primrose—not a single one of Joseph or the daughter I'd never met.

Countless trips to Jackson Hole in the old '50 Chevy pickup, snowed-in winter nights with tea and storytelling. Puzzles and reading in the library deep beneath us. Cleaning together, washing laundry, and baking.

My old lover, gray and wrinkled, lying on a bed, breathing her last caused a tear to trickle down my cheek. Had she been my fated mate, my seed would have sustained her life.

Chest aching, I closed my eyes, wetness dripping off my chin.

Primrose had prepared Dahlia's body for eternal rest— and flew her to the mountain's base where she buried her beneath a deep pile of rocks.

"You can shift?" I gasped.

Primrose pulled her hand away from mine but held my gaze, her calmness like a sea of glass beneath sunbeams of golden light. "Yes."

Strong.

My body slumped in my chair as I stared across the table. "Can..." I swiped at my wet face, ecstatic by the truth of my bloodline yet baffled by her existence. "Can you cloak yourself?"

She frowned, her puzzlement clear through the bond we had created.

I bent the light around me to explain, shimmering out of sight.

Her eyebrows shot upward, her giddiness making me smile. "How did you do that?"

I grabbed hold of her hand again, showing her through the blood bond between us, my ability creating the same within her as a Blood Born descendant learned from their elder—as I had from Father centuries earlier.

Instantly, she winked from existence but squeezed my hand. "This. Is. Amazing!" A heartbeat later, she reappeared, flashing a dazzling smile that made her look no more than a teenager.

"I'm twenty-two," she replied before I could ask the question that popped into my mind. "Sorry. Go ahead."

I peered into her eyes since I could see them again, noting the wisdom and knowledge of one who had lived a long life rather than her handful of years. "How old were you when Dahlia passed?"

"Eighteen. How old are you?" she asked, her head tilted to the side again. My granddaughter was beyond beautiful, a kind and caring spawn any Blood Born would be proud of.

I grinned, my chest swelling. "Four hundred and twenty-seven years."

Her jaw dropped open. "Will I live that long?" she asked, her voice breathless.

I pulled my hand away from my granddaughter's as her memory of Dahlia's aged face flitted through my mind. I reached for the serving spoon left in the skillet, needing to distract myself from what I'd lost. "Longer than a human, I'm sure, but not nearly the years I've had."

"Because I'm not a full Blood Born."

Once my plate was filled with chicken and potatoes, I glanced over at her. The tiniest bit of insecurity lay beneath her exterior. "How much do you know?"

"Not nearly enough." A hint of anger reached through the blood bond, causing my inner beast to whimper. Want to soothe and help Primrose rushed through us both. "You've visited the library—can you read the ancient language?"

She picked up her fork and stabbed her chicken. "No."

"Would you like to?" I asked, retrieving my own flatware so I could cut a bite off the breast on my plate.

"You'll teach me?"

"Easily." I found myself smiling, the ache of lost years and my mates left behind lessened by the opportunity ahead of me.

"Like how you taught me cloaking?" Primrose grinned and shimmered out of sight, her young, quick mind grasping what had taken me years to properly learn.

She's amazing.

"Yes."

"In that case—" she reached her hand over the table, fingers wiggling with the anticipation I could feel flowing off her like rocks tumbling down a mountainside "—show me everything."

Dinner forgotten, I gave my granddaughter the remaining knowledge, all the wisdom I had collected over the centuries, wondering how much was actually true.

CHAPTER 24
VANNI

Dolyn taking off without a word was like getting dumped all over again. With every hour that had passed, both Ashley and I felt sure he wouldn't return. My feet grew antsy, and even though Ashley clung to me, I couldn't calm myself enough to offer her the sense of solidity she searched for.

I put her over my lap and reddened her ass at her insistence, but even the release she'd soaked my thigh with didn't give her respite from worry.

Neither of us slept worth a shit on Dolyn's bed, and in the morning, we packed up a few days' worth of clothes. I booked a flight to Idaho Falls Regional, the closest I could get to the Tetons on short notice. Add a two-hour trip by car onto the end of the excursion, and we found ourselves exhausted and hard up to find accommodations in Jackson Hole, Wyoming.

Awareness of Dolyn had grown with every shortened mile between us, and both of our insides fluttered with anticipation. Mine, however, was laced with darkness, a deep-seated need to punish him for what he'd done to our female.

And myself.

Therapy had helped me work through most of my ex's abandonment, but my connection with Dolyn went far deeper than anything I'd experienced before. Even though we hadn't been intimate, the small touches we'd shared linked us together with an unbreakable bond.

He belonged to me, and I to him.

Need.

My teeth gritted over the voice I'd grown accustomed to but wasn't yet comfortable with. I tried to see it as another part of me rather than some sort of parasite, but I struggled with this new reality.

An inner beast.

Yessss.

He needed to shut the fuck up so I could sleep.

Ashley snuggled against my side on the lumpy mattress, the sheets smelling of our cum and sweat. Even though tiredness had tugged harshly on both of us, our naked flesh coming together demanded more than a snuggle.

The sun rose, and I felt more tired than the day before, my eyes gritty and mind hazed.

We'd made the right call in heading to where Elijah had told us his ancestral home lay, but where to go next and how to find his home escaped us. There was no listing of Dolyn Kemmerly—or anyone with that surname nearby. An old phonebook in the seedy motel room we'd managed to land a ways from Jackson Hole didn't offer shit, and exactly as Elijah had warned us, Dolyn wasn't on social media.

Thankfully, my club ran like a well-oiled machine, two of my dominants on staff more than able to manage the place in my absence. We would stay however long it was necessary to locate our mate.

We had breakfast at a little restaurant that made the most delicious homemade biscuits I'd ever tasted. Our waitress hadn't ever heard of Dolyn or anyone matching his description. Asking around town over the next couple of hours didn't offer any leads.

We felt Dolyn to the north, and the farther we went from Jackson Hole, the stronger the elusive cord between us became. Far from a pinpointed way, but a sense of rightness, a drawing of sorts that kept our focus on the snow-covered mountain range and gathering storm clouds.

The Tetons rose on our left, majestic and breath-catching, as otherworldly as Dolyn in that they appeared like a painted backdrop, much too beautiful for our earth.

"He'd said Grand Teton—not plural."

I nodded absently at Ashley's murmur, something she'd said a handful of times already. Gaze fixed on the range's tallest peak, I knew she spoke the truth. "Can you feel him?"

"I—I think so. It's more of a sense that I need to go that way."

I nodded, her explanation on point. Bundled in winter gear we'd grabbed before leaving New York, we sat cocooned in the SUV I'd rented, safe from the light snow swirling in eddies of wind that had begun to blow over the road.

Our third day without Dolyn had proved more taxing than the others as weariness from travel settled into our bones. I glanced over at Ashley to find purple bruises beneath her wide eyes, her shoulders slumped.

"What's the plan?" she whispered, purple-hued eyes cutting across the car's interior to gaze at the cragged peaks on my left.

"We'll find him, chain him to a fucking wall so he can't take off again, get some much-needed rest, then wake up and fuck him until he can't walk."

A spike of arousal shot across the cord between us, her tangy scent filling my nose and stiffening my cock.

She cast me a small smile. "Even tired enough to sleep for twenty-four hours straight, I crave you."

"Same, baby." I reached over and squeezed her hand before lacing my fingers through hers. The contact, the skin on skin I had longed for, for months, soothed me in ways I never realized I'd needed in my life.

Ashley had awakened my life with sunshine and warmth, thawing the coldness in my heart.

Then Dolyn had come in like a wrecking ball, making me yearn for things I'd never considered before.

Ours was a fucked-up situation, an out-of-this world circumstance, but I didn't want to live any other way. During the long flight, I relived our meeting Dolyn in my mind, and every second leading to where we'd ended up on a westbound flight for Idaho, knowing, somehow *assured*, that the three of us belonged together.

How the fuck that would work, I didn't have a clue. I hoped like hell that having dragonblood would make a threesome outside of the bedroom easier than I imagined. Three personalities, three individual minds and wants, regardless of the strange bonding of emotions—it promised to be one hell of a trying ride, especially with my past, Ashley's continued journey toward healing, and who the fuck knew what Dolyn's trauma entailed.

Considering his conflicting emotions and unease, I didn't imagine his past had been pretty.

Talking Dolyn into accepting us would be the first hurdle in our path heading to the happily ever after Ashley spoke of and I longed to give her.

I didn't imagine any picket fences or little cherub faces in our images. Instead, I envisioned a dungeon where I could keep my precious mates. Give them the darkness in my soul they both longed for. Offer them the pleasure their submission would ensure.

If Dolyn allowed himself to let go like I expected his beast drove him to do.

My dick thickened at the thought of having his complete submission. I wanted him under me, accepting every inch of my dick into his body, holding my gaze as I laid claim—and waste—to the soul he'd known until meeting me.

He belonged to me, and nothing was going to stop me from taking what was mine. I would not be denied—as his alpha, he would bow to me.

Yessss.

The voice in me whispered more with every passing day.

"I feel it too," Ashley whispered, squeezing my fingers and drawing my mind back to the SUV. "The darkness inside."

I shook my head at the absurdity of our conversation even though its truth resonated inside me. "Does it speak to you?"

"It's my newest best friend." Ashley laughed lightly, her voice shaky.

"Does the voice long for not just connection but pain?" I asked.

"Yes."

"And Dolyn?"

Ashley chewed on her lower lip, and I squeezed her hand to get her to stop. "He soothes the darkness inside." Her brow furrowed as though searching for words. "He's the gentleness I lost, the tender loving I never expected to find let alone enjoy. Does that make sense?"

I sifted through the emotions and hazy thoughts simmering from her, trying to understand her words. "I think so, yes."

She heaved a sigh but leaned forward a second later as we neared a closed-off intersection. "Turn left."

As though of the same mind, my brain had already made the choice to do as she said.

I pulled the SUV to a stop, eyeing the gate. "Stay here in the warmth."

She nodded, and I climbed out, the wind bitter and biting against my exposed face.

Better sense should have sent us southward toward Jackson Hole, but an urging kept me focused on moving nearer to the mountains.

The gate sat unlocked and swung open, the road beyond unplowed but easily seen with perhaps three inches of snow atop from a previous storm.

Seconds later, I climbed back into the SUV, shivering. "Goddamn, it's cold out there."

Ashley didn't speak, simply stared ahead at the looming snow-covered crags fading from sight beneath heavy clouds. She didn't mention waiting out the storm at our motel, and neither did I.

We drove in silence, deeper into the wilderness, the road narrowing and eventually fading into unplowed white. I pulled the SUV to a stop and put it in park.

"Now what?" Ashley asked, her voice small.

I stared into the darkening sky that promised more inches of snow than New York ever saw. Smart thinking would have taken us back the way we'd come, spending the night trying to sleep at the damn motel, and returning in the morning. My heart, the tug of Dolyn's presence before us, wiped being a responsible man from my head.

"We'll walk. Maybe Dolyn will feel us—come to us."

Ashley tugged on her woolen hat, zipped up her puffer coat, tugged on thick gloves, and hopped out of the SUV.

Doing the same as she had, I told myself we would find Dolyn. We *needed* him, the yearning a severe, driving force neither of us could ignore or deny.

Our beta, our full-blooded dragonblood was somewhere

in the foothills of Grand Teton, and nothing was going to stop us from locating him. The darkness inside me whispered an agreement, and I threw open my door, determined to seek out our fate.

CHAPTER 25

DOLYN

I woke from an erotic dream, sweating and dick leaking. Energy licked at my damp skin, heightening my pulse even though my heart thrummed with need.

Close.

I sat upright abruptly as I recognized the sensations swirling inside me. Darkness, pitch black as a tomb to a human, didn't keep my dragon's sight from making out every detail of my bedroom. The massive four-poster bed where I'd imagined fucking Vanni and Ashley, the washroom off to the side—and the lone pane of glass overlooking the valley far below.

I found myself striding across the warm rock floor and grasping the wooden frame of the window that was cloaked from the outside. Snow flew through the air, blinding my vision to within a mere twenty yards or so.

The beginnings of a mate bond shimmered through me, tugging me down—outside in weather no human would survive for very long.

My mates had come to find me.

I raced barefoot through the cavern to the old door

leading to the veranda. The slap of my palm slid it inward, and I stepped back from its path until it opened enough I could slip through.

Wind slammed me in the face, sleet biting at my naked body, but heat exploded in my core as their waning energy reached through the swirling whiteness.

My fragile human mates, lost in the wilderness below, were on the verge of freezing to death.

A roar ripped from my throat, and giving over to my beast nature, I leaped off the veranda, shifting in a blink. Our wings flapped and shot us forward like a bullet, our senses heightened. We couldn't see worth a shit in the storm, but the bond guided us downward—east and south toward our alpha and female.

My human half balked at the truth of the first but pushed thoughts of refusing to submit aside as the energy thickened between us, letting us know we drew nearer. Pain and numbness swirled from them, and our chest tightened, leaving us breathless.

Had hypothermia already set in? Were they beyond saving?

Another roar ripped from us, and we tucked our wings, diving as we pinpointed their location. The ground shook beneath us as we landed, and we stalked to an overhang and the two lumps huddled together somewhat out of the storm.

We blew a breath of warm air over them, immediately melting snow off their clothing, and Vanni slowly opened his eyes. The sense of loss and heartache emanating from him faded as his mouth worked.

"D-Dolyn?" he stuttered from the cold, his eyes widening.

Yes.

We hoped his inner dragon could hear us.

"Ashley…" Vanni turned, motioning stiffly toward her.

We focused our attention on our female. She lay

unmoving beside him, her face and lips pale. Another puffed exhale ruffled the snow-crusted hair around her face. Reaching forward with our front foot and extended, curved claws drew a gasp from Vanni, but he didn't move as we cradled Ashley and pulled her against our heated body. She stirred, and the relief, the rush of peacefulness through her eased our mind.

Vanni looked into our eyes and stumbled to stand. "You're fucking huge."

A beast-like chuckle rumbled in our chest, and we settled back onto our haunches, holding out our other front foot.

Vanni moved into our grasp and wrapped his arms around our ankle. The trust he showed, the sense of rightness we felt having them grasped against our chest caused overwhelming emotion to swell through every inch of our scaled body.

We leapt into the sky, clutching our mates close, trying to shelter them the best we could from the elements as we flew toward home. Pressed against our scales, they would feel the heat of the fire inside, the burning embers untouched by the cold. And, with our claws wrapped mostly around their core, all vital inner organs would also be protected from the winter wind.

After what seemed like forever, not nearly fast enough, we touched down on the veranda.

Primrose threw open the door and hurried outside, a blanket wrapped around her flapping in the wind. She whipped it off and wrapped it around Ashley as we shifted, my human half taking control. I grabbed my female before she could fall to the ground and hurried inside, Primrose slipping beneath Vanni's shoulder to help him along behind us.

A laser shot of dragon fire flew past my lips to the fire-place across the room, lighting the wood Primrose had stacked but never used because of the cavern's natural heat. Flames flickered upward, quickly catching the dried logs.

Clutching Ashely to me, I knelt before the fire, sending all of my love, my warmth, my desire through the weak energy shimmering between us.

Vanni dropped to his knees beside me, and Primrose helped rid him of his frozen hat and gloves. He grumbled as she tried to peel his coat off him.

"The fuck are you?" Vanni muttered, his tiredness like a living thing eating at my mind.

"Dolyn's granddaughter."

Silence coated the cavern except for the snap of the fire before us as Vanni stared up at her. His gaze roamed over her long, gold hair and returned to her face. "You have his eyes."

Primrose dipped her head, unsmiling, and tossed his coat aside.

"How the fuck old are you, Dolyn?" Vanni asked, his voice strengthening.

"Four hundred plus."

"Shit." He scooted closer, slipping Ashley's hat off her head and brushing the hair from her face with trembling fingers. "She seems okay through this cord thing between us. What are you feeling from her, Dolyn?"

I touched the energy between us, sifting through her pain, the beginnings of her awareness. "She will be fine."

"The best place for your female in is your bed," Primrose said. "Between the two of you where she belongs."

My brow furrowed. I'd shown her much of my own memories but had kept anything sexual to myself. "How do you know about such things?"

"I read, remember?" She met my stare. "And the emotions swarming off all three of you are as obvious to me as the green of your alpha's eyes."

I swallowed hard as my inner dragon purred. I hated the

truth of her words—and wondered how the fuck she guessed the truth.

"I *know* because I'm gifted."

"No shit," I muttered, standing and pulling Ashley's chilled, limp body into my arms. "You can actually read *everything* in my mind?"

Head tilting to the side, she peered into my eyes, her pupils swirling. A small smirk lifted her lips. "A little because you're my blood, but it's dragon voices I hear."

Growling over the complete lack of privacy from my grandchild, I turned and strode toward the hallway across the cavern.

"He wants you to follow him," Primrose told Vanni behind me before I could order him to do so.

I didn't turn to see if he would do as Primrose suggested, but the lantern light filtering behind me—and the tether of energy between me and my mate—let me know he did. My bedroom lay up a winding hallway, higher into the caverns of my home.

While I had no issue meandering about in the pitch-black, my mates would. Elijah had updated his place, and it was definitely time I did the same—but those thoughts, I would save for another day.

I pushed my bedroom door in with my foot and strode toward the bed.

Ashley stirred in my arms, and I nuzzled my nose beneath her ear. "You're safe, my female."

She let out a sigh, snuggling against me, but I set her on the edge of the bed and unzipped her coat.

"C-cold," she managed, her body shivering as Primrose set the lantern on the bed stand.

"We'll warm you up, promise." While my cock jerked at the thought of how *warm* I wanted our female, I focused on removing her clothing, right down to bare skin.

The rustle of cloth on the other side of the bed let me know Vanni did the same.

"I'm headed back to bed, but I'll leave the lantern," Primrose said, and the door shut quietly behind her.

"I have a million and one questions," Vanni muttered while climbing beneath the covers of my bed, goose bumps covering his trembling form.

"They can wait." I snipped the words and helped Ashley scoot to the middle of the bed.

Vanni wrapped his arms around her, and she snuggled into him as I climbed in behind, settling against her back.

The feel of her frigid skin on mine caused my brow to furrow, but Vanni's hand on her ass—against my lower abs— clenched my jaw. My shaft throbbed against Ashley's thigh as I fought off the need to shift higher so the backs of Vanni's fingers would brush against my cock.

A heavy, shuddered sigh rippled through Ashley's body between us, and I met Vanni's exhausted stare atop her head. Lust simmered like a cauldron between us. Heat and release were what my dragon craved, but I still struggled to accept.

Arousal, tangy and sweet wafted past my nose as Ashley stretched between us.

"You need to rest," I growled at her while holding Vanni's gaze.

A twinkle lit Vanni's eyes as he narrowed his eyes. "I think not."

CHAPTER 26

ASHLEY

A growl rumbled the chest pressed against my back at Vanni's words, and the one squashing my breasts replied in similar fashion.

Mates.

Eyes still closed, I soaked in their warmth, their heady scents as my body rushed to life with heat and need.

While my limbs felt heavy and on the verge of sleep, I couldn't ignore the sudden pulse between my thighs or the two thick cocks jutting into my leg.

I breathed deeply, hints of Vanni's cologne clinging to the whiskered neck against my face. Dolyn pressed against my entire backside, his hand soothing over my hip, to my knee, and up again, his touch gentle and tender as always.

Wetness eased from my pussy, coating my lower lips, and I gyrated against the hard bodies cradling me.

Vanni grasped hold of my ass with a possessive grip. "See?" he said with a low chuckle, heating my core even more. "She doesn't want to rest. Do you, baby?" He pushed my hair over my shoulder and scooted down to kiss my bared skin.

I tilted my head back, giving him better access to my neck as he rained open-mouthed kisses, nibbles, and licks leading toward my mouth.

My pussy pulsed with need—for both of them. "Please," I whispered a second before Vanni claimed my lips.

We both groaned at the contact, pulling a similar noise from Dolyn, who continued to stroke my thigh.

"Damn you," he growled, lifting my leg over his, spreading me wide. He buried his face in my hair and reached around my front to feather his fingertips along my bare pubic bone.

Whimpering against Vanni's mouth, I tilted my hips forward, needing Dolyn's touch lower. Vanni squeezed my ass cheek with the perfect sting that made my clit throb, and Dolyn's wandering fingers trailed down over the hard nub, straight into my dripping core.

"Oh." I tore my mouth from Vanni and clenched my eyes shut as Dolyn slid two fingers deep into me.

"See." Vanni's voice betrayed his smirk.

A war tugged through Dolyn, and while Vanni was sure of his position in our trio, Dolyn didn't approve of what he felt was pushing me past my limits.

I longed for a more solid bond among us, one that would settle the tumbling emotions radiating from Dolyn's troubled mind.

"I want you." I forced my eyelids up and nearly gasped at the brilliant green of Vanni's eyes, his adoration and desire for both of us swamping my mind.

Dolyn rubbed against the front of my inner walls with gentle strokes, and I moaned, fighting to keep my eyes open.

"Need you too," I said, lifting my arm behind me to grasp at the back of his head.

"It'll be too much, too soon," he grumbled, sliding his fingers in and out of my pussy.

"No." I spoke the word with a conviction I didn't quite feel, but I wanted to try. "Please."

Vanni shifted, rubbing his thick cock along my inner thigh, bumping and sliding along Dolyn's hand.

Dolyn hissed.

Vanni chuckled. "Why fight what we both want?"

"Fuck you, Vanni," Dolyn said.

"I suppose I could let you fuck me someday," Vanni mused, thrusting along the route he'd sent his hard length seconds earlier. "If you're a good boy."

A shot of lust laced the energy connecting me to Dolyn, and I couldn't help my smile. "Take me. Both of you," I demanded.

With a groan, Dolyn slid his fingers from my pussy, and Vanni didn't waste time replacing the head of his cock at my opening.

"Look at me, Ash."

I peered into Master's eyes as he pushed in, stretching me until fully seated against my womb. "G-God…"

"You're so fucking wet. Tight." He nudged in deeper against my cervix, pulling a gasp from my lips at the delicious ache.

"Go easy on her," Dolyn grumbled.

"Want him in here with me, Ash?" Vanni stroked deep. "Or in your ass?"

"We cannot spill together against her womb." Dolyn hissed, running the fingers he'd fucked me with over my pucker. Slick from my arousal, his rimming fingertips caused my breath to hitch with desire I never thought to experience.

"There," I whispered, ready for the final step toward healing. My innocence had been stolen in every way, and the hole Dolyn teased needed to be reclaimed as the others had already. "Take my ass, Dolyn. Own it, help me reclaim that part of me. I—I need to make new memories to overshadow the others."

A shudder rippled over Dolyn's chest still pressed against my spine, but he didn't mutter a peep.

"Let him in, baby," Vanni murmured against my lips, his breath sweet and hot.

"Ashley." Worry coated Dolyn's voice and his mind.

"Please," I whispered, turning my head to find his troubled eyes flaring with heat. "I want you. Need you inside me."

He pressed his lips against mine, gently pushing past my tight ring.

I grunted and bore down, allowing his finger to slide in deep.

"Mmm." Another smile coated Vanni's murmur as he slowly fucked into my pussy. "I can feel your finger through that thin membrane, boy. Yes," he hissed as Dolyn stroked, a gush of warmth inside me letting me know Vanni leaked his usual unnatural—or perhaps normal—amount of pre-cum. "Fuck." He buried and groaned, cock bucking inside me. "Use our arousal and stretch her good, beta." He pulled out fully, and I whimpered at the loss as Dolyn worked Vanni's cock a few times between my thighs, cockhead and knuckles brushing against my wet core.

Both hissed, their lust like flames over my skin. I burned from the inside out as we experienced arousal threefold.

Wet fingers returned to my asshole, and I bore down again, groaning as two breached me with ease. "Tingly," I gasped as he pressed in deep with a complete lack of sting.

"Mmm," Vanni hummed and slid back into my core, holding my head to his chest. "So sweet, baby. Your pussy was made for my cock."

I whimpered as they both fucked into me, Dolyn's scissoring fingers stretching me as Vanni continued to gently rock into my body.

Words weren't necessary. I could feel their rising desire, the rush to push for release, their determination to make sure I remained comfortable and present.

Vanni snaked a hand between us, gliding fingertips over my clit.

"Need…" I panted, so close to coming that my eyelids squeezed shut, brow furrowed as I tried to keep from tipping over.

"Please, Dolyn." I licked my dry lips. "I'm ready."

He eased his fingers out of my ass at the same time Vanni pulled free from my pussy.

I whimpered again but tilted my hips back, already knowing Dolyn's intent.

Gripping my waist, he thrust into the wetness Vanni had vacated.

"Yessss," I hissed, the heat of his shaft sinking deep inside me causing my pulse to thrum.

"Wait for us, Ash."

Eyes clenched shut, I nodded at my master's command, shivering—trembling, half delirious.

Dolyn pulled out of my pussy, and the blunt head of his wet cockhead pressed to my pucker. "Breathe," he murmured against my ear, voice low and ragged.

I did as told and bore down, allowing him to slide past my ring without resistance.

He growled, and I reached back to grab hold of his ass, digging my fingers into his hot, hard flesh to draw him closer.

"Please," I whined, backing against him.

He sank in deep, Vanni's pre-cum slicker than any lube, the tingling sensation a delicious addition of fuel for my simmering climax.

"Eyes on me."

I jerked my eyelids up and held Vanni's gaze. Fire burned in his green orbs, twice as brilliant as I'd ever seen. "Master."

He notched into my pussy and thrust, the double stretch between my thighs unbearably sweet, a delicious sting that faded as fast as it struck.

"Oh, my God." I moaned and panted, the desire in his focus as he filled me causing my heart to stutter.

Vanni wrapped his arms around me—as did Dolyn, and they clutched onto one another. Buried deep, they stilled, and the emotion swarming over me made my throat swell.

Alarm radiated from both of them.

"They're happy tears," I whispered.

"Let us love you, sweet female," Dolyn crooned in my ear, nudging into my ass.

I bit my lip until the tang of blood hit my tongue. Dolyn claimed he would never hurt me, but I needed something more. Ached for the burn I'd expected, the breath-stealing sting of having my ass stuffed full.

"Give it to her."

Dolyn grunted his hatred of being told what to do but pulled out a few inches and pushed back in.

My body shook although sweat broke out on my skin as I panted. "Again," I whined the word, attempting to writhe between their arms of banded steel.

Vanni retreated to the crown, and as he sank back in, Dolyn backed away.

"Oh God." I croaked as they took turns fucking into me— but it wasn't enough.

"Pinch her clit, boy. Nice and hard."

"No," Dolyn stated through gritted teeth while sinking balls deep into my hole.

"Do it, or I'll whip your ass raw."

"Don't threaten me with a good time," Dolyn snapped.

"Please!" I cried out, loving their verbal banter and conflicting emotions but needing to come.

Dolyn nuzzled into my hair and slid a hand between Vanni's stomach and mine, rubbing over my swollen clit.

"Harder. Please." Shuddering, I scraped my teeth against Vanni's pec.

"Now," my master demanded.

Dolyn's cock bucked in my ass as shame washed over him. "I'm sorry, my female." He dug his fingernails into my throbbing nub, and Vanni stabbed deep against my cervix.

I screamed against his chest, clawing at his back as my body pulsed with clenching pulls, desperate to draw him deeper. He and Dolyn slammed into me over and over, grunting like wild animals. Fingers dug into my hip with the bruising pain I adored, and I soared higher, crying out and clenching around them both.

Dolyn buried deep in my ass and stilled. Heat erupted from his throbbing cockhead.

"Fuck. Yes." Vanni stabbed into me twice more and erupted, a gush of his cum causing my insides to tighten.

A final pulse in my core milked him, my ring tight around Dolyn's girth.

All three of us breathed heavy, gasping for breath, tremors rippling through our bodies. Adoration, tender warmth, and satisfaction slid over me, our shared feelings mingling in my chest and heart.

I nuzzled against Vanni's hard pecs, releasing a heavy sigh.

Both cocks buried in me slowly softened as our heartbeats regulated in time with one another. Wetness leaked around Vanni's cock.

My limbs tingled, the lightness in my chest causing a smile so wide my jaw ached. The energy rippling from both men sent shivers over my skin, pebbling every inch of me.

"Okay?" Vanni asked, pulling his head back to peer into my face.

"More than," I murmured, eyes blinking slowly.

His gaze flicked over my head, and instant wariness tickled down my spine from Dolyn. Without a word, Vanni released his hold on my hip and slid his forearm along my skin as though reaching for Dolyn behind me. His arm flexed, and the two men crushed me between them, shoving Dolyn's groin tighter against my ass.

Flickers of renewed desire in him dampened my pussy around Vanni as I realized he must have grabbed hold of Dolyn's ass to pull him closer. "Mine," Vanni said, a challenge in his eyes.

Tension rolled off Dolyn, and I could imagine his jaw clenched.

"Don't bother fighting it, beta," Vanni said with a smirk and half-lidded eyes. "I'm going to own you, every inch, every emotion, and there's not a fucking thing you can do about it except submit to your alpha."

My pussy clutched at his length, but the arousal fled as a flash of anger rolled through Dolyn. He gently backed out of me, leaving me empty.

Vanni chuckled as Dolyn left the bed, his gaze tracking after him. "He will submit," he whispered as though to himself.

"You can't make him."

Vanni glanced down at me, a frown flickering over his dark brow. "You can't feel his desire to drop to his knees and worship me?"

The vision flooding my mind rushed arousal through me again. "A little."

"And you believe in this dragon shifter blood between us is real, right?"

"I do."

"Then our beta doesn't have a chance. He belongs to us— *between* us."

The truth of Vanni's words settled in my soul, and I closed my eyes as longing for that exact vision—Dolyn in me, Vanni in Dolyn—rushed through me like the strongest gale winds bent on tumbling the Tetons.

"Yes." My word rang in my ears even though I hadn't realized I'd spoken out loud.

"He's the bridge between us," Vanni continued filling my head with images of us all linked together. "His cock in you, mine in him."

Vanni's length thickened inside me, and he pulled out, gently easing into my sopping pussy in a lewd squelching noise.

A toilet flushed, but I lost myself in the glide of his length, the drag of him against my inner walls. "More." I gasped as he thrust against my womb.

With a growl, he rolled, pinning me beneath him, grabbing my legs and pressing them to the sides with a bruising grip on the back of my knees. "Open wide, baby. Take every inch." He slammed into me over and over, every brush against my cervix hurting in the best way possible.

I clutched at his arms, whimpering at the delicious pain, need rising to sear my skin.

"Go easy on her, you fucker!" Dolyn's growled words, the aggravation lancing over me, couldn't kill the passion rising inside my core. The bed dipped beside us, but Vanni held my stare, darkness swirling in his pupils.

"Harder." I groaned, and Dolyn cursed, settling near my head.

"Open up and suck him," Vanni said, lifting onto his haunches between my spread thighs. He stared down at where he pierced my body in short, harsh thrusts. "Take him deep, Ash. Make him blow his load down your throat."

I tipped my head to find Dolyn looming over me, teeth clenched as he jerked his swollen cock. He didn't thoroughly want this. Some part of him did, the same darkness inside Vanni—our beasts, I realized.

Three hisses of agreement whispered in my head.

Jaw unhinging, I opened wide.

With a groan—almost of pain—Dolyn moved closer, easing the head of his cock into my mouth.

"Give it to her," Vanni demanded, spreading my legs far enough an ache settled in my joints.

A rush of wetness slickened his thrusting cock, and I closed my eyes as Dolyn pressed in into my throat, cutting off my oxygen.

"Ashley—fuck." He groaned and pulled out, cursing again as I laved at his length with my tongue, hollowing my cheeks and trying to suck him deep again. "My female." Dolyn slowly slid back in, but needing more, I reached overhead and sank my fingernails into his meaty thighs.

"Mmm." Vanni murmured, still thrusting like a damn freight train into my quivering pussy. "She wants it all—give your sweet female what your inner dragon is begging for."

Dolyn slammed into my throat with a whimper as though losing control, and my heartbeat accelerated. Breath cut off.

"With me," Vanni said, and their thrusts came in time, owning me with a fierceness I couldn't stand against.

Submission to their onslaught hit me like an ecstasy of its own, flooding me with purpose and power.

I groaned around Dolyn's cock, all ability to think, to move outside instinctual muscle spasms, ripped from my mind. My body sucked them both deep, milking Vanni's cock, swallowing Dolyn's length.

As one, they shouted, hot cum shooting into me from either end, sending me headlong into a climax so powerful darkness hazed my vision.

CHAPTER 27
VANNI

Ashley passed out, completely spent, but the cord between us assured me she hadn't been hurt in any way. Similar exhaustion pulled at me, but after cleaning her up and biting back my chuckle at Dolyn's attempt to pretend I wasn't in the same room with him, I lay awake.

I didn't doubt a goddamn thing about the three of us. Being in the cavern-like home of Dolyn's had at first confused me. His scent everywhere, the pulsing energy of the mountain rippling through my bones...I belonged there. With them. The cord among the three of us had strengthened from our coming together but not nearly enough for the voice inside me demanding completion.

I wondered what that might look like, and the vision of Dolyn being the bridge between me and Ashley once more filled my mind.

The thought to demand Dolyn burrow his cock between her thighs and spread his cheeks in offering to me roused my dick, and I slowly jacked myself while staring in the dark.

Dolyn had extinguished the lantern, and although I

assumed pitch-black coated the bedroom, I found myself able to make out movement as he settled on his side facing us. A hint of gold glimmered, and I knew he peered at me, same as I fought to do with him.

"I've never wanted a man before," I said, unable to stand the tense and hungry silence between us. "I've never *taken* a man before."

Dolyn grunted but didn't reply.

"Have you?"

"What?" he asked on a heavy sigh.

"Fucked a man or ever wanted to be fucked by one?"

"Yes, and yes." He bit the words out as though annoyed, but all I sensed was lingering satisfaction and a hint of unease.

"Hmm." I narrowed my gaze, searching for the outline of his face in the dark. "My mate has given the gift of his virginity to someone other than me."

"Fuck off, Vanni."

"I am," I said with a lazy grin, gripping my dick harder, smearing the pre-cum beading at the head.

"Fuck." Dolyn's mutter widened my smile.

"Want a taste?" A few more muttered curses sounded in the darkness around us, Dolyn's discomfort intensifying. "Something you need to tell me, boy?"

He growled.

"Unlike your granddaughter, I'm not a mind reader, so how about you fill me in on why you have such an aversion to my cum."

"I don't desire it."

He lied, but I would get the truth out of him eventually. Tonight, I didn't have enough brain cells or vigor to punish his ass as I'd promised myself I would do once we'd located him.

"Did you like having your ass filled?" I asked instead.

"Yes." At least he hadn't hesitated with that truth. An echo hissed through my ears, and I wondered if our beasts could communicate more clearly than our human halves could hear in our heads.

"You'll like my cock in your ass ten times better," I stated with absolute assurance, stroking to my base.

Dolyn snorted and rolled onto his back. "Cocky son of a bitch," he grumbled to himself.

"You'll find out soon enough." My balls tightened, and I considered ordering him to finish me off. I peered in the darkness and could just make out the line of his wide shoulders to the dip of his waist. Need radiated off him like a heater, enticing and warm. "I can feel your desire for me, Dolyn."

He huffed a breath.

"Don't bother denying it. Your lust is potent and heady as fuck."

"Blow your damned load and go to sleep already," he stated sternly as though fed up, even as the scent of his arousal snuck up my nose.

I snickered and jerked harder, tugging upward and slamming my grip down to my base. "What is it about you that turns me on so much, hmm, Dolyn?" I gathered more precum oozing from my crown and thrust back up through my harsh grip, the sound of me fucking my fist wet and sloppy. "Your tight, round ass looks like it could take a lot of cane marks before I shove so damn deep inside you lose your breath."

Dolyn's low groan pushed me over the edge, and I swore as ropes of cum shot up over my abs.

Three climaxes in a matter of an hour, but at least this final one wasn't a gushing flood of spunk.

This awakened dragonblood thing was the shit though. I'd never come so much and so hard in all my years.

"Goddamn." I gasped and milked the last spurts of cum from my dick. "Just the *thought* of fucking you tips me over the edge. Can't imagine how good it's going to feel when you finally give in and let me shove my dick up your tight pucker. Gonna make it hurt so good."

He muttered a few more curses, and material landed on my chest. "Clean yourself and go to sleep," he hissed at me even as I imagined his cock bucked and leaked for release.

Chuckling, I actually obeyed my beta's command, and as I slipped into much needed rest, I realized I'd never been so happy in my life.

I woke to Ashley's lips wrapped around my cock, same as every morning since sharing a bed at Dolyn's suite back in New York. How many times had I shot my cum down her throat? She salivated for it. Begged, even while in the SUV from the airport to Jackson Hole.

With a groan, I grabbed hold of her head and held her still while fucking up into her lush mouth, jamming into her throat.

No admonishment of my roughness rose from the other side of the bed, and I glanced over. The lantern glowed softly from the bed stand, revealing Dolyn had gone.

His scent remained as did that awareness of his proximity, and I filled my lungs, longing and lust swelling through me, tightening my balls.

"Gonna come, baby. Fill up your belly like you're lusting for."

Ashley hummed with excitement, the scent of her arousal thickening in the air.

"Now." I shot, groaning with each spurt she swallowed, lapping and sucking as though insatiable.

"So good," she said with a sigh once I finished, kissing the tip of my softening dick. One last lick over the slit, and she crawled up my body, settling her sopping core against my groin. "I can't get enough of you and your sweet, tingly cum."

"Tingly?"

She nodded, her eyes full of amusement, a soft smile on her lips. "Best thing I've ever tasted."

"It's because he's your alpha."

I lifted my head as Ashley squeaked and rolled off me, pulling the sheet off me and up to her chin.

Primrose stood in the doorway I hadn't realized had been left open. "His cum will prolong your human life, same as Dolyn's will his once you've fully bonded." She pointed at me, and a rush of hot arousal swelled my cock at the thought of tasting Dolyn.

"And that—" she motioned toward my still stiff cock I put a hand over, "is because you're fated mates. You'll fuck like animals long after humans would slump in exhaustion."

"Excuse me, but *who are you?*" Ashley asked, her voice small even as jealousy rippled from her.

"Primrose. Dolyn's granddaughter."

"Holy…" Ashley cleared her throat. "He never said anything about having a granddaughter."

"Because he wasn't aware of my existence until he showed up."

"How long has it been since he's been home?"

"A very long time." Primrose stood in the doorway and went on to tell us both a bit of history I felt sure Dolyn would have preferred to share. But Primrose, while full of knowledge, didn't seem to have the best people skills. She had no filter when talking about her other grandparents, the death of her mother, how she didn't know her fathers, or that Dolyn had taught her the most glorious things by simply holding her hand.

"You've lived here all twenty-two years of your life?" I asked, taking in the threadbare robe around her shoulders that should have been tossed out the generation before.

"Yes."

"Don't get out much, do you?"

"No." Her whispered answer revealed more than mere fact.

"Now that we're here, you can leave," I told her.

She blinked, her amber-like eyes glowing in the lantern's low light.

"Vanni!" Ashley hissed, backhanding my chest.

"What? Primrose has been keeping this home in Dolyn's absence, giving up her childhood and teenage years." I shrugged. "She's free to go experience everything she's missed out on is all I'm saying." I peered at Primrose to find tears welling in her eyes, but I got a sense she wasn't upset with me.

"You understand exactly what I'm saying, don't you? You can hear that inner…thing inside me echoing my human thoughts."

She nodded and inhaled a deep breath. "Breakfast is in the kitchen. So is your beta. He's grumpy." Her gaze roamed over my nakedness, her head tilting to the side. "I would suggest fucking him."

Ashley gasped, and I snapped my jaw shut.

"Make him submit and claim him." Primrose continued as though her suggestion I own her grandfather's ass hadn't shocked us. "It'll lessen the war in his mind that kept him—and me—up all night before your arrival."

A lick of jealousy slithered through my stomach over her ability to know Dolyn's beastly thoughts.

She shrugged. "I'm gifted." Primrose turned and disappeared without another word.

"Let's go eat," Ash said, hopping off the bed as my mind reeled.

My stomach rumbled, but I yearned for something more than food.

I wanted that life-sustenance Primrose had spoken of. My mouth watered at the thought of Dolyn's dick in my mouth, and I rolled off the bed, determined to ease the need inside me.

"Shower first," I told Ashley, glancing toward the bathroom's open door.

The sweet scent of her arousal hit my nose, stronger than I'd noticed before. Was it possible that as the cord between us tightened I'd become more aware of her?

Yessss.

The darkness whispered inside me, and as I grabbed hold of Ashley's waist and pulled her up into my arms, her rush of desire—feelings of love—nearly buckled my knees.

"You're mine," I whispered, trying to read into the soul her purple-blue eyes revealed.

She brushed her lips across my mouth, her contentment and happiness swelling over me like waves. "Always."

Now if only I could get Dolyn to think and feel the same, I told myself while carrying Ashley into the bathroom.

CHAPTER 28

DOLYN

Late morning light flooded through the windows of the main living space. Not a speck of dust lined a single surface, not a streak or smudge on the glass letting in the rising sun.

I stood in the warm beams and sipped the coffee Primrose had left out, my mind full of conflicting emotions. I was torn, yet happy. In the short time alone with my granddaughter, I'd gotten to know her, and although young, her knowledge and her ability to hear some of my thoughts staggered my reality. In addition to her, fate had gifted me mates, a dream I'd given up on. But lingering distaste of being beta to a human male turned my stomach.

I took another sip of coffee regardless of the pit in my gut.

My head insisted neither Vanni nor Ashley were worthy of my blood, but the physical connection, the contact we had shared last night solidified the truth of who they were in the depths of my soul. I closed my eyes against the sunlight, remembering the exquisite pain Vanni had lavished on me, the bruising that had faded much too quickly because of my dragonblood and its ability to heal faster than a human.

Our mates will have no such benefits.

"Sure they will."

My eyelids jerked up at Primrose correcting my inner beast.

She meandered to the old-fashioned coffee percolator and poured herself a cup, Tiggy heeling on her left side.

"Explain," I demanded, wishing the dog had come to me like his swiveling head and needy gaze suggested he wanted to do. I even patted my thigh, causing him to whine, but he stayed by her. Such loyalty—he was an excellent beast, one deserving of much praise.

"An alpha's cum prolongs his mates' lives," Primrose explained as if I were a child.

"Meaning Vanni's will for Ashley, but what about him? He's mostly human."

My beast purred over my inadvertently admitting to Vanni's position in our trio.

I grimaced, my insides twisting hard enough my chest threatened to cave inward.

"As a royal Blood Born, yours will sustain him, as will the bond once you let go of your stubbornness."

Eyes closing, I fought to breathe evenly as my cock swelled inside its denim prison. I could see Vanni on his knees for me, drinking me down and begging for more. Not for the first time, I imagined bonding with my mates, and the desire to do so sent warring feelings through my mind and heart.

"Someday, I'm going to find the ones meant for me. I can't wait to share all I know."

Her statement ripped my thoughts off my own issues. My jaw clenched at the idea of two human males touching my granddaughter.

"Relax, Grandpapa," she said, her voice snippy. "While I appreciate your protective instincts, I don't need you to hold my hand. I've done well enough without you since birth."

Talk about a dagger to the chest.

She shrugged, too damn privy to my emotions. "Go on, Tiggy, you little love bug. I know you want to."

Tiggy leapt toward me but drew up in front of my legs, tongue lolling as he smiled up at me.

"Good boy," I murmured, crouching down to scratch behind his ears. He flipped onto his back, big brown eyes begging me for tummy scratches. "I'm going to spoil you rotten, yes I am." I chuckled as he sneezed, giving him exactly what he wanted.

Primrose snickered. She'd propped herself against the kitchen counter to watch me with her dog—*my* dog. Another sip of her coffee, and she straightened her old robe that fell to mid-thigh. "I'm leaving today."

I'd sensed her itchy feet but hadn't realized the extent of her drive. "Where are you going?" I asked while standing, Tiggy laying his head on my bare foot.

She glanced out the windows, at the snow-covered foothills falling below us. "I'm not sure, but now that you're here...I feel as though something is calling me out there into the endless world."

"It's hardly endless," I grumbled, trying to swallow down my disappointment she wanted to leave after our just having found each other.

"You need the cavern to yourselves for a while."

Yessss.

"You have to bond properly, and I have no desire to be around for *that*." She shuddered.

"We'll be discreet, I promise. Please stay."

Primrose snorted. "Vanni is *hardly* discreet. He was just

lying up there with his penis stiff as a rod, his attempt to cover that monster with a single hand laughable."

"What?" Anger and instant lust raced through me. My cock went hard in a blink.

"He and your female were kissing." She waved her hand. "Doing…*things*."

"In front of you?" I couldn't keep the anger from my voice even though the memory of touching and fucking roused me.

"Ashley hopped off him the second I walked in and buried herself under the sheet."

"Did you knock first?"

She tipped her head to the side as though baffled by my annoyance. "Why would I knock in my own home?"

I heaved a sigh. "You're not ready to expand your horizons, Primrose. There's so much you don't know about people. Privacy."

"I'm going." She glanced out the window again.

Feeling her stubbornness, and well aware who she'd inherited that character trait from, I didn't bother arguing. I pressed against my hard length, wishing the damn thing away, but it was no use. "Where does the pull come from?"

"The south."

I considered her words while sifting through her excitement, anxiety, and desires. While I had been certain Elijah and I had been the last dragonblood to roam the earth, I'd found that to be far from the truth. Perhaps there were two worthy of her blood, an alpha and beta who would match her drive and intelligence.

"There was a Blood Born clan in the Grand Canyon before my birth," I finally said, expecting the words would send her southward before the sun sank.

Her head jerked toward me, her thoughts without doubt

flying as fast as a dragon's wings would shoot her away from me.

"You'll shift to make the journey?" I asked, swearing I could feel her desire to leave immediately.

"I can get there faster if I do."

Rather than lecture her about men, relationships, and taking things slow, I held out my arms.

"No hugs until you put that away," she said, moving toward me with a smirk, her finger pointing at my bulge.

"Yeah. Sorry." Heat actually flooded my face—shame over my body's desires for the first time in my goddamn life.

"Don't be ashamed, Grandpapa," Primrose said, reaching up to touch my cheek, and I didn't argue the name she'd gifted me. As a beta, papa fit better than father, even if I wasn't too thrilled with my title—or station. "You're blessed to have found your mates. I only hope I'm able to do the same someday."

"You're always welcome home, Primrose."

"Thanks, but I'll definitely wait until you three get your relationship figured out—and can keep sexual actions in the bedroom where they belong."

Tiggy lopped around us as I clasped Primrose's upper body tight with my free arm, breathing in and memorizing the scent of rosemary from the soaps and shampoos she made. "A desire to bond with one's mates oftentimes overrides one's sense of propriety."

She stepped back, her eyes gleaming. "I can't wait to find that out for myself."

I swallowed my groan along with a mouthful of cooled coffee as she flounced away. Best she went out on her own, for if I shadowed my granddaughter, I would incinerate the first male to touch her. She disappeared down the hallway, and I returned my attention to the beautiful creature sitting at my feet.

"You were her faithful companion, but now you'll be mine. I hope that's okay with you."

Tiggy huffed a quiet bark and flopped again, showing me his belly.

"At least *you* see me as alpha," I muttered, squatting to give the good boy what he wanted. I ran my fingers through his thick fur, thinking about Primrose and the future she planned to seek out.

No one would truly be worthy of her. A direct descendant of the royal line, more dragonblood than human, she ought to be mated to a prince. She deserved someone like Elijah.

My brow furrowed as I remembered his mates, the female doubtless already bonded to him. Had she not been destined for him, I never would have found Ashley and Vanni. For a brief moment, a flash of a heartbeat, I considered sending Primrose to my ex-lover, thinking perhaps if a better option stood before Elijah, a true Blood Born, he might set aside the married couple.

My inner beast huffed an amused snort.

I closed my eyes.

There was no breaking a dragonblood bonding. Once mated, the energy among the three would not be torn apart —even by death.

Mostly human mates wouldn't live half the years my Primrose would, no matter the sustenance her alpha might provide their beta and vice versa. I had already lived more than three-quarters of my life, and still I wondered if I wouldn't be alone when death finally arrived to take me to the stars.

At least Dahlia and Joseph hadn't been by themselves when their end came.

Strangely, my heart no longer ached over the loss of them.

My mates' energy lingered overhead, reminding me why. I could sense them moving around…fucking without me.

Inner dragon whimpering his need, I hissed as my dick pressed against my jeans' zipper. But jealousy and hurt flooded through my human half, swarming the tensing of my stomach. Same as back in New York, I wanted to flee. Put distance between what I longed for yet feared.

I knew the truth of what I was—had recognized it decades ago—but acceptance did not come easily.

I pushed to my feet and strode toward the hallway that led into the cavern's bowels, Tiggy on my heels. I slipped into the darkness, my dragon sight making it easy to find my way deeper, giving me slight relief from my mates' energy and the reminder I couldn't escape my fate even if I wanted to. Tiggy stayed close, his nails clicking on stone behind me.

A few caves branched off, leading to areas I had yet to revisit since returning home, but I kept to the main dragon-created hallway that led to my favorite place in the caverns. A room that Primrose claimed she'd spent more time in than anywhere else. It was also where she'd gained some of her knowledge of the world outside the mountain and that of her Blood Born ancestors.

The library opened before me, the scent of ancient manuscripts and newer paper soothing the tumbling emotions in my heart, returning me to my childhood. I used to hide in these lower bowels to escape responsibilities and Father's harshness. Oftentimes, Papa and I would curl up on a couch, and I would fall asleep to his low voice reading from whatever text had caught his fancy.

I lifted my head and peered around the circular room and its ancient arches and rock-carved shelves lined with books. Manuscripts in the ancient language I'd learned as a young dragon. Books of a more modern era I had personally brought back to the cavern while living alone. Hundreds of years, thousands of books…it was no wonder Primrose knew the things she did.

Most of the ancient writings had been translated into the human language by Papa, and although his grasp on all spoken languages outshone what any mere human could, he'd chosen English due to the continent our family had settled.

It had been the work that had kept him occupied after his female, my mother, had passed. He'd succumbed to old age a mere week before Father, and I had never been so alone in my life.

Glory in what you've found.

Teeth clenched against my dragon's murmur, I moved into the massive cave, lighting a few lanterns to ease the strain on my dragon sight. While travelling through darkness didn't tire my eyes, attempting to read fine print without real light would give me a headache.

Lantern in hand, I followed the curved wall, my fingertips trailing over dust-free spines and shelves. I didn't know what I sought—other than escape. Iron stairs led to the balcony overlooking the cavern, that one, too, lined by shelves packed full of books.

Thinking to tire my mind by reading the ancient language would work to distract me, I pulled a tome off the far shelf and made my way back to the floor and old couches arranged in a square below.

Lantern on an end table and massive book spread open on my lap, I forced my eyes to focus as the language of old filtered through my memory.

A history of the dragonblood downfall.

No—choose another.

Lips pursed, I considered returning the book but kept on reading about how mankind had found a means of defeating the dragons long before we learned how to cloak our true forms.

My anger brewed, and while my inner beast begged me to shut the book, I continued on, feeding the racist thoughts inside my head, the ones filled with disdain for those lesser than Blood Born.

Vanni held me in my arms and fucked me against the shower wall, driving into me with such force I expected my back would bruise from where I pressed against stone. He had a vise grip on my waist, his fingertips digging into my flesh with a delicious burn, which combined with his deep-seated thrusts into me, sent me over the edge in a matter of seconds.

Although he fucked hard and enjoyed giving me the pain I craved, Vanni was gentle afterward, washing my body and hair with homemade products smelling of herbs.

I wondered over Primrose and her solitary life in the cavern and also what her plans were since the three of us had shown up. There was no question in my mind that Vanni and I would be staying with Dolyn for however long we needed to finish the bonding process and make a decision of where we would reside together.

Would the three of us being in the space she'd had all to herself for years bother her?

Did our humanness unsettle her as it still seemed to do with Dolyn?

Although he longed for us, his hesitation, his distaste for our lesser blood, festered inside me. I fought to keep my hurt contained, for I didn't want him to change his mind toward us out of pity.

I knew we weren't worthy of a full-blooded one such as himself, but I also felt he shouldn't simply toss aside what fate had destined for him—a life beyond loneliness and longing he'd experienced before meeting us.

We needed to sit and talk things through, the three of us communicating what we felt, what we wanted, and how to create the bond we all longed for. We also needed to discuss the rental SUV down the mountain, the lack of clothing other than the old T-shirt I wore that fell to my thighs, and the matching one Vanni had pulled on along with an old pair of jeans so outdated I wondered how they didn't fall apart at the seams.

Squeezing tightly to Vanni's fingers, I followed him down a hallway, the lantern in his other hand. Remnants of Dolyn's energy emanated from the light of the cavern opening ahead, and Primrose hadn't been joking about his grumpiness I could feel in rolling waves of tumultuous emotions the closer we drew.

My heart fell at the thought of a fight before the calm.

He seemed up in arms, ready to rip into someone—but the sense wasn't as potent as I'd expected when we walked into the cavernous room. I realized he'd gone deeper, down into the depths of this place rather than outside. Still, the fact he'd chosen to hide away from us caused my eyes to well.

I blinked away tears, and Vanni kissed the back of my hand while setting the lantern down on the counter and extinguishing it as natural light flooding through the many windows set in the far wall illuminated the living area generously. A gorgeous sight lay beyond the glass, but I was too caught up in my thoughts to appreciate the beauty of a white-covered Wyoming spreading out before us.

"We'll make this right," Vanni murmured, the soothing emotion I swore had to be love shimmering through the energy between us.

Nodding my trust in him, I attempted a smile.

He wiped his thumb under my eye, swiping off the droplet of moisture that fell. "None of that, or I'll have to beat his ass extra hard when I finally get him strung up."

A shot of lust licked at my clit, and I squeezed my thighs together.

"Hmm." One of Vanni's eyebrows rose as he studied my face. "You'd like to watch me punish our beta, wouldn't you?"

"Yes." I dropped my gaze from the heat in his eyes.

"Flogger, whip, or cane?"

I breathed an unsteady breath past my twitching lips. "Yes."

Vanni chuckled. "Naughty girl. What would Dolyn think, I wonder?"

"He wants the same."

My head jerked up for the second time that morning at Primrose's unexpected voice, my face heating. She meandered into the kitchen with a small bag in hand, the same vintage robe wrapped around her body as earlier.

"Does the all-knowing Primrose have any idea how I might sway him into eagerly submitting to his desires?" Vanni questioned, a hint of teasing in his voice as he poured two mugs of coffee from a percolator that looked to have seen better days.

"He needs to realize that you are worthy of him first. Once that's settled in his arrogant mind, he'll gladly fall to his knees before you."

Vanni groaned, sending a similar shiver of excitement through my blood.

"And when you're finally bonded, you'll never have to worry about what he's thinking or feeling ever again. It'll be as though he's speaking directly to your mind."

"You're serious?" Vanni asked, returning to my side and handing a cup of coffee to me.

She tipped her head to the side. "What reason would I have for lying?"

Vanni didn't reply, and Primrose turned her focus on me. "You aren't broken."

I sputtered the sip I'd taken of the piping hot brew. "I—I know that."

"Do you?"

I nodded as I considered all of the healing that had taken place in the previous couple of weeks.

"You were formed to match both alpha and beta," Primrose stated, her tone softer than earlier. "If changing the past removed your trauma, you wouldn't have found this love or have empathy in your heart for a certain tortured soul. You were crafted into the female your mates need, one who understands, a woman who is perfect as-is—scars and all."

My eyesight hazed over again, and Vanni wrapped an arm around my waist.

Warmth seeped into me, and I pressed in closer to my alpha and master, my heart...overcome, my mind full of Primrose's promise. "Thank you," I whispered.

A soft smile lightened Primrose's steady gaze.

My focus dropped to the bag in her hand. "You're leaving, aren't you?"

"I am." She moved toward the door and turned to face us. "I wish you the best of luck in getting past Grandpapa's stubbornness."

Vanni chuckled, but I found myself saddened she was departing so soon.

"When will you come back?" I asked, suddenly wishing I'd had more time with my beta's only living relative.

She glanced out one of the windows, blinking as though already long gone. "When I've found my mates."

"You aren't exactly dressed for the weather."

I glanced over her thin covering again at Vanni's statement.

"I don't need clothing." She shimmied the material off her body, and instant envy filled me over her lush curves—pert nipples on breasts still unaffected by age, tiny waist Vanni's hands would easily span, and shapely thighs I expected men would enjoy gripping while fucking into her.

"Calm yourself, baby," Vanni whispered against my hair, nuzzling against my scalp.

I realized a growl rumbled my chest, and I quieted with a gulp, my face heating as Vanni slid his palm down my back and over my ass cheek to squeeze.

"He doesn't want me, Ashley," Primrose stated, and considering she could basically read minds, I had to believe her. "Your alpha's desire burns for you and has since the day he first saw you." She smiled, and my breath caught at her beauty, the light in her eyes so similar to Dolyn's that my heart ached. "*That* is what I'm off to find for myself now that I can put Tiggy's care into Grandpapa's hands."

"Who's—"

She stepped outside before Vanni finished his question.

As one, he and I moved toward the window to watch her.

Primrose stood on the veranda's edge, bag in hand, head tipped back, and eyes closed as though breathing in freedom, expecting destiny to drive her forward in the way she ought to go. She bent her knees and leaped into the air, falling from sight.

I screamed, my coffee sloshing onto the stone floor. My

heart landed in my throat as a pale, golden dragon shot straight up into the sky, bag clutched in her front claws.

"Holy shit!" Vanni breathed. "Fucking hell! This shit is absolutely one hundred percent truth. Jesus Christ!"

I huffed a shaky laugh. "We didn't just imagine that, did we?"

"Nope." Vanni shook his head, staring after the massive beast diminishing in the distance.

"She's amazing—huge," I said, squinting to keep her in sight.

"Dolyn is even more impressive than his granddaughter."

I tore my gaze off Primrose's shimmering form as it faded in the cold, blue sky to peer up at Vanni. "When did you see him in his dragon form?"

"When he rescued us from the snow last night."

"He...what?"

"Held us in his claws and took us on the ride of a lifetime."

"Damn! I missed it!"

Vanni kissed the pout off my lips. "I'm sure he'll fly with you if you want. That man will do whatever the fuck you tell him to do." A glint lit his eye.

"What are you thinking? I'm getting something crafty going on in your energy...some manipulative tactic."

"Beg him to submit to me."

I pressed my lips together, expecting he would feel my disapproval.

"Fine." He huffed and sipped his coffee, a twinkle in his eyes as he stared down at me.

"What did he look like?" I asked, still annoyed I'd missed out on seeing our beta in his other form.

"His beast? Beautiful. Massive. Sexy as *fuck*." Vanni all but groaned the words, pressing down on his thickening bulge.

His arousal licked at my skin, dampening me between the

thighs, and he smirked. "Should we go find our beta and talk him into us?"

"Talk him into *me*—and you into him," I whispered, so turned on by the thoughts of bonding in that way my limbs shook.

Vanni's gaze narrowed, fire and darkness swirling in his eyes. "A bit of pain for him first, I'm thinking, for leaving us back in New York then not being in our bed when we woke this morning."

"Mmm." I squeezed my thighs together. "Can I watch?"

He chuckled and clasped my free hand with his. "If that's what my female wants, that's what she'll get."

"And if he fights?"

Vanni sobered as we stared at each other. "He could kill me with a mere flick of his fingers. All it would take would be a thin ribbon of the dragon fire I watched him shoot from his lips last night to light the fireplace."

A shiver covered my skin with goose bumps, and I swallowed, glancing at the massive stone chimney and the pile of blackened bits of wood on the grate. "Perhaps we ought to discuss things through with him before you attempt to dominate."

"I don't think he'll hurt me."

"How can you be sure?" I asked, studying his eyes, searching for the answer. I couldn't bear the thought of losing one of my mates, dragon or human. Such an event would leave me devastated, beyond hope of healing from grief no matter which was left by my side.

My inside friend agreed with a pained whimper, causing my throat to tighten.

"Had Dolyn wanted to harm me, he'd have given me more than a bruised cheek that night we first met."

Vanni had a point.

"He could have burst my body into flames for touching what he saw as his."

"I *am* his," I reminded my alpha.

Vanni's smirk appeared again, lessening the intensity of his stare. "You're also mine, and while I'm willing to share, I'm also the only one allowed to dole out punishment and pain. If he ever touches you, causes you pain outside the bedroom in any way…"

"He won't."

"How can you be sure?" Vanni echoed my question.

"I can feel it." I pressed my palm against my chest. "Here."

Vanni's gaze dropped to my hand and back to my eyes.

"Seems you've bonded more with him than I have. I can't tell what the fuck he's gonna do—just get slammed with his emotional reactions."

I squeezed his fingers and glanced toward the hallway Dolyn must have disappeared into. "Then let's go lay it all out on the table. Talk it out. Fuck it out. Do whatever it takes to make him fully ours so there won't be any question about his thoughts or feelings, like Primrose said."

Vanni dipped his head and started toward the hallway calling out to me, taking a quick sip of his coffee before setting it on the counter. I did the same. "You really believe this isn't some parallel universe, do you?"

"Yes, and I know you do too, otherwise, you wouldn't have left your club and building in Manhattan without a backward glance."

He frowned. "That's something else we have to figure out."

"What?"

"Packing up all our shit and getting it over here where it belongs."

Belongs, the voice in me echoed, and I'd never been surer

of anything in my life. If only we could make Dolyn realize
the same.

CHAPTER 30
VANNI

The cavern home had a strange effect on me. Like a shot of espresso and a handful of little blue pills, energy and the need to fuck had me on edge and hard in the old jeans I'd borrowed from Dolyn's bureau.

Everything in this cavernous place was outdated, some things in a state of disrepair, but not a single cell in my body wished to return to the luxury of my life before meeting Dolyn. The rock walls and ceilings, the scent of fire as though pulling from deep within the mountain, made me feel as though I'd found the home I'd always hoped for.

Home.

I nodded at the voice and instinctively led Ashley deeper into branching caves toward our missing mate, the slight hiss of the lantern and our breathing the only sounds. Claustrophobia used to be an issue for me, but nothing about Dolyn's lair caused me lightheadedness or led me to the verge of passing out. Rather, the lack of breath and headiness affecting me came from levels of lust I'd never considered possible.

I needed to prove my worth to Dolyn, even though I

didn't truly feel I had to, and I had no fucking clue how to go about doing it. The man was a dragon shifter for fuck's sake, far superior to any living creature. It was no wonder he fought the need to bond, to submit to an almost all-human alpha.

Couldn't blame the man, or dragon, rather, but it fucking hurt to be shunned, thought of as less than. Not enough. His stance brought back that shit from my past I'd been trying to forget about now that I'd found something ten times better.

Ashley squeezed my hand as though knowing what bothered me. She, unlike Dolyn, was perfect. In every goddamn way.

Soft and submissive, a bit of sass and caring. Considerate and modest, a diamond amidst piles of coal, a treasure I would love forever.

Love.

I considered the word I never expected to say or feel for another woman, but the voice within me spoke truth. I loved Ashley—I also loved Dolyn—and I needed to show them. All I could do was to offer them what they desired, give them the power over my actions, and pray the results led to their complete submission.

While manipulation would have worked to get me what *I* wanted, my mates' happiness and fulfillment would always come first to me.

Dolyn's energy clashed with mine before the cave ahead of us illuminated.

Would he flee again or face us?

Considering his roused pain and the burning anger I swore singed my skin, I expected both.

I swallowed, my stomach tight as we came into view of the biggest, most kick-ass library I'd seen in my life. Rock, shelf, balcony, books, couches, soft lamp light—

And Dolyn.

My gaze latched onto him the second I realized he sat on an old couch in the middle of the room.

All else fell away from my consciousness as he met my gaze, waves of pissiness and mistrust slamming into me—of me or his inner dragon, I couldn't tell.

The darkness in me swelled, rising and billowing, expanding in my chest and mind, filling me with the need to conquer. Zero doubt lay in me about my being alpha, and even though Dolyn could squash me like a damn bug beneath his heel, I didn't physically fear him. I didn't worry for my safety or my position.

Beta.

"Beta." The word left my mouth, a low rumble like the voice in my head.

He glared, and my cock swelled to the point of pain within a heartbeat.

I stalked toward him, gaze unwavering, steps sure.

He pushed to his feet, setting whatever he'd been reading aside, our focus still locked on the other.

I hadn't realized I'd released my hold on Ashley—or the lantern—until I crowded up in Dolyn's face, hands fisted at my sides, tension like a live wire, zapping over my skin. We stood almost nose to nose, shoulders nearly the same width, but his breadth—and strength—was so much more than mine.

Submit.

"Submit," I echoed and smiled, allowing the lust I felt for him to shine in my eyes as his frown deepened.

He held still, unbending as always.

"I said submit, boy."

The black of Dolyn's pupil swirled, heightening my breath. "Make me."

His growled words shivered over my skin, and my smile widened as I realized what he needed from me. "If that'll ease your conscience," I murmured, tearing my gaze off his arresting eyes to drink in the rest of his face—clenched jaw and lush mouth.

His strength wouldn't be topped, but I knew a thing or two.

A quick sweep of my leg and grasp on his arms sent him to the floor with an oomph, his face on the rock, my knee in the small of his back, palms wrapped around his wrists. Touching him had also opened up more of that cord between us, and I didn't doubt his desire. He trembled, and I leaned close to his ear. "Is this the answer, Dolyn? Need me to *take* what I want since you're too chicken shit to give it to me willingly?"

"Fuck. You." He pulled against my hold on his arms but without the full strength of his inner dragon.

I chuckled at his lackluster attempt to escape me. "Can you smell our female's arousal? Can you taste how wet she is because I have you right where you belong?"

Dolyn groaned, his eyelids slamming shut.

"Fight me, Dolyn," I whispered against his ear. "Make yourself believe you tried to withstand the draw to your alpha—your destiny."

With a growl, he snapped his head back, smashing his skull into my cheekbone. My grip on his wrists loosened enough he flipped me off him, and I crashed into one of the couches with a grunt.

I guessed I'd gone a little too far with my taunting.

Ashley gasped, but I kept my focus on Dolyn as he stood to his full height, his cock hard in his jeans, wetness from pre-cum wetting the denim. "You want it, try to take it."

His dick, his submission, his ass around my thrusting cock—I would have all three.

Yessss.

Our inner beasts hissed the lust I could feel like a tsunami rolling off Dolyn.

With a roar, I barreled forward, slamming into his stomach with my shoulder and sending us over the end of a couch and to the rock floor again. He smashed a fist into my side, and I answered with a punch of my own. Another snap of his head caught me in the chin, but I managed to stay atop him, our hard bodies pressing against each other.

We breathed heavily, stilling briefly as shared desire radiated between us. I flexed my ass, rubbing our denim-clad cocks together, and we both groaned.

Ashley's moan behind us ratcheted my need up another notch and caused a gush of pre-cum to soak my jeans.

I worked a hand between us and squeezed Dolyn's sizable girth, making his eyes roll back into his head. He didn't fight me but dug his fingers into my forearm as if to keep me in place. He shivered beneath me, the skin contact a temptation he fought to overcome.

Primrose's earlier words flickered through my memory, and rather than forcing him as Dolyn thought he wanted, I decided perhaps giving might work to set his mind free to accept what couldn't be denied.

"Let me touch you." I worked at the snap and zipper of his jeans, his hold on my arm tightening—but not yanking me away. At the first brush of my fingers against his straining dick, Dolyn whimpered the most delicious sound I'd ever heard. "Yours is the only cock I've held that wasn't my own," I told him, sliding my hand over his steel-like length.

Eyes closing, he thrust up through my fingers, his swollen head notching against my palm, wetting my skin with his slickness. "Fuck."

"I want that more than anything," I murmured, leaning close enough his panting breath caressed my lips, "but let me pleasure you this way right now."

I shifted toward his groin, and he grabbed hold of my hair. "Don't."

His strangled word paused me halfway down his body, my chin resting on his hard as fuck abs. "Don't what?"

He licked his lips, but kept his eyes clenched shut. "I... fuck."

I stroked his cock, and he groaned, thrusting upward again. "Tell me you lust to have my mouth on you," I said, unable to help myself.

"Fuck you."

I released his cock and yanked his jeans below his shaft's base, his balls still trapped inside the denim. "I'm going to suck you down, Dolyn. If you don't want that, you know your safeword."

He growled as a pearl of pre-cum glistened at the tip of his bobbing length but didn't speak.

"Dolyn—you have permission to fuck my mouth." I hesitated the space of two heartbeats before flicking my tongue over his slit. The sweetness of him exploded over my taste buds. "Fucking *hell*," I groaned as raw hunger awakened deep in my guts. I opened wide, and Dolyn yanked on my hair, shoving his cock into my throat until I gagged.

Yessss.

"Oh, God." Ashley's whimper only made me hotter, and I allowed Dolyn to use me, fuck my mouth, my throat, until tears ran down my cheeks.

Arousal far beyond the need to nut welled inside me like a never-ending spring of life, and the urge to bury inside him and douse his insides with my seed caused my sac to tighten.

I dug my fingers into his thighs and rubbed my aching shaft on the hard floor, groaning and moaning when he allowed me to breathe around his thick cock. Pre-cum continued to ooze from his slit, coating my tongue and making me lust for more.

I wanted it all—every goddamn spurt, every drop of cum his balls had to offer. Sweat broke out over my body as I humped the floor, Dolyn's grunts and the wet sounds of Ashley finger-fucking herself drove me to the brink of explosion.

Scraping my teeth against Dolyn's length as he withdrew sent curses past his lips and upped his pace.

Goddamn tears rolled down my face as he continued to gag me with every thrust.

Relax.

My throat opened at the crooning whisper, and I managed to swallow around Dolyn before he backed off the next time.

"Oh, fuck." Dolyn's whimper teetered me on the edge. "Can't—"

He buried deep in my throat, thick shots of cum jerking his dick against my tongue. He was sweet. Tingly—and I nutted in my jeans, groaning around his cock, swallowing the gift he offered—and wanting more. Ashley cried out from beside us, and fuck, how I wished she'd been sitting on his face where I could watch her come while he'd fucked my throat.

A mess smeared in my jeans, and I milked Dolyn dry, licking up his length, shoving the tip of my tongue into his hole in the hopes of one last taste of him.

His spunk was addictive—it was no wonder Ashley couldn't keep her mouth off my dick.

"So sweet, such a good boy, giving me what I need." I kissed the crown of his cock, up his abs, and pressed my weight completely on top of his hard body. "Kiss me."

His eyelids slowly opened, and the love, the desire in his golden eyes slammed into me, catching my breath. "No."

"That's not your safeword."

He glared.

I crushed my mouth against his. He bucked beneath me, biting and half-attempting to tear his head from my grasp on his ears, but I kissed him how he wanted me to, exactly as I felt through the strengthening bond between us. He *needed* force, taking rather than sharing. A hard nip to his lower lip opened his mouth to gasp, and I shoved my tongue deep inside, tasting him, trying to breathe his soul into my lungs, where he wouldn't ever be able to escape me.

He groaned and turned pliant—but only for a few seconds.

I found myself on my back, my head ringing as I stared up at the ceiling high overhead.

CHAPTER 31

DOLYN

"The fuck?" Vanni's murmur barely reached through the rush of wind in my ears.

I shoved my semi back into my jeans, my gaze flitting from his accusing glare on the floor where I'd tossed him like a pebble to Ashley, who lay trembling on a couch a few feet away, her eyes wide, lips parted.

The scent of the cum smeared between her naked thighs, parted beneath my T-shirt, drew me in like a goddamn black fly to sweat, my tongue needing a taste. I growled my desire, but she shrank into the old cushions beneath her, a hint of her fear thickening in the air between us.

I'd fucking given in like a cowardly wimp, like a needy little child who couldn't yet think for himself.

"What's the problem, big boy?" Vanni asked with enough venom I wanted to pop him in the nose as he struggled to sit, touching the back of his head with a wince.

"*You're* the problem," I hissed at him.

"Dolyn," Ashley murmured, but I ignored her.

I could sense his human-like pain—her dissipating satisfaction in release. They had to feel what I couldn't incinerate in my mind, so why bother trying to hide? I peered down at the alpha fate had destined me for, and the ache in his head, the frown marring his brow, didn't ease any of the hardness creeping around my heart as it should have.

"You're *human*," I reiterated my aversion to his other half.

His jaw clenched, and he pulled his hand away from the back of his head. Blood smeared his fingers, and Ashley gasped, dropping to the floor beside him.

Hands fisted at my sides, I stared as Ashley yanked off my shirt to hold it to the back of his head. Naked, she should have stolen my gaze, breath, and attention, but I found myself focused on Vanni's expressive face as he winced again —hurt because of the pleasure he had offered me.

And, I'd reacted like an absolute piece of shit, tossing him aside.

Elijah hadn't ever once allowed me to overpower him.

Vanni had let me hold his head with authority, shove my dick down his convulsing throat—but had it been because of the addiction my cum caused? Or had he given his beta control because he knew it was what I longed for?

He'd lapped at me as though he couldn't get enough, like he wanted to suck me hard again and fill his belly with another shot of life-giving sustenance.

My temples pounded with conflicting thoughts as Ashley removed her shirt from the back of Vanni's head to check on the amount of blood. "It's not too bad—I don't think you'll need stitches," she murmured, her concern over the human's wound rather than my aching heart, my goddamn mind on the verge of insanity...

"You aren't worthy of a full Blood Born." I hadn't meant for the words to come out so coarse, but the racist asshole Father had raised, fed with ancient texts, overshadowed the dragon within, begging me to accept what fate had *gifted* me.

"Well, thanks for that," Vanni said, his gaze narrowed as

he peered up at me, fire glinting in his green eyes. "We fly across the goddamn country, get lost in a fucking blizzard—because of shared desire to be with you—and this is how you treat us?" He shook his head, lips pursed. "Fuck. You. Dolyn. Fuck you and your selfish *fucking* pride."

A tear slid down Ashley's cheek as she tended to his wound, but she couldn't spare me a glance.

"You aren't worthy of *us*," Vanni continued, peering up at me, tension and anger radiating through the clinching tether between us. "I had hoped you would accept what is as obvious as the nose on your face, but if this is who you truly are inside, then I want no part of you."

A sob caught in Ashley's throat as she covered her face with her hands, the bloody shirt falling to the floor at her knees.

My dragon roared like a thousand knives stabbed into my heart, my soul. My claws shimmered, and the yearning to shift, explode into my full strength and size, shook my body. I gripped my head in my hands, desperate for the war to stop, begging Father's voice echoing in my mind to ease, to give me peace and allow me to accept my destiny.

Another sob from Ashley, and I lit from the room, dragon speed taking me through the caverns leading to freedom faster than any mere human could travel on foot.

Tiggy raced after me, and I mourned the poor beast had been forgotten in the library and doubtless seen our fight. Ever loyal, he followed as fast as he could to the front door. I paused to allow him time to catch up, swallowed hard, and bent to throw my arms around him.

"Be a good boy and watch over my mates—I promise I'll be back."

He licked my face and sat on his haunches.

I stood without looking into his big brown eyes. A blast of freezing air slammed into my body as I threw open the front door, but I ran and leaped off the veranda, my jeans shredding as my dragon rushed to take over my human-like body.

Tears swept across my scaled face as I shot forward, my wings shooting me beyond my mates' hurt—but not far enough to ease mine.

I continued onward, seeking refuge from the emotions, the pain, the torn desires wracking my brain, but I doubted I would find solace anywhere but in their arms.

With every flap on my sinewy wings, I sped eastward, the miles disappearing beneath me at a rapid pace. Rage continued to roil inside me.

I needed something.

An outlet.

A way to release the pent up frustration, anger, and disappointment in myself.

Being tied down and feeling the bite of Vanni's cane sounded divine, and my inner beast begged for me to return for the release we were desperate to experience.

But Father's voice continued to whisper in my head, centuries of his indoctrination still holding onto the reins of my mind.

Pastor—Jonestown.

My eyesight sharpened on the horizon rather than my internal strife at my beast's second suggestion.

Yessss.

I banked slightly, my heart racing in anticipation. Recalling all Ashley had told me, and the bit of investigation I'd done on my own into the man, led me toward a small town I'd studied but had never visited.

I'd promised myself revenge and had planned for it at some point in time.

Tonight, I would avenge my female, and hopefully, calm some of the storm raging inside me.

My insides still simmered hours later when I stood cloaked outside a single-story home alongside a white, clapboard church.

Jonestown Independent Bible, the sign along the road read.

The man moving about the house's interior was a mere wisp of a human. Stoop-shouldered and bald, he reminded me of a weasel, exactly as I'd thought upon seeing his professional headshot online. He disappeared down a hallway, and I tried his front door, pleased when the handle turned beneath my firm grip.

Ignorant redneck fool thought he was safe at his home in the middle of no-man's-land USA.

Huffing a silent snort, I let myself into his home. The house as a whole was neat and tidy, and the only indication of a mess was a stack of papers on the kitchen table to my right. A door beyond suggested a basement. It was locked, a key required to open the damned thing.

Sounds of clicking on a keyboard suggested the pastor busied himself for the time being.

A single flame of dragon fire melted the lock before me. Stairs led into darkness.

Teeth gritted, I descended into darkness.

The low ceiling demanded I bend slightly, and I glanced around, my enhanced sight allowing me to take in the boxes and crates. A wall of shelves held dozens of canned goods. Stackable washer and dryer units—two of them—stood against the opposite wall. A door nestled in between—also locked.

I strode forward, put my beast's fire to good use, and stepped into the small room beyond.

A single light bulb dangled from the ceiling.

I flipped the switch on the outside wall.

Brilliant white coated the walls, but the room gave off a

non-innocent air of staleness. Pristine sheets stretched tight over the mattress laying atop a metal frame bolted to the cement floor in the corner, and images of a young Ashley tied down and held against her will flooded my vision.

I bit my tongue, hands fisted at my sides as a flare of heat burst through my guts.

A worn box sat against the wall to my right.

My inner beast growled, suspicion raising the hairs on my arms.

Did the fucker keep trinkets? Memories to fill his filthy mind for when he needed to get off hours after preaching to a congregation who believed he walked on water?

I couldn't bear the thought of touching such filth. Refused to allow my skin contact with anything of his.

But if I wanted proof to ease my conscience for what I was about to do…

I elongated a single claw, preferring bone rather than flesh to rip into the box the pedophile's hands had touched.

Pictures spilled out across the floor.

Old grainy snapshots of a young girl bound on the bed behind me sat atop a stack of magazines.

Evil.

Simmering in agreement, I shifted the pile of photos, sliding them along the floor to reach those beneath. Dozens of images of the female lay before me, a few of a second even younger girl at the bottom. I didn't doubt the man upstairs was Ashley's abuser, but a few more flicks of my claw through the box's content didn't offer the pictures I'd expected to see.

Standing, I strode from the room and made for the stairs.

The man's heavy breaths sounded back through the hallway once I reached the main floor, the keyboard clicking having gone quiet.

I crept through the kitchen toward his office and stopped

in the doorway. Slouched with his back toward me, the man huddled over an old PC. My insides burned, the need to send the supposed man of God up in flames raging through me. While my ancestors killed humans without reason, I'd yet to take a life.

Tonight would be my first.

I lusted to hear his screams, watch his skin sizzle and blacken, his mouth gaping open until the flesh melted from his bones for what he'd done to those girls.

Swallowing back a snarl, I moved closer to the unaware man.

He sighed and sank into his chair, allowing me to clearly see over his shoulder.

An image of Ashley filled the computer's monitor and not from when she'd been a child.

She huddled in her winter coat, exiting the door of Tolzman Industries.

The fucker had been following her.

Cold eyes.

My roar caused her stalker to shoot upright and spin, knocking over his chair. Hands clasped over his ears, eyes wide, he scanned the room behind him.

Voice lowering to a growl, I shimmered into existence.

He screamed like one of the little girls he'd abused.

And I made sure he lived long enough to shriek again as I burned the house of sin down around him.

CHAPTER 32

ASHLEY

I held my face in my hands and sobbed, my heart torn as though a serrated knife had hacked its way through the tender flesh.

"It's okay," Vanni murmured, wrapping his arms around my waist and pulling me onto his lap, but I couldn't stop the tears. Surely, he experienced the same pain that I did—how could he stand knowing—*feeling*—Dolyn's energy leaving us again? Our beta's awful words were just as distressing, but his absence was ten times more painful now that our energies had become more strongly wrapped up together.

Vanni rocked me back and forth, clutching my cheek against his chest until I quieted, the soothing thump of his heart beneath my ear reassuring.

"He's gone," I whispered.

"Yes."

"What should we do?"

Vanni heaved a breath. "Long term? No fucking clue, but I wouldn't mind a shower right now."

I pulled back slightly, and he swept his lips up my neck, finding my mouth. With more gentleness than I thought him capable of, Vanni poured his love into our kiss, trying to ease my heartache by giving the kind of tenderness Dolyn had fulfilled me with.

I wished Vanni's sweetness, his caresses, could fill the part of me that needed more, but an aching emptiness remained deep inside me.

"I'm not enough," he whispered, tipping his forehead against mine, the hurt in his voice and through our growing bond causing my eyes to sting again.

"Same as I fall short for you." I pulled back and cradled his whiskered cheeks in my hands. "It's not that we're less—"

Vanni's snort cut me off, his brow furrowing and thunder filling his eyes. "Fucker needs to get that through his goddamn brain."

"Try to see things from his perspective, Vanni." I knew it was hard. I struggled to do the same, but thinking about past royal human lines of blood, rarely did a mere peasant take the throne alongside them. I expected Dolyn felt the same as those from ancient times did, but how could we help him overcome a sense of superiority he'd known as truth for four hundred-some years?

"We should go back to New York," Vanni muttered.

"No." I shook my head, the idea of abandoning the cavern turning my stomach to rock. "He'll return. We'll find a way to make him see we are worthy of his love. That bonding with us, regardless of our lesser blood, is what he's longing for."

Vanni grabbed the bloody shirt off the floor, wrapped his arms around my nakedness, and groaned while standing.

"Put me down."

"Never."

I grumbled, but wrapped my legs around his waist like he desired and laid my cheek on his shoulder as he started back the way we'd come in our search of Dolyn. He grabbed the lantern, easily carrying my much smaller frame with one arm. Relaxing against his rock-like chest, I closed my eyes, breathing a little easier.

"Hold onto me, sweetheart," he whispered, and I knew he meant beyond the physical.

The next morning, showered and in fresh—somewhat—old clothing from the fifties, we made our way to the kitchen and ate the sourdough bread Primrose had left out for us the day before. With only a wood stove's fire burned down to ash and no sign of matches anywhere, we were unable to make coffee.

I peered at Vanni across the table from me while Tiggy pigged out on a bowl of dog food we'd found in a lower cabinet. "Should we go look for Dolyn?"

Vanni's gaze shifted toward the windows. Swirling eddies of white hid the far expanse beyond. I'd never been in a blizzard before but expected what happened outside counted as one. "He's too far away."

"What about the SUV? Think you can find it again after this snow stops? We're going to need supplies if we stay here for any length of time." I glanced around the outdated kitchen. "I don't know how to cook on a wood stove." A small stack of firewood lay beside the empty fireplace. "How is it warm in here? There's no heat source right now."

Vanni glanced across the cavern and shrugged.

"We should go exploring." I eyed the oil lantern between us, the glass base of it more than half-full. Vanni had lit the wick earlier with a pack of matches in the bedside table drawer, but we'd left them there. "Shit."

"What?"

"We didn't bring the matches with us and turned the lamp off. How are we going to light it again?"

Without a word, we both stood and started rooting through every cabinet and drawer for a way to create flame, coming up empty.

Vanni rubbed a hand over his jaw, glancing around the vast cavern.

Tiggy eyed us from where he sat by the front door, head resting on his paws. We'd let him out after he'd eaten, and even though he'd hesitated to brave the snow, he'd gone onto the veranda to do his business and was scratching to be let back in seconds later.

"The night we got here, Dolyn started the fire with dragon flames from his mouth," Vanni said, releasing a heavy sigh.

"Of course, he did," I mumbled, hands on hips as I turned to glance over the main living area of his home. "We're lucky there's a pack of matches. Dragon shifters wouldn't have need of them. What do you think, Tiggy?" I turned to ask the dog.

He stared at us, and while he hadn't been aggressive or seemingly upset we'd invaded his home, he seemed…sad. But what creature wouldn't be when first Primrose then Dolyn had left him alone with two humans he didn't know?

I made my way over to him, and he thumped his tail without lifting his head. Bending, I petted over his head. "I'm hurting too, Tig. But we'll take care of you until he comes back, okay?"

Tiggy gave me a little lick, huffed, and closed his eyes.

Standing, I peered down the hallway.

"We have to go to our room."

I huffed at Vanni's statement I'd been about to make, anxiety over the pitch-black heightening my pulse.

He gathered up my hand and squeezed it tight. "With every day that passes, I swear I can see more than humanly possible in the dark. And even if I can't see enough to get us there, I'm pretty sure I remember the twists and turns."

"And if you don't, maybe our inner beasts do?" I suggested since I hadn't paid attention once while meandering the branching hallways that led to the sleeping chambers.

Yessss.

Both of us let out shaky laughs as the hissed assurance echoed between us.

"Let's go."

Within a dozen steps, we rounded a bend, and the darkness claimed my sight. I clutched to Vanni's hand, our steps slowing. "Tell me you aren't as blind as I am," I whispered, my voice seemingly loud in the stifling stillness.

"I'm not?"

"That sounded like a question," I hissed, grabbing hold of his upper arm with my free hand.

"Here," he said, and the lantern's handle brushed against my knuckles. "Hold this so I'm free to run my fingers along the rock."

Shivering, I took the oil lamp and dangled it by my side. "Do *not* let go of my hand."

"I won't. Promise."

We started out, moving slowly, the soft scrape of Vanni's fingertips along the rock wall accompanying the shuffling of our feet.

"I can actually make out the shadow of branching hall-ways ahead."

Left.

Relief flooded through both of us.

"That's what I thought," he murmured to the voices in our heads. "Thank you."

One branch led toward the master chamber as well as Primrose's, the other to a few guest quarters that hadn't been occupied in centuries.

"Come on." Vanni's footsteps moved faster, and I followed with a little more confidence. "We made it," he said, his breath leaving in a rush.

The sound of a door pushing inward met my ears, and sudden light from the window in the far wall made me blink.

"Thank God," I muttered, rubbing at the goose bumps on my arms that had nothing to do with cold.

Ten minutes later, matches in Vanni's back pocket and oil lamp lit, we descended into the bowels of the cavern.

"Which way?" he questioned at the first fork, and I pointed left since we already had been to the right and library beyond.

"Let's explore down there. Maybe we'll get lucky and find the pantry."

"Fuck, what I wouldn't do for a juicy steak right now."

I giggled even as my heart ached.

"What's so funny?"

"We won't need a grill with a dragon for our mate."

Vanni snorted. "Hopefully he gets his fine ass back here soon."

"What if he doesn't return, Vanni? Seriously—what are we going to do?"

He tugged me into his side and kissed the top of my head. "I don't know, Ash. One hour, one day at a time, alright? Primrose said something about being stocked up for the winter, so there's got to be a dragon hoard of food around here someplace."

I smiled but couldn't find the ability to laugh over his intended pun.

If Dolyn stayed away from his ancestral home as long as he'd done after last he'd visited, according to Primrose, we were doomed.

Shivering, I followed Vanni down the hallway, my throat tight and aching.

We searched the endless cavern high and low, exploring countless rooms hewn out of stone, the masonry areas so well-made not a lick of mortar showed in the cracks. The first and most important finding was a large pantry-type room below the kitchen. Primrose had stocked up for the winter like a true prepper, so at least we wouldn't starve. There were boxes of matches, candles, and batteries, so we wouldn't go without light either. Off the back of the pantry lay a decently stocked wine cellar that held dusty bottles, and we enjoyed two of them while eating canned beef stew we heated over an open fire Vanni managed to start.

We never found the source of heat, but the air did get warmer the deeper into the endless caverns we'd gone.

Tiggy had laid by the entryway all day except for when we let him outside to do his business, and his sad puppy-dog eyes felt like what Vanni and I experienced deep inside.

A yearning for what we didn't have, a desperation that grew with every hour.

Darkness fell outside, and rather than wasting oil or candles, we crawled into Dolyn's huge bed and held each other close, desire swirling between us—and reaching out for our third both our hearts ached for.

At least Tiggy had followed us down the hallway and curled up at the foot of the bed so he wasn't alone in the main living area.

I told Vanni all I knew about Elijah and how he and Dolyn had been together before meeting us. Vanni worried he'd pushed Dolyn too hard to submit and that he'd gone back to his ex.

A hard knot grew in Vanni's stomach, causing my own to tighten, but on the heels of his hurt came a sense of comfort.

I slid my leg between his and smoothed my hand over his

brow in the darkness, the cloud-covered sky outside the window not allowing a single moonbeam to illuminate the bedroom. "Your emotions just jumped from pain to pleased. What's going on?" I asked, my voice no more than a hushed whisper in the stillness.

"I was envisioning another man touching Dolyn. Tasting him. Fucking him." Vanni shifted, repeating his thoughts intensifying the unease in his guts. "Then I realized I can see you better than I could this morning while finding our way back the hallway to get the matches. Can you see me at all?"

I huffed the annoyance he probably already felt, considering how the bond between us had strengthened even in Dolyn's absence. "Not a damned bit."

"Maybe I've got more dragonblood than Dolyn believes."

I heaved a sigh and snuggled closer against Vanni's chest, head tucked beneath his chin.

He ran his hand over my hip and back up, tugging me so we pressed tight from chest to thigh. "Do you believe he at least misses us?"

"He'd better," I grumbled.

"He must, I mean, he's our fated mate, right?" Vanni hadn't really asked a question but spoke to assure himself. "He's got to feel what we are. That goddamn energy between us isn't imagined."

Our emotions—shared and singular—swirled between us as real as Vanni's fingertips drawing circles on my lower back. "It's definitely not," I murmured.

Tomorrow will be better.

Believing the voice in my head, I closed my eyes and allowed sleep to claim me.

CHAPTER 33

DOLYN

Morning light spilled through my bedroom window, and I considered the days that had passed since I'd rid the earth of that piece-of-shit human being who'd traumatized my female and those other young girls.

After drinking down his screams and reveling in my satisfaction, I'd flown into New York and stayed in my suite. Being away from my mates had made thinking easier, and even though I expected they mourned my disappearance, I wasn't yet ready to humble myself and return to take my place as their beta.

My emotions had been roused by reading ancient texts and Father's word in my memory, and I'd been an absolute asshole to Vanni. The reactions had been instinctual on my human half's part, and not for the first time, I cursed Father and the indoctrination—hardly "wisdom"—he'd pounded into my brain until I believed I was superior in every way.

What I wouldn't have given for another chance to talk to him. Confront him on his pressuring me into being something I clearly was not. Even knowing the truth now, I struggled to *accept* it. Unable to figure out what held me back from accepting what fate graciously offered, I continued to lag in making any decision regardless of my inner beast's pleadings to return to our mountain home.

He'd found a massive sense of peace while there, the feeling of being welcomed with open arms. We both adored our granddaughter, yet another situation I continued to consider heavily. Even though we'd shared our stories, and I'd taught her what I could through our blood bond, I feared for her safety.

And the gift she'd given me…

I smiled at the memory of Tiggy, my heart aching for missing him almost as much as my mates.

Go home.

Unrest should have had me up and moving, but I buried deeper into my silken sheets, wishing to ignore what lay ahead. But there would be no putting off the return for much longer. My chest felt cracked open with no female to soothe, no alpha to quiet my mind—

Elijah.

Eyes clenched shut, I huffed a heavy exhale. My beast didn't suggest we beg to submit to Elijah's hand. He assured me we had someone to talk to, a pure Blood Born who just might know exactly what I faced in my racist thoughts I struggled to heal from.

Had he accepted his mates without concern over their being mostly human? Did Jon, his beta, give him what he needed even though he didn't have enough dragonblood to shift? Would they be able to procreate even though their blood wasn't pure enough?

"Fuck." I scrubbed a hand over my face and growled. Could Ashley accept our seed and have the strength to carry *our* young? My stomach twisted into knots even though I'd felt sure she would. While we three might have dragonblood, would it be the proper potency to produce offspring?

Primrose existed because of me and my old lovers having created her mother. The Canadian twins who'd fathered her had come from somewhere. Surely, that history of our kind continued to be true.

But what if it wasn't? What if something had taken place in the twenty-something years since Primrose's birth? What if the dragonblood energy faded from the earth with every passing year? What if destiny intended our extinction, and no other Blood Born womb would support life?

Was a real bond even possible? I'd never witnessed one, had only read books and learned from secondhand experience through Papa and my mother.

But that had been close to four hundred years ago.

Too many questions and no answers had me climbing from bed, cloaking, and striding straight outside into the cold. I slid the slider shut and launched myself off my balcony. Muscle and bone expanded, skin morphing into scales, and I shot up into the sky, banking to head northeast.

While I trusted Elijah to tell me the truth of how he fared with his lovers, I needed to see with my own eyes that bonding with mostly humans was possible, that they would fit seamlessly as they ought to as fated mates of ones such as us.

With every flap of my sinewy wings, I flew faster, miles skimming past beneath me in a brown and snowy white blur. At least the sun's beams caressed my flank, the side of my face, and tucked legs as I travelled. The warmth seemed promising, an assurance that not just spring lay in wait but answers and confidence as well.

A couple of hours later, I landed on Elijah's veranda overlooking the White Mountains where his home nestled. Fresh snow covered the stone, the one-way windows only revealed to me because of my dragon sight.

I strode forward but had the decency to knock since I no longer had the right to let myself in unannounced.

The door yanked inward before I could draw breath.

Elijah stood across the threshold, freshly showered and in low-slung lounge pants, eyes an icy pale blue. He'd always been gorgeous to me, but for the first time, arousal didn't shiver my skin in his intimidating presence. "Dolyn."

"Can I come in?" I asked, my voice low and calm, my body vibrating over the possibility of him turning me away without the answers I sought.

He glanced down over my nakedness, merely making note of my lack of clothing, but stepped back, motioning me forward.

My inner beast breathed a sigh of relief, but I kept mine from being audible and revealing weakness.

No.

Lips in a thin line, I told myself what my inner beast had: I needed to stop with the shit Father had taught me that had discolored my thoughts toward myself.

A quick scan around the cavern revealed the absence of Elijah's mates, lowering my hope for good news. "Where are Jon and Dakota?"

"Hurrying to finish in the shower. They feel your presence and will be down shortly." He motioned toward the couch where a throw blanket draped.

My shoulders relaxed. "The bonding ritual worked, I take it?"

"Indeed, it did." Pleasure coated his tone, and I breathed a little easier at having one of my questions answered so quickly.

I wrapped the material around my waist, doing what I would have wanted him to do if the roles were reversed.

"Coffee?" he asked, ever the gracious host.

"Please."

Elijah headed into the kitchen. "You found your mates?"

"I have."

"And have you bonded with them?"

"Not yet—I wasn't sure it was possible with how human they are, but you lay that fear to rest." I settled at the island, watching the pure Blood Born work. Muscle rippled over his wide shoulders and back, but I had no wish to touch him. Kiss him. Bend over for him—

A snort drew my gaze to the top of the stairs as Elijah set a mug in front of me.

"What the fuck do you want *this* time?" Jon stood there in a pair of shorts, his longer blond hair dripping water onto his chest and running down into the waistband of his shorts. He had obviously felt my presence in his home and hastened to finish showering.

I grinned, loving how his eyes narrowed into a threatening glare. As if the man could hurt me. A chuckle rumbled in my chest over the fact he'd rushed to ensure I didn't make a move on his alpha. Jealousy was a delicious thing, and even though I would have loved to provoke Elijah's beta, I hadn't visited to get into a fight that would end up with Elijah's hands around my throat.

"I'm here seeking answers," I assured Elijah's beta. "Nothing more."

Jon's lips pressed tight, eyes wary with mistrust.

Their female, Dakota, arrived on the landing in leggings and one of Elijah's large button-down shirts that swallowed her up. Her wet hair twisted into a knot atop her head. She slid her hand into her husband's.

"Keep your eyes to yourself, asshole," Jon muttered at me.

Elijah stared at them as they descended, love and so much goddamned devotion in his gaze that my chest split in two.

My smile dissolved but not out of disappointment over having lost him to lesser beings. I wanted what the three of them shared, longed for it with every cell in my body.

The nearly-humans sidled up to their alpha, and Elijah kissed them both on the mouth in greeting. Jon shot me a cocky smirk after their quick lip-lock.

I was tempted to roll my eyes but refrained.

Elijah leaned against the counter, his mates bracketing his massive body, Dakota for what appeared to be soothing reasons with how she snuggled into him, and Jon with a satisfied grin. He trailed his hand over Elijah's pecs, down his washboard abs, his intent clear.

Elijah grasped Jon's hand before his beta could cup his bulge.

Biting back my snicker over Jon being denied and unable to physically stake his claim in front of me, I decided to address all three of them as equals since they'd been drawn together by fate.

"I'm sorry for disturbing what must still be the honeymoon phase."

Dakota's face flushed.

Jon smirked. "Don't see it ending anytime soon. We can't stop fucking. Elijah's massive cock, the delicious sweetness of his cum, how he perfectly fits us in every single way—it's heaven on earth. Fucking perfection."

"Enough," Elijah muttered, swatting Jon's ass.

It was his beta's turn to redden even though he gave his alpha a bratty stare that promised his punishment later.

My backside stung for the poor man. Elijah's arm packed one hell of a swing no matter the toy he wielded.

Deciding to spare Jon from the embarrassment he had brought on himself, I continued. "I'm in need of Elijah's wisdom as the only alpha royal Blood Born left on earth."

"You've accepted your position." Elijah didn't question,

but I nodded over him having caught me admitting his position of authority, something we'd constantly fought over in our years together.

"I know who I am, but I continue to struggle. I told you about my father and the supposed truth he'd poisoned my thoughts with when I was a child." I heaved a sigh and studied the coffee mug in my hands. A sip allowed me a moment to attempt to collect myself, but the rich roast from Elijah's French press distracted me with memories of sharing mornings with my ex-lover. I glanced around the wide-open living space where we'd attempted to love each other, noting the softer touches from a female creating a home to nest in.

Fresh flowers sat atop the coffee table, which suggested they'd flown or had driven to his place in Manhattan not too long ago. Two other throws draped across the couch's far arm, and a pile of yarn and knitting needles lay in one corner.

A bassinet stood beside the fireplace.

My gaze jerked toward Dakota. "Are you…" I swallowed, glancing down at her stomach. "Might I inquire if…"

She placed her hand on her belly, which I hadn't realized protruded thanks to Elijah's shirt. "Yes. We found a doctor with dragonblood in North Conway two days ago. After I showed her a vision of her future like I did with you, she believed the truth of what we were. Needless to say, her life has been turned upside down, but she verified my pregnancy that is progressing much faster than a human's. The three of us had been aware of our daughter's existence not long after conception, but an ultrasound allowed us to see her perfect little profile and button nose."

She has conceived.

Throat swelling, I lifted welling eyes to Dakota's, flicking my gaze over both of her mates and back again. "You've created life," I croaked, joy overflowing for the three of them and the possibility of having a similar future.

"We have." Elijah kissed the top of Dakota's head.

"Damned right we did." Pride laced Jon's words, and I couldn't blame him.

"Congratulations to you all," I offered, my smile returning even though my eyes remained wet. "I—I hope for the same someday."

"You've found your mates?" Dakota asked, leaning fully against her alpha, hand still on her lower abdomen.

Another rush of conflicting joy and pain flooded me. "I have."

"Elijah spoke with Ashley and assured her she wasn't in *The Twilight Zone*," Dakota said. "What of your alpha?"

"Vanni is…" What was with my voice trailing off when so many thoughts crowded my head? I huffed a laugh. "He's incredible. Stoic and yet a hilarious drunk when he lacks a filter. He's dominant in nature even if he is more human than beast. He's also gorgeous, the finest specimen I've seen upon this earth."

Dakota beamed at me.

Jon muttered under his breath something about *Elijah* being the hottest on the planet.

Elijah flashed a grin I hadn't seen in over a decade. "He is able to give you what you need?"

"Yes," I answered simply, remembering all too well how fulfilling it had been to kneel on the bench in Vanni's club and experience the strength behind the cane and whip he'd wielded to bring me pleasure.

"Then why are you here when you should be with them?" Elijah asked, not unkindly, his pale gaze full of happiness for me yet questioning my sanity over staying away from them. "You've recognized your place, which means you must feel the beginnings of a bond."

I nodded.

"Then there is no reason to question what has been destined since the time of your birth. They belong to you, and you to them. The three of you will complete one another in ways our parents could never have explained or prepared us for. Trust me."

Both Jon and Dakota gazed up at Elijah like he was responsible for the sun's rising every morning.

"You simply need to accept what is meant to be and submit yourself, Dolyn. Fully. No holding back."

Something I'd never done for him, and now I knew why. Elijah had never been mine, and I'd wasted ten years searching for a female who didn't exist for us.

Home.

Mates.

"I have to go." I stood, suddenly striding toward the door.

"Dolyn!" Dakota called out, halting my momentum.

She left her mates' side and approached on near-silent feet, hand outstretched. "May I?"

Swallowing hard, I nodded, remembering all too well what had happened the last time this gifted woman had touched my skin. I'd seen a vision of my mates and had experienced a bit of her own joy through the momentary connection between us.

Her slender hand rested against my left pec, and images rushed through my brain, stealing my breath and causing my cock to swell and tent the blanket wrapped tight around my waist.

"Oh, my." She giggled and stepped away. "You'd best get home, Dolyn. That bonding, the green fire wrapping tightly around the three of you, *well*." She laughed again and fanned her face.

Jon growled.

Elijah chuckled and held his beta's forearm with a firm grip to keep him from stalking forward.

I peered into Dakota's eyes, wanting her to see the depths of my thanks for her—and her possessive husband. "I hope you will allow our children to meet some day."

Her smile dazzled, and I understood Elijah's infatuation with his female, who was almost as lovely as my Ashley. "I would love nothing more. And if your female gives birth to a male, all the better," she said with a wink.

Jon snorted. "Not fucking happening, baby. You can get that goddamned thought right out of your pretty little head."

Ignoring his declaration, I spun away, ready to return to the ones who hopefully awaited my return. It wasn't as if they could escape the mountain, considering the weather when I'd left, but Vanni had the mental fortitude of ten men.

I wouldn't put *anything* past my alpha.

CHAPTER 34
VANNI

There was no TV or radio to entertain us as the days passed. The levels of our arousal intensified, but neither of us found true satisfaction like when we had enjoyed having Dolyn in the mix.

When not kissing, sucking, or fucking, we snooped around even deeper into what seemed like endless caverns, most empty and unused, covered in dust.

Rather than accompanying us, Tiggy had stayed by the front door, moping, chin resting on his front legs. No amount of hugs, words of love, or scratches pulled him out of his funk. Like him, Ashley started withdrawing into her emotions, anxiety and deepening sadness worsening with every hour.

While I attempted to distract her with exploration, we ended up in the library where I'd tried to make Dolyn submit to me.

But she didn't want to read.

Was tired of sitting on couches and talking about everything under the sun.

Her jaw and pussy ached from overuse.

At a loss, I watched her from where I sat on the couch, leaned forward, elbows on my knees. She stood in front of the library's cold fireplace, her back to me, arms crossed as though holding herself together. Yearning radiated off her, causing my lust to rekindle.

Needs Master.

Not lover.

The darkness inside me swirled, waking for the first time since Dolyn's departure with distinctive words.

"Shit," I murmured, head hanging with the realization of how badly I had failed my sweet submissive.

Follow.

An urge to exit the library brought me to my feet.

Ashley turned, her purple-hued eyes radiating desire that far outweighed lust.

I grabbed the lamp and held out my free hand. "Come."

Without a word, she obeyed and slid her palm to mine, crackles of energy licking up my arm. Instantly, her anxiety lessened, which boosted my confidence of doing the right thing. Ever trustful, she allowed me to lead her deeper into Dolyn's home, my feet moving as though they already knew the way to where my instincts demanded we go. We didn't traverse new territory, and I'd thought we had seen all there was—

Stop.

I pulled up abruptly, Ashley bumping into my back. "Hold this." I gave her the lantern and turned toward the rock wall, resting my palm on the stone at heart-level. No clue why I did so, but I felt an insistence that what I sought lay on the other side of the mass before us.

"What are you—" Ashley gasped as a loud grinding rent the air.

Like something out of a fantasy novel, a portion of the rock slid inward. Warm, stale air filled my nose but hardly unpleasant. Whatever room awaited beyond hadn't been used in years.

I reclaimed the light and lifted it high, stepping over the threshold into oppressive stillness.

A mother fucking dungeon opened up before us—and not the sort for prisoners.

A slow smile spread over my face, and my cock woke the fuck up at the ancient furniture made of solid wood scattered around the room. All sorts of implements of pain hung on the wall to my left, a long bench beneath covered with older toys. Chains hung from various areas around the room, connected to pulleys embedded in the rock ceiling.

"Oh God." Ashley's croak thickened my shaft even further, and I pressed on my bulge, taking note of the signs of disuse around us.

Considering the cleanliness of every single room we'd found in our explorations, it was obvious this was one cavern Primrose hadn't been aware of. A fine layer of dust covered everything—even the floor.

"Stay here," I murmured, handing Ashley the lamp. I eyed leather crops and floggers, not sure how well they would have held up over the years. A strange-looking flogger hung farther away, and I ambled closer, eyes narrowing. While I'd only seen Dolyn in his beast form once, I wouldn't ever forget the appearance of the golden scales that covered his massive body. "Get the fuck out," I murmured to myself while retrieving the toy that resembled tiny versions of his dragon's armor. The material was warm to the touch, a sense of familiarity trickling up through my fingertips to my chest and straight to my cock. Pre-cum oozed, soaking my jeans.

Beta.

"I'll be goddamned." I huffed a chuckle and returned my attention to the wall. A cane made out of the same material had me wishing Dolyn's juicy ass was available for me to take my aggression out on.

Soon.

A sadist could hope.

Having all I needed for the time being, I returned to Ashley's side.

She studied the flogger with its dozens of thin tails. "Is that…"

"Yeah, I think it is. Kinda perfect, if you ask me." I trailed the tails over her arm, and she shuddered.

"It's made from his scales," she said, the pulse in her neck thrumming. "I can *feel* him."

"Same." I clasped her hand, and we hurried back to the library since the furniture in the dungeon needed a thorough scrubbing before I would tie her to any of it.

Without being told, Ashley stripped and knelt on the couch, facing its back.

I set aside the lamp, rid myself of clothing, and swished the flogger a few times, getting a feel for it. The toy fit perfectly in my hand, the weight and ease with which it moved…*otherworldly.*

Smirking, I soothed my hand over Ashley's back, the skin beneath my palm satiny smooth and warm. Energy licked up my arm, the scent of her arousal flooding my nose. "Such a good girl for me."

She sighed, pressing into me.

"I'm sorry for not seeing to your needs."

"It's okay."

"It's *not*," I corrected her, pinching one ass cheek then the other.

She gasped and flinched.

"I'm going to make you fly, baby. What's your safeword, Ash?"

"Red," she whispered, laying her cheek against the couch's back cushion, a soft smile on her face, eyes closed.

I could sense her anticipation already led her toward subspace. It'd been too long since I'd cared for her in this way, and she had an abundance of anxiety and worry on her mind. From here on out, I would pay better attention to what my female required from her alpha and master. While I was only a piece of the puzzle of her life, I had a role to fill—and I would do so with all my ability and focus.

"Let's begin," I murmured and drew back my arm, reminding myself to take it easy since I'd never used a toy made out of goddamned dragon scales.

The tails hit her back with more thud than I'd expected for their thinness.

Ashley moaned. "Oh my God, that's *so* good, Master."

"Not too much?"

"No, Master."

I landed two more blows, the third slightly harder than the others.

Ashley shuddered.

"Color?"

"Green—so very green. It's like he's here..." Her voice trailed off, and I set my sights on sending her flying.

Lashes landed over her back and thighs. I hit her feet until they turned pink, and she squirmed, panting and begging for more.

Her desire and arousal flooded the energy between us, pulling the cord tight. I had no doubt I would climax without a single touch to my cock the second she shattered for me. But I didn't want that—I had plans.

"Widen your legs for me, Ash."

She obeyed without hesitation, offering me a tantalizing and mouthwatering view of her glistening labia and puckered, pink hole.

My cock dripped with the need to bury deep, to plant my seed where Dolyn's had been not so long ago.

Resuming with the flogger, I observed the subtle cues of her body. The tremors rippling over her skin. Her heaving torso as she attempted to fill her lungs while making the most delicious noises. A flush taking over her from neck to toes, only some from the pain I gifted her.

Haziness crept through the cord, and I landed two more intense blows before tossing the flogger aside and dropping to my knees. I buried my face between her cheeks, suckling the cream from her pussy, licking up over her asshole and back down.

Her sweet musk overcame my senses, all rational thought. Like an animal, I feasted with a hunger like I'd never known outside of tasting Dolyn's cum. Tongue in her ass, I stroked my rock-hard shaft, slickening copious amounts of pre-cum down my length.

"Gonna take this," I said, smearing more of my natural lube over her tight hole.

"Please," she whispered, on the verge of climaxing and drifting away.

Teeth clenched, I slipped a finger easily past the ring of muscle, sliding in without resistance. She groaned, and I pressed in another, scissoring to ready her for my girth.

"Master," she murmured, lost in a wave of passion.

What I wouldn't have given to have Dolyn with us, head shoved between her body and the couch, mouth latched to her clit to keep her focus off how I readied her ass.

A third finger ripped a grunt from her lungs, and I worked my way in, stretching her wide. Once she relaxed, I left her empty to line up my wet cockhead. One slow, steady push, and I sank into decadent silken heat.

"Fuuuuuck," I groaned as my cock disappeared into her.

"You're perfect, baby, swallowing me up. God*damn.*" Hissing, I pulled out and slammed in, jolting Ash forward so she plastered to the back of the couch.

She whined, lips parted as she panted, and I slid my arms around her waist, clutching her tight, my nose against her hair. Eyes closed, I gyrated my hips, sinking into her over and over again, my balls quickly tightening against my groin.

"Need you to let go, baby," I whispered, nosing her temple and breathing in the scent of her sweat and arousal. "Fly for me. Take me with you."

A low groan radiated between us, our inner voices hissing with pleasure.

Ashley came without sound, her hole clamped down on my cock.

Buried deep, I tumbled with her, thrusting with every thick spurt of cum through my shaft. Wetness leaked out around her rim, soaking the couch beneath us. Groaning, I squeezed her tight until I finished.

My breaths came in pants as I peppered her head, temple, and cheek with kisses.

She rested, her mind quiet. Empty.

A sense of satisfaction welled up inside me, and still deeply connected physically and emotionally, I laid us down on the couch, wet spot be damned. Murmurs of praise and adoration spilled from my lips as I petted every inch of her skin I could reach, even slipping fingers into her pussy a few times, stroking against the membrane along my semi.

While she rested, I shifted enough to pull my cock out an inch and push back in, slow strokes that built my need back up in a matter of seconds.

"Going to flood you again, sweet girl of mine," I murmured, caressing over her breasts.

She sighed and arched slightly.

All the consent I needed.

If only Dolyn would allow me to love and pleasure him as easily as our female did.

CHAPTER 35
ASHLEY

For the first time in days, I rested. Full-on silence in my head, muscles relaxed, and libido spent.

Vanni continued to stroke into my ass, and I squeezed my ring tight around him, desiring to help him feel good.

"Ash," he groaned, large hands sprawled over my chest, and he clutched me to him.

I laced my fingers through his, eyes closed, head still somewhat fuzzy as he gently chased his second orgasm. Heat tucked in close against my back, his heart thumping in perfect time with mine.

A small smile curved my lips. I loved this man. More than anything, I looked forward to completing our bond, being one with both him and Dolyn. Refusing to think on his absence and the hurt it caused my heart, I focused on my alpha, clenching my stretched pucker around his cock, coaxing him to fill me again like he'd promised.

With a deep growl, he buried deep.

Heat erupted in my ass, pulses of his cock throbbing inside me.

I moaned, tightening my fingers around his.

"Ash—baby. My love." His hot breath ghosted over the top of my head, his euphoria, the sense of contentment and release wafting over me like a gentle, springtime breeze.

A heavy sigh shuddered through me, and we lay still, slowly relaxing.

Vanni nuzzled my hair. "I made a mess of you and this couch."

"We'll both clean up," I murmured, still not ready to rouse fully.

"How are you feeling, baby?"

Brain somewhat more online, I took stock of my body. Zero residual pain lingered along my backside where he'd flogged me. Every impact had flooded me with a sense of Dolyn, like the toy crafted from parts of his beastly body made him present even though he hadn't been. I'd never enjoyed a scene more or fallen so completely into subspace.

"I'm perfect," I assured Vanni. "*You're* perfect, and I want you to use that flogger on me again when Dolyn returns."

"After I take the cane to his ass first."

I shuddered. "Yes, please."

He chuckled and slowly slid out of my ass.

A rush of cum gushed from my hole, and he groaned, attempting to shove it back in with his fingers.

"That is *not* normal," I said with a chuckle.

"Never used to come this much until I met Dolyn. It's like he woke something up inside me."

Twin voices agreed with my alpha's claim.

Vanni used his shirt to clean me up the best he could then carried me to the other couch and pulled me down, cradling my backside with me facing the library's far wall with its ancient-looking arches rising above recessed bookshelves. We lay in quietness, a purr-like sound humming between us.

My eyelids grew heavy, and I snuggled into his warmth.

Absently, he stroked a thumb over my nipple, but rather than arousing me, the caress soothed.

Look.

I blinked at the clear voice in my head, making my eyes focus on the distant, antique bookshelf. It was crafted out of wood when the others lining the walls had been carved into stone that wouldn't sag with age—

The old shelving *didn't* sag.

"That bookshelf still glows as though it got a fresh coat of poly and polish lately," I said.

Vanni lifted his head. "Probably because Primrose is a neat freak and had nothing better to do all winter long than clean this place."

"No. Look." I pushed up onto my elbow, gaze narrowing. "It's the only wooden one in this room, and it's set into the rock wall."

Closer.

"You heard that too, didn't you?" I asked Vanni.

He hummed an agreement and climbed off the couch, ass and thighs clenching as he moved across the cavern.

I stood, surprised to find my own legs sturdy when a scene like we'd shared usually left me rubbery as a wet noodle. Sidling up next to Vanni, I slid my hand into his. We both studied the piece of furniture that somehow didn't... belong.

As one, we both reached out with our free hands as though instinct dictated the movement. At the brush of our fingertips, energy licked over our bodies like flames, radiating heat and a sense of rightness.

"What the fuck?" Vanni ran his hand over the dustless shelf at eye level, and I did the same on the one below, my fingertips gliding along the wooden grain.

"It's warm," I breathed the words.

"Almost..."

I could sense Vanni's frown.

"Almost like it's *alive*." He pressed his palm flat on the shelf's back between two books, same as he'd done with the rock wall—door—leading into the dungeon.

The bookshelf shifted inward without a noise, causing both of us to flinch backward a step.

A burst of golden beams appeared around the shelf's curved edges before the entire bookcase slid to the left, revealing a cavern beyond.

Three orbs, close to two feet in diameter sat at the room's center on individual pedestals, their inner glow casting light on dozens of dimmed other orbs beneath arches lining the perimeter of the room.

Enter.

As one, we obeyed the echoing voices in our heads, stepping through the hidden doorway. A gentle warmth radiated throughout the circular cavern, smelling slightly of brimstone and earth. The scent reminded me of Dolyn.

Sadness seeped into my chest, and I whimpered, pressing a hand against my breast.

Vanni wrapped his arms around me, his own hurt mingling with mine and causing tears to well in my eyes.

"What is this place?" I croaked through the thickness in my throat.

"Maybe a mausoleum? But those aren't urns."

I had the sense Vanni was onto something. The three orbs at the room's center drew my attention. One gray, one blue, one…golden.

"They're scales," I breathed.

Touch.

Our feet moved us forward, hands outstretched as our inner beasts demanded.

CHAPTER 36
DOLYN

I landed near the rented SUV that still sat half-buried in fresh snow, a bag of clothing clutched in my claws. The mountain in front of me called out, urging me to return, submit to my alpha, and accept my place in attempting to repopulate the human world with Blood Born dragon shifters.

But responsibilities needed looking after first.

I'd taken care of Ashley's abuser, the largest and most important requirement for moving forward, but smaller details needed attending to.

My beastly form snorted at my human half, well aware of why I made him procrastinate.

Fear being the deciding factor, what Father had told me no royal Blood Born ever experienced. But I'd been hampered by the emotion my entire life, even though I attempted to smother it. Now, I acknowledged something I'd once seen as an imperfection but realized acted as another instinct to help protect our human half.

I'd always needed to be in control of things around me to be comfortable, and my relationships with Vanni and Ashley were no different. Once I completed the tasks before me and set things in order, I would feel free to take my place as beta.

A steady stream of dragon fire melted the snow around the vehicle Vanni had gotten from the airport and cleared the road they'd taken deeper into the wilderness to find me. Once shifted into my human form and dressed in the clothing I'd brought along, I pulled the agreement paperwork from the glove compartment and drove toward civilization.

Every mile into Idaho and away from my mates heightened the ache in my chest, but I pressed on. The cloaked flight back to Jackson Hole from the car rental place eased my breathing, but I wasn't yet done. I followed residual hints of Vanni's musk and Ashley's sweetness to the tiny hotel they had stayed in while searching for me, melted the lock to gain entry, and crashed on the bed they'd shared. The scent of cum covered the bedding and made my mouth water.

Need.

I ignored the beast and nuzzled into Vanni's pillow while clutching Ashley's tight.

One last night of putting off my destiny, and I would accept my fate.

I dreamed of my mates, of our coming together with the intense fire Dakota's vision had shown me. Being surrounded by my two lovers, the bond forging our hearts and minds together, flooded me with desperate need. I woke hard and aching but saved my release for the only two on earth who deserved my touch and pleasure.

I checked out of the motel room, their two suitcases they'd left behind in their search of me in hand.

Once away from human eyes, I shimmered out of existence and shifted. The flap of my wings blew the snow beneath me out in a swirling eddy, but I didn't waste longer than necessary watching it spin as though a tornado had rippled over the small stretch of land south of town.

I set my gaze on my mountain, on the cloaked door of my home I could easily make out with my dragon sight. The sense of drawing closer to my mates caused my skin to tingle and insides to quiver.

Would they be too angry with me for abandoning them a second time that they refused our bond? Had I hurt them with my remarks to the point they would deny what had been destined by fate?

My throat tightened, but I didn't push against the rising fear. I also refused to berate myself as I once would have done for choosing a wrong decision in my selfishness. Allowing forgiveness to myself didn't lessen my anxiety, but I finally felt as though I'd done something right. Self-care, Elijah would have called it.

Shifting back on the veranda, I hastened to press my hand against the front door. Stepping inside soothed like a warm blanket, a mother's caress to the forehead.

The scent of my mates, one soft and sweet, the other musky and similar to the brimstone far below the living quarters of our cavern, slid over me, tightening my groin and causing my mouth to water.

Yessss.

The clatter of toenails on the stone floor drew my attention to the other side of the kitchen.

"Tiggy," I murmured, dropping the two suitcases and holding out my arms.

He yipped and leapt toward me, paws on my shoulders, wet tongue from lapping at his water bowl snaking over my cheek with a sloppy kiss.

"Who's a good boy?" I crooned, scratching behind his ears, snickering when he wagged his tail so hard he almost toppled over. "Did you miss me, boy? Hmm?" Grinning, I gave him a quick pat to his head and stood.

The large living area was tidy, but the scents of my mates

and cum lingered on every surface. They had fucked on the couch, against the front door—on the kitchen table.

My gaze slid to the hallway leading deeper into the caverns.

"Stay," I ordered Tiggy with one last pet to his head.

Whining, he flopped onto the floor, head on his front paws.

Cock swelled and aching, I strode toward the cave that led down into the bowels of the mountain, my inner beast whimpering with the same need driving me forward.

My nose and my mates' energy led me into the library, and I pulled up short as my gaze landed on the wall to my right.

The door hiding my family's sacred mausoleum had been pushed inward without permission or authority. None save a royal Blood Born could open the vault holding my ancestors' incinerated bones. Only Elijah and I had the power to do such a thing. I hadn't done so, which meant Elijah had somehow located and infiltrated my home. I scented my mates beyond the threshold but not Elijah. Was he somehow able to cloak his presence in ways I'd never learned?

Forehead furrowing and shoulders tightening, I hurried forward to find out what his intentions were toward the two who belonged to me.

I pulled up short on the threshold, my breath leaving in a rush.

Completely enthralled, both Vanni's and Ashley's palms lay atop my mother's orb. Her aura rippled up their arms and around their bodies, lovingly embracing them both.

Warmth flooded through me, and heartbeat racing in my chest, I quickly scanned the room.

Elijah was nowhere to be found in the circular cavern.

My alpha—*Vanni*—was the only living male present. It didn't matter that lesser dragonblood flowed through his veins. My mother had sensed the beast inside him, the heart of who my alpha was, and had allowed him entry.

My son.

Wetness gathered in my eyes as my mother's beast whispered in my head.

You have always been worthy, more than enough to carry on our legacy.

Visions of Papa flitted through my head, causing my chest to ache.

Remember how he invested in and played with you. Adored every little part of who you are. Even now, he encourages you to follow your heart.

I wanted to question Father—

The law isn't always what one ought to decide their future upon.

My alpha father's actual voice rumbled through my mind for the first time in centuries, and I closed my eyes, memories flashing through me, bringing a tumble of emotions I allowed in the hopes of healing. Father showed me visions of discipline, hurtful words, punishments over my rebellion in my earlier years before I'd cowed beneath his authority.

I am sorry.

My muscles weakened as glorious solace swept through me.

I was wrong—and I see that now that I've passed beyond the realm of limited knowledge. I have made my peace with your papa, my kindhearted beta whom I adore. He has forgiven me for my mistreatment toward him, and I hope you will one day be able to do the same.

I swallowed hard, yearning to do that very thing, but as with everything when it came to my human half's stubborn side, I would need time to come to acceptance of his apologies.

Right now, I had more important matters to deal with.

My mother's light pierced through my mates' chests in a flash of opal brilliance. Their contentment and joy radiated through the tether among us that would hopefully soon be an unbreakable bond.

Vanni and Ashley were a gift and blessing beyond what I had ever dreamed possible. Deserving beyond measure.

I had been a fool, one poisoned by insecurities, a sense of superiority over their species when all that mattered was their hearts and souls.

Their inner dragons.

The energy rippling off them assured me they wished to be bonded with me—would stand in the way of anyone wanting to do me harm. My mates would remain by my side until we too left this land to reside in the beyond.

A sense of calm settled over me regardless of the fluttering inside the deepest reaches of me.

Mother's light lessened, but inner warmth radiated from my mates, Vanni's a vibrant green, Ashley's a pale gray, exactly as I'd seen in Dakota's vision all those weeks ago.

Scaled beasts shimmered briefly around them like auras, catching my breath and causing my eyes to well.

Yessss.

Mine.

"Ours," I whispered, as my mother's pearlescence ebbed, pulling back into her orb.

My mates' senses returned with a jolt, and they both spun. Only then did I take note of their nakedness, the scent of their combined cum in the air.

Ashley's eyes glowed, and the flow of desire for me, beyond the tender release I could offer her, flooded the slight tether between us.

"Ashley." I breathed her name as a prayer, and she tore from Vanni's hold on her hand and rushed toward me, throwing herself into my arms. She settled against me, all soft and warm, her legs wrapping around my waist.

Although my cock swelled and nudged against her core, I needed her mind more than her body. "I'm so sorry." My voice caught on a sob. "So fucking sorry for every goddamn—"

She took my mouth, and I drank in her sweet breath, the love radiating from her, washing over me, and melting my muscles. "You're forgiven," she murmured. "Take me, my love."

I sank to my knees, laying Ashley on her back beneath me. One shift of my hips led my aching shaft into the sweet haven of her embrace.

Home.

Longing for my alpha flooded my entire being as I buried in our female's warmth.

A shudder rippled through my body, and I planked on my elbows to meet Vanni's gaze as he squatted in front of me. "You're fucking my female, boy."

"I'm *making love* to our mate," I corrected him, pulling out and sliding into her slick heat. Her tight sheath pulsed, trying to suck me deeper.

One of his brows rose, a smirk playing on the corner of his mouth.

My cock bucked in response.

"You think you can just waltz back in like a naked, irresistible Greek god and all will be forgiven and forgotten?" Vanni murmured, his gaze trailing over our bodies, nothing but lust washing through our tether.

"You can punish me for being an asshole later," I said, holding his gaze, hoping he sensed my submission as I nudged a little deeper into Ashley's warmth. "Right now, we need you. *I* need you."

He smirked, already well aware of his mates' yearnings. "Say please."

Pleasssse.

My jaw clenched, a reaction born from years of stubbornness, but I deserved any shit Vanni thought to give me ten times over.

"*Please*, my alpha," I begged, all sense of self-preservation and pride set aside in my desire to mate. "Claim me as you have Ashley. Finish the bond to make the three of us one."

Vanni grasped my face in his hands, the aura of his beastly form flicking around him in swirls of green. Ancient words poured from his lips in a language he shouldn't know, the one of my people.

Our people.

Ashley's core tightened around my still shaft as Vanni's eyes began to glow, flames flickering to life around the three of us.

Vanni, a mostly-human male, had set our bonding in motion.

My body ached for him, craved him with a madness that hazed my vision, and had I not already been buried inside our female, I would have dropped to my knees in submission at his feet. "Please, Master," I croaked, my gaze dropping to his dripping cock.

I wanted his shaft buried deep in my ass, coating my insides with his seed, but I needed to taste his sweetness first. "Let me suck you."

He released his hold on my face and shifted forward on his knees, grabbing the base of his cock. "Show me what a good boy you can be for me, Dolyn."

"Yes, Master," I whispered and opened my mouth.

CHAPTER 37

ASHLEY

Vanni's cock disappeared between Dolyn's lips right above my head.

"Oh, God," I groaned as my core clenched down on my beta's length buried deep against my womb.

Dolyn shuddered, his chest rumbling against mine as Vanni's sweet flavor, which I could taste through our bond, coated his tongue.

The words Vanni had spoken, whatever language they were, had heightened my sense of them both, an awareness of their proximity stronger than I'd felt before.

Vanni pulled out, and Dolyn did the same to my pussy, leaving only his cockhead inside my body.

They both pressed forward as one, a euphoric spring of desire welling in all three of us.

"Such a good boy," Vanni murmured, gripping Dolyn's chin on the next synchronized withdraw and thrust.

My clit ached, and I clutched at Dolyn's shoulders, writhing against his flesh for more friction where I needed it most.

"You have to take me before our female finds her release,

Vanni," Dolyn said, his tone ragged with lust. "We must come as one in order for the bond to work. Not that I wouldn't mind trying again and again, but I've made us all wait long enough."

Vanni stood and moved behind us.

Moaning, I clung to Dolyn's back, fighting to keep my eyelids open. Tingles raced over my skin, my heart pounding inside my chest.

Dolyn lowered his head, his mouth claiming me with a hungry kiss that tasted of our alpha as Vanni kicked his knees wider.

I could feel both men's anticipation, Vanni's slick cockhead smearing and teasing over Dolyn's hole that ached to be filled.

"Goddamnit!" Dolyn growled. "Hurry up and fu—"

Vanni shoved into his ass with one brutal thrust.

My toes curled along with Dolyn's, both of our breaths lost at the exquisite sting racing through his backside.

I stared up into golden, glowing eyes, waves of emotion and need rolling through me.

Alpha.

Beta.

Female.

Our inner beasts echoed in my head, Dolyn's nearly weeping in relief at our finally coming together.

Whimpering, I lifted my head to brush my lips over Dolyn's again, desperate to have his tongue stroking mine.

Vanni's fingertips dug into Dolyn's hips, growls from his chest encouraging a similar sound from our beta. "You feel so good around my cock, Dolyn. Better than I fantasized." He pulled out to the crown, and one harsh thrust forward buried Dolyn inside me, ripping our mouths apart.

I gasped as Dolyn contorted his upper body to press his face into my neck.

My gaze met Vanni's behind him.

Drool flooded both of my mates' mouths in a rush, and awareness of their desire caused my inner walls to clench down on Dolyn's shaft.

"Please," I begged.

Vanni leaned forward, ensnaring my gaze with his glowing green orbs. "You want our pain, sweet girl."

I nodded frantically even though he hadn't asked a question.

He pulled out and thrust in time with Dolyn, our beta's arms beneath my back protecting me from the rock floor.

The sounds of wet fucking, panted breaths, and the scent of sex flooded the chamber around us as we chased fulfillment.

Whether or not Dolyn's ancestors watched our coming together, I didn't know. Didn't care. A deep craving to complete the bond drove us onward, and we strove toward the rapidly approaching peak.

Vanni grabbed Dolyn's hair in a tight fist, causing his back to arch.

I clung to Dolyn, keeping his mouth on my neck where instinctively I knew he needed to be in order for completion.

"Going to sink my teeth into your luscious flesh, beta," Vanni rumbled against Dolyn's ear. "Do the same to our female—and make it hurt even though you don't want it to."

Dolyn's reluctance shimmered through the lust, but he obeyed our alpha's command.

Sharp incisors pierced the skin where my neck met my shoulder, and I cried out at the delicious stinging pain.

Vanni's cock throbbed in Dolyn's ass. "Come, my mates."

Our climaxes slammed into each of us in unison, an eruption of cum and cries as Vanni bit our beta.

A surge of starbursts erupted inside me, lighting like a blast of fireworks through the cells of my body.

Awareness of my mates raced through my senses—a shared olfactory, emotional, and physical touch. The tang of blood coated my taste buds as another pulse clenched my pussy around Dolyn. Vanni throbbed inside Dolyn, spilling deep in his guts.

As seamlessly as we'd reached the pinnacle, we descended, shared gasps for breath and trembling muscles.

Two hearts beat with royal blood, I realized, not just Dolyn's.

I blinked my eyelids open, not having realized I'd nearly lost myself to subspace from merely coming together with my mates.

Vanni stared down at me, brilliant eyes wide.

Dolyn shuddered between us, his arms still cradling me, our alpha's grips on his hair and hip gentling.

"I am a direct descendant of the Blood Born meant to rule earth's skies," Vanni murmured what the three of us had become aware of.

"You were the key to unlocking all that I had ever wanted and dreamed of what fate had destined for me. For *us*." Dolyn's declaration caused relief to swell inside Vanni's chest and brought tears to my eyes.

Our emotions and continued thoughts of thankfulness and forgiveness pinged back and forth, Dolyn acting as a conductor, the bridge between alpha and female as fate had intended.

"I can sense you both in my head and heart," I said, my voice broken with happiness. "I—I can even feel Vanni inside you, Dolyn." I clenched around his softening length, causing both men to groan and shudder. "Oh, this is glorious." I smiled, tears pouring down my cheeks.

Peace surrounded us as our bodies remained locked. All three inner voices hummed their contentment, Dolyn's being the strongest and loudest.

"I'm sorry," Dolyn muttered, his lips caressing where he'd bitten me, the slight puncture wounds already sealing from the power of our bonding. "You're both worthy—always have been. I'm so sorry."

"I have plans to make you pay," Vanni said, his dick twitching in Dolyn's ass. A rush of need swelled inside of me at the images flashing in our alpha's mind.

Chains. Ropes. Floggers, crops, and that dragon scale cane.

Dolyn's dragon lusted over the thought of pain—and his human mind over giving himself freely to our alpha who shared similar desires. He shuddered atop me again, and I moaned, my pussy primed and ready for round two.

Vanni pulled out before either of my mates hardened fully, leaving Dolyn destitute over the emptiness in his ass.

I took his face in my hands and pressed a chaste kiss to his lips, one meant to reassure rather than rekindle.

Dolyn trembled in my arms, a heavy sigh sinking more of his weight against me. "Thank you."

Vanni returned with a shirt in hand. He knelt behind us, spreading Dolyn's cheeks wide. "So sexy." He shoved his fingers in deep, the squelch evidence to my ears of the copious amounts of cum he'd shot inside his beta. "So hot and wet. Almost makes me want to take your ass again, boy."

Another shot of lust roused my blood.

"Push it out."

Dolyn's face flushed at Vanni's command, his discomfort causing similar heat to rush through me.

He obeyed, eyes clenched shut, head hanging.

"Such a good boy for me." Pleasure coated Vanni's tone, his satisfaction settling over our minds and easing Dolyn's embarrassment as he smeared his spunk all over Dolyn's ass and thighs. "Mmm. Just like that. Again."

Another pulse of seed seeped from Dolyn's hole.

"So. Fucking. Sexy." Vanni cracked his palm against Dolyn's ass cheek, the slightest sting radiating across my backside.

I gasped, and Dolyn growled.

"Do not hurt her," he stated through gritted teeth.

I yanked on Dolyn's hair to meet his gaze. "I want to experience every bit of pain he gives you. Surely you felt how much I loved it?"

His brow furrowed, and he nodded.

Smiling up at him, I flung my arms around his torso, nosing along his neck and drinking in the scent of sex and cedar as the last of our alpha's seed leaked from him.

Vanni wiped him clean, and Dolyn finally slid from my body, taking longer to care for me.

He helped me to my feet but didn't release my hand as I sagged against him. Vanni entwined my other hand with his, creating a circle of one—heartbeat, mind, acceptance, and love.

"We were destined by our blood," I whispered, my eyes filling with tears. "By fate, we were meant to be together." I peered up at Dolyn. "You're mine." Giving Vanni my focus, I said, "I'm yours."

Dolyn squeezed her hand. "And you're mine." My heartbeat quickened, my rush of happiness flooded through our bond as Dolyn faced Vanni. "I'm yours, my alpha."

The darkness swirled in Vanni's pupils as the green of his eyes glowed with the inner fire. "And I belong to both of you." He dropped to his knees before us, his head bowed, offering Dolyn what Elijah never had.

True thankfulness wrapped all three of us in her embrace.

CHAPTER 38
VANNI

And I thought I wouldn't be able to love again, never mind with deeper meaning and intimacy than with my ex. What she and I had shared didn't compare to my connection with Dolyn and Ashley. While the whole no-privacy-in-the-head thing sometimes annoyed the hell out of me, I counted the gift a blessing when one of us got caught up in our thoughts and usually would have shut down.

That shit no longer worked.

There were no misunderstandings over tone or inflections. Talk about making for easy communication and a complete lack of arguing.

Within two weeks, we'd fucked everywhere. That honeymoon phase Dolyn had warned us about was no joke. We were insatiable for one another. Sometimes, Dolyn watched me give Ashley pain with her pleasure, but nothing got me hotter than Ashley's arousal when I took Dolyn to his limits.

He'd submitted his body to me completely, and while he never fully entered subspace, he often got that floaty feeling in the back of his mind that caused his inner beast to purr like a happy kitten.

Made me feel like a damned god to bring a dragon shifter of royal blood to his knees.

But I fell to mine for him too.

Often.

Couldn't have enough of his spunk shooting down my throat, the sweetness of his seed an addiction he gladly fed me whenever I grew hungry.

Daily, Dolyn took us out onto the veranda and attempted to teach us how to shift. While Dolyn claimed to see an aura flash around me consistently, I hadn't yet managed to stretch ligament, bone, and muscle, turning my flesh into scales.

Our dragons conversed constantly, the chatter bugs causing both Ashley and I to demand Dolyn show us how to muzzle the noisy bastards. But we both let them have their voice whenever our beta soared in the skies with us on his back or gently cradled in his claws.

Upon bonding, the cold no longer affected our human bodies. An inner fire had awakened, keeping us warm no matter the weather. Ashley and I had also gained a friend in Tiggy, who couldn't have cared less about our presence until we became one with Dolyn.

Oftentimes, he sat outside our bedroom door and whined until we finished draining orgasms from one another. His new favorite spot? The foot of the bed beside Ashley's feet.

The only place he didn't follow us was when we took to the sky.

"You can't be serious." I muttered, eyeing the cliff-like drop from the veranda of our cavern home two weeks to the day after our bonding. Of course, I knew he was, but I couldn't believe what he asked for.

The firm set of Dolyn's jaw raised my eyebrows.

Did my boy need a reddened ass?

Arousal shot through him. "No. I really do want you both on my back like we do every night—but I want our female to ride you while doing so."

"Goddamn, Dolyn." I shook my head even though my dick swelled at the thought—same as his. "If you want her cum leaking all over your scales, we can fuck right here on the ground, safe and sound, where no one will get hurt."

"But imagine her fear and your heightened pleasure from shooting across the sky while buried inside our female."

My inner dragon purred with delight as I eyed my beta's bare chest, his broad back as he turned to peer out over the frozen land falling away before us. Dolyn was desperate for both Ashley and I to learn how to shift so we could fly the skies with him. His inner beast loved to frolic among the clouds, but he hated being far away from us.

Holding hands as Dolyn had done with his granddaughter to teach her cloaking hadn't worked for us, unfortunately. We hadn't yet accomplished our goal of pleasing our beta in that way, but with each attempt through our bond, our inner dragons strengthened, giving us hope for our future.

Soon.

Expecting my beast spoke truth, I studied my beta as his thoughts continued down the path of cum leaking over his scales as wind swept over our faces. While I wasn't too keen on the idea, there wasn't anything I wouldn't attempt for him.

"We'll have to adjust those straps you created for me and Ashley, make it so I'm tied down rather than just hanging on for my life like usual when we fly."

Dolyn's eyes glimmered gold in the last of the sun's rays as his thoughts took another turn. "I would love to see you tied down."

I narrowed my gaze. "This will be the *only* time you see me such a thing."

A flash of his rare grin hit my chest like a lightning bolt.

"Then I'll take it, alpha."

Dolyn had found peace in our bonding, and although he loved to tease and feign fighting me for dominance, I always ended up on top.

Unless sucking his cock for the taste of his cum I craved.

An alpha Dom, getting on his knees for a male submissive…

I'd promised him more, and strangely, I actually looked forward to offering him the chance to dominate me.

He shot a glance over his shoulder, eyebrow raised, and I grinned and shrugged as pre-cum leaked from both our stiff dicks. His tongue flickered over his lip as his gaze dropped down to my throbbing length.

Sensing Ashley still lingered in our bedroom and could make it through the dark hallways thanks to heightened sight, I stilled, eyeing my beta, waiting.

He moved close, his focus on my chest and sank to his knees without a word, head bowed, hands clasped on his lap.

I ran my fingers through his hair exactly how he loved. "What do you want, beta?" I could feel the answer on his mind, but I loved giving him shit.

"A taste of your cum, Master."

I pressed on the base of my dick, jutting it toward his face.

"Then by all means—have a little lick."

His hot mouth closed over my swollen head, and I grabbed hold of his hair, pulling him in close, gagging him with my full length. "Such a good boy," I murmured what he enjoyed hearing, my balls tightening at the strength of his hollowed cheeks.

"So good taking me like this." I thrust in deep again, gagging him, loving how he grasped my thighs in desperation to keep me close. "Swallow around me…yes."

I groaned, fighting the need to blow my load.

On the verge of exploding, I pulled Dolyn off my dick.

"Enough." My voice came out strangled as I stepped back.

He peered up at me, his golden-brown eyes filled with lust and longing.

I smoothed my hand over his hair and cupped his cheek. "You please me, beta."

Overwhelming love and acceptance shimmered through our bond, and as much as I wanted to give him my whole load, I looked forward to filling our female as we soared through the air, our combined cum leaking over Dolyn's dragon body like he wished.

Both of our dicks jerked as though in agreement.

"Soon," I murmured as Ashley's presence drew near.

Naked as a jay, same as both Dolyn and I, Ashley stepped out onto the veranda, her arousal sweet in my nose. Her pupils were swollen, nipples tight and aching.

"I don't even have to be with you to get turned on by your shenanigans," she said, laughter in her voice. "That might be my favorite thing about this bond."

Dolyn promised us the desire to mate hard and fast—and frequently—would eventually lessen, but none of us seemed to look forward to that time. If a cavern or tunnel existed that we hadn't fucked in, I'd yet to see it, including the bed of the old truck deep in the bowels of our home.

Ashley walking toward us with a saunter in her step, heat in her eyes—and a whole lot of longing shimmering through our bond—made me hunger to order them both around. Tie him up. Make our female ride him while I flogged her back.

Or maybe have him take her while I whipped her thighs beneath his thrusting ass. An ass I enjoyed burying myself in more than I'd ever dreamed possible.

My beta. My female.

"I also heard a whisper saying you wanted me to fuck our

alpha while we go riding tonight." Ashley pointed out into the crimson-streaked sky.

"And did that voice tell you I'd be strapped down and unable to move?" I couldn't help but ask, knowing Dolyn's dragon would rumble in his chest. Need shot through me as his expected response did just that.

"Mmm." Ashley narrowed her gaze, hands resting on her flared hips, ones that no longer sported my bruises for longer than an hour when I gifted her the pain she craved as much as Dolyn did. "I've got to say—"

"Yeah, yeah." I rolled my eyes but knew she experienced my arousal at the idea of being under Dolyn's control. "Let's just get on with it."

Dolyn chuckled and leaped off the veranda, shooting my heart into my throat as it did every time he took to the sky.

His golden dragon banked, landing on the veranda's edge with a clatter of claws on stone. He blinked, the darkness in his pupils, the violence he kept contained, causing my dick to drip onto the stone beneath my feet.

Someday.

I rumbled an agreement with my dragon, the flare of lust in Dolyn's dragon eyes drawing my balls up tight against my body as he felt my desire to give him what he longed for.

Yes, I told him. *One day soon, you can tie me up—and you'll remember it's only because* I'm *allowing it.*

"I want to watch," Ashley said with a breathy moan, her arousal flooding my nose and the bond between us.

"Whatever you desire, my female," I said, crawling up onto Dolyn's back. The magnificence of his size, the sheer beauty of gold glinting in the failing light—I'd never seen anything so goddamn beautiful in my life.

It took a few bits of laughter and annoyed snorts from my beta like it always did, but Ashley and I managed to fasten in place the leather contraption he'd fashioned for us last week.

Legs strapped down tight against his body, I shifted my ass, his scales smooth beneath my bare skin and arousing as hell. "Get up here," I growled at Ashley, "before I grab my cock and jerk this load of cum from my balls all over Dolyn's pretty scales."

A growl rumbled beneath me, and I tipped my head back, fisting my cock. "Don't tempt me." I bit the words out, never more relieved to feel Ashley settle her thighs on either side of me. "Take me deep, baby," I said, lining my throbbing head at her opening.

She slammed down onto me, and Dolyn leaped into the air, my arms wrapped around our female, our hearts beating in time—twice beyond what they normally did—as our dragon carried us higher than I'd ever imagined, our cries of ecstasy lost in the wind rushing past our ears.

EPILOGUE - ASHLEY

I sat on the veranda's edge with Tiggy at my side, warm spring air wafting over my face as I gazed into the sky.

Both of my mates, cloaked and glorious, frolicked in their beast forms, bumping, diving, and rolling among the low, murky clouds that promised rain.

The chill of the stone beneath my naked backside didn't bother me, nor did the fact I hadn't yet been able to get my dragon wings to keep me in the air for longer than a few seconds.

Soon.

Even from the distance between us, I heard both Vanni and Dolyn's dragons echo my own's sentiment. Both Vanni and I had managed to shift after two months of practice. He'd only taken to the sky a week earlier, and I loved watching his black beast soar and dip alongside my golden god.

The smile remained on my face more often than not, a sense of contentment that doubled due to our bond. Never had I ever expected to find such joy and peace. While an occasional flashback or bad dream put me in a funk, my mates' connection with my thoughts and emotions allowed them to help me get ahead of trigger effects. Distraction was our favorite go-to, but learning what Dolyn had done in his absence had laid most of my trauma to rest.

My abuser no longer drew breath, and cold eyes wouldn't ever watch me again. There was no evil consciousness that would search me out and stalk me as he'd been doing for years. The man's computer had held damning evidence of his past sins, but rather than taking it to the authorities, Dolyn exacted justice the vigilante way, burning everything the man owned, body included, to the ground.

He felt zero remorse.

Same as me.

Were my parents out of their jobs? Perhaps. But, their lives no longer concerned me, just as mine hadn't to them all those years ago. Karma could be a bitch, and I left them to their fate.

As for me?

I sighed and scratched behind Tiggy's ear, my heartbeat starting to thrum as my beastly men drew closer, the power of their massive wings shooting them unhindered through the air. Every second, they loomed closer, heightening my breath. Need coiled in my abdomen, and the thought of shifting for us to breed in dragon form flitted through my mind, but I wanted hands on my skin. Lips and tongues worshiping me rather than a heated, hard fuck like our dragons tended to prefer.

Glowing eyes rested on me, their intent clear as the distance closed.

I scooted back from the veranda's edge, allowing them space to touch down one at a time. Once the first set of claws clattered on stone, the shifting began, quickly shrinking muscle and bone, morphing scales to skin.

Tiggy barked and ran to Dolyn, licking his leg.

My beta knelt, whispered into his ear, and like a good boy, Tiggy loped around me toward the open door behind me and disappeared inside.

I sprawled on my back, legs spread, propped on my elbows.

Vanni's focus slid over my body with laser focus, dark and menacing, causing goose bumps to erupt over every inch of me. Even my scalp tingled with heightened awareness. He palmed his shaft, a slow upward stroke making pre-cum leak from his slit.

My mouth watered, and I swallowed, glancing at Dolyn again.

His warm gaze rested on my face, the love in his heart catching my breath, his tenderness toward me causing my eyes to well.

Knowing their intent made my want expand, until I trembled, my core wet and aching.

Vanni fell between my spread legs and dove into my pussy like a starving man, his mouth and tongue searingly hot. I grabbed hold of his hair with one hand, hanging on for dear life, my other finding the back of Dolyn's neck as he knelt beside me.

Golden flames filled his irises, and I lost myself to the sweetness of his mouth as he descended on me. Everything but my need for fulfillment consumed me, a driving force toward completion. We fit together seamlessly, assurance of their devotion and my safety settled in my mind.

"Breed me," I gasped the second Dolyn allowed me breath. While I hadn't needed to speak what they already were well aware I wanted, both men loved hearing me voice my desires. The low tone of my whispered pleas made their ball sacs tighten and slickness ooze from their cocks.

Dolyn lay down, pulling me atop him, my back to his

chest. Arms crossed over my breasts, he slid me along his hard body until his cockhead kissed my swollen lower lips Vanni had been suckling on.

My alpha stood at our feet, wiping his forearm over his glistening mouth, dark gaze still between my thighs. "Fill her."

One slow shift of Dolyn's hips slid his thick shaft deep into my core.

I whimpered, digging fingernails into his forearms banded over me. "Please," I begged.

As though the word controlled our alpha, Vanni's stare slid over our entwined bodies as he sank to his knees. "Fucking gorgeous. My light and dark beauties." He smoothed his warm palms up the inside of my legs, thumbs rubbing along my opening stretched wide around Dolyn's shaft. "Mmm. So silky, soft, and wet."

He bent forward, teeth latching onto my clit.

I shrieked at the delicious sting, my climax tearing through my body.

Dolyn groaned beneath me but held still, buried deep against my cervix.

Panting and still craving more, I yanked on Vanni's hair, demanding he crawl over us and—

"Yessss," I hissed in time with my inner beast as Vanni's cockhead nudged against my opening.

"Let me in, Ash."

Curses spilled from all three of us as he notched and thrust forward, hard enough Dolyn moved across the stone beneath us. The bite of pebbles along his back, the ache in Vanni's full balls, and the sting of being overly full radiated through me, heightening my arousal, even though I'd already climaxed.

Insatiable, we clung to one another, my mates retreating

and filling me in synchronized motion, the sharing of thoughts and intent creating magic. The thrust of their cocks along each other's, the tightness of my core caressing them, intensified our pleasure.

Vanni feasted on my lips, the musk and sweetness of my arousal on his tongue causing Dolyn's mouth to flood with drool. My tender golden beta sank his teeth into my neck at Vanni's silent command, and I came with a rush, euphoria swirling through our bond.

Wet heat erupted against my womb's opening, both men's cocks sending seed pulsing deep inside me. My heart raced, fire dancing over my skin, and I blinked my eyes open to find Vanni's green flames licking around us as they always did when we came together like this.

Perhaps their seed would take this time, and I would gift them both the longing that had grown since our bonding.

It took three dragonblood to create life, and as our climaxes ebbed and we slowly stilled, save for heaving chests and thumping hearts, I focused on my womb, imagining cells coming together and forming new life.

Dolyn groaned over my thoughts, trying to shove his hard shaft deeper, probing at my cervix with a delicious, throbbing need. "Can't fill you enough, my female."

I snickered as cum seeped from my opening stretched wide around their combined girth. "We're making a mess all over your groin."

He hummed, nuzzling and licking where he'd bitten me, our dragonblood already having healed the slight wound. "I adore having evidence of your pleasure on my skin."

Vanni pulled out and knelt, sliding his fingers through the stickiness, and smeared our combined cum down Dolyn's thighs. He shivered beneath me, and I didn't need to see their eyes to know they stared at each other.

Our alpha's shaft continued to stick straight up from between the trimmed, dark hair on his groin. Hands tightening on Dolyn's legs, he trailed his gaze over our faces, our necks, Dolyn's possessive yet gentle petting over my torso.

Awareness of something slithered through our bond but not from the three of us.

My eyes widened.

Dolyn went still beneath me.

Vanni's gaze narrowed as he focused on my lower abdomen, a slow build of his sudden pride welling through us.

A whimper escaped Dolyn's lips against my neck, adrenaline rushing even as weightlessness flooded his chest.

"It feels as though we ought to celebrate," Vanni murmured, his tone low and promising.

Shivers raced through both me and Dolyn as images of our alpha's want flooded our minds.

Vanni face down in our bed, ass in the air. A spreader bar kept his legs wide, clear access to the part of him Dolyn had been desperate for. Arms beneath his body and wrists connected to the bar's center would keep him completely immobile for whatever his beta wished.

"Fuck." Dolyn grunted and sat, shifting me off his lap.

I stood and slid my hand into Vanni's as our beta knelt before his alpha, hands on his cum-slickened thighs, head bowed. Limbs loosened and heart rate slowing, Dolyn submitted himself fully, the joy he'd found potent and intoxicating. "Please, Master."

Vanni hummed his pleasure, stroking over Dolyn's hair. "Such a good boy for me."

Dolyn shuddered beneath his touch and praise.

"Come, my mates." Vanni offered his hand to Dolyn and helped him to his feet. "It's time to fulfill those fantasies."

Anticipation of watching Dolyn own our alpha raised the

hair follicles on my body, and I rubbed over my belly, a spring of thankfulness welling my eyes. "I love you both more than I imagined possible."

The same deep emotion returned twofold, radiating through all three of our hearts.

THE END

About the Author

Spicy romance author Lynn Burke believes everyone deserves healing and a happily ever after. She loves writing hot, inclusive stories of various pairings or triplings and creates characters who will steal your heart.

She is a USA Today Bestselling author, a wrangler of her three spawn, and a farmer's daughter who grows organic food. To escape reality, she hides in a quiet corner with her nose in a book.

You can find more about Lynn at her website: www.authorlynnburke.com

ALSO BY LYNN BURKE

Abel's Obsession

Divulging Secrets

Healing Storms

In Between

Reluctant Lumberjack

Resisting his Mate

Billion Dollar Love Anthology

Blood Born Series

Bonds of Worship Series

Dark Leopards MC

Darkest Desires Series

Devil's Outlaws MC

Elite Escort Series

Elite Escorts MM Series

Fallen Gliders MC

Forbidden Obsession Duet

Found by Fate Series

Midnight Sun Series

Missing Link Series

Pippen Creek Series

Risso Family Series

Sandy Ridge Series

Sinful Nature Series

Vicious Vipers MC